LIVE TO TELL

THE GOOD SISTER

"A chilling, captivating, and all-too-timely
tale of suburban suspense, *The Good Sister*
is guaranteed to keep you up at night—
and keep a closer eye on your kids, too!
I couldn't put it down."

Alison Gaylin, *USA Today* bestselling author

"Taut, tense, and incredibly suspenseful.
This chillingly creepy psychological thriller
is the perfect page-turner. Staub's powerful
and timely story-telling is captivating!"

Hank Phillippi Ryan, Agatha,
Anthony and Macavity-winning author

"Intense! Wendy Corsi Staub once again
delivers a masterful psychological mystery
that is both chilling and thrilling.
You will not be able to put *The Good Sister*
down until the very last page."

Allison Brennan

By Wendy Corsi Staub

WENDY CORSI STAUB

BLOOD RED

Mundy's Landing
Book One

wm
WILLIAM MORROW
An Imprint of HarperCollins*Publishers*

This is a work of fiction. Names, characters, places, and incidents are products of the author's imagination or are used fictitiously and are not to be construed as real. Any resemblance to actual events, locales, organizations, or persons, living or dead, is entirely coincidental.

WILLIAM MORROW
An Imprint of HarperCollins*Publishers*
195 Broadway
New York, New York 10007

Copyright © 2015 by Wendy Corsi Staub
Map courtesy of Brody Staub
Excerpt from *Blue Moon* copyright © 2016 by Wendy Corsi Staub
ISBN 978-0-06-234973-6
www.harpercollins.com

First William Morrow mass market printing: October 2015

10 9 8 7 6 5 4 3 2 1

For the Criscione,
Mackowiak and Gugino families,
with cherished memories
of late night laughs, group vacations,
Elks Club Christmas parties,
and softball fields—

and especially in loving memory of
Janet, Bob and Louie,
hanging out with my mom at the great
Card Club Picnic in the sky.

And for my guys:
Mark, Morgan, and Brody, with love.

Acknowledgments

With gratitude to my editor, Lucia Macro; her assistant, Nicole Fischer; publisher Liate Stehlik; and the many people at HarperCollins who played a role in bringing this book to print; to my literary agent, Laura Blake Peterson, and my film agent, Holly Frederick, at Curtis Brown, Limited; to Shawn Nicholls and Dana Trombley; to publicists Lauren Jackson, Pamela Jaffee, Danielle Bartlett, Jessie Edwards, and Caroline Perny; to Carol Fitzgerald and the gang at Bookreporter; to Peter Meluso; to Gae Polisner, Alison Gaylin, Kelly Kennedy Spagnola, Bob Belinke, and Hank Phillippi Ryan; to booksellers, librarians, and readers everywhere; to Mark Staub and Morgan Staub for the manuscript feedback and marketing support; and above all to Brody Staub for putting Mundy's Landing on the map—literally!

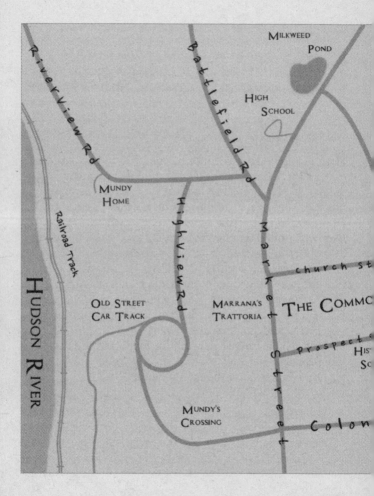

MUNDY'S LANDING

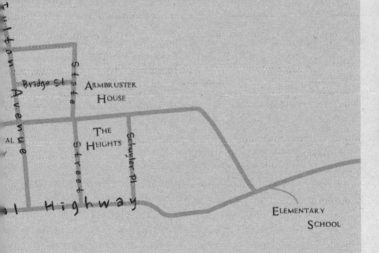

Fulton Avenue

Bridge St.

State Street

ARMBRUSTER HOUSE

AL.

THE HEIGHTS

Schuyler Pl.

Highway

ELEMENTARY SCHOOL

Prologue

March 22, 2015
Erie, Pennsylvania

She isn't the first redhead to cross Casey's path on this blustery Sunday evening. She's not even the best fit.

Earlier, there was a woman in the frozen foods aisle who had exactly the right look. Her hair was, if not naturally red, then at least dyed the appropriate cinnamon shade. It was pulled into a ponytail, but if the elastic band were to be yanked away, it would undoubtedly fall in waves to the middle of her back.

Casey's fingers clenched the metal hand bars of the crutches, itching to sink into that hair and pull hard so that her head jerked back and her neck arched, the creamy skin of her throat begging to be sliced open by a freshly honed blade. Her eyes were probably green, though she wasn't standing close enough to be sure. Even if the pupils weren't the distinct and exquisite blend of sage and olive that have always reminded Casey of military camouflage, the rest of her was dead-on.

She was petite, but not too skinny; fair-skinned at first glance. If it were summer, the faint scatter of freckles across the bridge of her nose and her cheekbones would be plainly visible, but in winter, you'd have to look hard to see them.

Yes, that first woman would have been perfect.

But she had a baby strapped across her chest in a sling and a toddler on board her shopping cart heaped high with boxes of diapers and cereal and cartons of milk and juice.

"Sierra, stop that," she said patiently as the child in the cart threw a sippy cup onto the floor yet again, laughing gleefully each time the woman stooped to pick it up.

Casey sensed her glancing over as if hoping to exchange a kids-do-the-darnedest-things eye roll.

Sorry, sweetheart. You're not going to get that from me.

Casey swung the crutches into motion and hobbled around the corner, leaving her behind. Clearly, she had her hands full already.

A little later, in the hardware section, there was another redhead. She was wandering up and down the aisles in search of something.

"Excuse me," she said to Casey the second time they passed each other, "have you seen rock salt anywhere?"

"No, I haven't."

"I bet they're sold out, too. Every store is because of the ice storm, but someone told me they had it here. Oh well, thanks."

"No problem." Casey watched her wander away.

She had almost the right build, albeit a little too padded, but her coloring was off. A true ginger, she had wiry shoulder-length hair and a ruddy, speckled complexion.

Casey decided to keep her in mind and move on. If no one better came along, she would do in a pinch.

Someone better has come along.

This new woman is in the pharmacy department, dropping off a prescription.

Feigning interest in an Ace bandage display, Casey

watches her approach the counter. She's alone, and she does have dark red hair, though that's where the resemblance stops. She's tall, curvy, and olive-skinned with Mediterranean features. But there's something about her: something about the way she walks, about the facial expression that radiates . . . goodness.

But you're not good, are you? And nobody knows that but you . . . and me.

An old man with a walker is heading in the same direction. Many people would have skirted around him, but the redhead takes her time, allowing him to get to the counter first. She waits patiently while he searches his pockets for his prescription bottles, at least half a dozen of them.

Seeing this, Casey nods with satisfaction.

When it's the woman's turn to hand over the prescription, the pharmacist checks the shelves. "I have it in stock, but it's going to be about fifteen minutes. Do you want to wait for it or come back tomorrow?"

She'll wait. She isn't in a rush. Good.

Casey leaves her behind in the pharmacy department, finds a cart, and maneuvers it awkwardly, tossing in enough items to fill several bags. The clock is ticking. There's a line at the single checkout lane.

Fifteen minutes . . . fifteen minutes . . .

At last, the cashier rings up the items, asking, "Do you need a hand getting out to your car?"

"No, thank you." Casey balances on the crutches and hands over cash.

"Are you sure?" According to her name tag, the cashier's name is Althea and she wants to know how she may help you.

"Positive," Casey says briskly, silently answering the name tag's printed question: *You may help me by moving a little faster, handing over my change, and then forgetting you ever saw me.*

The redhead from the pharmacy appears, heading toward the front of the store.

Althea persists: "I can call someone to—"

"No, I'm fine." The words come out too sharply, and Althea frowns. She painstakingly takes a couple of bills and coins from the drawer and starts to hand it over in an agonizingly unhurried manner.

Casey grabs the cash, thrusting it into the back pocket that doesn't contain a wad of dry cleaning plastic before wrestling the crutches and cart toward the door, a few steps behind the redhead.

Outside, sleet falls from the night sky and a gusting wind propels a wayward store flyer across the parking lot. The woman hastily puts up the hood of her jacket, obliterating the view of that glorious red hair, which gives Casey momentary pause.

Maybe she isn't the right stand-in.

Stand-in—that's how Casey has come to think of the women, like an almighty casting director who aims to spare the leading lady until opening night.

I decide who gets to live or die on any given day. It's all up to me. I control their fates.

Maybe there's someone else, someone better . . .

No. It's now or never. Casey has to leave town first thing tomorrow morning, and there will be no extending the stay and no coming back for her. Those are important rules, self-imposed and designed to stay one step ahead of the authorities.

One step? Try miles. They're so far behind they have yet to connect any of the stand-ins to each other.

The new candidate pauses to zip her jacket, allowing Casey to catch up to and then pass her, making a show of clumsiness with the cart and crutches, stumbling and nearly falling.

"Whoa—do you need a hand?" she asks.

Casey turns with a relieved smile. "That would be great. I'm still getting used to moving around on these things. Guess I didn't realize it would be so hard to push a cart."

"Here, I've got it." She grabs the handle. She's not wearing any rings, and the skin on her hands looks soft and smooth. Casey imagines her rubbing almond-scented lotion into them; imagines the fingers clutching and clawing, the nails broken, knuckles raw and bloodied.

"Where's your car?"

"Over there." Casey points out into a dark and distant corner of the lot before pushing the crutches into motion, leaning and hopping fluidly alongside the redhead and the cart.

"The store was a lot more crowded when I got here," Casey adds as they pass one empty space after another. "It took me forever to find what I needed and get out of there."

"I can imagine. You don't have a disability parking sticker?"

"No, not . . . yet. My doctor is working on it, though."

"What happened?" She gestures down at the blue mesh post-op shoe strapped to Casey's "bad" foot.

"My walkway was a sheet of ice on Tuesday. I slipped and broke it."

"That stinks." She nods, accepting the explanation. Just another casualty in a massive storm that brought down trees and power lines, caused a massive pileup on the interstate, and resulted in eleven lives lost.

Soon to be an even dozen, Casey thinks smugly. But of course, she won't be added to the official toll.

It'll be another of my little secrets.

They've almost reached the van parked beneath a burned-out lamppost.

Well—not burned out. The rubber tip of one of Casey's

crutches comes down on what looks like a sliver of ice, but of course it's a shard of glass from the overhead bulb that had been easily shattered with a well-aimed rock last night, long after the store had closed and the parking lot had emptied.

Casey pulls out the keys, presses a button, and the van's back hatch unlatches and rises slowly. No interior light though. It, too, has been disabled, long before last night.

"Thanks so much," Casey says as the woman parks the shopping cart near the rear bumper.

"No problem."

She smiles and starts to turn away, never seeing the metal crutch arcing into the air before it slams into her head; never feeling the hand that roughly jerks down the hood of her jacket and briefly caresses her long red hair before yanking her into the van.

From the *Mundy's Landing Tribune* Archives
Opinion
September 10, 2015

Protect Our Precious Children

To the Editor:

When my husband and I relocated to the Hudson Valley after having been born and raised in Manhattan, we were looking for a safe, old-fashioned small town where we could provide our treasured daughter with the wonderful childhood she deserves. We thought we had found it in Mundy's Landing.

Imagine our dismay when our Amanda came home from her first day of school yesterday and informed us that her fourth-grade class would be making an "educational" field trip in December to the historical society. Aware that the society houses macabre relics connected to the infamous murders of 1916, I was outraged and immediately called her teacher to protest. Ms. Mundy seemed unperturbed and informed me that this year's social studies curriculum encompasses New York State history, which to her way of thinking entails taking advantage of the fact that some of the most colorful chapters unfolded here in the Hudson Valley. She added that the trip is a long-standing tradition.

Just because something has always been done doesn't make it right! I invite fellow parents of our village to join me in taking a stand to protest this inappropriate local rite of passage. Aren't our children entitled to an anxiety-free school experience without exposure to a disturbing tragedy under the guise of education?

Bari Hicks
Mundy Estates

Chapter 1

November 30, 2015
Mundy's Landing, New York

Six minutes.

That's exactly how long it takes to drive between the elementary school where Rowan Mundy teaches and the riverside home where she lives with her family.

The route meanders along the brick-paved streets of The Heights, a sloping residential neighborhood. Its landmarks include her childhood home, the little white clapboard church where she was baptized and married, and Holy Angels Cemetery where her parents and father-in-law are buried alongside generations of local citizens. Among them: the trio of unidentified young girls whose murders during the village's sestercentennial celebration a century ago sealed Mundy's Landing's notoriety.

Most days, she drives on past all of those sites without taking note, her mind on whatever happened during the past few hours or on whatever needs to get done in the next few.

Once in a while, though, she allows herself to get caught up in nostalgia for long-gone loved ones and places that will never be the same.

Today is one of those days. Christmas music plays

on the car stereo, and the business district is decked out in wreaths and garlands that seem to have materialized overnight. She wistfully remembers cozy holidays when her parents were alive and her brothers and sister weren't scattered from East Coast to West.

Now her two oldest children are gone as well. Braden is a junior at Dartmouth; Katie a freshman at Cornell. Both were here for the long Thanksgiving weekend that just passed, but it was all too fleeting. They headed back yesterday in opposite directions.

"I hate this letting go thing," she told Jake, wiping tears as they stood on the front porch watching taillights disappear.

"They'll be home on break for a whole month before you know it, and you'll be counting down the days until they go back to school in January."

"No I won't."

"Oh, right. I'm the one who does that." Jake flashed his good-natured grin and went back to eating a leftover turkey drumstick and watching the Giants win in overtime.

Passing the Mundy's Landing Historical Society, which occupies a grand turreted mansion facing the Village Common, Rowan is reminded of an unpleasant phone call she received this morning from the mother of one of her fourth-grade students.

Bari Hicks moved to town from New York City over the summer, and has proven to be one of those people who always manages to find something to complain about. This week, she was calling to once again express her displeasure with the upcoming class field trip to see the Colonial Christmas exhibit.

The annual excursion has been a well-loved school tradition since Rowan herself was in fourth grade. Back then, this turreted mansion was still a private residence and the historical society was housed in the basement of the local library.

"I just don't think a trip like this sounds appropriate for children this age," Bari insisted back on curriculum night in September. *Appropriate* seems to be her favorite word. Rather, *inappropriate*. "My Amanda still isn't used to her new bedroom and she has enough problems falling asleep at night without being dragged through a gory chamber of horrors that's going to give her nightmares for years."

Although Rowan immediately grasped what she was referring to, she couldn't resist feigning ignorance.

"Oh, you must have this mixed up with the high school's haunted hallway fund-raiser, Mrs. Hicks. That's on Halloween, and I wouldn't dream of exposing my class to—"

"No, I'm talking about the historical society. The *murders*."

"Which murders?" That time, Rowan wasn't playing dumb. Mundy's Landing is famous for not one, but two notorious murder cases.

The first unfolded in the mid-seventeenth century, when Jake's ancestors James and Elizabeth Mundy were executed on the gallows for butchering and cannibalizing their fellow colonists. Their only son, Jeremiah Mundy, and his offspring lived such exemplary lives that the town was later named in their honor.

Mundy's Landing itself wasn't quite so fortunate in terms of redemption and reputation. Precisely two and a half centuries after the hangings, the so-called Sleeping Beauty murders marked one of the eeriest unsolved crime sprees in American history. The young female victims, whose identities were never known, were lain to rest beneath white granite markers simply etched with the year 1916 and the word *Angel*.

Those are the murders to which Bari Hicks was referring. "I heard the museum has bloody clothing on display, and the murder weapon, and a disembodied skull. Do you really think it's necessary to—?"

"There's no skull," Rowan quickly assured her, though she'd heard that rumor all her life, "and it isn't the actual murder weapon, it's just an antique razor blade someone's grandfather donated as an example, and the bloody clothing is only exhibited in the summer during . . ."

She couldn't quite bring herself to call the event Mundypalooza, the flippant popular term for the annual historical society–sponsored fund-raiser that draws crime buffs, reporters, tourists, and plain old fruitcakes from all over the globe.

". . . the convention," she chose to say instead, and hastily added, "We're only visiting the Colonial Christmas exhibit on our field trip. I promise Amanda will love it. All the kids do."

Bari aired her frustrations in a public letter to the *Mundy's Landing Tribune*, expecting to rally the villagers in protest. Today, Rowan convinced her to come along as a chaperone so that she can experience the long-standing tradition firsthand—and, ostensibly, protect her daughter from the evils of Mundy's Landing. It seemed like the easiest way to avoid additional Monday morning stress, but she regrets it already.

Now, winding toward home, she blinks against the glare of sinking autumn sun at every westbound curve. Lowering the visor doesn't help at all.

She worries about Mick.

In about ten minutes, her youngest son will be getting off the late bus after varsity basketball practice. Even if he's not plugged into his iPod—despite her warnings about the dangers of walking or jogging along the road wearing headphones—he'll have his head in the clouds as usual.

At this time of year, the angle of the late day sun is blinding. What if a car comes careening up the hill and doesn't see him until it's too late?

Long gone are Rowan's days of waiting in the mini-van at the bus stop on Highland Road, a busy north-south thoroughfare. Even on stormy afternoons—there are plenty of those in Mundy's Landing—Mick insists on walking home up Riverview Road, just as his older siblings did when they were in high school.

I'll walk Doofus, she decides as she brakes at the curb-side mailbox in front of their gabled Queen Anne Victorian perched on the bluff above the Hudson.

Doofus the aging basset hound was originally Rufus, but earned his current name when it became evident that he wasn't exactly the smartest canine in the world.

Rowan ordinarily lets him out into the yard when she gets home after a long day, but Doofus—although in-creasingly lazy—might welcome some exercise, and she can use it herself.

She bought a tasteless but slimming couscous salad for lunch today, courtesy of Wholesome & Hearty, the school district's new lunch program. But then someone left a plate of cookies in the teachers' break room after lunch and one of her students brought in birthday cup-cakes. Plus there's still half an apple pie in the fridge at home, leftover from Thanksgiving dinner.

There was a time when Rowan could gobble anything she felt like eating and never gain an ounce. Those days, too, are long gone. According to her doctor, she needs to exercise nearly an hour a day at her age just to keep her weight the same. And the hair colorist who's been hiding her gray for a few years now recently told her that her natural red shade was making her "mature" skin look sallow, and that the long hair she'd had all her life was too "weighty."

"I think you should try a short, youthful cut and go a few shades lighter, maybe a biscuit blond with honey highlights and caramel lowlights. What do you think?"

"I think biscuits and honey and caramel sound like something I'd want to eat right now if I didn't have to run ten miles to work off the extra calories," Rowan said with a sigh of resignation.

She finally agreed to the new hairstyle right before Thanksgiving. It got mixed reviews at home. Jake and Katie liked it; Braden, who resents change of any sort, did not; Mick informed her that now her hair wouldn't clash with the bright orange hoodie—emblazoned with a black tiger, Mundy's Landing High School mascot—that she wore to all his home basketball games.

"I never minded clashing," she said.

"I do. Can I dye my hair, too?"

"Nope. It's what makes you *you*."

"Isn't it what made you *you*, too?"

Yes, and whenever she catches sight of her reflection, she feels as though she's dwelling in a stranger's body.

Back at work today, her colleagues complimented her, her students questioned her, and the janitor told her she looks hot—which might be inappropriate, but as the forty-seven-year-old mother of three nearly grown kids, she'll take it.

She gets out of the car, goes around to grab the mail out of the box, and finds that it's full of catalogs. No surprise on this first Monday of the official holiday shopping season. Given the stack of bills that are also in the box, plus the two college tuition payments coming due for next semester, the catalogs will go straight into the recycling bin.

Money has been tight lately, and Jake is worried about his job as a regional sales manager amid rumors that his company might be bought out.

Lead us not into temptation, she thinks, tossing the heap of mail—which also includes a red envelope addressed to the family in her older sister Noreen's perfect handwriting, and a small package addressed to her—onto the passenger's seat.

As she pulls into the driveway and around back, she sees that there's garbage strewn by the back steps. The latch on top of the can snapped off when they overfilled it on Thanksgiving. Jake tried to pick up a new one the next day, but the strip malls on Colonial Highway were so jammed with Black Friday shoppers that he couldn't get near any of them.

As Rowan stoops to pick up a gnawed turkey carcass and wads of soggy paper towels discarded by woodland creatures, she tries to imagine Noreen doing the same.

Nope. It would never happen. Noreen, a busy Long Island attorney, runs her household—her life—without glitches.

As Rowan lets herself into the house and tosses the mail onto the cluttered counter in the butler's pantry, she marvels that her sister manages to send Christmas cards at all, let alone ahead of the masses. Yet somehow, she even hand-addresses the envelopes, rather than use those typed labels you can so easily print out year after year.

Rowan knows without opening this year's card that it'll have a photo of the svelte and lovely Noreen, her handsome trauma surgeon husband, and their four gorgeous kids, all color-coordinated in khaki and red or navy and white. Inside, there will be a handwritten note and the signature of each family member scrawled in red or green Sharpie.

Noreen has always managed to do so much and make it look so easy . . .

Which drives someone like me absolutely crazy. Which

is why, when I was a kid, I didn't even bother to try to follow in her footsteps.

She's so caught up in the familiar combination of envy and longing for her sister that she doesn't think twice about the package that came for her. She tosses it aside with the rest of the mail and takes her medication—the first thing she does every morning, and again every afternoon when she walks in the door.

It wasn't until Mick was diagnosed with ADHD back in elementary school that Rowan learned that it was hereditary.

With this disability, the apple doesn't fall far from the tree, the doctor told her, leading her to recognize similar symptoms in herself.

It was as if a puzzle piece she hadn't even realized was missing had suddenly dropped into place to complete a long-frustrating jigsaw.

If only someone—her parents, her teachers, her doctors—had figured it out when she was Mick's age. Now she understands why she spent so much of her childhood in trouble—academically, behaviorally—and why she so often felt restlessly uncomfortable in her own skin, even as an adult.

Things aren't perfect now—far from it—but at least she's more in control of her life, with better focus and the ability to quell her impulsive tendencies. Most of the time, anyway.

After swallowing the pill, she walks the dog down to the bus stop and returns with a grumbling Mick.

"Where's all the turkey?" he asks, poking his stubbly auburn head—exactly the same shade as her own—into the fridge.

"I tossed it last night."

"What? Why?"

"Because it was old, Mick. You can't eat leftovers after a few days."

"You didn't toss the pie." He pulls out the dish.

"Pie isn't poultry. That's still good."

She watches her son put the whole thing into the microwave and punch the quick start button, then open the freezer.

So much for Rowan's dessert plans. Oh well. She can't afford to indulge, and Mick can. Half a pie smothered in Vanilla Bean Häagen-Dazs is nothing more than a light afternoon snack for a famished, lanky sixteen-year-old athlete who begins every morning with a three-mile run.

The stack of mail still sits on the granite counter in the butler's pantry by the back door, along with her tote bag and the usual household clutter plus additional clutter accumulated over Thanksgiving: clean platters that need to go back to the dining room, a bread basket filled with cloth napkins that have to be washed, bottles of open and unopened Beaujolais . . .

She should get busy cleaning it up. She should do a lot of things. As always, now that the medication has begun to take hold again, it all seems more manageable.

After returning the platters and napkins to the built-in cabinets in the dining room, she asks Mick, "What time do you have to be at work?" Three nights a week, he's a busboy at Marrana's Trattoria in town.

"Five-thirty."

"I need you to do me a favor while you're there. Can you please get me a gift certificate for twenty-five dollars?" She pulls the cash from her wallet and hands it to him.

"Who's it for?"

"Marlena, the library aide. I pulled her name for the Secret Santa."

He looks at her as if she's speaking a foreign language. "I don't even know what that means."

"You know . . . or maybe you don't know. Secret Santa is something we do every year at work—we pick names and then we have to anonymously surprise the person with a little treat every day next week—"

"I don't really think a gift certificate counts as a treat, Mom. How about cookies or something?"

"No, the gift certificate is for the big gift on Friday."

"Big? You'd better do fifty bucks, then. Twenty-five seems cheap."

"The limit is twenty-five, big spender." She grins, shaking her head. "So, how much homework do you have?"

"Not a lot."

Same question every night; same answer. The truth is, he usually has a lot of homework, and it doesn't always get done.

"Look on the bright side," Jake says, whenever she frets that even with an early diagnosis, academic accommodations, and medication, Mick has shortchanged himself. "We won't be paying Ivy League tuition when it's his turn."

"No, we'll just be supporting him for the rest of his life."

"It might be the other way around. He's an enterprising kid. Maybe he'll invent a billion-dollar video game."

Maybe. Or maybe he'll turn himself around academically, find his way into a decent college, make something of himself . . .

You did, she reminds herself. *And if Mom and Dad were still alive, they'd still be reminding you they weren't so sure that was ever going to happen.*

"Did you get your grade back yet on the English test?"

"Which test?"

As if he doesn't know. She'd spent two hours helping him study for it last Monday night. "The one on literary devices."

"Oh. That test. Nope."

"Are you sure?"

"Yep. So stop looking at me like a detective who thinks the witness is lying." He flashes her a grin. "See? I know what a metaphor is. I bet I got an A-plus on that test."

"I hate to break it to you, kiddo, but that's not a metaphor. It's a simile."

"That's what I meant." Mick settles on a stool with the pile of mail, looking for something to leaf through while he eats, which will take all of two minutes.

"What's this?" He holds up the brown parcel addressed to Rowan.

"Probably something I ordered for you for Christmas. Don't open it."

"Is it the keys to my new car? Because don't forget, I'm taking my road test in less than a month."

"It is not"—she plucks the package from his hand—"the keys to your new car because there will *be* no new car."

"Then what am I going to drive?"

"You can share the minivan with me. And you already have the keys to that, so you're all set. Here—" She gives him the red envelope. "You can open Aunt Noreen's Christmas card."

"Bet you anything they made Goliath wear those stupid reindeer antlers again." Goliath is a German shepherd whose dignity is compromised, as far as Rowan's kids are concerned, by a costume every Christmas and Halloween.

"Don't worry, Doofus," Mick says, patting the dog, who lies on the hardwood floor at the base of his stool, hoping to catch a stray crumb with little effort. "We'd never do anything like that to you if *we* had a Christmas card picture."

"He wouldn't know he had a costume on if we zipped

him into a horse suit and hitched him to a buggy," Rowan points out. "Plus we do have a Christmas card picture. I mean, we *have* had one."

"When?"

"Back in the old days."

"When?" Classic Mick, persisting to demonstrate that he, as the youngest kid in the family, has suffered some slight, real or imagined.

It rarely works on Rowan, who as the lastborn of Kate and Jonathan Carmichael's four children is all too familiar with that technique.

"Back when we lived in Westchester," she tells Mick. She distinctly remembers having to cancel a family portrait shoot repeatedly to accommodate Jake's schedule. He was working in the city then, never home.

"Before I was born doesn't count, Mom."

"We had a few after you were born."

"We did not."

"Sure we did." *Did we?*

It's a wonder they even found time to conceive Mick back then, let alone take a family photo.

"I don't think so."

"Maybe not," she concedes. "After we moved here, I probably didn't send cards. But God knows we have plenty of family pictures. They're just not portraits." Her favorites—and there are many—are framed, cluttered on tabletops and hanging along the stairs in a hodgepodge gallery.

"That's not the same thing."

"You poor, poor neglected little working mom's son."

"Stop." He squirms away from her exaggerated sympathetic hug.

"But I feel so sorry for you!"

"Yeah, right."

She shrugs. Her mother never wasted much time feeling guilty for being a working mom, and she tries not to, either.

She used to be a stay-at-home mom. Giving it up hasn't always been easy, but she's never questioned that it was the right decision for her family, or her marriage.

Mick was three when she resumed the teaching career she'd launched back when she and Jake were newlyweds. She could have waited to go back until the kids were older if they'd stayed in the New York City suburbs and Jake had stuck with the higher-paying advertising sales job that kept him away for weeks at a time. But that would have been tempting fate, because . . .

She doesn't like to think back to those days. Things were so different. She and Jake were different people then: different from each other; different from the way they are now.

He quit his job and they sold the house and moved back to their hometown. The cost of living is much lower in Mundy's Landing than it had been in Westchester County, allowing Jake to take a lower-paying, less glamorous job as a sales rep in Albany. He was promoted within the first year, but they still couldn't make ends meet on one salary. She had to work, too.

"Oh geez! Poor Goliath!" Mick waves the Christmas card at her.

"Antlers?" she guesses.

"Worse. An elf hat. A whole elf costume. Look at this!"

Rowan takes in the sight of a humiliated-looking German shepherd decked out in green felt and red pom-poms alongside her sister's picture-perfect family. "Poor Goliath," she agrees. "But everyone else looks great. I miss them. Maybe we should try to get together for Christmas."

"Mom—you said never again, remember?"

"That wasn't me, that was Dad."

"That was all of us, including you. It took us a whole

day to get home in traffic last time we went to see Aunt Noreen for Christmas."

"That was a freak blizzard. It doesn't usually snow on Long Island over the holidays."

"Well, it always snows *here*."

Mick is right. In Mundy's Landing, Currier and Ives Christmases are the norm. On the bank of the Hudson River, cradled by the Catskill Mountains to the west, the Berkshires to the east, and the Adirondacks to the north, the village sees more than its share of treacherous weather from October through May. But as the hardy locals like to say, "We know how to handle it." Plows and salt trucks rumble into motion, shovels and windshield scrapers are kept close at hand, and it's business as usual.

Rowan opens three drawers before she finds a pair of scissors to slit open the packing tape on the box.

It's not from Amazon or Zappos or any number of places where she does most of her online shopping. There's no return address, just her own, computer-printed on a plain white label—yes, the kind overachievers like Noreen refuse to use for their Christmas cards.

Inside is a layer of crumpled newspaper.

Slightly yellowed newspaper, which strikes her as strange even before she sees what's beneath it.

"What is it?" Mick asks, looking up from his pie.

"I . . . I have no idea." She pulls out a flat black disk, turning it over in her hands.

"Who sent it?"

She shakes her head, clueless.

"I bet it's from your Secret Santa." Mick is beside her, rummaging through the box.

"That doesn't start until next week, and we leave the gifts for each other at school. We don't mail them."

"There's a bunch of those things in here," he notes, counting.

Yes . . . a bunch of what? Charcoal? There's a charred smell to the disks, whatever they are.

"There are twelve," Mick tells her. "Thirteen altogether, with the one you're holding. Unlucky number. Hey, this newspaper is pretty old. Cool, check it out. It's the *New York Times* from fourteen years ago. I was only two."

Fourteen years ago . . .

A memory slams into her.

It can't be. Nobody knows about that. Nobody other than—

"What's the date?" she asks Mick abruptly. "On the newspaper?"

"Whoa—it's November thirtieth, same as today! Think that's a coincidence?"

No. It's not a coincidence.

Nor is the fact that there are thirteen blackened disks in the box.

A voice—*his* voice—floats back over the years; fourteen years: *A baker's dozen . . .*

It happened fourteen years ago today. A Friday, not a Monday. In Westchester. It was snowing.

"Hey, I think these are cookies," Mick says. "Looks like your Secret Santa burned your treat."

Cookies . . .

Rowan's fingers let go and the charred object drops back into the box.

Either *he* tracked her down and sent this package as some kind of reminder, or a sick, twisted joke, or . . .

Someone else did.

Someone who knows her secret.

Driving along the New York State Thruway, northbound from New York City toward Mundy's Landing, Casey has had the same tune looping on the car's speakers for almost two hours now.

The songs are important. You can't just play any random tune when you're driving. That's one of the rules. You have to play a specific song, over and over, until you get to where you're going.

Sometimes it's country: Glen Campbell's "Wichita Lineman" or Willie Nelson's "On the Road Again."

Sometimes it's rock and roll: Journey's "Lights" or The Doors' "Riders on the Storm."

Today's song has great significance, a strong reminder of why this has to happen.

Every time it begins anew, Casey's fingers thrum the military drumbeat on the steering wheel with until it's time to howl the chorus again: *Sunday, bloody Sunday* . . .

By now, Rowan must have gotten the package that had been mailed on Friday from the city.

If her weekday unfolded the way it usually does, she was the one who reached into the mailbox this afternoon and found it.

Throughout the fall, Casey watched her, documenting her daily routine. Sometimes, that could even be accomplished from inside the school where she teaches. Security at Mundy's Landing Elementary is a joke. There are plenty of news articles online that would seem to indicate otherwise, dating back to the most recent school shooting and meant to reassure jittery parents that their precious children were well-protected under the new security measures.

It's true that all visitors have to be buzzed past the locked front door, but there are plenty of other ways into the building. It's surrounded by woods on three sides, so you can easily hide there watching for some deliveryman to leave a door propped open, or try tugging doors and windows until you find one that's unlocked.

Once, feeling especially bold, Casey even showed up at the front door wearing a uniform and got buzzed in by the secretary. She didn't even bother to request credentials or double check the made-up story about a faulty meter in the basement.

That was in the early morning, before the students arrived. Casey wandered the halls searching the teachers' names, written in black Sharpie on cardboard cutouts shaped like bright yellow pencils and taped beside every classroom. Rowan's was evident even before Casey spotted the pencil marked Ms. Mundy: she was in there talking to another teacher, and her voice echoed down the halls.

Some might find her chattiness endearing.

I used to.

Now it grates.

Four days a week, Casey knows, Rowan leaves school not long after the bell, just after three-thirty. But she always stays at least an hour later on Mondays. That's when she supervises the tutoring organization that matches volunteers from nearby Hadley College with local elementary school students.

Perched with binoculars high in a tree across the road from the house—a vantage that never failed to inspire a unique exhilaration in and of itself—Casey loved to watch her pull up in front of the mailbox at the foot of the driveway. She'd usually rifle through the stack of letters and catalogs quickly, toss them onto the seat, and drive on up to the house. But once in a while, something seemed to catch her eye and she'd open an envelope or package right there at the curb.

Sometimes, Casey seized the opportunity to stick around watching the house long after she'd disappeared inside, occasionally daring to scale a tree right on the property. Daring not because of the height—Casey has always been exhilarated by great heights—but because of the proximity to the house.

All any of them ever had to do was take a good, hard look, and they'd have seen me. But they never did.

Casey would sometimes stay late into the night until the last light was extinguished. Oblivious to a voyeur in their midst, the Mundy family went about their lives behind the sturdy plaster walls of the home that had been built well over a century ago—one hundred and twenty-seven years ago, to be exact.

Casey had left no stone unturned when it came to investigating Rowan's charmed life. One never knows when a seemingly irrelevant detail might come in handy.

An entire year of preparation has finally paid off.

November thirtieth has finally arrived.

The endgame has begun.

From the *Mundy's Landing Tribune* Archives
Real Estate
March 18, 2002

Just Reduced: Victorian Charmer
25 Riverview Road

Enjoy the ever-changing Hudson Valley landscape from the rocking chair wraparound porch of this lovely historic 3200-square-foot, 6-bedroom, 1.5-bath Queen Anne. Vintage features include elegant front entry, double parlors, formal dining room with built-in cabinetry, butler's pantry, full attic and cellar. Loaded with period charm including four fireplaces, stained glass transoms, and gabled dormers. Original oak, maple, and cherry floors, moldings, wainscoting, and pocket doors. Located minutes from business district on private 2 acre lot with mature trees and partial seasonal river views. Move-in ready. Your TLC and decorating touches will restore this gem to its bygone splendor.

Chapter 2

Mick Mundy has been eating in the wood-paneled dining room at Marrana's Trattoria since the place was known as Marrana's Pizzeria. That was long before the owners replaced the red vinyl table coverings with white linen and started charging twenty bucks for a plate of pasta. Which is ridiculous, according to Mick's father—although Dad's willing to pay even more than that for the Cavatelli a la Mama Marrana, the restaurant's sausage-and-cheese-smothered signature dish.

In the three months since Mick started working here, he's come to see the place in a new light. At first, it was a novelty to know what was happening behind the scenes—for instance, that the "world-famous" gorgonzola salad dressing is just Italian dressing from a big plastic jug with a handful of cheese crumbles thrown in. At this point, though, that's old news. Now that he's the one who has to scrape the leftovers from diners' plates into the garbage, he's even lost his taste for Cavatelli a la Mama.

Still, for the most part, he likes his job. The place tends to get busier as the week goes on, and those lucky enough to pull weekend shifts make decent money. But Mick often has basketball games on those nights and is stuck with Monday through Wednesday, when his portion of the waitresses' tips amounts to barely enough to put a few gallons of gas in the car.

When he actually *has* a car.

Which he never will if he winds up having to pay for it himself. Not with this job, anyway.

Monday nights always mean lousy tips, but tonight is surprisingly busy.

"Why do you think that is?" he asks Brianna Armbruster, seizing any excuse to talk to her as they stand shoulder-to-shoulder loading desserts onto a tray.

"No clue" is her reply.

"Maybe it's because no one feels like cooking after Thanksgiving."

"Maybe."

Brianna walks off with a swing of her red ponytail. Not in a snotty way—just . . .

Disinterested, basically. Which is the way most senior girls treat junior guys at Mundy's Landing High. It's not like he isn't used to it.

Still, he keeps trying with Brianna. Because this isn't school. He's not a junior here, he's a working man. This is the real world, where age doesn't matter. Well, anyway, it shouldn't, he thinks, staring after her. She fills out her waitress uniform—a basic black polo shirt and jeans— nicely.

He's known Brianna forever. You can't live in Mundy's Landing and not be acquainted with all the kids in town who are roughly your age. For two years, they played on the same youth soccer team. He didn't pay much attention to her, though—didn't fall in love with her—until the summer before his freshman year.

There he was, just riding his bike along Prospect Street on his usual morning paper route, tossing newspapers onto porches, when she jogged past with some guy. He hadn't seen much of her since she'd left middle school as a freckled tomboy with an overbite and orthodontic head-gear. Now the braces were gone, and she was wearing skimpy workout clothes, and he couldn't miss the fact that she'd grown up—not to mention out. He was so distracted he steered into a fire hydrant and found himself sprawled on the sidewalk with bloody hands and knees.

"Nice going, carrot top," the guy called, laughing.

Brianna whirled on him and pointed out that she, too, was a carrot top. He stammered a lame apology, which she ignored as she came over to make sure Mick was okay. She even held his arm as he got to his feet. He kind of wished he wasn't okay, because then she'd have to call an ambulance and ride with him to the hospital and keep a bedside vigil as he convalesced, maybe wearing a little white nurse's uniform, or—

"Could she be less into you?"

He turns to see Zach Willet grinning at him as he stares after Brianna.

"Yeah, she could be into *you*," he shoots back illogically.

"That makes zero sense."

"Cut me a break, will ya, Lou? Can't you see I'm love-sick over here?"

"Yeah, yeah, sorry 'bout that, Lou."

He and Zach always call each other Lou when they're here at work. He can't remember how it started, but it's become a *thing*, and they talk to each other in exaggerated mobster accents. Well, Zach's is dead-on, like he stepped out of the movie *Goodfellas*, but Mick's needs work.

They never hung out much in the past. Zach is part of a different crowd, the drama club kids. But they've gotten to be pretty good friends working together over the past few months.

Mick puts a plate containing a powdered-sugar-dusted cannoli onto his tray and consults the order.

"By the way—" Zach drops the wiseguy accent. "I heard she's going out with some college guy."

Mick's heart plummets. "What? Brianna? Since when?"

"Since a few days ago."

"Where'd you hear that?"

"I swore on my life I wouldn't tell."

That means it came from Gina Marrana, aka Jiffy Pop. Her parents own the restaurant, and she's the only other high school kid here tonight. She always seems to know everything about everyone in town. On slow nights, she brings Mick up to speed on the gossip.

"You swear on your life you won't tell?" Gina always asks, wearing her usual I'm-bursting-with-news-and-I'll-explode-if-I-don't-tell expression that spawned her nickname.

Mick always swears, although he's broken that vow quite a few times. But he's still alive, so . . .

"Why would Brianna go out with a college guy?" he asks Zach.

"Dude. Come on. Seriously?"

"Okay, well, what else do you know?" Might as well size up the competition.

"He's from New York but he's a freshman at Hadley and I think his parents have a summer house near Saugerties," Zach rattles off. "Oh, and he went to private boarding school in New England."

So he's rich. Mick thinks of the wealthy people—most of them from New York City—who have homes in the area. Back on Columbus Day, he served a middle-aged Manhattanite who called his a "country estate," which you'd think would make him a big tipper, but he left ten percent. Jerk.

"When you say going out," Mick says to Zach, "do you mean she's going to go on a date with him in the future? Or going out like boyfriend and girl—"

"I hate to break up your little chill sesh back here," Jiffy Pop herself interrupts, "but my mother's looking for you guys."

Zach follows her back out into the dining room as Mick goes back to his dessert order.

Tiramisu . . .

Biscotti . . .

Which reminds him of the crazy package that came in the mail today.

The way his mother reacted, you would have thought someone had sent her a severed human head instead of just a bunch of burnt cookies.

Mom tried to cover up how freaked out she was, though. First she claimed it was probably from her Secret Santa after all. But he reminded her that it wasn't exactly a present and anyway, she'd said that didn't start until next week. Then she said it was just a joke, and that one of her old college friends had sent it.

He didn't believe that for a second.

She didn't seem amused. She seemed terrified.

Even more troubling: she told Mick not to tell his father about it.

"You want me to lie to Dad?" he asked, just to be clear.

"No! I don't want you to lie. Just don't mention it unless, you know, he asks about it."

"So, like, if Dad comes walking in and says, 'Hey, by any chance did someone send Mom a weird package in the mail today?' then I can say—"

"Don't be a wiseass, Mick." She was almost her usual self in that instant, but in the next, she was digging through the box like a *Survivor* contestant digging for the hidden immunity idol.

That's what Mick told her, adding, "That's a simile. Pretty good, huh?"

She failed to appreciate his literary genius, which

wasn't like her. She just told him to go get changed for work. And when he returned to the kitchen ten minutes later, she nearly jumped out of her skin.

"Are you all right?" he asked as she pressed a hand to her chest like she was having a heart attack.

"I'm fine."

But she wasn't. She was totally pale and jumpy, and she locked the house when they left. She never bothers to do that.

"Why don't you want Dad to know?" he asked her when they were in the car heading toward the restaurant.

"Know what?" she asked, even though he knew she knew exactly what he was talking about.

"About that package."

"Oh, because my friend Carolyn sent it, and . . . you know Dad doesn't like her."

Mick barely knows who Carolyn is, other than that she went to the University of Buffalo with Mom and lives outside Rochester. "Why doesn't he like her?"

"He thinks she talks too much."

"He thinks all your friends talk too m— Look out!"

Mom slammed on the brakes. She'd almost driven right through a stop sign into oncoming traffic.

"Geez, Mom, you could have gotten us killed," he said mildly.

"I'm sorry! Oh my God! I'm so sorry!" She just sat there for a second with her forehead resting on the steering wheel. Then someone honked behind them and she drove on, but he could see her hands shaking and she kept biting her lip.

Mick is sure there's a lot more to that box of burnt cookies than a stupid joke. Too bad he can't mention it to his father.

Then again, he didn't swear on his life.

Casey's headlights illuminate a green sign announcing the next exit. From there, it'll be just a fifteen-minute drive up the local road until the picturesque cluster of gabled rooftops and steeples comes into view.

It's been a long day on the road already, but Casey had no problem making the two-hour detour in rush hour traffic. Too many days have passed without seeing Rowan. A glimpse of her might be too much to hope for, but sometimes it's enough just to drive by the big old house and imagine her inside, utterly unaware that her perfect little world is about to come crashing down around her.

From the exit, it takes fourteen minutes to reach the chamber of commerce billboard that reads Welcome to Mundy's Landing.

Alongside it is a traffic sign indicating that the speed limit has dropped from fifty-five to thirty and is "strictly enforced."

When Casey first visited, there was a third sign here as well: a temporary one directing visitors toward the center of town and the historical society on Prospect Street, the hub for the annual convention colloquially known as Mundypalooza.

Casey took full advantage of the hordes of tourists that descended upon the little village to commemorate its claim to fame as the murder capital of the world—unofficially, of course. It's not as though the local government has embraced that slogan and printed it on bumper stickers.

Yet.

The local election campaigns this fall pitted the old guard against fresh blood. Casey followed them with interest. John Ransom, Mundy's Landing's longtime mayor—whose bloodline reportedly links him to the notorious first settlers, as with many other longtime locals,

including Rowan's husband—doesn't like to acknowledge, much less draw attention to, the infamous murder
sprees that unfolded here in the mid–1600s and then
again almost a century ago.

Ninety-nine years, five months, and seven days ago, to
be precise.

Casey enjoys being precise.

Mayor Ransom was soundly defeated by a relative
newcomer who'd won the vocal support of local business owners. They might not admit to capitalizing on the
village's bloody past, but they certainly benefit from the
annual invitation that draws increasingly large flocks of
crime buffs, historians, and media from all over the world
every summer.

Can you solve the Sleeping Beauty murders?

The question was printed on posters taped to every
store window and lamppost in town and echoed in countless newspapers and all over the Internet.

How amusing.

What does it matter now whether the killer is identified? It's not as though the culprit still roams these
brick-paved streets by night, preying on innocent school-
children. Solving the ancient murders would accomplish
nothing—other than to erase the very reason for Mundypalooza's existence.

Clearly, the powers-that-be haven't thought of that.

Fools.

With next summer marking not just ML350—the
town's three-hundred-fiftieth birthday—but also the cen-
tennial anniversary of the unsolved Sleeping Beauty murders, the upcoming Mundypalooza promises to be more
popular than ever. By then, Casey's work here will be
done. Too bad, because it would be even easier to get lost
in increasingly larger crowds, moving in and out of circles
that orbit and intersect those of Rowan and her family.

It's tricky, at this time of year, to slip in and out of their world unnoticed. But not impossible.

"Sunday, bloody Sunday . . ." Singing, Casey drives slowly past the Mundy home, turns around in a driveway down the road, and drives past it again. It would be nice to spot Rowan's silhouette in the window, which has happened many times. But it doesn't happen tonight.

It would be even nicer to park the car a short distance away, slip back through neighboring yards, and climb the massive elm behind the Mundy house. Perched high in its branches at night, camouflaged by dense foliage, Casey watched the family inside their home throughout the summer and into early fall.

That became too risky after the leaves fell.

But eventually, frustrated by the lack of proximity, emboldened by the knowledge that November thirtieth was looming, Casey tried a new tactic.

The Mundy family is careless about locking doors: their cars in the driveway and even the back door of the house are often left unlocked. Not that it matters. They keep a key hidden under a planter on the back step.

Casey began to prowl the house when they weren't home—and once, in the dead of night, when they were. Those stealthy maneuvers were dangerous, but they allowed a heady, perhaps even addictive, sense of power, as well as some mementos that have come in handy.

The family dog—an ignorant creature—barely stirs when Casey comes around now, other than to happily chew the chunks of steak fed to him with gloved fingers.

But those days are over. Now isn't the time to throw caution to the wind. You don't painstakingly scale a towering tree only to remove your safety harness just short of the apex.

But this *is* a special night; one that calls for a celebration.

And I know just the place . . .

The Village Common is aglow with white twinkle lights. The surrounding streets are quiet, though hardly deserted. The red brick Village Hall, stately Dapplebrook Inn, and cobblestone library building are aglow. The Olde Opera House marquee advertises a current showing of a popular art house film. Restaurants are busy, and a couple of shops have extended holiday shopping hours. There are only a few available parking spaces in the municipal lot. Casey pulls into one of them and waits for the song to come to an end before stepping out into the chilly night air and striding toward Marrana's.

Back when Rowan and Jake got engaged, long before they decided to move back to their hometown, they built their dream home—a shared imaginary one. They pictured themselves in a house with fireplaces and wooden floors and staircases; with tall paned windows and a ginger-bread porch.

They pictured themselves *here.*

Neither of them had ever been inside it, or even noticed it during all the years they'd spent growing up in Mundy's Landing. Yet the moment the Realtor drove them up to the house the real estate ad described as a Victorian charmer, they both knew it was meant to be theirs.

It was so ideal that Rowan sometimes wonders if it had been lurking somewhere in the back of her mind all along, an indelible fragment of some childhood memory that had long since evaporated.

The house had every feature they'd fantasized about and then some, but layer upon layer of "modern up-dates" had masked the original charm. Previous owners had painted the nineteenth-century woodwork, paneled over the wainscoting, layered the inlaid oak floors with shag carpet, and obscured vintage tin ceilings and crown moldings above popcorn drop ceilings.

That was fine with Rowan and Jake. The house was a bargain fixer-upper, well within their budget. Restoring it had encompassed the better part of a decade and a good chunk of money, but it was worthwhile.

Their dream home has become a reality, something Rowan doesn't tend to take for granted. Most evenings, when the day is fading and the rooms glow with lamplight, hushed aside from the electric hum of the dishwasher or television, she soaks up the cozy ambiance.

Tonight, as usual, she's settled into the quiet nook off the foyer that serves as her home office. A few hours stretch between now and bedtime, to be filled with lesson planning or reading or poking around on the Internet, something she doesn't get to do at her day job, unlike many of her friends.

Officially, this room—which has solid cherry pocket doors, a marble fireplace, built-in bookshelves, and vintage wall sconces that were originally gas—was intended for the entire family to use. Unofficially, it's hers alone, cluttered with her books and files and decorated with tag sale finds: a fainting couch upholstered in rose velvet, a doily-topped pie crust table, an antique baby buggy with a yellowed christening gown draped over the handle.

Hearing the familiar opening music for NFL's *Monday Night Football* coming from the TV in the living room across the foyer, she quickly sets aside the stack of social studies tests she'd been grading.

Rather, trying to grade. And pretending to grade, when Jake slid open one of the doors and poked his head in here earlier to ask what had happened to the pistachio nuts he'd bought over the weekend.

"They're in the top left cupboard," she told him, red

pen poised as though he'd just interrupted her from doing
something other than fretting about the mysterious package she'd received this afternoon.

"No, they aren't. I just looked."

"They're there."

"They're not," he volleyed back, and they embarked
upon yet another discussion of the sort they've had countless times over two decades of marriage.

"Mick must have eaten them," Jake decided.

"Mick doesn't *like* them."

"No, he just doesn't want to be bothered with the shells.
But if he was hungry enough—and when isn't he?—then
he probably . . ."

Shut up!

That was what Rowan wanted to scream at her unwitting husband in that moment. Didn't he realize how insignificant his stupid pistachio nuts were? Didn't he know
she had other things to worry about?

No. He didn't.

Still doesn't. Thank God. She's not about to bring it
up, and Mick was already at his busboy job when Jake
walked in the door after work. He won't be home for at
least another hour. By then, with luck, he'll have forgotten all about the package that came in the mail, which is
currently stashed in a dark corner of the attic. She wanted
to throw it away, but with the garbage can latch broken,
raccoons might get into it overnight and leave it strewn
across the steps for the whole world—*Jake*—to see.

Right now, he's safely occupied with *Monday Night
Football* and the pistachios, which of course he found in the
top left cupboard after all, right where she said they'd be.

It's not that she runs a highly organized household.
Far from it. But after two decades of marriage and one
of medication, there is a certain order to the chaos. Jake
somehow has yet to fully grasp it.

She pushes the stack of social studies papers aside, drops the pen, and opens her laptop. Before she allows herself to start typing, she looks over her shoulder again to make sure Jake hasn't resurfaced in the doorway.

Satisfied that she's alone, Rowan opens a search engine, resigned to searching for the man who's been on her mind ever since she realized what was in that box.

Cookies.

Burnt cookies.

Thirteen of them.

"Why thirteen?" he asked on that snowy afternoon, watching her carry the baking sheet over to the oven. "That's unlucky, isn't it?"

"Not for me," she said. "When I was a kid, my sister taught me how to bake, but she always wanted me to put exactly a dozen balls of dough onto the sheet for every batch. She was a real stickler for recipes and rules."

"And you weren't big on rules?"

She allowed herself to grin naughtily at him. "Never."

She knew she was flirting. Somehow, she didn't care.

The kids were safely in the next room, parked in front of the television watching *How the Grinch Stole Christmas*. Not the old cartoon Rowan remembered from her childhood, but the recent movie with Jim Carrey. She'd bought the DVD the week before and intended to save it for Christmas, but pulled it out to occupy the kids while the adults were in the kitchen . . . baking cookies.

She finished telling him about her sister: "Whenever she wasn't looking, I'd put an extra ball of dough on the baking sheet—and then I'd snag the extra cookies for myself when they were done, and still have an even dozen."

She remembers feeling his eyes on her as she put that last cookie sheet into the oven. Remembers the silence that fell between them and that she could hear Faith Hill

singing "Where Are You, Christmas?" on TV in the next
room. Remembers setting the timer for eight minutes.

Remembers . . .

Remembers how they wound up in the laundry room
off the kitchen. They didn't even notice the stove buzzer
when it went off. But they certainly heard the blast of the
smoke alarm ten, maybe twelve minutes later.

Thank God for that.

Saved by the bell.

The cookies were burned.

She dumped the batch into the kitchen garbage after
he was safely out of the house. She remembers putting the
closed white kitchen bag inside a black trash bag, closing that tightly, and putting it inside another bag before
carrying it out to the trash can. She was uneasy about it
being there for the next few days until garbage pickup, as
if it would somehow incriminate her should Jake stumble
across it.

Her heart stopped that night when he stood in the
kitchen stomping the snow from his boots, sniffing the
air, and asking her if she'd burned dinner.

"No," she told him, "just toast, earlier."

The lie rolled off her tongue as impulsively as it would
have fifteen years earlier if her parents had caught her
breaking curfew or if the vice principal had found her
cutting class in the gazebo. Old habits—shameful ones
you'd worked hard to obliterate—die hard.

That was the first lie—and one of the few—of their
marriage, and such a silly, unnecessary one. She could
have said cookies instead of toast. That simple truth
wouldn't have alerted him that while he was working his
ass off to earn a living for them, she was in their next door
neighbor's arms.

Richard Walker.

She types the name into the search engine, heart pounding, and hits Enter.

The joy went out of Mick's evening when Brianna Armbruster cashed out her tips and went home almost an hour ago, soon followed by Zach and just about everyone else. He's more than ready to call it a night, but a couple of solo diners are lingering and he can't leave until they do.

They're both alone at tables for two, and finished their meals long ago with dropped checks waiting to be paid. If they didn't have their backs to each other, Mick might think they were interested in each other, each hoping the other might make a move. But they appear to be in their own little worlds: the guy is sipping bourbon and reading a book; the woman drinking tea and endlessly typing on an iPad.

Standing in the corner of the dining room with Patty, the waitress who's stuck here with him, Mick is quickly running out of things to talk about. She's a lot older than he is, and she's not a sports fan, which eliminates most topics that come to mind.

"So . . . did you start your Christmas shopping yet?" he asks.

"Started and finished it on Black Friday, except a couple of gift cards I need to pick up."

"Gift cards—thanks for reminding me!" He reaches into his pocket and pulls out the money his mother gave him. "I need to get a gift certificate to Marrana's for my mom."

"No offense, but maybe you should get her something a little more personal. Does she like jewelry? Because they have those new Trinkettes over at Vernon's Apothecary."

"New what?"

"Trinkettes—you know, the bead charm bracelets with the little stick figures. All the high school girls are wearing them."

Brianna isn't, and anyway, that has nothing to do with this.

"My mom has been out of high school for a few years now," Mick reminds Patty, "and anyway, *I'm* not giving *her* the gift certificate. She's giving it to someone at work for a Secret Santa. That's this thing where they leave each other little gifts every day next week, and then on Friday they—"

"I know what a Secret Santa is," Patty cuts in.

"You do? Am I the only person who's never heard of it before?"

"Pretty much," she says, walking over to the cash register. "Okay, I'll ring up your gift certificate." In a lower voice, glancing at the two customers who show no signs of leaving any time soon, she adds, "Too bad I can't ring up their checks, too, so we can get the hell out of here."

"Maybe we can flicker the lights or something."

"Not allowed. The first rule Mrs. Marrana ever taught me was never to rush customers out the door."

Mick doesn't bother to point out that Mrs. Marrana herself rushed out the door earlier and will never know. Patty has worked here much longer than he has, and she's probably even more eager to get home to her boyfriend than Mick is to go finish an overdue chemistry lab. If he doesn't hand it in tomorrow, it'll cost him a letter grade. That wouldn't be that big a deal if he wasn't barely hanging in there with a C-minus.

Patty hands him the gift certificate, then quietly tells him she's going to the ladies' room to put on some lipstick. "If they leave, lock the door and flip the sign right away."

"Don't worry, I will."

As she walks away, Mick weighs the wisdom of flickering the lights while she's gone.

"Don't even think about it," she murmurs without turning her head, and Mick can't help but grin.

It fades when he glances again at the two customers who stand—or rather, sit—between him and freedom.

How can people be so dense?

Both appear to be in their thirties or maybe forties. He can never tell how old older people are. Both are wearing businesslike clothing; neither wears a wedding ring. The guy has a beard and glasses; the woman is slightly overweight with strawberry blond hair and a pretty face. Mick watches her absently lift the little teapot to add more hot water to her cup, only to realize it's empty. As she glances around to summon a refill, he quickly busies himself sorting clean silverware that's already been sorted. Twice.

"Excuse me?" she calls pleasantly. "Can I please get some more water for my tea?"

"Um, actually . . . we're closed."

She looks at her watch. "What time do you close?"

"Well, the kitchen closes at nine-thirty on weeknights, so . . ." He shrugs and adds, "I'm really sorry."

Her pleasant tone and expression evaporate. "I'm not asking for another entrée. Just some hot water so that I can finish my tea."

You just did, he wants to say.

Instead, he offers another unapologetic apology.

She scowls and looks over at the man at the next table, clearly expecting him to speak up and protest this outrage. He turns a page of his book as if to punctuate the fact that he's ignoring them both.

With a beleaguered sigh, the woman goes back to typing on her iPad, probably posting a negative online review about the rude busboy at Marrana's Trattoria.

Five minutes later, she's still typing and Patty is still in the ladies' room when the man abruptly snaps his book closed, reaches for the check folder, glances at the bill, and tucks a few bills inside. He stands, retrieves a navy peacoat from the rack, and heads for the door with a cursory "Thanks."

"Good night," Mick calls after him, hoping the female customer will take the hint.

She does, so promptly that for a moment Mick wonders whether they'd arranged some kind of secret rendezvous without him noticing.

But as he locks the door and flips the sign, he sees them walking in opposite directions down the street, neither taking a backward glance.

This isn't the first time Rowan's looked for Rick since she moved away from Westchester County. But never before has it seemed so important to find him.

The problem with a name like Richard Walker is that you can never be sure you've found the right one based on the name alone. There are hundreds of Richard Walkers scattered through the tri-state area, and thousands beyond.

She scans page after page of search results, looking for a listing that fits everything she knew about him before they lost touch thirteen years ago. She remembers that his favorite color was orange, that he was left-handed, that he was obsessed with airplanes as a little boy, that his family's house burned down not long before he graduated high school.

Those details don't count, but they come rushing back at her along with countless others, none of which are useful. She doesn't recall—or more likely never knew—concrete details like his birth date and graduation years and wedding date; the name or location of his Midwestern hometown, his parents' names, or even what he did for a living.

He'd grown up dreaming of becoming an airline pilot, but that hadn't happened because, as he told her, "I could barely afford college, let alone flight training, and the military didn't want me."

"Why not?"

"Smoke inhalation from the fire—I had a collapsed lung, and it took me a long time to heal."

He was between jobs when she knew him, and she can't even remember what his career had been, only that it had nothing to do with aviation. It was insignificant in the grand scheme of things.

She clicks on one Richard Walker entry after another, looking for details that might fit. He'd be in his late forties or early fifties, and is probably still somewhere in New York. The package was postmarked there, and packed with a crumpled local newspaper.

Why the hell would he do such a thing after all these years?

The man she'd known hadn't seemed capable of a malicious prank.

Okay, so maybe he didn't send the package.

Maybe it was someone else.

His wife, Vanessa? Had she, after all these years, somehow found out what happened?

But nothing happened! Not really.

That's what Rowan told herself afterward. And, all right, when time eventually burned off the fog that seemed to have settled over her in those days, she knew it wasn't "nothing."

But it wasn't what it might have been, what it undoubtedly would have been if the smoke alarm hadn't gone off, or if she'd ever dared let herself be alone in a room with Rick for even five minutes after that day . . .

But I didn't. I made sure.

Even if Vanessa *thought* something had happened, it's hard for Rowan to imagine her doing something like this. She was a Wall Street executive, the breadwinner while Rick stayed at home with the kids, two of whom were hers from a prior marriage.

Rowan would wave at her sometimes as she scurried to and from her car in a suit with a satchel over her shoulder and a cell phone pressed to her ear. She'd wave back distractedly, setting herself apart from the wistful working moms who loved to tell Rowan how lucky she was to be at home with the kids; lucky that she never missed a parent conference or a choir concert or had to scramble on sick-kid days and snow days . . .

She only recalls one snow day when they were living in Westchester. November thirtieth. That was the day.

Maybe Vanessa found out about—

But nothing happened! Nothing happened!

Or was it someone else?

Only one other person besides Rick Walker knows about that day.

You shouldn't have told! Why did you tell?

The words that have been marching through Rowan's mind all night like a news crawl are the same ones she'd thought as soon as she'd unburdened her deep, dark secret years ago.

So many difficult moments in her life were impulse-driven, especially back then. But at least she confided in someone she trusted. Someone who promised never to tell.

But promises can be broken.

From the driver's seat in the municipal parking lot off Market Street, Casey has a clear view of Marrana's restaurant when the last remaining waitress and busboy emerge. The woman locks the door after them and has a quick word with the kid before lighting a cigarette and walking off down the street smoking it.

Rowan Mundy's youngest son is left alone on the deserted sidewalk to wait for his ride home.

It's an interesting, and tempting, scenario to be sure. Ever the opportunist, Casey clenches the wheel hard, trying not to imagine what it would be like to squeeze the kid's skinny neck instead.

But that's not part of the plan. Not this stage, anyway.

It might be different if Brianna, that cute little red-headed waitress, had been the one to walk away alone in the dark. She's young, but maybe not too young to be a stand-in. Casey regrets not having been seated in her section, and that her shift ended so soon.

You weren't the only one.

There was no mistaking the wistfulness on Mick Mundy's face when Brianna left.

The kid pulls a cell phone out of his pocket, texting and leaning as he waits for his ride home. Wearing an expensive down jacket, one leg bent with an enormous basketball sneaker resting against the brick outer wall of the restaurant, he looks as though he doesn't have a care in the world. Casey knows that is hardly the case.

Eavesdropping on Mick Mundy's conversation with Patty the waitress, Casey noted that the kid didn't mention that the girl he likes barely acknowledges him. He did, however, confess that his lousy grades might preclude him from going to Vermont for an upcoming ski weekend—never mind that they won't get him into a decent college. He also mentioned, a few times, that he was really hungry and that his feet hurt. Mick Mundy's concerns don't seem to focus very far beyond the immediate future.

Considering that his two older siblings and his father were your classic high school overachievers, that charac-

teristic must be attributed not to age, but to heredity—
maternal heredity, that is.

Mick doesn't just look like his mother. He acts like her.

Yes, he's afflicted with the same attention deficit disorder. But that's no excuse. Even with medication, he goes
careening through life with the same reckless attitude,
thinking only of his own immediate needs, heedless of
consequences his selfish actions might inflict upon other
people's innocent lives.

Mick and Rowan will never learn the error of their
ways unless they're made to suffer the way they've made
others suffer.

And they will. Very, very soon.

But not yet. Just as it was very important to wait until
November thirtieth to alert Rowan that her transgression
has not been forgiven or forgotten, it's only fitting that the
last days of her life be laced with anguish and dread.

As for Mick, Casey has yet to decide whether his
punishment includes execution—or simply witnessing
the hideous death that will soon befall his mother. Time
will tell. Plenty of sons lose their mothers at a young age.
Some are crippled by the loss; others are made stronger.

Headlights swing around a corner, illuminating the
sidewalk in front of the restaurant.

Casey is expecting—hoping—to see the familiar minivan, but it's a dark SUV with Rowan's husband behind
the wheel. He pulls up to the curb, the kid jumps into the
passenger seat, and they're gone.

But that was excellent; it really was. To have spent
this night, of all nights, incognito and in the company of
Rowan's son . . .

To have been the source of the kid's frustration, holding him captive in the restaurant with the unwitting as-
sistance of a fellow patron . . .

Heady with power, Cascy starts the engine, looks into the rearview mirror to back up, and is struck by the still-unfamiliar reflection. This look wasn't initially meant to be a disguise, and yet . . .

You look nothing like yourself. She wouldn't know you if she saw you.

Casey dared to get close enough to Rowan in public to test that theory a couple of times. It was at once vexing and exhilarating to have her brush on past in the supermarket aisle with an oblivious "Excuse me." Casey was tempted to grab hold of her and confront her, but managed to keep cool and move on as if they were total strangers; as if their lives—all their lives—had never intersected; as if they hadn't been forever impacted on that fateful day fourteen years ago.

It would be nice to imagine that the memory has tormented her all this time. But chances are—Rowan being Rowan—that she hasn't even thought about it in years.

It doesn't matter.

Casey is certain she's thinking about it tonight.

The house is still, other than the ticking mantel clock and an occasional creaking floorboard overhead that lets Rowan know Mick is still awake in his room. He's probably not doing his homework, as he claimed when he got home from the restaurant. More likely he's goofing off on the Internet while shooting wads of crumpled notebook paper into the hoop on the back of his door, having long ago misplaced the Nerf basketball that came with it.

Ordinarily, she'd have caught him in the act and told him to get to work or get to bed.

Ordinarily, she'd be in bed herself by now.

But when Jake turned in after the football game ended, she told him to go on upstairs without her.

"It's late. What are you doing?" he asked around a yawn.

She couldn't claim to be grading papers; he'd caught her on the computer.

"Christmas shopping," she told him.

"Can't it wait?"

"Cyber Monday deals end at midnight. I'm saving us a ton of money."

That was enough to send him upstairs with a simple "Great, good night."

Now it's after midnight, and Rowan has yet to buy anything, but she's fairly certain she's finally zeroed in on the right man.

She sits staring at the Facebook profile of a Rick Walker who appears to be the right age and works for an unnamed firm in Manhattan as an administrative services manager. At least, that's what it says here.

It might be a lie.

Everything can be a lie when it comes to social networking.

She can't access his private photos, but the headshot on his profile page bears some resemblance to the man she used to know. Yes, he's wearing sunglasses in the picture, and has a receding hairline, and is clean-shaven, while her Rick usually had five o'clock shadow.

Your Rick? Don't think of him as your Rick. Nothing happened.

Be that as it may . . .

This Facebook profile could very well belong to the Rick—Vanessa's Rick—with whom *nothing* happened fourteen years ago tonight.

She studies his friends list looking for mutual connections or familiar names, but doesn't find any, including his wife's. That's not surprising. The Vanessa she remembers doesn't strike Rowan as the type of person who'd waste time on social networking.

There are a few Facebook profiles that share her name, but none could possibly belong to her.

Rick Walker's younger two kids, whom she remembers with varying degrees of fondness, would be around the same age as her own. Their names don't appear on his friends list either, although that doesn't mean anything. Of her own three offspring, only Katie was willing to connect to her via social networking, and Rowan is fairly sure that she screens her Facebook page to keep her mother from seeing all but the most innocuous posts. Either that, or her daughter is leading an unusually dull social life for a college freshman.

After investigating Rick Walker's public Facebook profile as thoroughly as possible, Rowan looks for him on other social media and is quickly overwhelmed. It's just too hard to tell whether any of the Rick Walkers out there are the same man she used to know.

She can always send him a Facebook friend request and see if he accepts it.

But you don't want to be friends with him, she reminds herself. *That makes no sense after what he did to you, sending that package . . .*

Maybe it was just his way of telling her he still thinks about her after all these years. Maybe he meant it as a misguided grand romantic gesture.

Too bad it came off as merely creepy, and . . . all right, frightening.

Regardless of his motives, she has two options now: confront him, or ignore him. And ignoring just isn't her style—especially when she's angry. Which she is, more so by the moment.

How dare he barge into her life again?

She impulsively sends him a friend request, then sits staring at the screen under the irrational assumption that he'll accept instantly so that she can give him a piece of her mind.

When that doesn't happen—not instantly, and not in the space of another ten, fifteen, and then twenty minutes—she regrets having sent it. Now the ball is in his court, leaving her feeling even more helpless than she would if she'd ignored him.

She abruptly closes out of the Facebook screen, pushes back her chair, and starts to get up before thinking of Jake. He seemed to accept her Cyber Monday shopping story. But what if he decides to snoop through her computer to see whether she bought anything for him?

He's not a ten-year-old kid hoping for a new Xbox, she reminds herself. Yet she reaches again for the laptop and clears the browsing and search histories, just in case.

Satisfied she's covered her tracks, she turns off the computer and flicks off the desk lamp as a sudden gust of wind rattles the panes and stirs the sheer lace curtains that cover the windows. They're closed, of course. And poorly insulated. Still . . .

She's rarely spooked in this big old house. But there have been times, over the past few months, when she could have sworn she saw someone out there in the night, looking in, and once she had the eerie feeling that she was being watched in her second-floor bedroom.

When she mentioned that to Jake, he asked, "So which do you think it is? A ghost or a Peeping Tom?" His tone made it clear that he thought they were equally unlikely options, and she dropped the subject.

But now, standing alone in the dark, unsettled by the moving curtains, she feels a familiar twinge of apprehension.

Is it any wonder? It's been a hell of a day. Time to put it behind her at last.

As she starts to turn toward the doorway, a human shadow materializes outside the window. She sees it in the corner of her eye, amid the silhouettes of shrubs and trees in the yard, and a gasp catches in her throat.

Spinning to face the glass, she realizes that it's only the maple sapling she and Jake planted one spring to replace a mighty oak felled by a fierce winter storm. Braden took a photo of them that day, arm in arm, wearing jeans and holding shovels. It sits framed on her desk.

"A hundred years from now, our great grandchildren will tie a swing to its branches and push our great-great grandchildren in it," she told Jake as he dragged the hose over to soak the soil at its base.

"I like that you're assuming the house will still be in the family and that the kids will want to stay in Mundy's Landing."

"Why wouldn't they? We did. And this house is our happily-ever-after."

It was one of those rare days when she appreciated it all: the house, and the life she and Jake had built there together. The day before and the day after were undoubtedly fraught with the usual tensions, but on that April day, in that moment, it all seemed idyllic.

Dogged by the memory of it—and by a fresh wave of fear-tainted guilt—Rowan scuttles up the stairs to bed, heart pounding.

As she slips beneath the covers beside her snoring husband, she wills sleep to overtake her quickly; a complete and dreamless sleep.

But she finds herself staring up through the skylight above their bed at the bare tree branches moving against the night sky, thinking of the past and the mysterious box in the attic. Now, not only does she feel as though she's inhabiting a blond stranger's body whenever she looks into a mirror, but she's been enveloped by the strange sense that she's inadvertently trespassed into someone else's life.

Oh, who is she kidding?

It's like she's been thrown back into her *own* life, the one she'd tried so hard to leave behind with her teenage years.

Fourteen years ago, having long since transformed herself from a rebellious kid to an upstanding wife and mother and fourth-grade teacher, she'd nearly ventured back into dangerous territory. Teetering on the familiar good girl/bad girl precipice, she could easily have lost sight of who she really is and what matters most. But in the end, that hadn't happened. Sheer conviction kept her on the straight and narrow. That was all that counted.

That, and the fact that Jake and the kids would never find out.

Or so she believed.

Now someone—*Rick? Damn you, Rick!*—wants her to be aware that her secret was never safe; that she isn't safe at all, even now. Her entire world can unravel in an instant, and she's no longer in charge.

Sleep refuses to claim her just as it did fourteen years ago tonight, dooming her to greet the cold and gloomy December dawn with restless exhaustion and the sense that the battle she thought she'd won long ago has begun anew.

From the *Mundy's Landing Tribune* Archives
Society Page
June 20, 1993

Rowan M. Carmichael Weds
A. Jacob Mundy IV

Surrounded by family and friends, Rowan Mary Carmichael exchanged vows with Asa Jacob Mundy IV in a double ring ceremony at Holy Angels Church on Saturday afternoon.

The groom is the son of Mrs. Laura Mundy III of Mundy's Landing and the late Asa Jacob Mundy III. The bride is the daughter of Jonathan "Mickey" Carmichael of Mundy's Landing and the late Katherine Devlin Carmichael. Given in marriage by her father, she wore her mother's silk gown, which had a V-neckline and was accented with Alençon lace appliques, and she carried a bouquet of peonies and roses.

The bride's sister, Noreen Carmichael Chapman of Oyster Bay, was matron of honor. Bridesmaids were Liza Mundy of Austin and Carolyn Kaliszewski of Buffalo. Edward Mundy, cousin of the groom, was best man, and ushers were Mitchell and Daniel Carmichael, brothers of the bride. Andrew Carmichael, the bride's nephew, was the ring bearer.

Following a honeymoon in Cancun, the newlyweds will make their home in Westchester County, where Mrs. Mundy will begin a teaching position in the fall. Mr. Mundy is employed as an advertising executive in New York City.

Chapter 3

The work week passed without further incident. For that, Rowan is grateful. She hasn't allowed herself to completely forget about the package of burnt cookies, still tucked away beneath the attic rafters, but she's gone from dwelling on it in a constant state of paranoia to accepting that it happened and trying to move on.

That's much easier to accomplish in some moments than in others. During the days when she's busy in the classroom, she barely has time to think about it, much less check her Facebook page to see whether Rick Walker has responded to her errant friend request. But her nights at home have been marked by frequent and futile Facebook patrols and by restless worrying and wondering and very little sleep.

By the time Friday night rolls around, she's feeling utterly drained. She'd much prefer climbing into bed in her pajamas to climbing into the bleachers in the high school gym. But Mick has a home game, and she never misses one.

Her friend Nancy Vandergraaf does a double take as Rowan settles onto the bench beside her. "Rowan! I didn't recognize you without your red hair. What happened?"

"I got old," she says wryly.

"If you're old, then I'm ancient."

Nancy, who used to be Nancy Morrison, graduated Mundy's Landing High two years ahead of Rowan and steadily dated her brother Danny. He went on to marry his college sweetheart and lives in California, while Nancy married—and later messily divorced—Danny's former best friend, Christian Vandergraaf. Rowan wasn't living here when that particular small-town drama unfolded, but Nancy had long since filled her in. She talks a lot and spares very few details.

She particularly enjoys bringing up their shared high school past, which she remembers far more fondly than Rowan. Nancy was a class officer and honor student whose glory days unfolded beneath this very roof, while Rowan was the quintessential party girl whose memories of that era are often shrouded in a haze of forbidden substances.

"So where's Jake tonight?" Nancy wants to know.

"He's having dinner with a couple of sales reps in Albany but he's going to try to make the second half of the game." Rowan presses a hand to her mouth as a yawn escapes her. "Sorry. Long week."

"Tell me about it." Nancy launches into a drawn-out personal drama involving a plumber, a flea-ridden dog, a cold sore, and a Christmas gift that's been backordered until February.

Nancy, whose only child plays on the team with Mick, is one of those irritating people who, if you're tired, will tell you she's more tired; if you're busy, she's busier; if you've had bad news, she's had worse. Sometimes Rowan nips her monologues in the bud, but tonight, she lets her talk. The tirade blends with the chatter of the gathering crowd around them and the cheerleaders' chants and the squeaking of basketball shoes on the polished hardwoods as the team warms up.

Then Nancy interrupts herself to whisper, "Look at

Diane Westerly pretending she has no clue who's sitting behind her."

Rowan looks. "What do you mean?"

"You're kidding, right?"

"Wrong. Who's sitting behind her?"

"Lynda Carlotta!" When that fails to get a reaction, Nancy adds, "You didn't hear?"

"Obviously not." Rowan rubs her burning shoulder blade, not really caring whether she hears now, or not.

"Diane's having an affair with Jim Carlotta."

Affair.

The word brings Rowan right back to Monday, and the box filled with burnt cookies, and Rick Walker.

"How do you know that?"

"Everyone knows. Everyone except Lynda, anyway." Nancy shakes her brunette head. "I can't believe she'd do something like that."

"Like not knowing about her husband's affair?"

"What? No, I'm talking about Diane! She's the horrible one, not Lynda. I mean, they're friends."

"What about Jim? They're *married.*"

"He's horrible, too," Nancy agrees in an offhanded way that somehow implies the cheating husband isn't quite as blameworthy as the backstabbing woman.

Or maybe Rowan is reading too much into the conversation. Maybe she's identifying with Diane Westerly, a perpetually frazzled stay-at-home mother of four, imagining how she might have, in a brief, wayward moment, found herself in the arms of a man whose kids have long shared sandboxes and cafeteria tables and carpools with her own.

As Nancy talks on, Rowan surreptitiously pulls her cell phone out of the back pocket of her jeans and sneaks a peek at her Facebook account. There's one new notification: *Rick Walker has accepted your friend request.*

She jumps to her feet, heart racing.

"Where are you going, Ro? The game's about to start."

"I know, but I forgot I have to . . . call someone." She's already weaving her way down the bleachers, seeking empty spots on benches for her boots. It's slow going, and several people expect her to stop and chat. She brushes them off and keeps going, clutching her phone in her trembling hand and heading toward the nearest set of doors.

At last, she steps outside into the cold night air. Only then does she exhale. She hadn't even realized she'd been holding her breath.

A light sleet is falling, landing in droplets on the back-lit screen.

"Moisture isn't good for electronics," she hears herself telling Mick, who's always leaving his own phone by the tub or kitchen sink.

"It's okay," he invariably responds.

"It's *not* okay."

After all these years, the maternal ritual plays out in her head like an oldies soundtrack on the radio, so much a part of her that she barely takes notice.

Her feet carry her on a familiar route across the back parking lot toward the gazebo that was donated by her sister's senior class upon their graduation. Noreen Carmichael had spearheaded the fund-raising efforts and proudly wielded the scissors at the ribbon-cutting ceremony.

How well Rowan recalls her parents' pride in her sister on that sunny June day over thirty years ago. How well she remembers their shame when she herself was caught on that very spot a few years later, cutting class and smoking—just regular cigarettes that day, thank goodness.

It wasn't the first time she'd gotten into trouble, but it was memorable for a couple of reasons. She wasn't just

given detention, she was suspended. Dad yelled, Mom
sobbed; they doled out the usual grounding and warnings and threats, none of which got through to her. It took
a tragedy for Rowan to wake up and make the promise
she's bent on keeping to this day.

Directly on the heels of Rowan's disgrace, Mom was
diagnosed with acute myelogenous leukemia, a fast-
moving, virulent form of cancer. She lived mere weeks.
In one of her final lucid moments, she begged her youngest daughter to "be a good girl."

And from that day on, I was.

Stepping into the gazebo, Rowan heads for the bench
where she held court on many a defiant day—and night—
surrounded by fellow mavericks who have long since
faded from her life. Perhaps a few managed to redeem
themselves, moving away, joining the military. But most
of those kids burned out quickly after high school and
more than one died young, their granite headstones in
Holy Angels Cemetery a somber reminder of the road not
taken.

Ironic, Rowan thinks, that in this spot at this time of
year, when the branches are bare, there's a pretty good
view of Milkweed Pond. That's where she and Jake went
skating on their first date twenty-five years ago. It was
Christmas night, and snow was falling like moonlit glit-
ter, and their paths were forever altered the moment they
kissed. She vividly remembers praying that he felt the
same sparks and promising God that she would never ask
Him for anything else if this perfect man could just fall
in love with her.

He wasn't perfect, of course. But she didn't notice or
care. If someone had time traveled back to that moment
from the future to assure her that she would wear Jake
Mundy's wedding ring and bear his children and share
his bed for the rest of her life, she'd have been ecstatic.

And if that same someone had told her that one day she'd resent that Jake snores and doesn't know how to cook, that he whistles in the shower and considers khaki and gray compatible clothing colors, that she would eventually—even just fleetingly—find someone else more attractive and appealing . . .

She'd have said that was impossible.

Even now that it's actually happened, that last part seems impossible.

Beneath the shelter of the octagonal wooden roof, she pushes away her first-date memories of Jake on a sickening tide of remorse. Again, she focuses on her phone.

She is, indeed, now Facebook friends with Rick Walker.

Now that she's been granted access to his private profile page, she can see that he's not prone to frequent updates and when he does post something, it's nothing particularly relevant: photos of meals and sunsets and a few shared cartoons and articles about golf courses—did Rick even golf? Is this the wrong man?

Even as she wonders whether she's befriended some random stranger, she clicks on his private photo album and suddenly there he is: the man she used to know. He's wearing a dress shirt with rolled-up sleeves and a tie, standing between a pair of middle-aged women, neither of them Vanessa. He has more wrinkles and less hair, but the grin is familiar.

She's so taken aback at the sight of him that she doesn't immediately realize that she also has a new private message—from him.

Rowan, wow, what a surprise. Thanks for finding me here. I actually found your profile last year when I first got on Facebook but I didn't know if I should send you a friend request. I'm glad you made the first move. You look great in your pictures and I'm happy to see that you and Jake are still together and the kids seem to be doing well. I'm working in Manhattan and living in New Jersey, single and dating, with an empty nest. I'd love to connect in person sometime so let me know if you're ever in New York.

Shaken by the casual words, and by his admission that he's single and dating, she reads the message several times, searching for hidden meaning.

Wow, what a surprise . . .

I'm glad you made the first move . . .

I'm happy to see that you and Jake are still together . . .

One moment those phrases seem to resonate irony; the next sincerity.

Either he sent the package and he's baiting her, or he's utterly oblivious—in which case, he needs to be told. But not, she decides, in writing.

I'm going to be in New York this weekend, she types back quickly. *Can we get together for coffee?*

Thinking better of it, she stands with her thumb poised over the Send button, thoughts flying through the scenario.

Jake doesn't have to know she's going to New York. She'll tell him she's going to have lunch with her sister.

Then again—what if Noreen happens to call?

Asking her sister to cover for her is out of the question.

She'll just have to tell Jake she's going to spend the day Christmas shopping.

But—the same excuse? Is it getting tired?

No—she knows he won't question her. She and Katie have spent plenty of Saturdays from dawn to dusk at the Woodbury Common Outlet Mall down in Central Valley, well over an hour away. She hasn't had the heart to go back there since her daughter left for college, but with the holidays looming, she'd probably have gone alone sooner or later.

But lying to her husband . . . is that a good idea?

Of course not. It's a terrible idea.
But what choice do you have?

The truth: that's her choice. Maybe she should just tell Jake that she's going to the city for the day tomorrow. Leaving out the part about meeting Rick would make her guilty of omission, but not a lie.

That's the kind of reasoning Rowan might have used in her troubled youth when her undiagnosed disability left her frequently suffering the consequences of her impulsive tendencies. Time and again, she disappointed the parents who loved and trusted her.

"Don't you let her down," her ravaged father told her the day she made her deathbed promise to her mother.

"I won't, Daddy. I promise. I'll make her proud, and you, too."

She could see the doubt in his green eyes and spent years trying to erase it. She isn't convinced she ever fully did.

But Jake . . .

Jake never once looked at her that way. Unlike Mom and Dad, he never knew her as a truth-bending opportunist.

If she tells him she's going to the city, he won't ask questions. He might want to come with her, though. When they were living in Westchester, they made an annual excursion to see the store windows on Fifth Avenue and the tree at Rockefeller Center. The kids were little and the crowds were overwhelming and it probably was never as much fun as it was supposed to be, but Rowan has fond memories of the city at Christmas and she knows Jake does, too. She can imagine him saying, *We'll both go, and Mick can come, too. Maybe we can grab Knicks tickets . . .*

No. No, that won't work. Maybe she should just forget about seeing Rick Walker in person. Maybe she should just write back right now and ask him what the hell he thinks he's doing, tracking her down and sending an anonymous package.

As she stands weighing her options, her phone rings in her hand, startling her. Her thumb comes down on the Send button and the message she was just deciding to delete goes zinging out into cyberspace.

Ten minutes later, back in the bleachers, she sneaks a peek at her account and finds a reply.

I'd love to see you! I'm free all day tomorrow. Name the time and place.

Okay. So there it is. She's going, which means she's lying.

Reminding herself that it's for Jake's own good, she watches the rest of the game grimly and is relieved when he doesn't show up after all.

She's in bed when he gets home, pretending to be asleep.

Another lie, on the heels of the note she left for him on the kitchen counter: *Going shopping first thing in the a.m., probably won't be back till dinner.*

Old habits . . .

Dammit.

But it'll be the last lie ever, she promises herself as her husband begins to snore peacefully beside her.

Saturday dawns damp and dreary, perfect for staying in bed. That's where Jake and Mick are when Rowan leaves the house after too little sleep and too little coffee. Extra caffeine would only make her even more nervous, if that's possible.

In the large master bathroom—which had been a sleeping porch before she and Jake renovated the house—she dresses in jeans, boots, and a black turtleneck. After surveying her reflection, she pulls a gray cardigan over the turtleneck. No need to display her curves. Then she decides that the cardigan isn't flattering and swaps both sweaters for a blouse and blazer. Unbuttoning the top two buttons, she glimpses cleavage and hastily buttons both. Now she looks like a prim schoolmarm. She settles on just the top button open: casually comfortable.

The hair and makeup are just as befuddling. Letting it hang in loose blondish waves is potentially sexy, which she doesn't want, yet now that it's shoulder-length, a ponytail is too stubby and severe. Her lashes and thin lips tend to disappear without cosmetic enhancement, but the liner and lipstick she wears on a daily basis suddenly seem suggestive. She doesn't want him getting ideas.

Oh, come on.

He probably already *has* ideas, unless he really is the one who sent the package, in which case he's all but summoned her presence this morning. But if he's expecting a walk on the shady side of memory lane, he's in for an unpleasant surprise.

In the end, she skips the lipstick and eyeliner, goes with the ponytail, and turns her back on the mirror. Downstairs, she finds Doofus blissfully snoozing on the rug and has to shake him awake.

"You'd make a lousy watchdog, you know that?"

He wags his tail, apparently mistaking it as a compliment.

"I don't suppose you've seen my keys?" she adds, unsuccessfully searching the cluttered kitchen surfaces, a daily occurrence.

She lets the dog out into the yard and takes her medication on an empty stomach. To stave off the predictable tide of nausea—evocative of morning-sickness-meets-wretched-hangover—she belatedly gobbles a couple of saltines as she continues searching for her keys. After finding them in the pocket of last night's jacket, she coaxes Doofus back inside too soon even for his taste.

"Sorry, but I've got to run," she explains, dumping some food into a bowl for him and convinced he's gazing reproachfully after her when she finally hurtles herself out the door.

The pavement is slick and shiny as she winds her way south along Highland Road, riding the brake in anticipation of joggers and deer. Tendrils of mist obscure portions of the highway she knows so well.

Growing up in Mundy's Landing, she longed for the day she could leave the village behind. But when it finally arrived, she found herself longing to go back home. It took her well over a decade to do that. After a year as a commuter student at Hadley, the only college willing to admit her, probably only because the admissions people were local and knew about her recently deceased mother, she transferred to her mother's alma mater, the University of Buffalo. Like Mom, she majored in education, not because she particularly wanted to become a teacher, but because it made her feel closer to her mother and it made her widowed father happy.

Weary of western New York winters, she went south to Virginia for her master's. But while she was back home over Christmas break, she met Asa Jacob Mundy IV, though no one ever called him that. He was just Jake. He was seven years older than Rowan, having graduated high school just ahead of her oldest brother, Mitch.

Like most graduates of Mundy's Landing High School during their era, Jake had gone away to college and stayed away. His father had died fairly young and his mother was still living in Mundy's Landing, but she's long since settled in Texas with Jake's older sister, Liza.

Jake hadn't strayed so far: he was working for an ad agency in New York City when Rowan met him.

They were married the June after she got her master's degree. She'd had her fill of steamy Southern summers and welcomed the chance to move North again. She found a teaching position in the New York suburbs and that's where they settled. Her father adored Jake—not just because everyone likes Jake, but because he was a hometown boy, a Mundy.

Dad lived to walk Rowan down the aisle and hold her firstborn, but died while she was pregnant with her second. He never met the daughter Rowan named for her mother, or his own namesake, Mick; never got to see her come full circle back to Mundy's Landing.

Not a day goes by that she doesn't long for her parents or remember the promises she made to them both and struggled so hard to keep.

What would they think of her now?

They wouldn't be proud of me—that's for damned sure.

Resisting the urge to feel sorry for herself, Rowan swallows over the lump in her throat and merges onto the thruway headed toward New York City, determined to make things right again.

The drive should take only two hours, but three and a half have passed before she's finally pulling into a parking garage in the West Fifties. It was pouring by the time she reached the northern suburbs, and steady traffic gave way to notorious holiday gridlock within the city limits.

She'd expected to have plenty of time to gather her emotions before meeting Rick, but she's got less than fifteen minutes to make her way to the Hell's Kitchen restaurant he'd suggested. She covers those blocks beneath a dripping umbrella, pausing on every corner to exchange texts with Jake, who's back home and filled with the usual questions about where to find things that have gone missing in the laundry room or kitchen. A phone call would be easier, but she knows there'll be no passing off the rumbles, honks, and shouts of urban street noise for a shopping mall.

She signs off with a quick "TTYL" when she arrives at the designated meeting spot.

It appears to be more of a no-frills coffee shop than the upscale café she was for some reason anticipating. He suggested it, saying it was close to the West Side Highway and the PATH trains to Jersey, where he now lives . . . alone.

That his marriage to Vanessa didn't survive probably shouldn't surprise Rowan, but it does.

There but for the grace of God, she thinks, pausing in front of the door to silence her phone. Then, taking a deep breath, she steps inside the restaurant.

She recognizes Rick Walker immediately, sitting alone in a booth with his back to the door. There's something strikingly familiar about the poised, pensive posture: elbows propped on the table, raised cup clutched in both hands, head bent.

Either he's got her right where he wants her, or he's in for one hell of a nasty surprise.

"Table for one?" a waitress asks, and she shakes her head and points toward Rick.

"I'm joining someone."

The woman waves her on, but Rowan hesitates, unwilling to approach him. She reminds herself that she's anonymous here; no one is watching her, judging her. But it isn't easy to push aside the guilt and trepidation.

At last, she walks over to the table and steels herself for the confrontation whose script has been running through in her head all night.

"Rick?" Her voice works. So far, so good.

He looks up, lights up with a grin that crinkles the corners of his eyes just as she remembers. He sets down the mug—tea, she sees, noting the string dangling over the edge. He always chose tea over coffee.

"I'm surprised you don't," he said once, soon after they met.

"Why?"

"Because you grew up in an Irish household."

"So you assume we drank tea?"

"You didn't?"

"Sure we did. And whiskey, too, and we ate corned beef and cabbage every night and wore kilts and danced jigs . . ."

"And hid pots of gold at the end of the rainbow, right?"

"Exactly," she agreed with a laugh.

Snippets of that lighthearted exchange float into her head as he gets up to embrace her like a long-lost friend.

"Rowan. It's so good to see you. I almost didn't recognize you without your hair."

"I still have hair." He does, too, but it's thinning.

"I meant your long red hair. But you look great. Sit down."

She'd been worried until this moment that she'd take one look at him and become infatuated all over again. But that isn't the case, and it's not just because he's a middle-aged man now. His looks were never the draw in the first place. It was more that Rick understood her—or rather, she perceived that he understood her—far better than Jake did at the time.

Unlike her husband, he knew his way around the kitchen and the supermarket; the playground and the pediatrician's office; the preschool parking lot and—perhaps most important—the circle of moms. Neither of them could relate to the designer stroller–pushing crowd that populated their suburb. Rowan and Rick seemed to be the only two parents on the playground who hadn't grown up in Westchester, didn't come from money, and didn't have doting parents willing to write fat checks and babysit the grandkids. Nor had they swapped demanding corporate careers to spend days at home with their toddlers. They used to laughingly speculate that some of those moms managed their kids the way they used to manage their corporate minions.

Jake would never have grasped the humor in imagining a brisk memo delivered to a sandbox with a cc to a crib, bearing the subject line "Potty Training Objectives" or "Naptime Agenda."

Rick got it. He got her.

She used to wonder whether she'd married the wrong man.

Now I'm positive I didn't, she thinks as she sinks into the booth, missing Jake already. What a difference fourteen years—a lifetime—has made. She'd give anything to be at home where she belongs, instead of here with Rick, exhuming memories.

The place feels familiar. They sometimes took the kids out for lunch after preschool pickup, to a diner just like this one. Maybe that's why he chose it.

Yes, and one of his boys—or was it Braden?—was going through a stage when he'd eat nothing but simple white carbs. Bagels, cereal, buttered pasta . . .

Funny that she doesn't remember whether it was his son or her own, but she clearly remembers sitting across from Rick in a corner booth crammed with kids and crumbs, talking endlessly about parenting challenges she might have discussed with the other moms if they weren't so cliquey, or with her own mom if she were still alive.

When she'd become a mother a decade after losing her own, Rowan was surprised to find herself grieving the loss all over again and feeling lonelier than she had in years. Then Rick came along, and he was interested in her day-to-day existence because he shared it. He actually cared about potty training technique and transitioning away from naps and training wheels . . .

When she discussed those things with Jake, he always seemed to be either disinterested or oppositional. "Why do you bother asking me for my opinion if you don't want to listen to what I have to say?" he'd ask.

"I didn't ask for your opinion. You offered it."

"They're my kids, too."

"I know. But it's fine. I'm the one who's with them most of the time, so I'll deal with it."

And she would—often with plenty of helpful input from Rick Walker.

And yes, she did think he was good-looking back then. Not conventionally tall, dark, and handsome like Jake. But Rick had warm brown eyes and a quick grin and was hilariously funny, and so sweet and caring with his kids—and with her kids, and with her. He was always complimenting her on her laugh, her parenting skills, her hair—especially her hair.

"I've always had a thing for redheads . . ."

The comment hadn't seemed particularly inappropriate at the time. She'd been too caught up in her infatuation, wondering what it would be like to kiss him, and then one day . . .

She knew.

How exhilarating to realize he'd been longing for the same forbidden connection all those times they were together. How satisfying to indulge blatant desire after all those years of keeping her emotions and behavior in check.

And how utterly foolish, and selfish, and sinful, and terrifying.

They size each other up across the table.

What's supposed to come next?

An accusation, she believes. But the words she'd rehearsed refuse to form on her lips, so she busies herself shrugging out of her coat and arranging her paper napkin on her lap. Meanwhile, he starts to talk. And talk. He doesn't sound anxious, but maybe he is, because he won't shut up and give her a moment to gather her thoughts and her nerve.

He's telling her how happy he is that she wanted to get together, asking her how things are, how everyone has been.

"Jake? The kids? Are they grown up now? They must be."

"My older two are in college. The youngest is still at home with us."

"That's Mickey. You gave him your maiden name, Carmichael, as a first name, and you used to call him Mickey, like they called your dad."

"We still do, only now it's shortened to Mick," she tells him, unnerved. Does he just happen to remember those details? Or did he find them somewhere online?

He must remember. Her father's nickname wouldn't have been officially documented in any public record or forum.

"Mick. Rhymes with Rick," he says.

She never thought of that. She wants to assure him that it's pure coincidence, and that it has nothing to do with him, but of course he knows that.

He must.

Right?

"How about your kids?"

"None of them are named after me."

"That's . . . I didn't mean that."

"I know what you meant," he says, " but I was thinking about how when Liam was born I really wanted to name him Rick, not just after myself but after my father, but Vanessa didn't want to because her firstborn was named after her ex and after he left, she couldn't stand to hear the name. So she didn't want to name our son after me, I guess because she figured sooner or later, either I'd leave or she'd hate me or maybe both."

She doesn't know what to say.

After an awkward moment of silence, he says, "You know what I want to know? Did you ever get your Victorian?"

"What do you mean?"

"Don't you remember how much we both hated our raised ranches when we were living in Westchester? I was always fantasizing about moving to a farmhouse somewhere, and you wanted a big old Victorian. You used to talk about exactly what it would look like: gingerbread porch, pocket doors, high ceilings . . ."

He's describing her house. Does he know? Has he seen it?

"And you were going to furnish it entirely in period furniture," he goes on. "You were so crazy about that era. Remember how we'd go to tag sales so that you could look for antiques? That one time, it took us an hour to walk two blocks with all the kids because we had to use one of the strollers to push that big old fringed lampshade you found."

Unsettled by the memory—particularly when she recollects that she'd casually lied to Jake about how much it had cost—she quickly changes the subject. "Wait, you haven't told me about your kids. How are they?"

"Liam and Erin are both in college, like your older two. And Vanessa's boys have been grown up and out on their own for years now. They're both still in the city, but ever since she died, it's been—"

"She *died*? I thought—I mean, I assumed—you'd gotten divorced. I'm so sorry. I didn't—"

"It's okay. We were divorced a while back, and then . . . she died."

What is there to say to that, other than "I'm sorry," again.

To think she'd considered that Vanessa—poor dead

Vanessa—might have been responsible for sending the package.

But . . . Rick? Could he really have sent it?

The waitress appears, providing a brief respite from the conversation as Rowan orders the coffee she'd sworn off earlier. She needs it desperately now, having expended every ounce of energy she possessed just to propel herself to this place—not just physically, but emotionally. Now that the initial confrontation is over, the sheer exhaustion of the night before—the *week* before—has caught up with her. She's finding it difficult to sort through her thoughts, and the conversation has already drifted so far off script that she has no idea how to steer it back.

She toys with the upside-down coffee cup on her scalloped paper placemat as Rick orders a toasted sesame bagel.

"Cream cheese?"

"No, butter, thanks, Bernice," he tells the waitress, and Rowan remembers that he always did have a folksy way of addressing waitstaff by the first names printed on their name tags, and that he never did like cream cheese. He always ordered his bagels with butter. Sesame bagels. Real butter, not margarine—which he specifies to Bernice an instant after the memory flits into Rowan's mind.

"Real butter." Bernice nods, writing it down. "Anything else?"

"Just ice in a go-cup with a lid and a straw and a lemon."

A new wave of memories: he'll keep adding hot water to his tea as they sit here, and when he leaves, he'll dump what's left into the cup and take it with him. Voilà—iced tea. Two beverages for the price of one, he used to say, and she thought it was clever. Now it seems like cheating.

"What about for you, hon?" The waitress has turned to Rowan, pen poised on her pad.

"Just the coffee, thanks. I'm not hungry."

"You can share my bagel if you change your mind," Rick tells her after Bernice leaves.

An image flashes into her brain: Rick leaning across the table feeding her as they laugh together.

It's not a memory; it never happened—and never will happen.

How dare he offer to share his food?

Irrational anger flares within her.

He has no business getting so . . . so cozy with her, especially considering that they haven't been alone together since the moment fourteen years ago when they were jerked back to their senses courtesy of the blasting smoke alarm.

"Rick." She clenches her hands in her lap. "About the package . . ."

He just looks at her, waiting. Not a hint of recognition in his eyes.

If he were responsible, there would at least be a telltale flicker, right?

But if he didn't send it, and Vanessa is dead, then who else could it have been?

"You sent it. I know you did."

He blinks. "Sent what?"

"The box."

"What box?"

"Come on, stop playing stupid. I know that you—"

"All righty, here we are." The waitress is back to turn over Rowan's cup and fill it with steaming black coffee.

"Cream?"

"Please."

They gaze at each other in uncomfortable silence as the waitress briefly steps away and returns with a small silver cream dispenser.

"More hot water?" she asks Rick, gesturing at the little teapot in front of him.

"Please. Although I think I'm *in* hot water," he replies, "and I'm not sure exactly why."

"Don't worry. I'm sure she'll tell you," Bernice returns with a sly grin, probably assuming this is one of those typical men-from-Mars, women-from-Venus conversations.

After she's gone, Rick tells Rowan, "I'm not playing stupid, I swear. Apparently, I just *am* stupid, because I have no idea what you're talking about."

"You didn't send the package."

"To you? No. What kind of package?"

"Come on, Rick. Please. It had to be you."

He frowns, shaking his head. "As much as I'd love to take credit or blame for whatever was or wasn't in it . . . I can't."

She wants desperately to believe him. Oh hell, maybe she *does* believe him.

Now who's stupid?

"What happened, exactly? Someone sent you something? What made you think it was from me?"

She hedges, unwilling to go there just yet. Or ever again.

"It was just a guess. I'm sorry. I honestly thought it was you."

"But *why*? What was it?"

There's no way around it. The only way to explain the situation is to acknowledge that—despite all her self-denial—something did happen between them that snowy day. Yes, it could have been much worse, and yes, she nipped it in the bud, but the uncomfortable reality can never be erased.

Clearing her throat, folding and unfolding the corner of her paper placemat, she begins, "Do you remember . . ."

She trails off.

Maybe he doesn't remember.

No, of course he remembers. He must.

Unless she was just one in a long line of extramarital conquests that eventually led to the demise of his marriage to Vanessa . . .

"I have a pretty good memory," he prompts, and there's a gentle undercurrent in his tone that causes her to look up sharply.

He's thinking of that day. She can tell by the look on his face.

She shouldn't have come here; shouldn't have hunted him down or lied to Jake or snuck away to the city on a weekend afternoon when she should be home taking care of her husband and son, who can't even find their clean socks or the grape jelly when she's gone, dammit, dammit . . .

Off she goes on the emotional roller coaster again, but when it careens back around to the starting point—the anonymous package—she knows she couldn't have done this any other way.

You don't ignore something like that, and you don't share it with your husband.

Whoever sent it was counting on her to act, and she's acting.

"Who else knows?" she asks abruptly. "About what happened that day?"

He doesn't even pretend not to know what she's talking about. "The snow day?"

"The snow day. Yes."

"No one. I never told anyone. Did you?"

She hesitates.

"Did you tell Jake?"

"Jake? No!" She shakes her head vehemently. "Did you tell Vanessa?"

"Are you kidding? No way." He rubs his temples briefly. "Why are we here, Rowan?"

"Because someone sent me a box of thirteen burnt cookies wrapped in an old newspaper from that exact day fourteen years ago."

He absorbs her words. "November thirtieth."

"You remember the date."

"I told you, I have a pretty good memory. For some things, anyway." He stretches a hand across the table, reaching for hers.

She snatches it out of reach, nearly spilling her coffee. "What are you doing, Rick?"

"Sorry. I'm sorry." His hand becomes a fist, pressed beneath his chin as he stares at her. "You're upset. I was trying to . . . I mean . . . look, I don't know what I was doing, but—"

"I should go."

"Wait—who the hell sent that package?"

"You didn't?"

"Why would you think that?"

"You know, the smoke alarm and the burned cookies that day . . . and you once told me you lost your childhood home to a fire, and you had smoke inhalation injuries, and I thought maybe . . ."

She's babbling. He's looking at her as though she's lost her mind. Maybe she has.

"What does that have to do with anything?"

"It doesn't. Forget it. But if it wasn't you, and you never told anyone . . ."

"Then *you* must have told someone."

She did.

She told one person, years ago, not long after it happened. She confessed her secret in a moment of weakness, needing to unburden her guilt, and she regretted it immediately afterward.

"Who did you tell, Rowan? Because obviously, whoever it was sent that package."

She's shaking her head before he finishes speaking.

"There's no way. She wouldn't do something like that. Not in a million years."

"Who?"

"My sister."

From the *Mundy's Landing Tribune* Archives
Obituaries
May 12, 1985

Katherine D. Carmichael

Katherine "Kate" (Devlin) Carmichael died at home yesterday following a brief illness.

She was born in Mundy's Landing on April 17, 1941, to the late Seamus I. and Mary O'Hara Devlin. She graduated from Mundy's Landing High School in 1958 and from the University of Buffalo in 1962 with a bachelor of science in education. She had been employed as a teacher at Saint Helena's Parochial School since 1974. A devoted wife and mother and avid homemaker, she enjoyed sewing, knitting, cooking, and gardening. She was an active parishioner at Holy Angels Catholic Church, where she served as president of the Blessed Sacrament Society and sang in the choir.

She is survived by her devoted husband, Jonathan "Mickey" Carmichael, whom she married on July 14, 1962; their four children: Mitchell, Daniel, Noreen, and Rowan; three brothers, Seamus (Eileen) Devlin of Schenectady, Thomas (Joanne) Devlin of Mundy's Landing, and Rev. Robert Devlin of Boston, Massachusetts; two sisters, Margaret (Anthony) Bartone of Punta Gorda, Florida, and Maureen Devlin of Saint Louis; and many nieces, nephews, and cousins.

A wake will be held at Dunnewyk Funeral Home at 225 Fulton Avenue in Mundy's Landing tomorrow from 2:00 to 4:00 and 7:00 to 9:00 p.m. A Mass of Christian Burial will be celebrated Tuesday morning at ten o'clock at Holy Angels Church, followed by interment at Holy Angels Cemetery.

Chapter 4

As Noreen Carmichael Chapman pulls her Mercedes SUV into the private subdivision after dropping two of her four kids at Saturday lessons, she notes that the Holdens have yet to put up their Christmas decorations. The other half-dozen brick mansions on the cul-de-sac off Cove Neck Road, including the Chapmans', are tastefully decked in live wreaths and garlands. At dusk, the surrounding landscape will come alive with white twinkle lights and spotlights.

The Holdens, when they finally do get around to decorating, won't use the local florist service to hang their greens and set up their lights, unlike every other house here. They probably won't dare to set up an enormous blow-up snowman, as some of the neighbors irrationally fear, but there will be a crèche on the lawn and they'll use strings of bright-colored bulbs, each as much an abomination in this up-market neighborhood as their absence would have been in Noreen's hometown years ago.

Growing up in her parents' well-worn Dutch Colonial in a village that had seen better days, she always envisioned a different sort of future for herself, and one very much like the life she now lives: transported to a classy New York City suburb, married with children and a career and enough money that she's never had to make a week's

worth of groceries last a month the way her mother sometimes did.

Mom never seemed to mind, though. And she gladly
went back to work as a teacher at the parochial school
when Rowan started first grade, though her paycheck
barely covered gas money to get there, Dad often pointed
out with a laugh. Mom always responded that she loved
being back in a classroom so much she'd do it for free.

Whenever autumn rolled around, Dad supplemented
his insurance salesman's paychecks working weekends at
the local hardware store so that Santa Claus could pay
his annual visit in December. Christmas gifts were one
of the few things that were never in short supply in the
Carmichael household.

And love—there was always plenty of love to go
around.

We just didn't appreciate it then.

Pulling into the large circular driveway in front of her
house, Noreen briefly considers leaving the car parked by
the door, but quickly decides against it. Having survived
the chaotic Carmichael household, she thrives on domestic orderliness: everything in its proper place. Not to mention *everyone*—though that particular objective has been
elusive of late.

Opting to exercise control wherever she still can, she
pulls around into the four-car garage, even though she has
to leave again shortly to deliver the kids from their lessons to a sports practice and a birthday party.

Kevin's work at an understaffed, overburdened inner
city hospital keeps him away for days at a time. Their
eldest, Sean, is enrolled at Notre Dame University but
spending a semester abroad in Paris. High schooler Shannon is away this weekend at a debate team tournament.
That leaves just Noreen to shuttle the others, Sabrina and
Samantha, from one weekend activity to another.

She'd willingly traded her commute to a large Manhattan law firm specializing in CEO and celebrity divorces for motherhood and a local practice in Garden City. Her work is mostly confined to weekdays so that she can be here whenever her kids are—which is not as often as it used to be. They're growing up, busy with their own lives.

She presses the alarm keypad and lets herself into the house. Her heeled boots tap hollowly across the hardwoods, accompanied by the steady hum of the housekeeper, Luz, running the vacuum upstairs.

In the marble-tiled foyer, she takes off her coat and hangs it in the cedar-lined closet. The woodsy fragrance mingles with the scent of furniture polish, this morning's coffee, and the fresh evergreen garland draped along the curving banister and hall balcony above.

Next weekend, the florist who decorated the house inside and out will bring in a pair of fresh-cut ten-foot balsam firs. They'll be elegantly trimmed with white lights and Waterford ornaments and velvet bows: one in ice blue to complement the living room decor, the other in maroon to match the great room. Right before Christmas, one more tree will be delivered, this time to the beach house in Southampton where the Chapmans always spend the holiday itself.

This year . . .

This year might be different.

When the time comes, though, she'll take it in stride just as she has everything else, just as she's always taught her kids to do. Change is never all bad any more than it's all good.

She closes the closet door and finds herself looking into the full-length mirror remembering her son's high school graduation day. As he stood in this spot checking his reflection and adjusting his cap and gown, she stood by with a camera, wondering where the years had gone and wondering where Kevin had gone, wondering why he never seemed to be here when he should have been.

And now you know.

"Why do they call it commencement?" Sean asked her, wise beyond his years. "It's not really about the beginning. It's the end."

She told him what her own mother had told her when she left for college decades ago: "Because it's easier to say good-bye if you focus on what lies ahead instead of what lies behind you."

The irony, of course, is that Mom's immediate future held the hardest good-bye of all. Noreen chose not to remind her son of that, and as she studies her own reflection, patting her wind-tousled hair into place, she wishes she hadn't thought of it now.

On the sidewalk outside the coffee shop, Rowan buttons her coat in the drizzle, watching Rick do the same.

She wishes she'd never come here. She's run out of things to say to him—ran out after the first five minutes, which they spent speculating about who might have sent the package. But they stayed for another half hour, mostly sharing details about where their lives had led them since they'd left Westchester.

It turns out Rick and Vanessa moved away not long after Rowan and Jake did. He said Vanessa was tired of the long commute, so they moved to Hoboken, which was much closer to her office in the financial district. Like Rowan, and like her mother before her, he went back to work when his youngest started preschool.

"What do you do?"

"These days, I'm in administrative services."

"Really? Where?"

"Trust me—you never heard of it."

She asked him if he had a card, and he said, "I gave

you my cell number when we messaged on Facebook, if you need—"

"I know, but I like something tangible."

He searched his pockets and, then told her he didn't have a business card on him. Maybe it was the truth; maybe not. Maybe he works in administrative services; maybe he doesn't. Maybe he was evading her; maybe she's just paranoid. Who the hell knows?

He didn't talk much about the divorce, other than to say it was a long time coming and they stuck it out until the kids were more or less out on their own. And he hasn't revisited Vanessa's death at all.

She's curious to know how it happened, but it's not the kind of thing you come right out and ask. And he didn't volunteer the information, though he's spoken pretty freely about some things.

When she asked where in New Jersey he's living now, he gave her the exact address in Weehawken, adding that it's almost on the very spot where Aaron Burr and Alexander Hamilton famously dueled to the death. "You probably teach your students about that in social studies, right? Fourth grade?"

She was almost positive she hadn't told him which grade she's teaching.

A little later, he let it slip that he knows where Katie is going to college.

"Winters can be brutal that far upstate," he commented when she mentioned her daughter in passing. "My kids didn't have the grades to get into Cornell, but I thought maybe they'd like Ithaca College, so we drove up and looked. It was snowing like crazy, and that was in late April. They wouldn't even get out of the car to take the tour. Liam wound up in Texas and Erin's in California. They're both at decent colleges but nothing like Cornell."

Had she even told him where Katie goes to school? She was almost positive that she hadn't.

To be fair, he'd admitted in his message last night that he'd found her on Facebook long before she found him.

But she never mentions her job there because the principal frowns on social networking. And Katie's Facebook profile is privacy-protected, so even if he'd spotted her on Rowan's friends list, he wouldn't see anything more than her name and headshot.

Okay—so what if he snooped around online to find out where she works, and where her kids go to college?

Maybe she's reading too much into his motives. Plenty of people look up old friends and neighbors online. It doesn't have to mean anything ominous.

But it might, and she's anxious to be alone with her thoughts in the car, on her way home.

"I'm glad we finally got to see each other again after all these years," he says as she fishes in her bag for her umbrella and keys and parking stub. "Even if it wasn't just to catch up and talk about old times. When you figure out who sent that package, let me know."

"I will."

"Maybe it didn't have anything to do with . . . you know. That snow day."

She just looks at him.

"You're right," he says quickly. "It must have something to do with it. But I didn't send it, and I swear I never told a soul, and if the only person who knows is your sister, then maybe she was just playing a joke."

"Noreen would never joke about that." She shakes her head, remembering her sister's reaction years ago to her secret.

Noreen came down hard on her, claiming that an extramarital emotional affair is as damaging as a physical one. Maybe she was right, but Rowan resented her just the way she used to when they were kids, resented that her sister made perfection look so easy.

"I have to go," she tells Rick, jangling her car keys. She has to detour to Woodbury Common Outlet Mall before she can go home.

Jake will be expecting her to walk in the door with shopping bags. If she doesn't, he'll question her, and she'll have to lie again. This way, her initial lie will become a half truth.

"Does Jake know you met me here today?"

"No."

"Are you going to tell him?"

She's tempted to pretend that she is, but hears herself say, "No. I'm not."

"Where does he think you are right now?"

"He was sleeping. I didn't talk to him."

"You just took off?"

"No, of course not. I left him a note. It was no big deal." She shrugs, unwilling to tell him the details of her lie to her husband, hating that she lied to Jake, who means everything to her, but can't lie to Rick, who means nothing.

"Easy way out," he says.

"What?"

"I once left a note, too. It's the easy way out."

"What are you talking about?"

"When I left Vanessa the first time, that's how I did it. Left her a note while she was sleeping, saying I couldn't do this anymore, and walked out."

"The first time?"

"It took a few tries before I managed to make it stick."

Poor Vanessa, she thinks.

Wow. The emotional affair is over, if she had the slightest doubt.

I didn't, she assures herself. *Not for a second.*

If only she hadn't been forced to open this door to the past in the first place.

If only she could be sure it would remain closed from here on in.

Why is it, Mick wonders, that whenever he wouldn't mind having the house to himself—which is pretty much all day, every day—his parents are around, yet the one day it would have been useful to have at least one of them home, they're both gone?

He'd woken up early planning to go on his morning run, but rolled over and went back to sleep when he saw the crummy weather. Hours later, he re-awakened to his dad calling through the bedroom door that he was heading out to run some errands.

"Where's Mom?" he asked groggily.

"At the mall."

"When will she be back?"

"Not till tonight."

"How about you?"

"Later" was the vague reply.

Mick fell back to sleep for another hour. When he finally got out of bed, he realized he'd have to ride his bike into town. Not fun even on a nice autumn day when you're sixteen years old and have a driver's permit, but positively torturous in this icy December rain.

But he's determined to carry out the plan that popped into his head last Monday night when he should have been working on his homework.

Operation Secret Santa, he calls it—not that he's even shared it with his friends. Well aware that he's walking the fine line between pathetic loser and romantic hero, he figures no one will be the wiser if the plan fails. But if it works out, he'll tell the world what he did, and the world will think he's a genius.

Better yet, Brianna Armbruster will have fallen head over heels in love with him and dumped the college guy Zach told him about.

When that happens, everything—even spending all the tip money he was saving for his ski trip and pedaling this uphill mile in freezing rain—will be worthwhile.

Mick warms himself with thoughts of the future. When he and Brianna are married with kids, they'll talk about Operation Secret Santa the way his own parents often talk about the good old days when they first fell in love.

It's hard for Mick to even imagine Mom and Dad meeting and dating back when they were only a little older than his brother and sister are now. But he's heard the story often enough—about how they were both home in Mundy's Landing for Christmas, and Dad was in Vernon's Apothecary looking for a present for Grandma Mundy, and Mom was there buying "something embarrassing," as she always puts it. Even if Mick had the slightest desire to know what it was, there's no interrupting his parents when they volley the story back and forth.

"She heard me telling the saleswoman that I was browsing for something for my mom," Dad says, "and for some reason, she decided to put her two cents in."

"Because he was looking at the gaudiest earrings you ever saw."

"And you wanted me to buy her perfume that stunk to high heaven."

"It was Giorgio Armani. Your mother loves it."

"Now she does—"

"Thanks to me."

"Thanks to you," Dad agrees, "but I still think it stinks."

"But you bought it for her. And you bought me a beer that night when we ran into each other again down at the Windmill." That's a local pub.

"And you dumped it on my lap."

Mom would insist that it was an accident, and Dad would say it was on purpose. Then they'd argue about whose idea it was to go see a movie together on Christmas Day, because neither of them bothered to make sure the theater would be open. It wasn't; nor were any of the restaurants in town. To salvage the date, they went skating on Milkweed Pond behind the high school. Mom remembers that they had the ice all to themselves and that it was snowing; Dad is convinced there were other skaters and that there was no snow.

The only detail that was never disputed by either of them: that even on that first date, they knew they would be together forever.

Mick locks his bike on the rack in front of the library and walks toward the shops and restaurants that line the village square. The Windmill is still there, a few doors down from Marrana's.

Someday, he and Brianna will go there, and they'll skate together on Milkweed Pond, and they'll share their love story with their kids. It'll start with the moment Mick fell off his bike in front of her that summer before freshman year—they'll leave out the fact that she was with another guy who called Mick a carrot top. The next part will be about how he left her anonymous little Secret Santa gifts every day for a week, and on Friday came the big gift, the one that won her heart . . .

What will it be?

Not a twenty-five-dollar gift certificate to Marrana's, that's for sure.

But he has a pocket full of tip money and all afternoon to figure it out.

Vast and iconic, the white-columned James A. Farley post office branch is always extra-crowded in December, not just with people mailing holiday cards and packages but also with hordes of Good Samaritans. This is where Operation Santa Claus began over a century ago, with people picking up letters from needy children and anonymously buying gifts for them.

The tradition is going strong on this rainy Manhattan Saturday. Casey has to weave past crowds of do-gooders to join hundreds of customers on the long line that snakes toward the service counter.

No one amid this chaos is likely to question—or later remember—a plain brown-paper-wrapped package.

It takes nearly an hour to reach the counter, but that's just fine. There's a redheaded woman standing just a few people ahead in the line, her long hair a tantalizing reminder of the pleasures that lie in store very soon . . .

As a child, even during the hardest years, Casey was always anxious for Christmas. But that giddy anticipation was nothing compared to this.

Another stand-in might be necessary after all. Not here, though. That would break all the rules of the game, rules that are there for very good reasons.

If something were to go wrong now, then none of this will have any meaning. Casey's efforts will amount to nothing, and a guilty woman will go unpunished.

I couldn't bear that. I can't take any chances. I have to stick with the plan, follow the rules, wait it out.

It's the redhead's turn to step forward to the counter. As she moves out of reach, Casey fists fingers that long to grasp that beautiful hair and yank her backward.

"Next!"

Casey places the package on the counter, keeping an eye on the redhead a short distance away.

"Is there anything fragile, liquid, or perishable inside?" the postal clerk asks.

"No." A lie.

"Do you want insurance or tracking or delivery confirmation?"

"No thanks."

"You sure?"

"Positive."

The clerk, a diminutive Asian woman, takes her sweet time typing on her keyboard with glossy purple fingernails that clash with her close-cropped red hair.

Casey's hands clench and unclench, clench and unclench.

She slaps a label on the box.

"When will it get there? Do you know?"

The clerk glances at the label. "I doubt Monday, but you never know. Probably Tuesday. Wednesday or Thursday at the latest."

"That's not very specific."

"You could have sent it priority so that it's traceable or—"

"I didn't want to do that."

"Then you take your chances. It's Christmastime. Things are crazy here."

Yeah. No kidding.

Everything about her is irritating. What a pleasure it would be to slice into her belly and see her flesh rip open, oozing gobs of white fat and red blood.

But it wouldn't bring pleasure in the usual way.

She's all wrong. Her dye job is unnatural, and her hair is short. Things would be different if it were long and silky like Rowan's, or like that of the young woman standing nearby . . .

The woman who's going to get away if this bitch doesn't speed things up.

Dispatching the clerk would be strictly business, resulting in the same perfunctory pleasure you get when you've finally swatted a fly that's been buzzing around the house.

"That'll be six dollars and five cents."

Seething with impatience, Casey hands over a twenty-dollar bill.

"Do you have a nickel?"

"No."

Wearing a disapproving expression, she takes change from her drawer, counting it twice before handing it over. "Have a good weekend."

"Oh, I will." *Believe me.*

Casey pockets the money and turns to see that the redhead—the other redhead, the potential stand-in—is just finishing up, too.

Yes, it would be against the rules, self-imposed or not.

But as the saying goes—and as Rowan herself clearly agrees—rules were made to be broken.

From the *Mundy's Landing Tribune* Archives
Community Notebook
July 1, 2004

New Hires at Local Schools

At Mundy's Landing Elementary, a new fourth-grade teacher will replace retiring teacher Eloise Duncan in the upcoming school year. Born and raised in the village, Rowan Carmichael Mundy attended MLES and was a student in Mrs. Duncan's classroom just over twenty-five years ago, as was her husband, Jake. The couple moved back to their mutual hometown in 2002 and live on Riverview Drive with their three children, all of whom are students in the public school district. Asked how she feels about being employed at her alma mater, Ms. Mundy smiled and stated simply, "It's home, and I'm glad to be back."

Chapter 5

On Saturday evening, when Rowan drives around the bend and her house comes into view, she knows immediately that something is terribly wrong.

Night fell over an hour ago, but the windows are dark from attic to basement, and the porch light and lamppost are off.

She'd exchanged text messages with both Jake and Mick shortly before leaving Central Valley to make the long drive home. Mick was already gone, out for pizza with friends before tonight's varsity hockey game, but Jake was home and suggested that they go out to dinner.

Date night? Marrana's?

Sounds great! she'd responded even though it's the last thing she feels like doing.

She has to force herself to keep driving toward the dark house, her heart pounding wildly as her mind flits through the possibilities, each horrific in its own way.

Jake knew she'd lied about where she was going this morning and decided to give her a taste of her own medicine, or . . .

Or he'd found the burnt cookies in the attic and figured out what had happened between her and Rick fourteen years ago and had walked out on her, or . . .

Or someone broke into the house and attacked him . . .

Or . . .

Or he dozed off watching TV before it got dark, she realizes with relief as she turns into the driveway and spots a telltale faint blue flicker in the living room window.

Ironic that her mind didn't even go to that innocuous scenario despite the fact that it happens regularly.

It's because her guilt has been festering all day.

As she was driving back from Manhattan, she'd worked herself into a panic about the box in the attic, worried that Jake might have decided to put up the outdoor Christmas lights this afternoon to surprise her.

They're also stored in the attic—yes, on the opposite end, but still . . .

Every year, she has to nag him to string the lights in the shrubs and along the porch eaves. This year—the one year she's been trying to keep him out of the attic and thus hasn't mentioned it at all—would be the one year he'd do it.

And if he'd gone poking around up there and found the package . . .

Oh, come on. One plus one doesn't add up to five.

She tried to convince herself that a box filled with burnt cookies and old newspaper couldn't possibly lead Jake to conclude that she'd been unfaithful. But by the time she arrived at the mall, paranoia had gotten the better of her.

She tried to call Noreen, but her sister didn't pick up her cell or at the house. She left a message, trying to sound casual: "Loved your Christmas card. Call me back whenever you have a chance."

Noreen is one of those people who walks around with her phone in her pocket when it isn't in her hand. She always returns calls promptly. This time, she didn't.

Maybe she's busy.

Of course she's busy; she's always busy.

Rowan takes a deep breath as she pulls around to the back of the house and parks beside Jake's Jeep. After turning off the engine, she rests her forehead against the steering wheel for a moment, spent.

You're okay. Pull yourself together. You've got this.

She gets out of the minivan and grabs the shopping bags from the back. She'd more or less raced through the outlet center snatching up things she thought Jake and the kids might like for Christmas, along with a belated engagement gift for her nephew Andrew and his fiancée, who live in Chicago near her oldest brother, Mitch.

Her efforts resulted in a convincing pile of paper shopping bags and the promise of hefty store credit card bills come January.

By then, though, this will all be behind her. She'll have figured out which of two possible scenarios is the more likely.

Either Rick was playing out an elaborate charade today, lying about having sent the package or at least about having told someone what had happened between them years ago, or . . .

Or the one person in whom Rowan confided is responsible in some way for the burnt cookies.

But Rowan just can't imagine it. Her sister is much too classy—not to mention too busy—to pull something like that. Besides, although Noreen might be sanctimonious at times, she would never deliberately hurt Rowan.

It's far more likely that Rick is behind this.

He seemed earnest today—for the most part—but how well does she know him, really?

Not well at all, anymore. There had been a time when she knew him as well as she knew her own husband, but people change.

I need to talk to Noreen, she thinks as she juggles the

shopping bags to unlock the back door. *I'll call her again, and if she doesn't pick up, I'll tell her it's really urgent.*

There's a brand-new garbage can sitting beside the back steps, the latch firmly in place. Now she can get rid of the evidence at last.

In the dark living room, she finds Jake dozing on the couch in front of a college basketball game. There's a bag of chips and a soda can on the coffee table—sans coaster, as usual, but she's not about to chide him for that. Not today.

"Hey," she says, startling him. "Sorry. I'm home."

"Welcome back." He yawns, stretches. "How was the mall?"

"Great." She holds up her bags. "How was your day?"

"Great."

"What'd you do?"

"This, pretty much. And some errands."

"Did you have a chance to refill your prescription?" He's been on medication to lower his cholesterol since his last physical, much to his dismay, and he keeps allowing it to run out.

"Forgot."

"Did you remember to pick up some dog food?" She'd texted him that they were running low.

"Forgot," he says again, "But I did buy a new trash can and drop off my shirts at the dry cleaner."

"Terrific. No more rancid garbage in the backyard, plus you'll look nice and spiffy while your cholesterol is spiking and the dog is starving to death."

"Spiffy? Who says spiffy?" he retorts, but in his usual good-natured way.

She smiles, glad things are back to normal, then reminds herself that things were never *not* normal. Not on Jake's end.

And that's the way it's going to stay, she vows, drinking in the gallery of happy family photographs beside the stairs as she heads up to change for dinner.

The call to her sister will have to wait until later, or tomorrow morning. Tonight is date night with her husband, and Jake deserves her undivided attention at last.

Noreen is finally finished driving the kids around.

For today, anyway. What a whirlwind. She just dropped Sabrina and her friends at a bat mitzvah in Great Neck, and someone else's mom is picking them up at midnight. She ran to the mall with Samantha to get a birthday gift for a friend, then delivered her and the gift and a trio of other girls to the birthday girl's sleepover. Shannon won't be home until tomorrow and Sean won't be home until Christmas and Kevin is still at the hospital and God only knows when he'll be home.

She texted him earlier to make sure he'd seen the billing statement for Sean's spring semester tuition. No response. He's probably in the OR. She's used to that. He nearly missed the delivery of their fourth child because he was miles away in surgery when her water broke. The contractions progressed so quickly that she was pushing by the time he got her message.

The labor room nurses reassured her that he'd be there on time for the birth—and in the end, they were right—but everyone else seemed more disturbed by her husband's absence than she was.

I can take care of myself. I've never needed anyone there holding my hand or, God forbid, looking over my shoulder . . .

Rowan called her cell phone twice today; called the house, too. Not urgent, according to her messages.

As always, the thought of her younger sister is accompanied by an intermingling of nostalgia, affection, and deep-seated antagonism. Her relationship with Rowan is perhaps the most complicated one in her life—and considering the state of her life at the moment, she's in no hurry to return her sister's call.

In the master bedroom, she folds the jeans she'd worn today back into the bureau drawer and hangs her silk blouse in her walk-in closet. She pulls on a cozy long-sleeved T-shirt, a pair of fleece-lined yoga pants, and soft yarn socks. At times like this, small doses of comfort go a long way.

Downstairs in the butler's pantry that connects the kitchen to the formal dining room, she takes a hand-blown crystal goblet from a glass-fronted cabinet. It's part of an elegant set of four she and Kevin received for their wedding, courtesy of his long-dead great-aunt Martha. They'd registered at Tiffany's to please his family and Macy's to please hers. She wound up returning nearly all the gifts from her side in exchange for store credit, which she never did use.

The irony is that she never used most of her Tiffany's gifts, either, including these glasses. She was always afraid they would break. Tonight, who cares? Everything is fragile; everything is breaking.

She picks up the bottle of Pontet-Canet Bordeaux she pulled from the wine cellar when she got home and inserts a butterfly corkscrew imprinted Mundy's Landing Wine & Liquor. She took the corkscrew from a drawer at her parents' house after her father died. He didn't just use the bottle opener on top to pop the caps off his beer bottles; he opened cream sodas for Noreen and her brothers and sister on special occasions.

She made sure Rowan didn't see her pocket the corkscrew that day as they were cleaning out the kitchen—not because she thought her sister might want it, but because she didn't want Rowan to know that she did.

She twists the cheap corkscrew into the cork and pulls,

gratified when it glides out with a slight, almost celebra-
tory popping sound.

She really should let the Bordeaux breathe, and she
really shouldn't be drinking alone, but to hell with rules
tonight. She tucks the corkscrew back into a drawer beneath a stack of linen dish towels, pours some wine into
her crystal goblet, and sips.

She plunks the glass on the counter a little too hard,
but it doesn't crack. Nor does her face, when she allows a
smile to touch her lips for the first time all day.

There, see?
Better already.

Sometimes, you can discover more about a stranger just
by watching her from afar for a little while than you'll
ever know about loved ones.

After leaving the post office, Casey followed the redhead to a bookstore just off Union Square. She counted
out pocket change to buy a small cup of coffee and proceeded to nurse it for several hours while she sat in a
comfortable chair reading magazines off the rack. At a
table nearby, Casey pretended to be engrossed in a thick
textbook plucked from a shelf in the science section,
while noting every detail about the redhead.

She took only one magazine at a time, turning the
pages carefully and making sure she didn't spill a drop
of coffee on the merchandise. She read each magazine
cover-to-cover and when she finished, she returned it to
the proper slot on the rack, rather than placing it haphaz-
ardly or leaving it where she was sitting, the way other
so-called customers were doing. Her choice in reading
material was eclectic: the highbrow *New Yorker* and
Paris Review were followed by *Us Weekly* and *Sports Il-
lustrated*.

So she's brainy with a frivolous and athletic streak;

she's conscientious, and she's either frugal or flat broke. She's also most likely unattached, judging by her bare ring finger and the fact that she never once looks at her phone or sends or receives a text. These days, lovers in her age group constantly check in with each other electronically.

Dusk has fallen beyond the plate-glass windows when at last the redhead stands and stretches. She takes her time putting the last magazine back on the rack and doesn't seem to notice Casey making a hasty exit to the street, leaving the textbook sitting open on the table.

Never once looking over her shoulder, she walks north on Broadway through Chelsea, turns left at 28th Street, and walks west, following it as it curves past the Penn South residential complex toward the Hudson River. She crosses Eleventh Avenue and covers half the final block before unlocking the door to a small, narrow apartment building.

Casey can't follow her inside, but makes note of the address and the fact that there's a large Con Edison facility directly opposite the building. Interesting. Maybe it's some kind of sign that this is meant to be.

Less than a minute after the redhead disappears inside, a light goes on in the fourth-floor apartment. As if to confirm that it's the right place, and provide yet another sign, she appears in the window briefly, a real-life Rapunzel with coppery hair.

Then she's gone again, leaving Casey to gaze thoughtfully at the grillwork ladders and platforms that zigzag up the front of the building, right to her window. Watching her from the fire escape would almost feel like watching Rowan through the skylight, from the high branches of the elm tree in her yard.

Adrenaline spikes through Casey's veins, undiminished by the voice of reason: *What if someone sees you up there and calls the police?*

Pedestrian and vehicle traffic on this block is relatively light. A nosy neighbor in the same building or even on the same side of the street would have to stick his or her head all the way out the window to even see the fire escape. That's not likely on a gloomy December night. There are no residential buildings facing the apartment from across the street, only the windowless Con Ed facility. Still . . .

You're too smart to take stupid chances.

Smarter than anyone. Smarter than everyone.

Casey walks away, vowing to forget about her even though another bleak Sunday looms just ahead.

From the *Mundy's Landing Tribune* Archives
Lifestyles
June 10, 1966

For Modern Mundys,
History a Source of Pride, Not Shame

Their ties to this village stretch back over three centuries and are well documented at the Mundy's Landing Historical Society in the basement of the Elsworth Ransom Library. According to director Miss Ora Abrams, "The Mundy family tree includes a Revolutionary War general, a wealthy industrialist, and a hero who went down with the *Titanic* after saving the lives of several steerage children."

She added that the society's former curator, her great-aunt Etta Abrams, graduated from Mundy's Landing High School in 1900 with Maxwell Mundy Ransom—who until his hospitalization last winter resided at his ancestral home here on Battlefield Road. He served in the House of Representatives during the Great Depression and was instrumental in New Deal legislation.

Miss Abrams said, "It's a rich legacy of which any family would be proud."

Make no mistake: they are.

"Am I honored to be descended from the original Mundys of Mundy's Landing? Absolutely," John Elsworth Ransom told the *Tribune* last week. "When I was young, my uncle Max would sit me on his knee and tell me about his boyhood adventures with his pal Frank—who grew up to become President Franklin Delano Roosevelt. I wanted to grow up to become just like him."

Fresh from his final semester at Harvard Law School, alma mater of both his uncle and FDR, with political aspirations and the New York State bar exam looming, he's well on his way.

Asked, however, about more distant family members—namely, James and Elizabeth Mundy—Mr. Ransom was noticeably less effusive. His maternal bloodline descends from their daughter Priscilla Mundy, who was born in England in 1658 and crossed the Atlantic in the spring of 1665 with her parents and older siblings, Jeremiah and Charity. The family narrowly escaped the Great Plague, which killed 100,000 people, fifteen percent of London's population.

They arrived on what is now the island of Manhattan. Having been surrendered by the Dutch Republic a year earlier, its name had changed from the Province of New Netherland to the Province of New York, after James, Duke of York. The ship sailed a hundred miles north up the Hudson River, landing in an idyllic spot at the mouth of a creek on the eastern bank. Today, the location is designated by a stone marker at what is now Schaapskill Nature Preserve.

During the ferocious winter of 1665–66, the frozen river stranded a long-awaited ship loaded with sorely needed supplies. When it finally arrived in the spring, only five of the original thirty-odd settlers had survived: James and Elizabeth Mundy and their three children.

There's no arguing the fact that husband and wife resorted to cannibalism to keep their family alive as their fellow settlers were dying of starvation. They weren't the first early American colonists to do so, and the longtime consensus among historians, local and beyond, is that they didn't murder anyone. But in June of 1666, newly arrived colonists convicted them of murder and hanged them with their children watching.

While most modern scholars theorize that the Mundys were guilty only of consuming the flesh of those who were already dead, a stumbling block emerged in 1947. An archaeology team from nearby Hadley College unearthed a partially shattered, severed skull found among discarded human bones behind the Mundy homesite. A medical examiner concluded that it belonged to a young woman and contained fractures consistent with a sharp blow to the head. That can be attributed to an accident, yet some historians consider it evidence that the Mundys themselves killed their victims before eating them.

Today, the skull reportedly rests among the seventeenth-century artifacts in Mundy's Landing Historical Society's private collection. John Ransom hasn't viewed it, nor is he interested in doing so.

His distant cousin Asa Jacob Mundy, a direct descendent of Jeremiah Mundy, the doomed couple's only son, concurs. "All I care to know is that this village was named for Jeremiah's great-grandson, Enoch Mundy. He was a brave general in the Revolutionary War and a hero to many. My father taught me to be proud of my heritage, and I've taught my son and daughter the same thing."

Mr. Mundy's namesake son, who goes by Jake, may be only seven years old, but the boy is well aware of the hefty legacy that goes along with being born and raised in a town that bears one's own name. "My great-great-great-great-great-great . . ." He paused and looked up at his father to ask, "How many greats, again?"

The senior Mundy laughed and patted his son's dark crew cut. "Too many to count."

The child declared that he would settle on ten, and counted off the generations before breathlessly punctuating them with the remainder of the sentence: ". . . Grandfather was named Jeremiah Mundy and he was very brave. He sailed all the way across the ocean when he was just a boy like me."

Questioned privately by this reporter, his father

admitted that young Jake wasn't aware of the tragic postscript to his ancestor's arrival in the New World. "Sooner or later, I'm sure he'll find out," he said with a shrug. "We all do."

Chapter 6

Sitting across the table from Jake, Rowan watches him study the menu as though he hasn't eaten at Marrana's dozens of times before. Hundreds of times, probably.

She admires the familiar furrow between his dark brows and his full mouth and the masculine angle of his stubbly jaw, even though she's always preferred him clean-shaven.

"What are you having?" he asks without looking up.

"I'm not sure. I forgot my reading glasses at home and I can't see the specials."

"So you're my blind date then, is that it?"

"Good one," she says, deadpan: her usual response to his corny jokes.

"You can borrow my readers in a second," he tells her, focused on the menu again. "Maybe I should order something different this time."

He always says that, then—after much deliberation—orders his usual Cavatelli a la Mama. And salad with blue cheese dressing, hold the cucumbers, and a glass of Chianti, just one, because he's driving. But he'll urge her to have two and she will, and she'll tease him that he's hoping to take advantage of her when they get home, and he'll tell her she's absolutely right. He'll have a cup of coffee and dessert—spumoni in summer, cannoli in winter—

while she finishes her wine, and then they'll drive home at around nine and he'll walk the dog while she falls into bed. She'll try to stay awake but most of the time she won't, and he'll give her a good-natured good night peck on her cheek and go back downstairs to watch *Sports Center*.

There was a time—all right, there have been many, many times—when the predictable rhythm of date night made Rowan long for the passion they shared back in the early days of their relationship. Tonight, however, maintaining her vow to focus on Jake, she finds herself cherishing every mundane marital moment.

"Yeah," he says abruptly. "I know."

She blinks. "What?"

"I know I should have shaved. That's what you're thinking, right? I can tell by the way you're looking at me."

Ordinarily, that would be exactly what she's thinking.

"It's okay, Jake. I know you hate to shave on weekends."

"Yeah, but I really did mean to do it this morning. It's getting gray."

"The beard?"

"See?" He strokes his whiskery chin. "You're married to an old man, Ro."

"You're not old. You're middle-aged, and you're married to a middle-aged lady."

"Nah, you're a hot blonde now. If I'm not careful someone's going to steal you away."

She tries not to flinch, smile pasted firmly on her face. "I doubt that."

"Maybe I should dye my beard."

"Blond?"

He grins. "That might look kind of cool."

"I like the gray. It's distinguished."

"You think?"

"Sure." She can't hold back an enormous yawn.

"Past your bedtime?"

"Pretty much. If you're finished with your reading glasses there, Gramps, your blind date needs them before she falls asleep at the table."

Precious normalcy. It can all disappear in an instant.

Before Rowan can look at the menu, Annabelle Bingham stops by their table on her way back from the ladies' room. They've shared a friendship since their own school days at Mundy's Landing Elementary. The bond, like most, was stronger during some eras than others. Unlike Rowan, Annabelle walked the straight and narrow in high school, as swim team captain and honors student.

"Date night?" she guesses, greeting Rowan and Jake with hugs.

"Yes, how about you?"

"Nope, three's a crowd, as usual." She points across the room to where her husband, Trib, and their son, Oliver, are sitting.

Trib's real name is Charles, but his nickname was bestowed in elementary school because his family owns the *Mundy's Landing Tribune*. His father passed away not long ago, making him editor-in-chief.

"Did you and Trib really make an offer on 46 Bridge Street?" Rowan asks Annabelle, having heard through the local grapevine that the house-hunting couple has set their sights on one of the most notorious homes in town.

Located in The Heights, 46 Bridge is one of the three houses where the Sleeping Beauty corpses turned up, and the only one still owned by the same family that had been in residence back in 1916. In fact, until she died just shy of her 105th birthday, Augusta Purcell was the last known living witness to the crime.

Her nephew and sole heir, Lester, is determined to keep the house from being exploited and reportedly refused an immediate offer from Ora Abrams on behalf of the historical society. Nor, according to the rumor mill, will Lester allow Realtors to show it to anyone he doesn't pre-approve, in an effort to weed out Mundypalooza groupies. He's determined to sell only to a longtime local family as a private residence. That's going to be tricky considering that local families aren't just familiar with the home's bloody past, they're also fully aware that curiosity seekers think nothing of trespassing, peering in the windows, or even snatching souvenirs from the storied Murder Houses. A few summers ago during Mundypalooza, someone stole the mailbox from 19 Schuyler Place with the residents' mail still inside.

"News travels fast around here," Annabelle says mildly, and changes the subject. "Where's Mick tonight?"

"Hockey game," Rowan says.

Jake adds, "It's not like he'd want to be with us if he were free, though."

"Oliver never wants to be without us." Annabelle's smile is wistful.

Rowan taught Annabelle's son in her fourth-grade class two years ago. Diagnosed with generalized anxiety disorder, he's being treated with medication and therapy.

She asks Annabelle how he's coping with middle school this year.

"Let's just say it's been a rough transition," she says, and Rowan notices the worry lines around her eyes and dark circles beneath them.

"I'm sure it'll get better."

"I hope so."

Rowan curbs the impulse to mention that living in one of the notorious Murder Houses, as the locals call them, might not be the healthiest thing for an overly anxious kid. It's none of her business, and she knows that the Binghams aren't very well-off and may have little choice. They fit Lester's criteria, and the mansion at 46 Bridge Street is an absolute steal in this inflated real estate market.

"Anything look good?" Jake asks as Annabelle heads back to her table and Rowan puts on the glasses to glance at the specials.

"Everything looks good. I'm starved. I haven't eaten since . . ."

The conversation with Annabelle had distracted her. For a moment, she'd forgotten about her day, and the diner, and Rick. Now it comes rushing back and her appetite completely disappears. Again.

"Didn't you stop at the food court for lunch?"

"It was too crowded. Long lines." She pretends to study the menu, struggling to hold it steady in her hands. "I can't decide between the lobster ravioli and the eggplant rollatini."

"Get both."

"Both? No way."

"How about if I get the ravioli and promise to share?"

You can share my bagel . . .

Rick, barging into her head again, dammit.

"No, thanks," she tells Jake abruptly. "You have to get the Cavatelli a la Mama."

"Why?"

"Because it's what you do. It's what *we* do. We don't share."

He starts to laugh, then takes a closer look at her face. "Wait—are you serious?"

"Yes! No. I mean . . . I don't know."

"Ro? What's going on?"

"I'm sorry. I'm just . . ." She's just exhausted and emotional and terrified that everything is going to change; that she's going to lose Jake.

"Hey." He reaches across the table, finds her hand, grasps it. "Are you okay?"

"I'm fine, I'm just . . ." She forces herself to look up at him. His face, viewed through the reading glasses, is a blur. "I'm just so tired, and . . . it's hormones, I guess. I told you. You're married to a middle-aged lady. This is what you get. Isn't it fun?"

She manages a laugh, and he squeezes her hand.

"I love my middle-aged lady," he says, "and someday I'll love my little old lady, too."

She swallows hard, unable to find her voice. She's grateful when the waitress, the owners' daughter, Gina, comes over to take their order: the usual for Jake, eggplant rollatini for Rowan. She notices that Jake doesn't call Gina by her first name, even though he's known her all his life and it's printed right there on her name tag in case he can't remember what it is.

Back when she was regularly eating lunch in diners with Rick and the kids, she got it into her head that Jake was a little standoffish. Now she decides that Jake is appropriately unobtrusive and Rick a little too presumptuous.

Left alone with Jake again, she finds him watching her intently.

"What? I should have shaved this morning?" she quips, rubbing her chin, and he laughs.

She asks him about his dinner last night, and whether Mick had done any schoolwork this afternoon, and if he heard from Braden or Katie today. He volleys back questions of his own—perhaps too many questions?

He's just asking about your day. There's nothing unusual about that.

She resists the impulse to change the subject, telling him about her hours spent shopping, stores she visited, gifts she bought. Maybe it's just her imagination, but he seems to be watching her more closely than usual as he sips his wine and nibbles a roll from the bread basket, almost as if he's . . . suspicious?

Or is it something else?

A new and frightening possibility flutters at the edges of her consciousness, but she pushes it away, unwilling to let it in.

At the high school hockey game with a couple of his friends from the basketball team, Mick is surprised—and relieved—when Brianna Armbruster climbs into the stands just as the team skates onto the ice. She's with a group of female friends, all fellow seniors, all really pretty. But not nearly as pretty as Brianna.

If she really were seeing a college guy, as Zach had claimed, then shouldn't she be with him on a Saturday night?

Mick decides that she should and would, choosing to ignore the little voice inside his head pointing out that unless the college guy lives on a nearby campus, he's probably away again until Christmas break like Mick's older siblings are.

It's much more appealing to assume that Brianna has since broken up with the guy, or that Zach got it wrong in the first place, tormenting Mick with some stupid rumor that isn't even true.

He's at the game, too, sitting a few rows ahead with two girls from the drama club. They're both seniors and halfway decent-looking, but nowhere near as pretty as Brianna's friends and nowhere near as beautiful as Brianna herself.

Mick finds himself growing annoyed, watching Zach and the two girls keep up a steady stream of chatter, barely paying attention to the action on the rink. It's one thing for a drama girl to do that, he decided, but Zach is a guy and should know better, even if he's never played a sport in his life. Not that that's why he's getting on Mick's nerves tonight. And it's not because he's here with senior girls, or because Zach is the one who told him about Brianna dating a college guy, which he never should have done, regardless of whether it's true or they've broken up.

They probably haven't, Mick speculates glumly. He can't help but notice that she spends most of the first period typing on her phone. A few times, she nudges her friends and shows it to them. Watching them all lean in to exclaim over whatever was so fascinating on the screen in her hand, Mick is pretty sure it's not Brianna's latest moves in Words with Friends. There's just something specific about the way girls talk and giggle when they're discussing a guy, as opposed to some other random thing.

When Brianna finally looks up from her phone and turns around to talk to someone behind her, she spots Mick. His heart soars when she waves and gives him a big smile. At least he's pretty sure she's looking at him.

All right, there's a small chance that she might be smiling and waving at someone behind him. But he doubts it. Especially since he would look like a real idiot, smiling and waving back so enthusiastically.

Right before the end of the first period, Brianna and her friends head for the door, probably headed for the ladies' room along with a million other girls. Either that, or they're going out to sneak cigarettes in the gazebo, which Mick doubts. She's not that kind of girl.

Zach is also on the move, but Mick avoids making eye contact with him as the crowd heads en masse toward the student council concessions table.

"Hey, can I borrow five bucks?" asks his friend Van— short for Christian Wilhelm Vandergraaf III.

"For what? An apple and a box of raisins?" Mick asks moodily. The school is no longer allowed to sell candy thanks to some health fanatic mom who pushed them into enforcing a new district wellness policy.

"For whatever. I'm broke and I'm starved."

"Well, so am I." Mick spent his last dollar on admission to the game, after blowing the rest of his money on Brianna's gifts.

She's nowhere to be seen in the crowd milling around the lobby, but here comes Zach with his senior female friends.

"Hey, Lou, how's it goin'?" he asks in his *Goodfellas* dialect.

"It's going," Mick responds in his regular voice.

"Good game, right?"

"How would you know?"

Zach frowns. "What's wrong with you?"

"Nothing. What's wrong with you?"

Taking the hint, Zach shrugs and drifts away.

"How come you're being such a douche?" Van asks. "I thought you liked that kid."

"He's okay."

"How come he calls you Lou?"

"How come you call me a douche?" Mick returns, keeping an eye out for Brianna.

He finds her back in the bleachers, texting away on her phone, with her friends watching over her shoulder.

Mick settles in to watch the rest of the game, keeping an eye on her and wondering why his life is suddenly so depressing.

When her cell phone rings just past midnight, Julia Sexton is curled up on her futon wearing yoga pants, eating stale microwave popcorn, and drinking a bottle of Bud Light from the fridge—the most inexpensive Saturday night she's had in months.

She's a hundred dollars short and five days late on the December rent for this studio apartment on the westernmost fringes of Manhattan's Chelsea neighborhood.

She mailed a check this afternoon to the absentee

landlord, accompanied by an apologetic note explaining she'd send the rest of the money as soon as she has it. She came home from the post office to a nasty voice mail he'd left her.

She didn't listen to the whole thing, but she got the gist: *pay up or get out.*

Luckily, he doesn't have her cell phone number. The incoming call is from Dana, her former roommate and the reason Julia is in this mess in the first place, having moved in with her boyfriend in Brooklyn last month.

"Dude," Dana says, "what are you doing?"

"The only thing I can afford to do since you stuck me for the December rent on this place: nothing."

"I gave you notice!"

"A month."

"That's long enough to find a new roommate."

"In a tiny studio? No one I know was looking to move, and I'm not about to share three hundred square feet with a total stranger," Julia reminds her. They've been over this before. "Nothing against Alex, but I'm kind of hoping you're calling to tell me that you guys broke up and you're moving back in with me?"

"I'm calling to tell you that Alex's band just got a last-minute gig at this club in Williamsburg. They go on at around one-fifteen. They're getting paid in free drinks, me included, and you can come as my guest."

"I don't know . . . the weather's crappy." She goes to the window and looks out.

Her fourth-floor walkup overlooks the Con Edison facility directly across the street, with its barbed wire–topped chain link fence. Rain is coming down in sheets, splashing into a gutter river, and the block is deserted.

"Don't be lame, Jules," Dana says. "Come on."

"It's a fifteen-minute walk to the subway from here."

"So take a cab."

"There are no cabs, and I'm broke, remember?"

"Okay, but you have a MetroCard, so grab an umbrella and get your ass moving. Alex's friend Marc will be there. Remember him from the Halloween party?"

Julia remembers him. Tall, dark-haired, bearded, tattooed. Her type—unlike her ex-boyfriend, a pasty banker who considered her songwriting career a little hobby.

Mind made up, she arranges to meet Dana. She hangs up and quickly changes into jeans, boots, and a V-necked black sweater that just barely reveals the top of her own tattoo. It's a ladybug. As soon as she saves up enough money, she's going to get another, maybe a butterfly with polka-dotted wings this time. She likes polka dots. They mingle nicely with her freckles.

She puts on lipstick and a raincoat, brushes her long red hair, and takes one last look out the window, hoping to find that the deluge has miraculously ended or that 28th Street is suddenly teeming with available taxis . . .

Which you can't afford anyway, she reminds herself.

Good thing there are no cabs there to tempt her. It's still pouring out; the street is still deserted.

Or is it?

Frowning, she leans closer to the window, spotting a figure across the street wearing a hooded slicker.

Whoever it is isn't smoking or walking a dog or even walking at all. Just . . . standing. In the rain.

Must be a security guard for Con Ed. They usually hang out on the other side of the chain link fence, but the lot there is probably flooded. It happens sometimes.

It's good to know someone is out there keeping a watchful eye on the block. She usually doesn't worry about her safety in this neighborhood, even this late at night, but you never know.

Julia grabs her umbrella and wallet, containing only a

MetroCard, her ID, and a five-dollar bill that has to last her until payday next week.

Then she turns off the light and heads out the door.

Mick was really hoping he'd get to talk to Brianna before the crowd dispersed after the hockey game, but she and her friends took off the minute it ended.

He thought she might rematerialize at the Dunkin' Donuts across from the rink, always mobbed with high school kids on weekend nights. He even hung out long after his friends left. But Brianna never came, and his cell phone battery died, because of course he'd forgotten to charge it. He was forced to walk all the way home alone in the dark and pouring rain.

A local cop, there getting coffee, did offer him a ride as he left. "You're Braden Mundy's brother, right?" he said.

"Yeah. How do you know him?"

"We were Eagle Scouts together. I graduated a year ahead of him. And I had your mom as a teacher, too. Come on, I'll give you a lift home."

Mick had momentarily hoped his perfect brother might have had a run-in with local law enforcement at some point in his otherwise charmed hometown life. He turned down the offer.

He regrets it now.

It's not that he isn't perfectly capable of making the walk. He's jogged it a million times. But that's always during the day. Even plugged into familiar music on his iPod—which wouldn't make Mom happy—he's a little unnerved now that he's left the brightly lit village streets behind. He jogs up the last stretch of Riverview Road toward home, past the scattering of neighboring houses, all of them set back from the road, windows darkened at this hour.

It must be nice to live in town, closer to the school and civilization, not to mention the Armbrusters' house on Prospect Street.

Not that he's afraid, isolated out here in the middle of the night, but still . . .

Okay, maybe he's a little afraid.

When Mom texted him on the way home from dinner earlier, he assured her he'd have a ride home later. It hadn't been a lie—not then. He was planning to leave with his friends. He still could have called home and his parents would have come to get him, but if Brianna showed up late after all, he didn't want her to see him getting into the family minivan on a Saturday night.

He told his parents not to wait up. Dad will anyway—or at least he'll be dozing in the living room in front of the television. Mick is hoping that's the case tonight.

This isn't the first time he's gotten home late, and he knows from experience exactly how to get away with it.

He turns off the music and removes his headphones. Now he can hear the rain dripping and the accelerated rhythm of his own breathing and his feet crunching through the last of the fallen leaves, and . . .

And something rustling in the bushes.

Spooked, he's tempted to dart up onto the porch. The light is on there, and that's the door he's supposed to use when he comes in at night.

But if he does, Dad will hear him and he'll be in trouble.

Reminding himself that the rustling is probably just a raccoon or maybe a deer, as opposed to a bear or a psycho killer, he slips around to the back. Even if that door is locked—it usually isn't—it's far enough from the living room, where his father and Doofus are undoubtedly snoozing, that they won't be awakened by the sound of a key turning, the creaky door, and footsteps.

Tonight, he finds the door locked. It has been all week,

he's noticed, ever since Mom got that weird package. He's barely given that a passing thought, but now he realizes that she hasn't been her usual talkative self when he's seen her—which, granted, hasn't been much.

Having forgotten to carry his key tonight, Mick retrieves the one they keep hidden under a planter on the back step.

He unlocks the door, puts the key back, and steps inside out of the wet chill at last. He carries his sopping sneakers as he tiptoes across the floor. The house is hushed and dark, other than the glow and volume of the television spilling into the foyer. No snoring, but he does hear a momentary jingle of Doofus's tags.

Ordinarily on a night like this, Mick would be glad that Doofus lacks even the slightest canine instinct to investigate the fact that someone has just entered the house. Still skittish from the desolate walk home, though, he finds himself wondering . . .

What if that someone wasn't me?

Yeah? Who else would it be? A psycho killer? A bear?

Mick reminds himself that Brianna's supposed college boyfriend probably wouldn't be worrying about stuff like that. Nor would he have to worry about letting his parents know he's made it safely home.

Well, tonight, Mick's not going to be doing that, either. He quietly slides the dead bolt on the front door and flips the porch light switch. He leaves his down jacket hanging over the newel post.

When Dad wakes up, he'll know Mick is inside and assume that he just didn't hear him come in.

"I tried to wake you up when I got home," Mick will tell him tomorrow. "You didn't budge."

It's not far-fetched. Dad is a sound sleeper and a loud snorer, even though he's not snoring tonight.

Mick stays close to the wall as he climbs the wide stairs. The treads don't creak as much when you place your feet all the way to the right. Safely on the second floor at last, he goes past the bathroom to his room without bothering to brush his teeth and wash his face, again aware that his parents wouldn't approve. Nor would Mom be happy that he's tossed his wet clothes onto the hardwood floor by his hamper, or that he's changed into a short-sleeved T-shirt and basketball shorts instead of the flannel pajamas she keeps buying for him.

They have so many rules. You'd think they'd loosen up by the time they got to the third kid, but it seems to Mick that he gets extra attention—unless, of course, he actually *wants* attention.

As he reaches past a stack of textbooks to plug his phone into the charger on his desk, he remembers that he was supposed to work on a social studies paper this afternoon. Mom is going to ask him about it first thing tomorrow.

But it can wait, he decides, sitting down with a notebook and pen.

Right now, he has to compose the Secret Santa note he's going to leave for Brianna on Monday, along with the first gift. Each day, he'll give her a little bead charm bearing a stick figure that represents something they have in common. On the fifth day, she'll get the silver Trinkettes bracelet that holds all the beads and has room for lots more, as the lady in the gift shop pointed out.

"See that? You can give your girlfriend a new bead on every special occasion."

Mick didn't bother to tell her that the bracelet's recipient isn't exactly his girlfriend.

Yet.

When it's over and the girl lies face up in the mud, her eyes vacantly staring at the black night sky, Casey stands over her, panting.

It's still pouring out. If Casey hadn't come prepared, the rain would quickly wash away the blood that oozes everywhere the blade slit through her perfect skin.

I won't let that happen. I'm always prepared, always one step ahead.

Casey hums softly, fishing around for the wad of dry cleaner's plastic that always comes in handy at times like this. You can tuck it into your pocket and carry it around all day, and no one will ever know it's there. You can do the same with a folding barber's razor, but sometimes, when you sit down or lean against something, the hard bulge of the handle presses into your flesh. Then you remember that it's there, and you forget that you promised yourself that you won't use it, even if a perfect opportunity were to present itself as it had this afternoon.

No, wait, technically it was yesterday afternoon that Casey first spotted the redhead in the post office. It's morning now. Sunday morning.

Sunday, bloody Sunday . . .

Casey waited until midnight to return to West 28th Street. The block had been rendered desolate by the hour and the rain, but the light still shone like a beacon in that fourth-floor apartment. Soon Rapunzel reappeared in the window again, this time wearing a coat. Was she coming or going?

Going, Casey realized when the light went out a moment later. It wouldn't be necessary to scale the wet and slippery metal fire escape after all.

That was a pity for someone who had always embraced the challenge of climbing to new heights—literally—and yet . . .

She came to me.

Casey unfurls the plastic wrap and drapes it over her body to keep the rain from diluting the blood and wash-

ing it away. Only the girl's head remains exposed, waiting
for the razor, still sticky with blood, to finish the job.

Quinn's Bar and Grill on West 44th Street is busy when
Rick walks through the door. Ordinarily he'd head for
the bar, order a draft beer, and mingle with the regulars,
hoping a stool might open up before closing.

Tonight, though, he spots an empty high-top table in
the front corner, away from the crowd, and heads straight
for it. Settling onto a stool facing the plate-glass window,
he stares at his own reflection framed by a garland of red
and green ornaments strung with white Christmas lights.

"What'll it be tonight, love?"

Any other night, he'd flirt with his favorite waitress, a
sporty blond Aussie, but tonight he doesn't even make eye
contact. "Jameson straight up."

"Tough day, hmm?" Without waiting for a reply, she
heads back to the bar, leaving him alone with his thoughts.

Tough day, indeed.

Tough night, too.

He thought he was prepared to come face to face with
Rowan Mundy again after all these years, but . . .

He closes his eyes, seeing her face again. Not the
face that had haunted him all these years, though. She'd
changed. That shouldn't have caught him off guard, because he knew she'd aged—everyone ages—but for some
reason, he felt betrayed, seeing her in person.

Her face was still pretty, but her girlish freckles had
faded and so had the light that used to gleam in her
green eyes when she looked at him. This Rowan was
more mature, laugh lines at the corners of her mouth
and eyes confirming that years had passed and they'd
been good to her. She'd picked up a few extra pounds on
her petite frame, but the curves were flattering. Her hair,
though . . .

Her hair. Her crowning glory is gone.

Of all the changes he should have anticipated, that never entered his mind. Why would it? In all of the photos on her Facebook page, that long, wavy dark red hair had been cascading over her shoulders same as always.

When he first glimpsed her this morning, a part of him wondered, perhaps irrationally, whether she'd cut it short and dyed it at the last minute just to spite him.

"I've always had a thing for redheads," he'd told her once—after they'd become friends, but long before he dared to take it further. "My first love was a redhead."

"No way, really?"

He'd told her about Brenda. She'd actually been interested, asking questions and making comments, unlike Vanessa.

Vanessa never wanted to hear about Brenda; never wanted to acknowledge that there had been women in his life before she came along.

Ironic, since she'd actually been married before he came along. He might have benefited from hearing a little more about her ex-husband. But, being Vanessa, she compartmentalized. She was always good at that.

Unlike Rowan, who wore her heart on her sleeve. He'd fallen a little in love with her the first time they met, even though she was pregnant with her third child at the time.

The moving truck was still in the Walkers' driveway when Rowan came walking over, juggling a plate of homemade brownies and the chubby hands of her little son and daughter. It was summer, hot and humid. She was wearing a spaghetti-strapped floral print maternity sundress that revealed a good amount of cleavage as well as her swollen legs. Her freckles were out in full force and her hair hung in loose, damp waves and clung in tendrils to her flushed cheeks.

"Welcome to the neighborhood," she said, offering

him the brownies. "I'm Rowan, and this is Braden and Katie. We live next door."

She was warm and earthy and flushed and real, while he was married to an ice princess. He was enamored on the spot, even as her kids squirmed out of her grasp and made a beeline for the elaborate tree house perched in the branches of an oak tree in his new backyard.

"Guys, get back here! They know better," she told Rick. "Sorry. They've been looking at that through the fence for years, dying to play on it."

"The kids who lived here before we moved in were teenagers. I bet their parents wouldn't have minded if they'd come over."

"You bet wrong," Rowan said with a laugh. "They were pretty fussy about their yard and my kids can be a handful."

She cast a glance at the steps, where his four were contentedly reading or coloring with crayons. "Okay, I'm totally impressed. How do you get your kids to behave so well? You've got twice as many as I do."

"Not for long," he said, gesturing at her enormous stomach.

"Right. It's another boy."

"That's good. Boys are easier."

"Who said?"

"I did. We have three."

It was months before he even mentioned that the older two of his sons belonged to Vanessa's deadbeat first husband. "He was a lousy dad," he told Rowan.

"Well, it seems like you're making up for it."

"God knows I'm trying."

It was spring by then, and he was pitching a Wiffle ball to his boys and Braden while the girls set up housekeeping in the tree house and Rowan sat on his back steps nursing newborn Mick.

Vanessa had fed their babies formula, despite his protests that breast milk was healthier.

"I bottle-fed my boys and they turned out just fine," she said, and made it clear that since she was the one who'd have to nurse, she was the one who'd get to decide.

She'd gone right back to work after her maternity leave was up. She had no choice. She was the breadwinner. When they were living in Westchester, she and Jake Mundy often caught the same weekday train into the city and the same train back to the suburbs at night, while their spouses entertained the kids and each other.

Those days were so pleasant, and so innocent . . . at first, anyway.

Rick eventually acknowledged, if only to himself, that something was starting to brew between them. He picked up on Rowan's loneliness and wistfulness when she spoke of her husband. He felt the same way about Vanessa, whose commuting time had quadrupled with the move, and who was constantly stressed about the hefty mortgage payments they'd taken on and the volatile state of the economy.

Years later, discussing his failing marriage, his old friend Bob asked Rick if he had doubts about whether his wife truly loved him.

"No," he said, "it's the other way around."

"She doubts that you love her?"

"Yes. And so do I."

As that steamy summer traipsed toward fall, Rowan's baby weight melted away and the circles beneath her eyes began to fade. She started laughing more, worrying less about her kids. They shared parenting concerns and confided in each other, sharing things they hadn't even told their spouses. Nothing significant, really. Just little things that came up during the long hours they spent together; things their spouses weren't around to hear or wouldn't have found significant.

Months passed, a year and then two. They relied on each other the way neighbors do, borrowing items and carpooling, recommending pediatricians and babysitters and kid-friendly barbers. Their time together ebbed and flowed depending on the weather and the season and the kids' schedules. He could count on seeing more of her whenever school was out for breaks and summer. He grew to dread September's abrupt curtailment of carefree summer days spent with Rowan and all the kids in the yard or park or pool.

Then came the sunny Tuesday morning two hijacked planes flew into the World Trade Center. She showed up at his door barefoot with her youngest child in her arms, cell phone in hand.

"I've been trying to call you, but the lines are jammed," she said breathlessly. "Did you hear?"

He hadn't.

She'd come running because she was worried about Vanessa and didn't want him to be alone. But his wife's office was out of harm's way, and Rowan assured him that her husband had landed safely in Chicago the night before, away on a business trip.

He gave her toddler something to play with and then the two of them stood shoulder-to-shoulder in front of his television watching the horror unfold. At some point— when another plane hit the Pentagon, or when the first tower collapsed, or the second?—she cried. His arm went around her, pulling her close, comforting her.

Everything changed that day, in many ways. Globally, locally, politically . . .

Emotionally, romantically, physically.

I was already in love with her by then. Not just infatuated. In love.

It didn't matter that she was married, or that he was.

In the days that followed the terrorist attacks, they

drifted back into spending time together even without the kids around. They had coffee and watched the endless news reports. As September turned to October and then November, life slowly drifted back to its usual rhythm. There was no longer any compelling reason to spend mornings together, vigilantly keeping an eye on CNN and reminding each other that they were safe.

Yet they kept seeing each other. Her son Mick was always with her, the safeguard against anything inappropriate happening between them while their spouses were absent.

Then came the snow day.

They spent the morning on the hill in the park, with all the kids and their sleds. Then she promised them hot chocolate and home-baked cookies, so they all trooped back to her house. Mick wanted to watch the Grinch movie with the big kids in the living room, and Rick and Rowan found themselves alone together in the kitchen, and . . .

Even now, he curses the fateful intervention of the smoke alarm. They were close, so close . . .

Afterward, if she'd been willing, Rick would have embarked on a full-blown affair. Hell, he might have walked away from Vanessa if she'd asked him to; maybe even from the kids.

She wasn't willing. She distanced herself immediately. He hardly saw her again that winter, and the next thing he knew, it was spring and she was moving away.

He tried to convince himself it was for the best. Vanessa was his wife, the mother of his children, a good, steadfast, beautiful woman. She loved him and didn't deserve to be left twice in a lifetime.

Had he ever stopped loving Rowan, though?

Vanessa didn't think he had.

He'd lied to Rowan today, when he'd said he hadn't told anyone what had happened between them on the snow day.

He'd told two people. One was his best friend, Bob. The other was Vanessa.

He hadn't confessed to his wife right away. He never intended to do it at all. But after the Mundy family had packed up and moved, Vanessa said she was glad to have them gone.

"Why would you say that? They were the ideal neighbors. Our kids miss them like crazy."

"They'll survive. But will you?"

He looked sharply at her and he saw in her eyes that she knew. Maybe not exactly what had unfolded between him and Rowan, but she knew how he felt about her.

There was no denying the accusation in Vanessa's eyes, or in her words when she came right out and asked him what had gone on.

He told her the whole truth.

It almost killed her.

In the end, maybe it had.

"Here you go, love." His Aussie pal is back, setting down a cocktail napkin and topping it with a glass filled with amber-colored liquid. "What are we drinking to this evening?"

"I can't think of anything worth toasting."

"Rubbish. There's always something or someone worth toasting, isn't there?"

"You know what? There is."

"All right, then. Cheers."

"Cheers." Rick raises his glass, not to her, but to his own reflection in the rain-spattered plate-glass window.

From the *Mundy's Landing Tribune* Archives
Local News
January 6, 1975

Longtime Institution to Shutter

Thomas N. Westerly, proprietor of Westerly Dry Goods on Market Street in the village, announced yesterday that the store will close at the end of the month.

Established by his grandfather Nelson Westerly more than eighty years ago, the small department store thrived until early this decade. Mr. Westerly attributes its demise to a confluence of factors that include the decline in population, the economic downturn, and, in the wake of inflation, shoppers abandoning the business district in favor of two recently opened discount chain stores on Colonial Highway as well as the new Dutchess Mall in Fishkill.

"We just can't compete," Mr. Westerly said from his office on the second floor of the brick building, where his desk resides in the shadow of a framed sepia photo that shows his grandfather sitting in that very spot in 1920. Other than the merchandise itself, little has changed inside the building Nelson Westerly built in 1893. However, a glance out the window reveals nearly deserted sidewalks, countless available parking spots, and empty storefronts that bear Going Out of Business Sale or Space for Rent signs.

Asked what he'll do next, Mr. Westerly shrugged sadly and shared a situation echoed by many local merchants: "This store is the only livelihood our family has known for three generations. I had hoped my son would step in when he graduates from college next year. Now, I guess we'll have to figure out something else."

Chapter 7

Even on weekend mornings, Rowan's body clock wakes her early, drop-kicking the day's to-do list into her brain before her bare feet even hit the hardwood floor. Most Sundays, she has time to walk the dog, shop for groceries, and put them away long before she leaves for ten o'clock Mass at Holy Angels.

But when she opens her eyes today, she finds that the light falling through the skylight is all wrong. It isn't morning at all. According to the digital clock on the nightstand, it's nearly noon.

Jake's side of the bed is empty; probably has been for hours. She stretches and yawns, thinking about coffee and wondering how she'd managed to sleep so late.

The house is quiet.

She must have been really tired, or . . .

Oh.

Yesterday comes rushing back to her; not just the day but the awful week. Her well-rested Sunday morning contentment evaporates in an instant.

She closes her eyes, wishing she could beam herself back to last Sunday, when she was up early to make pancakes for Jake and all three of her kids before church as Thanksgiving weekend wound to a close. On that morning, her heaviest burden was the knowledge that Braden and Katie were heading back to college before nightfall. It had been ages since she'd given Rick Walker more than a passing thought.

Flash forward a week, and she's thought of little else.

Rick was, predictably, the last thing on her mind last night before she fell asleep, but at least she hadn't dreamed of him. She yawns and starts to stretch, realizing that she'd been so exhausted she hadn't dreamed of any—

Hearing the distinct sound of a floorboard creaking overhead, she freezes.

Someone is in the attic.

She bounds out of bed, opens the bedroom door, and sees that the door leading to the third floor is ajar. A shaft of yellow light spills into the dim hallway.

Not pausing to throw a robe over her makeshift nightshirt—one of Jake's old T-shirts—she hurries toward the hall bathroom, where the shower is running. Mick must be in there. Jake would use the one off the master bedroom. Still, she opens the bathroom door a crack and calls, "Jake?"

"Hey!" Mick, cranky, is behind the shower curtain. "Geez, Mom! I'm in here!"

"Sorry." She closes the door again and calls from the foot of the attic stairs. "Jake?"

"Up here."

Cursing softly, she climbs the narrow staircase. The rudimentary treads are rough beneath her bare feet; a splinter stabs into her toe. She ignores the twinge of pain and the prickle of goose bumps on her legs as she ascends into the cold, cavernous space beneath the sloping Victorian roofline.

Irregularly shaped, draped in cobwebs, and crisscrossed by rough-hewn beams, the space stretches in every direction to low knee walls and paired dormers. Its dusty floor, slatted walls, and towering ceiling are made of aged wood that seems even darker at night or on a gloomy winter day, as the only lighting is a bare bulb perched high in the rafters. While she shudders at the thought of the bats that undoubtedly lurk up there and occasionally swoop their way downstairs in warmer months, Rowan has always found that the attic holds a certain appeal.

Its corners have yielded interesting relics of bygone eras: a child's tin toy, coins, buttons, even a stash of empty Prohibition era liquor bottles. There's a partial view of the Hudson River through the west-facing windows at this time of year, when the leaves are off the trees. She doesn't even mind the smell that wafts in the air: it reminds her of library books and sawdust and the archive room at the historical museum.

Arriving at the top of the stairs, she can hear rain pattering on the roof and a strong wind swaying the ancient trees that surround the house. She hugs herself, shivering, looking for Jake. "Babe? Where are you?"

"Here," he calls from the shadows in a corner opposite the one where she hid the box. Thank goodness.

"What are you doing?"

"Taking a break. I spent the whole morning getting ready for the meeting."

"What meeting?"

"The regional sales meeting."

"When is it?"

"Wednesday," he says in a tone that tells her she should have known that. "In Saratoga Springs."

"Oh—that's right. My field trip is Wednesday, too. There's a lot going on these days."

"When isn't there a lot going on?"

Oh, Jake. You have no idea.

Unless he does have an idea and he lured her up here to prove a point? The point being . . .

That he's a terrific husband, and she doesn't deserve him?

With a grunt, he drags a carton across the floor as a gust of wind rattles the windows, sending a draft over her bare legs.

"What's in there?" she asks.

"Light strings. I already carried down the other stuff."

Her heart skips a beat. "What other stuff?"

"You know. Decorations. The ones that go inside—not for the tree."

She wonders, fleetingly, if he stumbled across her secret and is covering up.

No. They've kept the holiday decorations in the same spot—the spot where he is—ever since they moved into the house years ago. He'd have no reason to go rummaging anywhere else up here. Not today, anyway.

She pushes her doubts away just as she did last night at the restaurant, when she got it into her head that there was hidden meaning in everything Jake said and did.

If he had found any reason to be suspicious of her, he'd bring it up directly. That's how he rolls.

"Do you need a hand?" she asks as he backs out of the corner carrying a large box.

"Nope, got it." He ducks his head to avoid bumping it on a low beam. He's wearing exactly what he had on yesterday and left in a heap on the bedroom floor when he dressed for dinner: a faded pair of jeans and his old bleach-stained New York Knicks sweatshirt.

"Hey, guess what I found?" he asks, and her heart stops.

"What?"

He balances the box against his hip with one hand and holds out a sprig of plastic mistletoe with the other. "You brought it when you came to visit me in Manhattan the Christmas after we met. Remember?"

She remembers. She used a thumbtack to hang it in

his bedroom doorway while he was at work, and it later fell onto their heads while they were kissing. That night, they shared a bottle of champagne to celebrate the end of her semester. When they went their separate ways the next morning to spend the holidays with their respective families—he and his mother were flying to Texas to visit his sister that year—Jake predicted they'd never spend another Christmas apart.

He was right.

And we never will, she vows fiercely. "Where did you find that old thing?"

"On the floor. It must have fallen out of one of the boxes we kept from back before we had the kids. I really need to clean this place out one of these days. There's stuff just thrown everywhere."

"That's way down on your honey-do list. Come on, let's go downstairs and I'll make pancakes."

"It's way past breakfast, sleeping beauty."

"Then we'll have them for lunch," she says, wishing he hadn't called her that.

Right now, she doesn't want to think about the Sleeping Beauty murders: dead schoolgirls eerily turning up tucked into beds all over town—girls no one had ever seen before, whose identities were never known.

"Hey, why aren't you dressed?" Jake looks her up and down. "Aren't you cold?"

"Freezing. I just got out of bed, and I didn't know where you were."

"That's what you get when you sleep for almost fifteen hours straight," he says lightly, setting down the box, unzipping his sweatshirt, and handing it to her.

"You don't have to—"

"It's okay, I worked up a sweat up here." He picks up the box again and heads down the steep flight of steps.

She wraps the sweatshirt around herself. It's soft and

warm and it smells like fabric softener and like him. She shoves the mistletoe into the pocket, puts up the hood, and bunches the fabric in both hands, pressing it to her nose so that she can breathe the comforting familiar scent as she follows him down, limping along on her splintered toe. When they reach the second floor, she turns off the light, closes the attic door, and locks it.

"Wait—we still need the rest of the decorations."

"Mick can grab them later. Go ahead downstairs. I'll be there in a minute."

Agreeable, and looking forward to pancakes, he whistles as he continues on down to the first floor.

Chiming steeple bells in a nearby church are getting on Casey's nerves.

"Dammit. Dammit! Shut up!"

The bells continue to peal, reverberating the reminder that it's a Sunday.

Casey has always hated Sundays.

No—that isn't true.

There was a time, back in childhood, when life was good and Sundays were especially idyllic. Sleeping late, eating home-cooked dinners with everyone at the table, watching sports on television—unless it was nice enough outside to throw a ball or Frisbee around with the neighborhood kids . . .

Ah, the good old days.

More recent Sundays may not have entailed cozy family time, but there's something to be said for a day of rest, even if it's occasionally a lonely one.

Then came that terrible Sunday last year.

Sunday, bloody Sunday . . .

The U2 song drifts into Casey's head, drowning out the church bells.

"They're my favorite band. I've seen them in concert

a few times," Rowan once said, many years ago. "I'd love
to go again . . ."

It sounded like an invitation.

She was such a flirt. Damn her.

Now the lyrics march through Casey's brain, lyrics
about wanting to close your eyes and make it go away . . .

But you can't do that. You can't escape.

Casey reaches for the first scrapbook, always kept
close at hand.

On the first page is a yellowed newspaper clipping announcing Vanessa De Forrest's birth; on the last is her
obituary. Displayed on the pages in between are painstakingly preserved mementos.

This is my time capsule, Casey thinks. *Just like the one
buried in Mundy's Landing.*

Just short of a century ago, during the sestercentennial
celebration, even as a madman raged through the village
leaving young women's corpses in people's homes, the
residents of Mundy's Landing sealed a chest filled with
artifacts and buried it in a vault beneath the marble floor
of Village Hall. It's designated to be unearthed on July
sixteenth next year.

Reading about it last summer, Casey first grasped the
importance of assembling a tangible record that will out-
live these precious, fleeting moments—something that
announces, "This is what it was like in my own personal
here and now. This is what happened."

The scrapbook was a labor of love. But when Casey
leafs through the pages, pleasant memories aren't all that
come rushing back.

Blood . . .

When Casey thinks back to that ghastly day, that's
one of the things that stands out more than anything else.
There was so much blood. It was everywhere, glistening

puddles and delicate smears of crimson: on the floor, on her white nightgown, in her hair . . .

Her blond hair was soaked with so much blood that it appeared red. The irony wasn't lost on Casey.

All that blood, all that red . . .

She was more beautiful, somehow, in death than she ever was in life. Her face had finally released its perpetually constricted expression. It hadn't even been noticeable until it was no longer there. Now, at last, she was at peace.

But I wasn't. My ordeal was just beginning.

Casey closes the first scrapbook abruptly and pushes it aside, frustrated.

It didn't have to happen that way. It's all because of Rowan.

Damn her.

Damn her!

It had been obvious even years ago that Rowan was to blame for everything that had gone wrong. Faced with the undeniable truth on that bloody Sunday, Casey felt something snap inside.

She has to pay.

That was how—that was when—the quest for vengeance had begun: unexpectedly and yet not, on that dreadful morning just over a year ago when Vanessa De Forrest died a horrible, lonely death. For Casey, restraint gave way at last, and wrath spewed like a swarm of lethal hornets.

That was the beginning and I'll decide when and where it will end.

Only the *how* has been predetermined: Rowan will die a tortured, bloody death.

What about the kid?

The question of Mick has weighed heavily ever since Casey connected with him at Marrana's Trattoria last Monday night.

If Mick were to die, there would be no frightened feminine whimpers, no long, lovely hair to caress, no sweet-scented skin to nuzzle or scattering of freckles on feminine curves, or hidden tattoos in provocative places . . .

Casey thinks of the girl last night, Rapunzel—also known as Julia Sexton, according to her identification.

Casey had cleverly stolen her wallet, just like all the others. Their deaths appear to be the result of a mugging, making it harder for the cops to identify their bodies. It's such fun to create little stumbling blocks like that for the so-called authorities; such a pleasure to watch the police and media and family members try to make sense of a seemingly random homicide.

Until now, Casey has had to follow those proceedings from afar.

This front row seat promises to be much more satisfying, although there are certain risks involved with a victim found closer to home. For that reason, Julia Sexton must be the last of them.

Except, of course, for Rowan.

Setting the scrapbook aside, Casey paces over to the window. The church steeple rises against a steel gray sky, its bell tower having fallen silent.

Even if Casey can't fight off the growing urge until it's time to deal with Rowan Mundy, nothing can happen so close to home again. Breaking the self-imposed rule once was daring enough. Twice wouldn't be daring, it would be stupid; maybe even disastrous.

Having studied the methodology of the Sleeping Beauty Killer and other famously elusive and equally brilliant murderers, Casey is well aware that they managed to evade capture because they remained focused and methodical.

Ted Bundy started out that way, but then he sloppily

escalated his crimes and failed to resist the allure of an entire sorority house filled with women. That disorganized spree proved to be his undoing.

It won't happen to me. I'm much stronger than he was, much smarter.

They'll never catch me. Never.

Five minutes late for noon Mass, Noreen steps out of her car and hurries through the wet snow toward Saint Ignatius by the Bay.

At least she made it this week. It's been a while—was it October, maybe?—since she's attended Mass.

Things have been too hectic at home.

Not that that's an acceptable excuse. Even when the kids were babies, or later when all four were playing sports, they almost always managed to get to church together as a family. Sometimes it took so much effort to get six people out the door on Sunday mornings—five of them complaining—that she'd wonder why she bothered to insist. But then they'd slip into their pew and that familiar sense of peace would settle over her, and she'd know it had been worthwhile.

These days, Noreen attends Mass alone, if at all. And when she does, she's not so sure that it's even worthwhile. Ever the respectable Catholic, she doesn't like to be reminded that she's committed mortal sins, or where those sins—past and upcoming—place her in the eyes of the church. But you can hardly forget that something is amiss when you're hurrying alone up the wide steps where you posed as a bride twenty-three years ago—and later, cradling four different babies in white christening gowns.

She remembers her father's initial distress when she told him that she wouldn't be getting married at Holy Angels in Mundy's Landing. He was more upset about that, at the time, than he was a year later when Rowan married a Protestant.

He eventually came around when Noreen explained that she didn't want to walk down the very aisle where her mother's casket had made its final journey.

"Last time I set foot in that church was the saddest day of my life, Dad. I don't want to get married there."

How could he argue with that?

Of course, she didn't tell him that she also happened to prefer the aesthetic of this elegant brick structure overlooking the Long Island Sound to her hometown parish. Unlike the stone and stucco Protestant churches that preside over the Village Common, Holy Angels is a small clapboard structure perched like an afterthought on a side street in The Heights.

According to Rowan, who's still a member there, not much has changed at the old church over the years. Anyone who doesn't arrive half an hour early Christmas and Easter to get a spot in the pews still winds up sitting along the wall in folding chairs, or standing conspicuously in the aisles. The Carmichael family invariably stood, much to Noreen's humiliation. Rowan told her that the Mundy family now does the same, but it doesn't seem to bother her or her kids.

Nor does she seem to mind that the Holy Angels congregation is perpetually in fund-raiser mode, always trying to replace or repair something: choir robes, hymnals, the notoriously leaky roof. When Rowan and Jake were married in the church on a rainy day—which was supposedly good luck—the flower arrangements had to be strategically placed on the altar to catch the drips from the ceiling, and the Communion host became as soggy as the bride's veil. That would never have happened here at the cathedral-like Saint Ignatius, even if the weather hadn't been picture-perfect on Noreen's wedding day.

Was that sunshine bad luck? she wonders now, as she slips alone through the massive wooden doors into the church.

The congregation is standing, still singing the opening hymn. She hurries down the aisle toward the pew she and Kevin and the kids shared for years. But when she reaches it, she finds that it's already occupied.

This isn't the first Goldilocks moment she's had lately, and it's certainly the most benign.

Still, it stings to see that new family has taken over the pew: three adorable children and another baby on the way, a pretty mommy in a maternity dress, and a handsome daddy who efficiently slides his daughters over to make room for Noreen to sit on the end.

She forces a grateful smile, trying not to betray her resentment.

It's not their fault. They didn't do anything wrong.

Then again, neither did Noreen. She did nothing wrong, made superhuman efforts, in fact, to do everything right—everything, dammit!—and look how things have turned out for her.

Ire begins to simmer like lava, threatening to erupt in a bloodcurdling scream. Fighting it back, she reaches for a missal and opens it, blindly looking for today's readings.

"What page is it?" the younger of the little girls beside her asks loudly, talking to her older sister as they flip through their own missals.

"Shh!"

"But what page?"

"Here," the big sister whispers, "give it to me."

"No! I can do it myself!" the little one protests, turning the pages so determinedly that she tears one, only to be quietly reprimanded by her sister and her parents.

That's me and Rowan forty-odd years ago.

Except these two girls, one blond and one brunette,

look nothing alike, while Noreen and Rowan could have passed for twins. Identical on the outside, but oil and water within.

She thinks about her sister's phone call yesterday. In her message, she said something about liking the Christmas card. Was she being genuine? Or was it a veiled jibe?

No, she can't possibly know the truth just by looking at a card. Anyway, everything really was fine back when the photo was snapped. That was last summer, before Sean left for his semester in Europe, before things fell apart.

It was Noreen's deliberate decision to mail out the cards as though nothing had happened, and one she has yet to regret, even now.

Remorse simply isn't her style.

Then again, neither is avoidance. Isn't that what she's done where her sister is concerned?

I have to call her back.

What if she wants to spend Christmas together?

Chances are, she doesn't. Their approach to the holiday doesn't mesh much better than anything else about their lives. Rowan's family is so laid back and disorganized that the last time they shared a holiday, Noreen wound up serving Christmas brunch after sundown.

Her nephews and niece were as taken aback to discover that the Chapmans hadn't decorated their own tree as her own kids were to find out that their cousins had— and enjoyed it.

"But ours is like the 'before' version of the Charlie Brown Christmas tree compared to yours," Rowan told Noreen with a grin. "Want to trade?"

"I'm sure it's beautiful."

"It's not. It's scrawny and the trunk is so crooked it fell over twice and we lost all of the fragile ornaments."

"Oh no."

"That's what you get when you let the kids pick it out.

But they made some new decorations after it fell. Remember how Mom used to have us make them when we were kids?" she added fondly. "We used cookie cutters to make the shapes out of cookie dough."

"It was just flour, salt, and water."

"No wonder it didn't taste very good." She laughed. "Yours were always perfect, and you helped the boys so theirs were, too. Mine were a mess."

"Only because you wouldn't let me help you."

That was Rowan. She liked to do things her own way—usually the hard way, and the wrong way. Funny how she seems to look back on her own difficult childhood as if it were idyllic, while Noreen, whose youth seemed unblemished as it unfolded, can clearly see the flaws in retrospect.

Given Rowan's penchant for trouble, Noreen would have predicted that her kid sister would wind up in a gutter somewhere, destitute, alone, and miserable. Too bad Mom didn't live to see her turn herself around. Then again, if she had lived, it probably never would have happened.

It wasn't until they were both grown women that Rowan revealed the reason she'd changed so drastically. "I promised Mom I'd behave," she told Noreen on the long ago day when they'd met in Mundy's Landing to clean out their childhood home after Dad died. "She was always so worried about what I was up to."

"Because you were always up to something."

"Exactly. She was afraid of what might happen to me if she wasn't there to watch out for me. I had to promise her that I'd be okay. It was the only way to give her peace of mind."

"She knew I'd have watched out for you, and so would the boys."

"You all had your own lives by then. You and Danny

were away in college, and Mitch was doing his residency in Chicago. It was just me and Dad living here after Mom died."

"So you didn't think I'd be there for you?"

"I wasn't your problem," Rowan said. "I had to grow up and learn how to be responsible for myself."

"Well, I'm glad you did. Some people never do."

Noreen refused to participate in guilt trips—self-inflicted, or otherwise. She'd devoted a good part of her youth to damage control on behalf of her sister, and often being mistaken for her, to the point where she'd joke about wanting to wear a badge that said, "Don't worry, I'm the good one."

There were times, even in adulthood, when Noreen grew weary of her own prim, holier-than-thou façade. But she was playing her role, the one her family always expected of her; the one she expected—still *expects*—of herself.

And all you have to do is keep it up awhile longer. No one has to know that your life has unraveled until it's absolutely necessary—and that includes Rowan.

From the *Mundy's Landing Tribune* Archives
Special Feature
January 18, 1992

Historical Society to Sponsor Second Annual Convention

The Mundy's Landing Historical Society may be unceremoniously housed in cramped quarters in the basement of the Elsworth Ransom Library on Fulton Avenue, but crime buffs worldwide have long believed its archives hold the key to one of the most notorious unsolved murder cases of the century.

During the steamy summer of 1916, as Mundy's Landing celebrated its sestercentennial with parades and pageantry, a serial killer was lurking. One by one, over a period of days, local families awakened to find the brutally slain corpses of young girls tucked into vacant beds in the house. In perhaps the eeriest twist of all, no one in the family—indeed, no one in town—recognized any of the victims.

Though the case was subsequently sensationalized in national headlines accompanied by composite sketches of the girls—dubbed "Sleeping Beauties"—they were never identified. Their unclaimed remains were buried in Holy Angels Cemetery, and the killings stopped just as abruptly as they'd begun. Local authorities chased a number of leads to dead ends. By the following year, as the United States entered World War I, the case faded from the public eye, though never entirely.

Theories have continued to abound over the decades, courtesy of armchair sleuths who have suspected everyone from Mundy's Landing's most illustrious citizens to a mysterious vagrant reportedly sighted in the area.

Last summer marked the seventy-fifth anniversary of the crimes, and Director Ora Abrams organized a historical society fund-raiser to commemorate the occasion. Her goal: to eventually move the non-profit museum into larger quarters.

"We just don't have room to permanently display most of what we have in the archives," she told the *Tribune* from her tiny, windowless office. "But the library board agreed to let us use the upstairs conference rooms to create a special convention exhibit. We weren't certain it would draw attendance beyond our little village, but it did."

Well beyond.

Last July's daylong event was a success. Several weeks later, in a confluence of events, an ABC News producer happened to be visiting friends at their summer home outside Mundy's Landing around the same time serial killer Jeffrey Dahmer was arrested in Milwaukee. Through her friends, the producer learned of the Sleeping Beauty case and visited the exhibit, where she met Ms. Abrams.

"She was absolutely fascinated by the story," Ms. Abrams remembers, "and I wound up showing her some items from the private collection."

While she wouldn't elaborate, those items are rumored to have included bloodstained clothing and a number of other artifacts deemed too sensitive or too gruesome for the permanent exhibit.

The producer later returned to the village with a correspondent and television crew from the news-magazine program *20/20*. The Sleeping Beauty murders were included alongside Jack the Ripper and the Zodiac Killer in an unsolved crimes segment last fall.

According to Ms. Abrams, the resulting groundswell of interest has resulted in a drastic uptick in daily visitors at the historical society, leading her to make the fundraiser an annual event. "We see everyone from historians to detectives to even a true crime author researching a book about the case. We've given the public an unprecedented opportunity to try their hand at solving it."

On New Year's Day, she issued a press release bearing the headline: CAN YOU SOLVE THE SLEEPING BEAUTY MURDERS?

Whether that's even possible remains to be seen, but providing access to relevant artifacts might shed additional light on the case and, at the very least, raise sorely needed funds.

Local residents who belong to Friends of the Museum can preview the special exhibit directly following the Independence Day parade and ceremonies in the Common on Thursday, July 2. It will be open to the general public July 3 through 5. Tickets can be purchased at the historical society beginning this week.

Chapter 8

Last night at Marrana's, when Rowan somehow got it into her head that Jake was looking at her strangely, she'd almost believed he sent the box of burnt cookies himself.

What if he'd snuck into the house unexpectedly on that snowy afternoon while she was with Rick?

He wouldn't sneak in, though. He'd have no reason to think he might be interrupting a clandestine tryst . . . or would he?

Even if he did, he couldn't possibly have anticipated that would be the day, the moment when Rick would finally make a move.

Anyway, if he had walked in on them, he'd have burst into the room throwing punches at Rick. That's the kind of guy Jake is; always has been—even-keeled temperament until something drastic sets him off, and then look out. He wouldn't have waited fourteen years to mail an anonymous package.

Still, it had a Manhattan postmark. Jake's regional sales job occasionally takes him there. It hasn't lately, though . . .

As far as you know.

She's too well aware just how easy it is to make the two-hour drive to the city and later claim to have been elsewhere.

As she takes her medication, brushes her teeth, combs her hair, and throws on jeans and a sweatshirt—her own this time, not Jake's—she tries to convince herself that the man she married would never be capable of doing something so sneaky or hurtful.

Just like he believes you'd never do anything sneaky or hurtful?

Glimpsing the stranger in the bureau mirror, she steps closer, forcing herself to take a good, hard look. Awash in guilt, she finds it difficult to even make eye contact with herself.

I don't know her, she thinks, staring at her reflection. *And I don't like her.*

It isn't just that she still expects to see her familiar red hair. Her face looks older, etched in the shadows of worry lines and dark circles.

How is it that Jake hasn't figured out just by looking at her that something is terribly wrong?

Maybe he has.

Remembering the way he'd studied her across the table last night, she turns away abruptly and walks over to the bed. What she wouldn't give to crawl back under the covers and hide for the rest of the day. Not just from Jake, but from herself.

Maybe she should just tell him the truth.

She dismisses the thought before it's even fully formed.

He might not believe that what had happened between her and Rick had stopped short of a physical affair, or that it was completely meaningless. He probably wouldn't grasp that it had grown out of the circumstances of their lives back then; circumstances that no longer exist. She made a stupid, selfish mistake, but it's one she would never make again. She's older and wiser; their marriage has evolved; she loves Jake and would never . . .

She can hear herself saying all of those things to her
husband as clearly as if the conversation actually took
place. It isn't difficult to imagine his response; the terrible
devastation in his voice and the angry accusation in his
eyes weigh on her as vividly as an ugly memory.

No. It can never happen. She'll never tell him. She
loves him too much to inflict that level of pain.

She forces herself to make the bed, same as she does
every morning. Normalcy. It's all about normalcy.

Downstairs, she steps around the box of indoor decorations Jake left near the foot of the steps, and is relieved
to find Mick in the kitchen. He's wearing a striped T-
shirt with plaid shorts—shorts, in December! Stripes
and plaid!—and standing in front of the open refrigerator
gulping milk straight from the carton.

Ah, normalcy.

Seeing her, he hastily puts the milk carton back.
"Sorry. I forgot to get a glass."

"It's okay."

"It is?"

"I mean, no, it's not okay, but . . . I'll let it slide this
time. Did you run this morning?"

"Yup."

"Did you remember to take your medicine?"

"Yup."

"Did you eat something with it so you won't get an
upset stomach?"

"No, I was about to."

At too many maternal questions, a scowl begins to
work its way over his freckled face, but she deftly erases
it with a final one: "Want me to make some pancakes?"

"Yeah! I can eat about twenty, so make a lot."

Rowan isn't sure she can even choke down one.

*Burnt cookies: the weight loss magic bullet. You don't
even have to eat them, and they'll kill your appetite for*

a full week.

Jake appears with the Sunday paper in its blue plastic bag from the foot of the driveway. As usual, Mick promptly asks to see the sports section. As usual, Jake reminds him that the paper has been sitting outside since dawn and that Mick was perfectly capable of retrieving it then.

"Come on, Dad. That's not fair. You read all those other sections, too. I just want to check the Knicks score from last night."

"They lost."

"Yeah, no kidding. Let me—"

"You can have the sports section when I'm done with it. Here, help yourself to one of those other sections. Maybe you'll learn something. And by the way—what time did you come in last night?"

"Around twelve, give or take."

"Give or take a few hours?"

"No! A few minutes."

"Don't lie to me, Mick."

"I'm not! I told you I was home. You must not have heard me."

Standing at the stove, listening to the predictable rhythm of their testosterone-fueled argument, Rowan finds herself breathing a little easier.

For now, anyway.

Running late, with a pounding hangover headache, Rick takes the PATH train into Manhattan at noon.

He'd lied to Rowan on Friday night when he'd said his schedule was wide open this weekend. In reality, he had—*has*—plans for Sunday brunch with his closest friend in the world. He'd have canceled if today had been his only opportunity to reconnect with Rowan, but as it turned out, he didn't have to.

That's good, because he really needs someone to talk to right now, and Bob Belinke is one of the few people he trusts.

They met in kindergarten back in their hometown Appleton, Wisconsin, and bonded—rather, clashed—when they both wanted to play with the same toy plane at recess. Bob was equally obsessed with all things aviation-related, and they both wanted to become pilots when they grew up.

Bob learned to fly at sixteen, had his private license at eighteen, went to Aeronautical University, went to work for the FAA as an air traffic controller in Illinois, Oklahoma, and Kansas, and even owned his own plane, while Rick . . .

Well, at least someone's dream came true.

Bob retired to Florida over a decade ago, but he's an avid traveler and pops up in New York every so often. This weekend, he's on an overnight layover on his way home from Scotland and England, and he'd e-mailed Rick last week to see if he was free.

It's been a while since I've heard from you, he wrote. *I worry. How are you doing on your own?*

On his own—he's always been on his own. Even when he and Vanessa were still married and going through the motions of supporting each other, they lived separate lives. He felt more alone in their relationship than he has since it ended with her death.

But he wrote back to Bob simply *Hanging in there*, and arranged to meet today at the same diner where he wound up meeting Rowan yesterday.

It's near Bob's hotel and the PATH station and—most important—it's affordable. He hasn't told Bob about his recent layoff. He hasn't told anyone, even the kids. With two in college, bills stacking up, and Vanessa's life insurance settlement still in limbo, Rick isn't going to be brunching at the Peninsula anytime soon.

Walking in, he spots Bob sitting a booth away from the one he and Rowan shared only twenty-four hours ago. The same waitress is handling the section. What was her name? Bertrice? Beatrice?

She spots him heading to the table and waves, cheerfully busting his chops: "What, are you a stalker or something?"

"Only for you—" He can see her name tag now. "—Bernice."

Standing to greet him with a warm handshake, Bob asks if he's a regular here.

"This weekend I am," he replies, thinking no one in the restaurant is going to mistake Bob for a regular. He's wearing a bright blue polo shirt and has the tanned, relaxed vibe that may be de rigueur in Florida but is rarely seen in New York City.

There was a time, not long after they were married, when Rick imagined himself and Vanessa living that life someday. It was a short-lived fantasy. Even if they had stayed together—even if they could have afforded for Vanessa to retire and she'd been willing to move South— the lifestyle would never have suited her.

"Can you see me on a golf course, wearing a visor and Lilly Pulitzer?" she'd asked, wrinkling her nose when he brought it up. "All that pastel. I could never."

"You don't have to dress like that. It's not in the Florida rulebook."

"I bet there *is* a Florida rulebook and it comes with coupons for bug repellent and early bird specials."

"Why do you hate Florida so much?"

Why do you hate everything?

Ignoring the question he'd asked, Vanessa added, as if

to answer the one he hadn't asked: "And the sun. I hate the sun. I burn and I freckle."

Rick had to bite his tongue to keep from saying he likes freckles.

With Vanessa, he had to bite his tongue to keep from saying a lot of things.

It wasn't healthy. A lot of marriages aren't. Some survive anyway, but most end in some kind of heartache, Rick thinks glumly as he throws his jacket on the hook beside the booth and slides onto the bench.

"You're looking good," he tells Bob.

"So are you."

"Yeah, right." Rick is well aware that the return compliment is perfunctory. He looks about as great as he feels today.

"I like your shirt."

"Now you're really laying on the bull."

"What? I like your shirt. Why is that bull?"

"Because men don't say they like each other's shirts."

"They do when they've rooted for the same team together all their lives. I thought you wore that just for me."

Looking down, Rick sees the familiar Green Bay Packers logo, grins, and nods. Might as well let Bob think he's wearing this T-shirt in honor of their shared hometown, which is only a half-hour drive from Lambeau Field, as opposed to it being the only clean item of clothing in his drawer.

He asks Bob about his trip and finds himself envious again as his old friend describes his adventures in England and Scotland, plus a journey last winter to Antarctica, which is where he was when Vanessa died and why he was unreachable for several days afterward.

"The farthest from New York I've been is Appleton," Rick tells him, "and I haven't even been back there in years."

"Why don't you come down, spend some time on the beach and the golf course . . . If you haven't been traveling, you must have some vacation time coming."

Rick sidesteps that, saying, "I haven't even touched my clubs in over a year."

"Then let's plan something."

Rick pretends that's a possibility. He's good at that—letting people treat him as though he's not flat broke, or lugging around this burden of guilt like a boulder on a chain.

The waitress arrives at the table with a pot of hot water and a selection of tea bags. "I didn't know if you wanted caf or decaf."

"Thanks for remembering, Bernice, but I'm actually having coffee today. Black and strong." He makes a point of looking her in the eye when he speaks with her. People in the service industry appreciate that, and when you use their names, Vanessa told him years ago. It establishes respect and trust.

She was right about that—about a lot of other things she taught him back when they first met, often saying that he was "a little rough around the edges." She was right, of course—and he didn't resent her for it in the beginning.

"Uh-oh. Tough night?" Bernice asks sympathetically, but he chooses not to answer that.

She fills his coffee cup, refills Rick's, and takes their orders: sesame bagel with butter for Rick, a Western omelet with a side of sausage for Bob.

"Hey, he has a better appetite than your friend yesterday did," she tells Rick with a wink.

"You're dating?" Bob asks after she's bustled away.

"What makes you think that?"

"Bernice said you were here yesterday with someone."

"She said *friend*, not *date*."

"I'm pretty good at deductive reasoning."

"Sorry, Sherlock, you're wrong about this."

"I don't think so." Bob has been a Sherlock Holmes buff since they started their own detective agency when they were kids. "Who was she?"

"Old friend."

"Female."

"Yes. And don't look so smug. You had a fifty-fifty chance of getting that one right."

He's trying to keep it light, but Bob is earnest.

He's also the only person in the world Rick told about his near miss with adultery. Besides Vanessa, anyway.

And she doesn't count, because she's no longer even in this world anyway—thanks to me.

Rick had told Bob about it in a moment of weakness. Now he wishes he'd kept his mouth shut. Bob knows him better than anyone, and he is a damned good detective. The next thing Rick knows, he'll have guessed that Rowan was his lunch date yesterday.

I don't want to talk about that. Not even with him.

Rick tries to change the subject, but it isn't easy. Bob is sincerely concerned about his well-being and thinks he should be dating.

"I think it's healthy for you to move on, after . . ."

"Vanessa and I had both moved on," Rick feels obligated to point out. "You know, long before she . . ."

"Died," Bob supplies when he trails off.

"That's one word for it."

"Rick, I know it has to be hard. You don't need to—"

"It's not as hard as it could have been, though, right? She wasn't my wife, she was my ex."

"Look, I get that. I have twice as many exes as you do, remember? That might make it slightly less complicated, but it doesn't make it easy. In some ways, it might even make it harder. You and Vanessa were together for a long time. I'm worried—"

"Don't worry."

Ignoring the interruption, Bob goes on, "I'm worried you're in denial. I know you loved her. She was the mother of your children. The way she died was horrific."

Remaining silent, Rick reaches for a spoon and stirs his coffee.

Bob talks on, asking questions but not forcing the answers, and talking about the past; about all the positive things that had come out of his marriage to Vanessa. "For what it's worth, I always thought you guys were a solid couple."

"And that is why you're a lousy detective. We were never a solid couple, unless you count the very beginning."

"You mean the first night, or . . ."

"The first year after we were married, maybe even longer. But we weren't right for each other."

"What about that woman—your neighbor?"

"She's ancient history," Rick says quickly. "Anyway, I'm talking about long before I met her."

"So then . . . Look, I know it's none of my business, so you can tell me to go to hell if you don't want to talk about it."

"No, it's fine. I haven't seen you since she's been gone, and . . . I can't pretend it didn't happen. It's probably good for me to get some of this out in the open, and I already told you I can't afford therapy right now, and there really aren't very many people in my life who want to listen."

"I'll listen."

There's a long silence.

"You're not talking."

Rick shrugs. "I guess I'm thinking about things I could have done a little differently."

"You mean before—"

"When Vanessa and I were still married."

"Like what?"

Rick thinks of Rowan. Thinks of how he told his wife, in considerable detail, how he felt about her. "I made a really bad decision on a really bad day."

"Who hasn't?" Bob shakes his dark head. "Listen, I've made plenty of good decisions on good days and bad decisions on good days based on good information that turned out to be bad . . ."

"And here I thought I was going to be the only one who was incoherently hung over today."

"Hey, I may be jet-lagged, but I'm not hungover. I'm trying to help you see that we do the best we can in any given moment. Don't beat yourself up because of what happened to Vanessa, Rick. It wasn't your fault."

Rick says nothing, just stirs his black coffee, biting his tongue to keep from telling Bob that he's wrong about that.

Dead wrong.

Gazing down at the nude, violated corpse of a young female, Detective Sullivan Leary shivers as much from the grisly sight as from the bitter chill. She clasps her bare knuckles against her mouth, blowing on them, and her breath snakes misty wisps into the gloomy air.

"I told you that you should've grabbed your gloves." Her partner, Detective Stockton Barnes, shakes his head. "It's colder than a witch's tit out here today."

"Is that any way to talk in front of a lady?"

"I don't think she can hear me," he replies with a nod at the dead woman.

That Barnes fails to consider Sully a lady, much less curb his tongue in front of her, can be attributed to the fact that they've been working together for quite a long time now. Longer than either of them worked with any other partner, and longer than the duration of both their failed marriages combined.

No one understands Sully the way Barnes does. No one makes her more frustrated, no one makes her laugh harder, and no one has her back the way he does. In many ways, they're like an old married couple.

Their relationship is far more productive and rewarding than the ones either of them shared with their ex-spouses, but it's strictly platonic. So far, anyway.

Once in a while—a very great while, usually when they've adjourned to the pub for a couple of whiskeys after a long, hard day on the job—Sully finds herself wondering what it would be like to throw caution to the wind and let the man kiss her.

Assuming he'd even want to.

You never can tell with Stockton. He likes to tease her that he'd never be attracted to a "scrawny little white woman" like her.

"I like ladies who have a little meat on their bones," he commented just the other day as they sat at the bar unwinding after attending the funeral of a rookie who'd been shot responding to a domestic disturbance. Ordinarily, they don't indulge in whiskey during the day, but the service had stirred Sully's grief for her beloved father, who'd passed away in September. Barnes was doing his best to cheer her up—by busting her chops, as usual.

"And what would your daddy have said about you dating a black man?"

"What is this, Alabama in 1962? He might have had a problem with me dating a fellow cop, but he wasn't a racist."

"He was a cop himself, and so was his father," Stockton pointed out.

"And so were his brothers and uncles and grandfather and great-grandfather, but . . ."

"But he wouldn't have wanted you dating a cop."

"Listen, I'm a big girl. I make my own decisions."

"So what are you saying, Gingersnap?" That's his pet name for her. Early on in their relationship, she asked him to stop. That did a lot of good. "You saying that you *want* to date a cop?"

"What, are you kidding me? I married one the first time around, and look how that turned out," she said, and that was that. For the time being, anyway.

Someday they might find their way into each other's bed. That, or they'll be best man or maid of honor at each other's second weddings.

Sully shoves her hands into the pockets of her insulated navy blue coat and leans over the dead girl.

The body was found in a clump of shrubs between Twelfth Avenue and the Hudson River a little while ago, phoned in by a man who'd been chasing a terrier that had escaped its leash.

Now he protectively cradles the little dog in his arms, standing alongside the usual assortment of curious onlookers plus a couple of reporters and a television news crew, all clustered beyond blue police barricades. Within the perimeter cordoned off by yellow tape, a forensics team takes measurements and snaps photos. On a car radio somewhere nearby, Johnny Mathis is singing that it's beginning to look a lot like Christmas.

It isn't, but it might be true by nightfall. The forecast calls for the first snowfall of the season, though Sully isn't convinced it's really going to happen and in fact accepted a friendly little wager from Stockton as they were driving over here from the precinct.

"It hardly ever snows in Manhattan in December. That would be too perfect. It only happens in small towns and in movies," she theorized. "In real life, the snow doesn't fall here until the holidays are over and there's absolutely nothing to look forward to but baseball and that's still months away. It's like, kick 'em when they're down."

"The snow is like that?"

"It is."

"Sadistic snow, is that it?"

"It's New York. What do you expect, Barnes? Kind, gentle snow?"

So now, if it does happen to snow within the next twenty-four hours, she has to take the subway to Stockton's Bronx apartment in the morning and clean it off his car. If it doesn't, he has to wear a Mets cap to Yankee Stadium on opening day in April.

"Now who's sadistic?" Stockton muttered, parking the car as they arrived at the scene. "You're a Yankee fan, too. You hate the Mets as much as I do."

"But not as much as I love seeing you squirm."

They went from laughingly shaking hands on their bet to suitably somber the moment they stepped out of the car half an hour ago.

"This is a damned shame," Stockton murmurs as they gaze at the dead girl.

She's lying on her back in the frozen mud, her fair, freckled skin spattered in her own blood and covered in multiple stab wounds. When found, she was covered in a sheet of dry cleaner's plastic: "shrink-wrapped like a bodega cucumber" was Barnes's poetic description when they first saw her.

The plastic shroud is a peculiar signature, one they've never seen before. The forensics team stripped it away after taking countless photographs, leaving the girl's dead flesh exposed to the December chill.

Why was it there in the first place? She was stabbed, not asphyxiated. Was her killer trying to protect her from the elements? Was it some kind of fetish?

"She's not a junkie," Sully comments, observing no

sign of needle marks and noting that the victim is slightly built, but healthy and athletic-looking as opposed to malnourished or emaciated.

"Nope. She could be sniffing, though."

"She could. But she's not a working girl, either. Look at her makeup and earrings." She's wearing very little eyeliner and no mascara to enhance her sandy lashes, and her earlobes are adorned only with tasteful studs set in silver.

"Those are diamonds, though," Stockton says. "Maybe she's a high-class call girl."

Sully holds a magnifying glass up to one of the earrings, studies it for a moment, and shakes her head. "Not the real thing. They're cubic zirconia."

"How can you tell?"

"No inclusions," Sully says briefly, not bothering to explain that real diamonds of this size wouldn't be this flawless.

"I'll take your word for it. But these days, even a highclass call girl might have fake diamonds."

"Yeah, but she'd still get a manicure—not to mention a pedicure." Leaning in to examine the victim's feet, she adds, "Those heels have never been touched by a pumice stone."

"Again, I'll take your word for it. Is that a tat?"

Sully follows Stockton's pointing finger back up to the torso. At first glance, the small tattoo perched between the gashes near the victim's collarbone is almost entirely camouflaged by blood and freckles. It's a deeper shade of red, though: a ladybug.

"They're supposed to bring good luck," Stockton says as she moves the magnifying glass in for a better look.

"Guess it didn't work for her."

Somebody's daughter, somebody's friend . . .

Right now, somewhere in the city, someone might be

wondering where she is. Sooner or later, with any luck, she'll be reported missing.

Until then, without clothing or ID, she's a Jane Doe.

There's no clue to her identity other than the tattoo. That and the fact that she's completely bald.

"What do you think?" Stockton asks. "Chemotherapy or fashion statement?"

"Neither." Sully's breath puffs white in the air as she leans in, spotting something.

"What makes you say that?"

"I think whoever killed her shaved her head," she says, staring at the clump of long, red hair tangled amid the dead leaves on the ground.

After finishing their pancakes, Rowan unpacks the decorations Jake carried down, and he dispatches Mick to get the other box of Christmas lights from the attic, which—predictably—results in a flash-fire argument.

As she unwraps the snow globe the kids chipped in and bought her years ago at Vernon's Apothecary, she can hear Mick stomping around the attic and Jake stomping around the kitchen. She winds the key in the bottom of the snow globe to hear its tinkling rendition of "Winter Wonderland."

Jake sticks his head in. "I'm going to walk Doofus. Tell Mick not to disappear. I'll be back in five minutes."

"Why don't you tell him?"

"Because every time I tell him anything he gives me an argument."

When Mick comes down carrying more boxes, she relays the message, and adds, "Can you please try to get along with your dad? For me?"

"I try, but he always yells at me."

"He says the same thing about you. Try harder."

She heads into the living room to hang five stockings

by the fireplace and arrange the porcelain crèche on the mantel, shoving aside a bunch of framed family photos to make room. She should probably put them away until January, but she likes to look at them.

A few minutes later, she hears Mick and Jake laughing good-naturedly about something as they head outside together.

Leaving the rest of the decorations in the hall, she goes straight to her study, closes the door, and dials her sister's cell phone number.

Now, as before, it rings a few times and goes into voice mail.

"Hey, it's me again. I hope everything is okay there. Listen, I need you to call me back, okay? It's kind of important. Call my cell."

She dials Noreen's home phone and is relieved when someone picks it up on the first ring. It's her niece, Sabrina.

"Oh, hi, Aunt Ro."

"How are you, kiddo?"

"Good, but I thought you might be my friend's mom calling. She's supposed to pick me up for tennis and we're late."

"Tennis? In December?"

"I play at the club."

Club—as in the North Shore country club Noreen and Kevin joined years ago, which didn't thrill Dad when he found out.

He'd long disapproved of Hudson Chase, the local country club, which for years wouldn't consider Irish Catholics, among others, for membership. "You can bet your sweet keister that changed when JFK got into the White House," Dad used to say. "And do you think I joined that country club after I was allowed to?"

"No way!" Rowan would shout on cue as a child, as Noreen just rolled her eyes.

"My ride is here," Sabrina blurts into the phone. "I've gotta go!"

"Wait! Is your mom home?"

"She went to church but it must be over by now. Call her cell."

"I tried. She didn't—"

"I have to go. See you, Aunt Ro."

"Bye, sweetie," Rowan says to the dial tone.

She can see Jake and Mick through the window. They appear to be arguing again, both gesturing wildly at a tangled light string on the ground.

She sighs, wishing Braden were here. Her even-tempered firstborn has always been the buffer between frustrated Jake and hotheaded Mick.

Aware that either her husband or son might come stomping into the house any second, Rowan quickly dials Noreen's cell again.

The phone rings several times and then goes into voice mail.

Maybe she put it on silent mode during Mass and forgot to turn on the volume afterward. But even if she did that, she'd probably have it on vibration mode.

Maybe she doesn't want to talk to you.

But why wouldn't she?

She doesn't know why I'm calling.

Or does she?

Frustrated, Rowan hangs up without leaving yet another message. She doesn't want to text or e-mail her. Putting it into writing would mean risking that somebody else might see it and ask questions.

The house is quiet, other than the occasional jingle from Doofus's dog tags as he changes nap positions in the next room. Outside, the rain has stopped, though the wind continues to blow.

She turns her attention to her laptop. Opening a search engine, she types *Vanessa Walker*.

As before, the results are inconclusive. Nothing that pops up matches what she knows about Rick's wife; not even when she adds the word *death*, or Rick's name to the search. But when she throws in New Jersey—bingo. Among the results, she finds an obituary whose accompanying photo shows a vaguely familiar face.

The woman's name is Vanessa, but her last name isn't Walker. It's De Forrest.

That's right, Rowan remembers now. Rick's wife had kept her maiden name—or was it her name from her first marriage? She can't recall which it was, only that it bothered him that she wouldn't take his last name. He mentioned that once, adding that Jake must be glad she'd done that when they got married.

"I'm sure he'd have been okay either way," she said. "It was my decision."

"*Everything* is Vanessa's decision," he replied darkly—indicating, perhaps, that the marriage was in trouble very early on.

Rowan glances out the window. She can see Jake and Mick out by the boxwood clump near the lamppost, still trying to untangle the first string of lights. Assured that she has the house to herself awhile longer, she reads on.

Rick isn't mentioned in the obituary; nor is the first husband. Only the names of her four children, a brother, and her mother, all of whom survive her, and her father, who does not. Basic details about her life are listed: birth date and place, graduation, job. The exact cause of death is absent, but that's often the case in obituaries. Sometimes there's a mention of a battle with a long illness, but not in this case. Sometimes, too, the family requests memorial contributions to a specific charity, which can sometimes serve as a clue. Again, there's nothing like that here.

How did Vanessa die?

Rowan combs the article again, searching for some detail she might have missed.

She finds one almost immediately, and can't believe she overlooked it the first time.

It doesn't reveal how Vanessa died, but it reveals when: last year—on November 30.

From the *Mundy's Landing Tribune*
Weather
December 8, 2015

Forecast

Today: Mostly pleasant with bright sunshine. Light and variable wind SSE at 7 to 10 mph. High: 42 F.

Tonight: Increasing cloudiness with temperatures falling below freezing. Low: mid–20s F.

Tomorrow: Mostly cloudy with snow squalls developing by late morning. Chance of snow 80 percent. Northwest wind at 8–13 mph with gusts to 30 mph. Accumulation 1–2 inches before tapering off in early evening. High: high 20s F. Low: mid 20s F.

A look ahead: Winter storm developing over the High Plains may bring widespread heavy snow to the region Friday into Saturday.

Chapter 9

Beyond the window, the world is dark except for swirling snow in a street lamp's glow. Dawn is still a few hours off, but Casey was prodded awake by a restless ache that hasn't subsided the way it usually does after a successful conquest. If anything, it's more persistent than ever.

You can't surrender to it. You have to focus on other things; stay busy, stay strong.

Focus . . . focus . . . focus . . .

Where are my glasses?

Ah, there, next to the television. It's on, tuned to the Weather Channel as always. There's a blizzard brewing out West, but it's too soon to tell the impact or even the path. Something to keep in mind, though. A significant storm could change everything.

Humming softly, Casey puts on the glasses and picks up the antique leather strop that came with the barber's razor purchased last summer.

The idea to swap a modern blade for an antique one had been inspired by a visit to the Mundy's Landing Historical Society.

Just such a blade had been a prominent part of the special exhibit celebrating the Sleeping Beauty murders. Some, including local hypocrites who laugh all the way to the bank, might argue that *celebrate* is the wrong word.

But even they can't ignore that the annual festival incites a carnival atmosphere. Last year, a vendor was selling T-shirts imprinted with the word *Mundypalooza* and an illustration of the suspected murder weapon: a folding blade like the one on exhibit and the one Casey purchased at a nearby flea market.

I wouldn't buy a tacky T-shirt, though. That's for damned sure. Some people just don't know where to draw the line.

Casey is pleased to discover that the strop works equally well to sharpen scissors. Several pulls on one blade, several pulls on the other, and the pair is good as new.

Casey places it beside the waiting scrapbook on the table and stands holding the strop, thoughtfully stroking the length of it as if caressing the long hair of a loved one.

Julia Sexton was supposed to be the last stand-in.

But it doesn't hurt to be prepared, just in case . . .

Casey stands and walks over to the kitchenette, where the straight razor still sits in the drying rack.

It was gratifying, yesterday, to watch blood that had dried an ugly shade of brown become vivid red again as it ran into the white porcelain sink, though it gradually diluted to a watery pink. After the last drop had swirled down the drain, Casey filled the sink with steaming bleach water and soaked the razor for a while, obliterating every trace of blood and human DNA.

Now it's ready to go again. All it needs is the painstakingly sharpened edge that offers not the slightest bit of resistance, cutting through skin and tendons and muscle like gossamer strands of hair.

Marching her fourth-graders through the quiet halls of the elementary school on Monday morning, Rowan punctuates yet another shush with the phrase she wearily uses all day, every day: "People, please!"

Wriggly and chatty thanks to the season's first snow-fall and a rousing game of crab walk soccer in gym class, all but a few perpetually obedient kids ignore her.

Most of the doors that line the corridor are propped open, thanks to the school's ancient boilers necessarily transforming some classrooms into saunas in order to keep others from becoming walk-in freezers. The issue dates back to Rowan's childhood. How well she remembers being held captive at her desk, distracted by her more fortunate schoolmates who had been temporarily sprung from their own stuffy classrooms. Her own fourth-grade teacher, Mrs. Duncan, would relish the irony that she's become the person wearily dishing out the *people, please*s.

"Ms. Mundy, Billy touched me again," Amanda Hicks whines as they enter the stairwell, where their echoes bounce off beige tile.

"It was an accident! I couldn't help it."

"Billy, please keep your hands to yourself," she says wearily, biting her tongue to keep from calling Amanda a tattletale.

"But she stopped walking on purpose so that I would crash into her!"

Rowan doesn't doubt it, but she didn't witness the incident and she ignores the accusation. Any reprimand to Amanda would guarantee another phone call from her mother, and one conversation with Bari Hicks is more than enough in one day. While the class was in the gym, she spent fifteen minutes on the phone explaining the logistics of this week's field trip to the local historical society, which Bari's chaperoning.

She doesn't see why she has to ride the bus over with the group, because buses are loud and bouncy and make her queasy.

"We need to have a certain number of chaperones on

the bus with the kids," Rowan explained. "I counted you
into that equation."

"I can take Amanda in my car, and a few of her
friends. They'll be much more comfortable. I have plenty
of room." Her car is a luxury SUV that seats eight, but
Amanda only has two friends to speak of, both of whom
are her neighbors in Mundy Estates.

"The district doesn't allow that. I can try to find someone else to chaperone if you're—"

"No, no, I'll do it. But I wish you had told me I had to
ride the bus in the first place."

Ordinarily, Rowan would muster infinite patience, but
this morning, overtired and preoccupied, it was all she
could do not to snap at the woman that any idiot with half
a brain knows that chaperoning a field trip means traveling *with* the kids.

*But somehow, I managed to keep my cool. Now all I
have to do is try not to explode—or fall asleep—for the
rest of the day.*

She'd lain awake nearly all night wondering what happened to Vanessa De Forrest last November thirtieth.

Several times yesterday, she almost called Rick to ask
how Vanessa had died. But she couldn't. She was afraid
to do that, afraid of him.

She wants to believe the date is a mere coincidence,
and might have convinced herself of it if she hadn't received the package last Monday.

Who, besides Rick, would have reason to force her to
open that ominous door to the past?

Jake?

Rowan refuses to let her mind venture very far in that
direction.

She's never felt so alone in her life.

*You can't talk to Jake, you can't talk to Rick, you can't
talk to the police . . .*

You can talk to Noreen if she ever calls you back . . .

But now that Rowan knows about Vanessa, that no longer seems vital.

Her head is spinning with possibilities at this point, and only one thing is certain: she has to protect her secret, at least until she finds out who is threatening her with it.

They've reached the second floor of the school, filing down another hallway lined with drying snow boots, closed lockers, and open classrooms.

"People, please. Others are trying to work."

"Hey, Ms. Mundy," someone calls, "what's that?"

"What's what?" she asks before catching sight of the small red and green gift bag hanging from the doorknob of her classroom.

The students swoop in like tag sale early birds on a crate of Depression glass.

"It's a present!"

"Who's it for?"

"Let me see!"

"Stop pushing!"

Some days, it doesn't take much to turn a group of fourth-graders into tiny kids. This is one of them.

Amanda viciously wrangles the bag from someone's grasp and bestows it with a beatific smile more befitting gift giver than gift snatcher. "Ms. Mundy, it's for you."

Wary, Rowan takes the bag. The tag dangling from a rope handle bears her full name, printed in well-defined, evenly spaced, perfectly straight or rounded letters. The printing style is distinctive among elementary school teachers. Early this morning, she left a similarly addressed gift box on the table in the deserted teacher's lounge for the library aide.

The principal's secretary wandered in and spotted her leaving the bag. "Let me guess. Secret Santa?"

"Ho ho ho."

"'Tis the season," the secretary responded with a grin. She was wearing a jingle bell around her neck on a red silk cord and mentioned that it had been left by her own Secret Santa, tied to the Reserved sign in front of her numbered spot in the employee parking lot.

Yes. 'Tis the season. Ordinarily, Rowan wouldn't bat an eye at an anonymous gift, but this year things are different. Yes, she's fairly certain the package contains her Secret Santa's Monday offering, but she can't entirely erase the nagging doubt from her mind.

"Aren't you going to open your present?"

"Not right now."

"But don't you want to see what it is?"

"Not right now," she repeats to whichever of the girls is asking the question. For a change, it isn't Amanda.

"Wow, what a Grinch." This time, it is Amanda, and while the word *Grinch* is innocuous in the grand scheme of things a fourth-grader can call a teacher, it throws Rowan right back to the snow day again.

This is ridiculous. It's consuming her life, and it has to stop.

You have to confront Rick. Better him than Jake.

For now, she stashes the gift bag in a desk drawer where it won't distract the class—or her.

Bob Belinke should have been taxiing down a runway hours ago. Instead, he's in a taxi at the airport and heading in the wrong direction.

As much as he loves the Manhattan skyline looming in the gray shroud beyond the cab's furiously swiping windshield wipers, he'd prefer to be headed home to the tropical sun. He's chilled to the bone and his skin is leathery after alternate blasts of wet cold wind and dry overheated air.

He spent enough years working in aviation to have anticipated travel complications when he heard the snowy forecast last night. Strong wind and an inch or two of snow are more than sufficient to snarl air traffic at JFK, but he was hoping for a mere delay. Unfortunately, the inbound flight he was supposed to board was diverted by a mechanical problem. Rather than hang around the airport all day hoping to squeeze onto another flight with connections amid residual delays, he opted to rebook for tomorrow morning.

Maybe it's just as well.

Now I can call Rick and make sure he's okay.

He's been concerned about his old friend ever since they parted ways yesterday afternoon.

"You've got to let go of the guilt," Bob told him on the street outside the restaurant. "It's going to eat you alive. What happened to Vanessa wasn't your fault."

"How do you know that?" Rick snapped. "You don't, okay? You only know what I've told you."

Bob was taken aback. It took him a moment to figure out what to say to that. "It's time for you to start healing. Don't isolate yourself in this. You still have friends, and you still have a family, too, for that matter. Talk to them."

"Everyone has moved on. No one wants to hear from me."

"You don't think your kids would want—"

"Come on, Bob, you might not be a dad, but you were a stepdad, and you were once a kid yourself. You really think that after all that's happened these guys will welcome the old man barging in for a good old-fashioned heart-to-heart? They've picked up the pieces and moved on, and they're busy with lives of their own. Vanessa's kids have jobs, and my kids are in the middle of finals, and none of them want to hear from me right now."

"They might surprise you. But I'm here for you if you want to keep talking. I don't have to be anywhere this afternoon."

"I do."

Bob refrained from asking where; refrained from saying anything more than "Call me if you need me. Anytime."

Rick said that he would, but he won't.

That's okay, Bob thinks as the cab enters the Manhattan-bound lanes on the Van Wyck Expressway. *I'll call him, as soon as I get back to the hotel.*

After getting the kids off to school early this morning, Noreen crawled back into bed. She meant to snooze for another fifteen minutes, but fell asleep for a couple of hours. Now she wakes up to the sound of the housekeeper vacuuming down the hall and is glad she's in the master bedroom this morning. Otherwise, if Kevin were home, Luz might have found her in the guest room down the hall, where she's been spending some nights lately.

If the housekeeper is aware that Noreen's perfect life has fallen apart, she hasn't mentioned it. Still, she must have noticed someone's been sleeping in the guest suite whenever Kevin isn't doing an overnight shift at the hospital. Noreen is always careful to remake the guest bed when she gets up in the morning, but she can never get the coverlet to lie as smoothly as Luz does. When she slips back in at night, she often finds that the sheets have been changed.

Luz is discreet. Good for her.

It's more than Noreen can say for Kevin.

He didn't come home last night, and she's pretty sure he wasn't at the hospital. Maybe he'd stayed at his new apartment, since he started paying rent on the first of the month—though she doubts that, as it's still purportedly unfurnished. He said he doesn't want to fill it with "just any old furniture" and intends to pillage the house for pieces as soon as the kids are informed of the impending separation.

But Noreen isn't stupid. She's certain he's found a soft landing spot somewhere.

At least his absence spared her another long night on the mattress in the guest room. It's a perfectly decent mattress. But it cost significantly less than the five-figure premium king-sized one in the master suite.

"You can sleep here too," Kevin says whenever he's home overnight. "I don't mind."

That makes her want to scream, *Well, I do! I mind! I mind!* but of course she never does.

She rolls over, huddling deeper into the goose down comforter as the thought of her soon-to-be-ex-husband settles over her like a clammy blanket on a raw day.

Back in September, when he said they had to talk, she assumed he wanted to discuss their upcoming wedding anniversary.

She was wrong.

"This isn't working," he said, and for a moment she thought he was referring to the cell phone clasped in his strong, well-groomed surgeon's hands. He wasn't wearing his gold wedding band, she noticed belatedly—but only after he clarified that it was their marriage that wasn't working.

"We've grown apart," he said, and had the audacity to heap on a few more clichés: "I want us to stay friends," and "There's no one else," topped off by "It's not you. It's me."

"Really?" she said with a bitter laugh. "Really? It's not you, it's me? Can't you do any better than that?"

He could not, other than to assure her, once again, that there's not another woman.

She didn't believe it then, and she doesn't believe it now. You don't walk away from a life like the one they've built here unless you're walking toward something you think is going to be better.

But it won't be, after a while. It never is, in these situations. Sooner or later, Kevin is going to come crawling back.

Or maybe he won't be able to leave her after all, despite having presented it as a fait accompli.

She's always given him plenty of space. She's never complained about him being gone so much. She brings in a good income and she takes good care of the house and the kids and the dog and herself. She may be closing in on fifty, but there's not an ounce of flab on her body. She avoids the sun and has regular injections to keep facial wrinkles at bay, and she'd never permit a strand of gray in her long red mane.

Hell, she's handled enough divorce cases to know that she's not the kind of wife men leave; she's the kind of woman they leave their wives for. In fact . . .

She shakes her head, pushing away the thought of the man who would have done just that, if she'd let him.

But I wasn't about to walk away from Kevin, and I was so positive he'd never walk away from me.

Yes, well . . . live and learn.

Aware that she has a client meeting in less than an hour, she throws aside the covers and stretches, glad she showered the first time she got up. All it takes now is ten minutes to splash water on her face, put on some makeup, brush her teeth and her hair, and throw on a suit.

Downstairs, she pours lukewarm coffee into a mug and goes over the kids' afterschool schedules as she waits for it to reheat in the microwave. Shannon has an SAT prep class, Sabrina has a piano lesson, Samantha a Girl Scout meeting. Three different directions, but with enough time between them that Noreen can get each girl to where she has to be and back home again.

Piece of cake, she thinks, removing her coffee from the microwave, dumping it into a plastic go-mug, and heading for the door.

The kids haven't been informed of the looming separation. With Sean overseas until just before Christmas, the news has had to wait; it's the kind that should be shared in person with all the kids at once. They'll undoubtedly be caught off guard by it.

Noreen certainly was.

Her three daughters, who have been living obliviously under this roof as the marriage unraveled, will be upset when they find out, but it's her son who will take it the hardest. Sean is by far the most sensitive of her brood, and he's been homesick this semester. Just last night he texted that he can't wait to come home for Christmas and reminded her that he doesn't have to be back on campus at Notre Dame until mid-January.

I was thinking you and I and Dad can do some skiing while the girls are in school, he wrote.

Sounds fun, she replied, which was better than a vague *We'll see*, much less letting it slip that he's going to spend part of that break helping his father settle into a new apartment.

Kevin wants to officially move in on January first. "That'll give the kids some time to absorb the separation."

"Ten days. Great."

Even she hasn't absorbed it yet, and she's had three months.

"You must have seen this coming," Kevin kept insisting.

She denied it. But looking back, she can't remember if she was lying to him, or to both of them. When, exactly, did she fall out of love? When did he? Does it matter?

Aside from her clients, plenty of couples she knows

manage to keep their families intact when the romance
fades. They just live separate lives, and no one outside the
marriage is the wiser.

*Why do we have to be different? Why do we have to
endure a divorce?*

No one knows better than Noreen what that can do to
children, not to mention finances.

Now the world will know she failed spectacularly at
something she'd considered one of her greatest successes.
For twenty-three years, she was proud, perhaps smugly
so, that she'd married so well.

And now . . .

*I have no control over my future. None. He's decided
what's going to happen to me, whether I like it or not.*

In the front hall, she takes her coat from the closet and
picks up her leather satchel filled with legal briefs for the
meeting.

Her gaze falls on the wedding portrait in a Baccarat
crystal frame on the table by the staircase. Just looking at
it, she feels a fresh scream beginning to swell inside of her.

She reaches a trembling hand toward the photo, dis-
placed by Luz and her dust cloth.

The burgeoning scream, were she to allow it to escape
her throat, would undoubtedly shatter the frame along
with every window in the house.

As always, she suppresses the rage.

She gently nudges the frame back a bit, away from the
table's edge, once more at a perfect forty-five-degree angle.

There. That's better. Much better.

She gives a satisfied nod and walks out the door.

Having wasted the early morning hours prowling the
streets for a suitable stand-in, Casey gave up when the
commuters began to swarm.

Back at home, a nap would have been welcome, but sleep refused to come. A long hot shower—not a bath, never a bath!—helped a little. So did some tea and toast, yet Casey remains fidgety as the day wears on.

Out on the street beyond the window, a light drizzle washes into the gutters the last traces of snow that had fallen overnight. There was barely enough to stick, but it was sufficient to keep all but the hardiest New Yorkers from venturing out early unless they had to. Casey's interest lies not in those hardy types, but in the sweetly feminine and vulnerable—precisely the kind of woman who would choose to spend a stormy morning safely snuggled at home.

At least the futile early morning wanderlust resulted in one fruitful find: a copy of the *New York Daily News*, with its front page photo of a West Side crime scene and the headline: MYSTERY WOMAN SLAIN.

She's not a mystery to me.

How gratifying to be the only person alive who knows her name. And how amusing to find that the accompanying article shares so few specific details about the crime. The authorities hold them back, hoping to eventually trap the culprit into revealing things only the killer would know.

They won't trap me.

Casey settles at the table with the newspaper and takes great care to cut out the article with freshly honed scissors. On the reverse side is an article about the anniversary of the Pearl Harbor bombing.

Ah, today is December 7—the date lives in infamy, right up there with September 11.

And November 30.

Casey smiles contentedly. The second scrapbook is coming along as nicely as Vanessa's, filled with precious relics of a productive and cathartic year. A time capsule, if you will.

Really, the collection rivals the archival exhibits at the Mundy's Landing Historical Society. It might even, when all is said and done, compete with whatever lies buried in the vault beneath the marble floor of Village Hall.

Casey thinks back to a rainy summer afternoon when the museum was packed with visitors. They were so stupidly oblivious, caught up in dusty old murders when a modern mastermind was right there in their midst, scheming something far greater.

One day, these scrapbooks will be part of just such an exhibit. People will travel from all over the world to see it.

They'll try to solve the case, try to figure out who I am—but of course, they won't be able to. I'll always be one step ahead of them, just like the best of the best: the Sleeping Beauty Killer and Jack the Ripper and the Zodiac . . .

Casey flips chronologically through the pages of the scrapbook. *So many memories. So many beautiful girls. I'll never forget them.*

Ah, here's the blank page. This is where Julia Sexton's story will begin—and end.

First, the proper tools: a ruler to measure the page and then the clipping, three times. That's the rule. You measure once, twice, thrice, and then you use a pencil to mark the spot. It has to be a number two pencil, because it brings back the memory of the yellow cardboard cutouts taped on to the wall outside each classroom at Mundy's Landing Elementary School.

I want the one that says Ms. Mundy, Casey decides. *I have to have it, for Rowan's scrapbook.*

Like Vanessa, Rowan has her very own volume. Already, hers is filled with souvenirs. Some were gleaned from Casey's excursions through her house; others were relevant items picked up here and there along the way. The latest addition: the customer copy of the dinner check from Marrana's last Monday night.

The quest to get the pencil cutout will present a bit of a challenge, but nothing insurmountable. In fact, another visit to the school would present the perfect opportunity to deliver another little gift.

Contemplating the new plan, Casey pastes the newspaper article precisely in the center of the page, then reaches into a drawer where the rest of the relics are waiting.

Julia's wallet, minus its meager contents, was discarded in a Dumpster a few blocks away from where she died. Sooner or later, it'll find its way into the landfill or into the hands of the NYPD. Either way is fine.

They'll never suspect me.

Even if, by some bizarre turn of events, Casey's tracks aren't covered as well as they should be, it won't matter.

A whole new life will be under way very soon, far from New York City and far from Mundy's Landing. Julia Sexton will be nothing but a distant memory, albeit a pleasurable one. For the police, she'll represent yet another unsolved homicide.

Now who's the authority?

Positioning her driver's license, MetroCard, and five-dollar-bill on the page, Casey feels the edgy compulsion beginning to take hold again.

It was all so perfect: the secret ladybug tattoo, sweet-smelling skin, the throaty pleas for her life to be spared . . .

She'd been so wonderfully terrified in those all-too-fleeting final moments when she grasped exactly what was about to happen to her.

I wanted to savor it this time, but I got carried away again.

Quickly, much too quickly, it was over. Julia lay life-lessly cradled in Casey's arms. It was time to kiss her good-bye.

Next time, it will be Rowan's turn.

And then it will be over for good, and Casey will move on.

Just one more . . .

Two, if you count Rowan's son.

And I'm not counting him, Casey thinks with disdain.

Anyway, it won't be enough.

If I could only have one more stand-in, I'd make it last. I wouldn't just pounce on someone who strikes my fancy. I'd get closer and closer and when it's time, I'd make sure she suffers.

Vanessa's voice floats back from Thanksgiving Day just over a year ago, the last time Casey saw her alive. It was just the two of them.

"No, I didn't make any hors d'oeuvres," she said. "They only ruin your appetite."

"But I'm starved."

"Good. Everything will taste much better if you're truly famished. Know what I mean?"

"I know exactly what you mean."

But I didn't really. Not then.

Anyway, Vanessa's philosophy didn't keep Casey from complaining that dinner was taking too long.

"Come on, cut it out."

"Cut what out?"

"Being so hangry."

"You mean hungry."

"I mean angry because you're hungry. *Hangry.*"

Who wouldn't smile at something so clever?

I did, even though I was hangry. And now . . . I'm even hangrier.

But she was right—everything tastes much better when you're truly famished. And I'll be sated very soon . . .

Resolving to stick to the plan, Casey picks up the final memento of last night: silken strands of Julia Sexton's long red hair, tied—just for now—with a white satin ribbon smeared with blood.

From the *Mundy's Landing Tribune* Archives
Front Page
November 4, 2015

Mayor Ransom Ousted in Landslide

Democrat John Elsworth Ransom, whose roots extend to the first settlers of Mundy's Landing and whose tenure as mayor stretches back to dawning hours of the twenty-first century, was soundly defeated by Republican Dean Cochran in yesterday's local election.

Cochran, a native Californian, is a commercial real estate developer who relocated to the area in 2011. He has since been instrumental in the development of Mundy Estates, a luxury townhome development where he currently resides. Celebrating his victory last night at party headquarters, he said, "The people of Mundy's Landing are prepared to prove that it is, indeed possible to march toward the future while keeping the past firmly in our collective sightline."

The incumbent mayor expressed disappointment that constituents had "placed their confidence in a candidate whose tenuous ties to our community and lack of a viable political track record may jeopardize the dignity and integrity of our hometown."

Sworn in on January 1, 2000, lifelong resident Ransom had promised a new era of prosperity and revitalization of the central business district. Indeed, despite the recession, Mayor Ransom's four consecutive terms saw nearly two dozen empty storefronts along Market and Broad Streets transformed into thriving locally owned restaurants and boutiques, successfully keeping national chains such as Starbucks and CVS from setting up shop within the village proper.

"I'm as much a fan of mom-and-pop operations as

the next guy," Cochran told voters during an election eve rally. "But why limit ourselves? Chain stores exist alongside small businesses in economically vibrant communities across the country. Let's embrace the expansion that will ultimately restore our beloved village to its glory days as a Hudson River boomtown."

A vocal proponent of the budding local tourism industry, Mayor-elect Cochran is currently in discussion with several major hotel corporations interested in developing the vacant parcel of land on Colonial Highway where Valley Cove Pleasure Park stood a century ago. He points out that the vast majority of attendees for the annual Mundy's Landing Historical Society–sponsored Scene of the Crime Convention— colloquially known as Mundypalooza—are forced to find lodging elsewhere. "Let's keep those visitors— and their open wallets—right here in town," he said during the campaign, prompting Mayor Ransom to accuse him of "exploiting murder for politics and profit."

The convention, during which crime buffs, armchair sleuths, and curiosity seekers from around the globe try their hand at solving the Sleeping Beauty murders of 1916, was perhaps the most hotly contested issue in a tension-fraught mayoral race.

Ransom has eschewed the event since its inception in 1991, while Cochran serves on the planning board for the 2016 convention, which marks the hundred-year anniversary of the crime spree and coincides with ML350, a planned celebration to commemorate the village's 350-year-old heritage and the public opening of a time capsule buried a century ago.

Chapter 10

"**I** have good news and bad news," Bob's voice greets Rick when he picks up his cell phone on Monday afternoon. "Which do you want first?"

No brainer: "The bad." How bad can it be compared to all that's already happened?

"My flight was canceled. I'm stuck in New York overnight."

"That stinks," Rick says mildly.

"The good news is, I'm free for dinner if you are."

His immediate instinct is to make up an excuse. He knows he said too much yesterday about Vanessa; knows Bob is concerned about him and will want to discuss it again.

No thanks. But when he opens his mouth to say he has to work late tonight, "Sure—dinner sounds great" comes out.

"Great. Let's go to the Blue Water Grill in Union Square. I haven't been there in a while."

"I don't know, I'm not really—"

"My treat," Bob adds quickly.

"You don't have to do that."

"I want to. If I'd been around when Vanessa died, I could have, you know . . ."

"You could have sent a fruit basket and a card. You

don't have to spring for dinner at a fancy restaurant." The quip might have worked in person, but over the phone it lands with an obnoxious thud.

I sound like an asshole, Rick thinks. *Maybe I am an asshole.*

"I'd have been here for you if I could have been, Rick."

"I didn't mean it that way. I meant . . . never mind. Vanessa always said my communication skills weren't great."

Her communication skills, however, were stellar. She always managed to tell him precisely what she thought of him, right to the bitter end.

Rough around the edges. That's me.

Except with Rowan. With her, he was the man he could never be for Vanessa, even from the start. Why?

Was it because Rowan, who was down to earth, unlike his wife, didn't intimidate him? Or simply that he loved her, and he'd never loved Vanessa?

Sometimes Rick wonders how he and Vanessa wound up together in the first place—and how they'd managed to last as long as they did. When they met, they were both lonely. She was looking for a father for her children, and he was looking for . . .

Not passion, because he'd met plenty of women who were far less reserved and if not more attractive than Vanessa, who was truly striking, then at least more appealing to him. And he wasn't looking for a meal ticket, though she'd accused him of that during the final days of their marriage. Not companionship, either, because Vanessa was on the verge of being too busy for him even when they met. After they met, forget it. She had no time for him.

Maybe if she'd been more attentive to his needs, he wouldn't have strayed.

He regrets having said that to her during their last

fight, the one during which he'd confessed—all those years later—that he'd stopped loving her years ago and fallen in love with Rowan.

Yeah. Communication isn't his forte. Either he says too much, or too little, or the wrong thing.

"I'll help you work on those communication skills," Bob offers. "And I want you to think about taking my advice. Like I told you yesterday, if you would just reach out to the people who care about you, you might—"

"I did that."

"And . . . ?"

"We'll talk."

"See? That's good. It's a good start."

Realizing Bob misunderstood, Rick doesn't bother to correct him. He meant he would talk to Bob about the kids, not that the kids had agreed to talk to him when he'd reached out to them.

He'd followed Bob's advice and made four phone calls—to his stepsons, and to his son and daughter. All four went straight into voice mail. None has been returned so far.

He spends the rest of the afternoon alternately trying to figure out how to get out of having dinner with Bob and looking forward to it.

It's been ages since he ate in a place with cloth napkins and a wine list that extends beyond house white and house red. Besides, brunch yesterday was a good distraction from thinking about Rowan. Maybe dinner tonight will be an even better one.

"And who can tell me the year the first settlers arrived in Mundy's Landing?" Rowan asks her class as their afternoon history review winds down. "Raise your hands, please. No shouted answers. Let's see . . . Shane?"

"Sixteen sixty-five?"

"Good. And do you know where they came from?"

"Holland?"

"No, the Dutch had lost control of New Netherland the year before to which country?"

"England!" Billy blurts, resulting, predictably, in a reprimand from Amanda Hicks, whose hand has been waving in the air since the history review began.

"You were supposed to raise your hand! Ms. Mundy, he was supposed to—"

Mercifully, Amanda's final tattle of the day is curtailed by the final bell.

"People," Rowan calls above the explosion of chatter and scraping chairs, "please hand me your review sheets on the way out. And I'm still missing a few permission slips for our field trip. They were due on Friday. You need to get them in or you're not going!"

Predictably, she's inundated by questions about the review sheets, the homework, the permission slips, including "What permission slips?" and "What field trip?"

At last, she's alone, holding a sheaf of papers, including a permission slip that appears to be from last September's field trip, and a single boot someone just found on the floor under a desk and no one recognizes.

She closes the classroom door and then locks it, something she never does—not from the inside, anyway. But she has only a few minutes before she heads down to the tutoring room, and the gift bag she stashed in her desk earlier has been on her mind all afternoon. It's time to find out whether it's an offering from her Secret Santa, or her Secret Stalker.

First things first. She tosses the boot into the lost and found crate with all the other single boots and shoes—and there are many. Then she puts the papers on her desk, tosses the old permission slip into the blue recycling bin, and plucks out the things that don't belong there: an apple core, a cellophane wrapper, a mitten. The garbage goes into the garbage can, the mitten into the lost and found.

You're procrastinating. Just look inside the bag.

She opens the drawer, takes it out, and takes a deep breath.

Go ahead. Hurry up.

She gingerly pushes aside the white glitter-dusted tissue paper tufting from the top.

What if there's a layer of yellowed newspaper beneath it?

Then that's it. I call the police, she decides.

There's no newspaper, only a small balsam-scented jar candle. She recognizes the label from the gift department at Vernon's Apothecary on Market Street. She was just talking about these candles in the teachers' lounge last week.

Okay. Okay, this is good.

And even if it didn't turn out to be just a harmless little gift . . .

How could she have considered calling the police?

Even if she asked them not to make the case public or involve her husband, this is a tiny village. Everyone gossips. *Everyone*. It would get back to Jake, and she'd have to tell him.

Besides, what happened last week wasn't a crime. It's not as though the cops will put the anonymous package sender on their most wanted list and alert the FBI.

Your life isn't hanging in the balance here. Your marriage, maybe, and definitely your personal integrity and peace of mind—but not your life. Not unless . . .

Again, she thinks of Vanessa.

Again, she wonders . . . and keeps right on wondering as she endures the next ninety minutes going through the motions with her students in the tutoring room.

When at last the school day drags to a close, she's come to a decision.

Alone in her car, she takes her cell phone from her pocket and begins dialing.

More than twenty-four hours after discovering the body, Sully continues browsing through photos of young women who have recently gone missing in the tri-state area. There are always so many—far too many. But she's no closer to identifying the victim than she is to finding her killer.

"Sully."

Something in Stockton's tone causes her to glance up sharply from her computer screen. Seated at his adjacent desk and focused on his own computer, he's shaking his head. "Come and look at this."

She jumps up and hurries over. "Did you find her?"

"No, but I found this in the unsolved case files."

Leaning over his shoulder to see the screen, Sully finds herself looking at a female corpse.

Nude . . .

Covered in bloody slashes . . .

Bald.

She curses softly. "Who is she?"

Stockton wordlessly clicks over to a new screen, revealing another photograph. This one shows a smiling young woman with long red hair.

"That's the victim?"

"Right. It's a selfie she posted on Instagram a few hours before she went missing last March in Erie, Pennsylvania."

"So she still had her hair when she disappeared."

"But not when her body turned up a few days later, dumped by the side of a road."

"Son of a bitch shaves their heads."

"Looks that way."

Forensics already confirmed that the strands of hair

that turned up near their victim had been cut or shaved off, as opposed to ripped out in a struggle.

"Are there others?" she asks, pulling up a chair.

"Aren't there always?" Stockton asks grimly, and clicks over to another case file.

Mick has been looking for the right opportunity to anonymously present Brianna's first Secret Santa gift from the moment he arrived at school this morning. Having memorized her schedule back in September, he did his best to stay one step ahead of her as she went from class to class. That plan resulted in three tardy slips on his own schedule, and the small gift bag containing the bead charm was still in his backpack when the final bell rang.

That leaves him with two options: he can either deliver the gift to her house, or slip it into her bag or coat when she leaves them in the employee closet at the restaurant tonight.

If he waits until then, though, the mystery will be over on the first day. She'll guess that it's from either him or Zach. The only other guys who work on Mondays are Mr. Marrana and the dishwasher, both of whom are married.

After the last bell, he detours several times past Brianna's locker and her friends' lockers. No sign of her, or of them. Now running late for practice, he stops by his locker to grab his jacket and gym bag, brooding. Maybe this was a stupid idea all along. Maybe he should just forget the stupid gift, and Brianna, too.

He slams the locker door, turns around, and nearly crashes into Zach Willet.

"Sorry," Mick mutters, and starts to move on.

"Hey, Lou, you okay?"

"Um, not really."

"What's wrong?"

Mick turns to face him. "Are you sure about that college guy?"

"What college guy?"

"The college guy!" he repeats, wondering how Zach can possibly be so ignorant. "The one Brianna's seeing!"

"Am I sure what?"

"That she's seeing him!"

"Stop shouting at me, Mick." Zach never calls him by his real first name, and he looks irritated.

Well, that makes two of us.

"You know what? Forget it." Mick turns and walks away.

"You know what? I will," Zach calls after him.

In the gym, the coach gives him extra laps for being late. Before he starts running, Mick says, "I just want to let you know that I have to leave early today for a doctor's appointment."

The coach nods but he looks a bit suspicious, probably assuming it's a ploy to get out of running the extra laps. To prove that it isn't, Mick runs them hard and fast, and succeeds in purging some of the frustration that's been percolating all day.

Ninety minutes later, as he covers the few blocks from the school on Battlefield Road to Brianna's house on Prospect Street, he belatedly realizes that this wasn't a great plan after all. Now he can't catch the late bus with the rest of the team, which means he'll have to walk all the way home. Plus, if Mom shows up at the bus stop again like she did last Monday, she'll freak out when he doesn't get off.

He pulls his phone out of his pocket, deciding to send her a preemptive text. He can say that he's getting a ride home with one of the seniors on the team, or—

No, he can't. His phone battery is dead.

He'll just have to deal with the consequences. Tomor-

row, he'll make sure it's charged—and come up with a
better plan for delivering Brianna's gift.

Prospect Street runs along the south side of the Village
Common, parallel to Church Street and perpendicular to
Market Street and Fulton Avenue. East of the Common,
it climbs into a hilly residential enclave known as The
Heights. Mick's parents both grew up in that neighborhood, Mom on State Street right around the corner from
the Armbrusters' two-story yellow house with black
shutters.

Dusk is falling. The lights are on in some of the houses
he passes, and there are even a few Christmas trees glow-
ing in front windows.

Not at Brianna's house, though. The first floor is dark,
and there are no cars parked in the short driveway beside
the front walk. Both her parents work up in Albany, Mick
knows. They probably aren't home yet.

He looks to make sure no one is around before he
stops to stare up at the light spilling from a second-
floor window. Is that Brianna's room? Is she there right
now, getting ready for work beyond the drawn blinds? Is
she . . . dressed?

He promptly pushes that tantalizing notion from his
head, telling himself that it's probably her kid brother's
bedroom anyway.

Still, she's probably home. And when she leaves to
walk to the restaurant, she'll come out the side door that
faces the driveway. He recalls from his paperboy days
that the Armbruster family rarely bothered to shovel the
walk that leads to the porch because they don't use the
front door.

After another furtive glance to make sure the street is
deserted, he strides up the driveway, unzipping his backpack as he goes. He reaches the side door, finds the gift
bag, and hangs it on the knob. Halfway down the drive-

way again, he thinks better of it and backtracks. This time, he opens the door and hangs the bag on the inside knob, where it will keep the door ajar. That way, she can't possibly miss it when she leaves.

Again, he turns away; again, he turns back with hesitation.

What if someone sees it before she does and steals it?

Glancing toward the street, he sees that one of the neighbors has materialized with her dog, standing by the curb.

Terrific.

Unfortunately, the leashed terrier isn't as clueless as Doofus, and immediately starts barking. The old woman turns, spots Mick, and gives him a long, suspicious look before recognition dawns.

"How are you, Mick?" she calls with a cheerful wave as her dog continues to bark. "How's your mom?"

"I'm great, Mrs. Gershin," he responds in a low voice, hurrying away from Brianna's house. "Mom's great."

"What's that?" she pretty much shrieks above the barking, and he looks at the upstairs window to make sure Brianna hasn't been summoned by all the commotion.

"Great, we're all great," he tells Mrs. Gershin. "Everyone's great."

Maybe he should ask her not to tell anyone she saw him here. He can explain about the Secret Santa.

No—that's a bad idea. She's elderly and hard of hearing even without the yappy dog. He'd have to shout to get the point across.

It's better just to get away while he can. With any luck, Mrs. Gershin isn't just deaf, she's also senile and will forget she ever saw him here.

Seeing Rowan's number pop up on her cell phone, Noreen immediately excuses herself from the client meeting.

If it had been going well, she might have stuck it out and made a mental note to return the call later.

But it isn't going well. The man sitting across from her and her partner Jennifer at the conference room table— the wealthy businessman who's trying to hide a five-year-old love child and major assets from his wife of forty years—reminds her of Kevin.

Welcoming the opportunity to step into the short hallway outside the conference room, she answers the call. "Rowan?"

"Oh my God. There you are. What's going on?"

"What do you mean?"

"I've been trying to reach you for days. Didn't you get my messages?"

"I got one." Maybe two. Or possibly three, she realizes, though she's not about to surrender to any guilt trip her sister intends to lay on her. "You said it wasn't important."

"Only the first time, and I lied. You always call me back. Why didn't you?"

"I've been busy."

"You're always busy, but—"

"I'm sorry. Is everything okay?"

There's a pause. "No."

Ah, there it is anyway: guilt, trying its best to ooze in despite Noreen's intentions, and bringing with it a ripple of concern.

"What's wrong?" she asks, pacing the short length of the hall, past her office, Jennifer's office, the restroom, and the tiny waiting area. "Are the boys okay?"

The boys—it's what their parents always called their older brothers. Mitch and Danny were the boys; Noreen and Rowan were the girls. The boys were always a solid unit, while the girls were frequently at odds with each other. Then again, Rowan was pretty much at odds with everyone in the family at any given time.

I spent so many years trying to smooth over her messes. Is it any wonder that I'm wary when she calls, even now?

"The boys are fine. It's me. I'm not fine."

"What happened?"

"Are you alone?"

"Yes." *More alone than you'd ever imagine.*

"I need to talk to you about something. I wouldn't bother you if I had anyone else to turn to, but . . . I don't."

"Did you try the supermarket cashier and the guy who does your gutters?"

"Noreen, come on, this isn't a joke. I need you."

Hearing the vulnerability in her sister's voice, she softens. Just a little. She perches on one of the two waiting room chairs and begins straightening the pile of magazines between them. "Tell me. I'm listening."

"Do you remember what I told you years ago? About . . . something I almost did?"

"The affair with your neighbor?"

"Shh!"

"I told you, I'm alone—and even if I weren't, no one here would have any idea who I'm talking to or what I'm talking about."

"I know, but still . . . for once can't you just be . . ."

"Warm and fuzzy? Is that what you want?"

That gets a laugh out of her sister—not a long or remotely merry one, but at least it defuses the tension.

"Forget it. Warm and fuzzy isn't you. And . . . I need *you*. Do you remember what I told you that day when you asked me why Jake and I moved back to Mundy's Landing?"

Noreen does, very clearly.

"I know you thought I was taking a step backward and that I might get myself into trouble again," Rowan said that day, "but . . . I was actually trying to keep myself out of trouble."

It was then that she confessed the real reason she'd wanted to leave Westchester.

"I was worried about my marriage," she told Noreen, who at that point would never have dreamed that she should have been worried about her own.

"Why? Did something happen? Did Jake have an affair?"

"It wasn't Jake."

"*You* had an affair?"

"Almost, but I stopped it."

Here we go again, she thought. Just when she thought Rowan had her act together and was going to be okay.

"With whom?" she asked her sister.

"Wow, even when you're completely scandalized, you use perfect grammar," Rowan commented, shaking her head. "Do you remember my neighbor Rick? You met him and his wife, Vanessa, that time you and Kevin came over for Mick's first birthday."

Noreen couldn't have picked Rick out of a crowd, but she remembered the party. It was a sprawling backyard affair complete with a rented bouncy house and a cotton candy machine. Hordes of bouncing, sticky, screaming kids on a sugar high.

She remembered Rick's wife, too. She was attractive, with dark hair and porcelain skin, but a little uptight. She seemed uncomfortable with the other women at the party, most of whom were in full-blown stay-at-home-mom mode. Noreen found herself relating to her, but it was Kevin who spent a lot of time on the deck talking to her while Noreen shielded their children's fragile skulls from the baseball bat her sister kept handing to frenzied toddlers to use on the piñata.

She opted not to pick a fight with Kevin about it on the way home. When it came to their marriage, she chose to let a lot of things go over the years.

And now you're second-guessing them all.

At least she isn't the only one whose marriage is less than perfect. Then again, her sister had gone to great lengths to save hers, moving upstate just to get away from temptation.

"That's a little drastic," Noreen commented at the time. "Couldn't you just have avoided him?"

"No. I didn't trust myself to do that. Sometimes I can be . . . you know."

Yeah. She knew. Self-control had never been Rowan's forte.

Not about to relinquish her long-held role as her sister's moral compass, Noreen felt obligated to scold the weakness and near indiscretion. They never discussed it again.

"Did you tell anyone about it?" Rowan asks her now.

Noreen stops straightening the magazines. "You made me swear I wouldn't, remember?"

"I do remember. That's why I'm asking. Did you tell anyone?"

She hesitates, not wanting to admit the truth.

Back then, she told Kevin everything.

She wished she hadn't told him about that, though. He asked more questions than she cared to—or even could—answer, including some that made her squirm. She even wondered whether deep down, her husband had a crush on her sister. Maybe he was drawn to the proverbial bad girl now that he'd dutifully married the good one.

At the time, Noreen couldn't relate to wanting to walk on the wild side, though she can now. Not that she'd ever admit it to her sister, much less to her soon-to-be-ex-husband. Let Kevin take the blame for their failed marriage. She's perfectly content to play the role of the wronged and heartbroken wife. No one ever has to know that isn't quite the case.

Yes. You take your comfort where you can. Some nights, you find it in cozy socks and good wine; other nights, though not lately, between the sheets in an unfamiliar bed, in someone's muscular arms.

Kevin would be stunned if he knew he wasn't the only one who'd ever strayed. But he'll never know or even suspect. If he goes through with the divorce, she'll make good and sure that he's the only villain.

Noreen may not have gotten much better at honoring certain vows over the past decade or so, but she's definitely mastered the art of keeping a secret.

Her own, anyway.

Rush hour on the subway is always crowded, and today is no exception.

It might have been tolerable if Rick could have boarded the downtown express at his midtown stop and stepped off in Union Square five minutes later, but something has gone seriously awry. For the past half hour, he's been stuck underground on a stalled train, standing shoulder to shoulder, chest to back, back to chest—or perhaps breast; it's hard to tell—with a throng of strangers who are silently, and sullenly, resigned to their fate. The lone exception: a deceptively normal-looking businessman with frenetic eyes who's loudly informed everyone, repeatedly, that there's no cell phone service in this spot.

That means Rick has no way of letting Bob know he'll be late for their dinner. Hopefully, Bob'll figure it out. Or maybe he'll assume Rick isn't going to show up at all.

Maybe I shouldn't, even if I ever get off this train.

Then again, he and Bob don't have to rehash Vanessa, or—God forbid—Rowan, or the kids, or anything else remotely personal or unpleasant. They can just talk about sports or old times or Bob's travels. Something safe.

The speaker clicks on to broadcast a garbled announcement from the conductor: something about police activity on the track ahead.

"What did they say?" someone asks from somewhere behind him.

"MTA code for someone jumping in front of the train" is the reply. "This happened the other day, too, and that's exactly what they said. Police activity."

"Yeah, well, it's the holiday season. Suicide rates are up."

"It's the most . . . wonderful time . . . of the year," a new voice sings.

"What, just because some idiot loser is miserable, we all gotta suffer now?" yet another passenger chimes in. "You gonna kill yourself, you gotta be considerate of others. You know what I'm sayin'?"

"Hell, yeah. Do it at home. Gun to the head, noose to the neck . . . No fuss, no muss. Well, maybe a little muss."

The jokes roll on, because this is a city of extremes. When hordes of New Yorkers find themselves captive in a stressful situation, group interaction tends to go one of two ways: dark humor or explosive anger.

Rick is steeped in the latter by the time the train starts moving again—backward. Downtown express service has been disrupted for the foreseeable future. Dispatched at the previous station, he opts not to wait on the platform to catch the next downtown local with the crushing crowd.

As he makes his way up several flights of steps to the sidewalk, where another gloomy, wet December dusk has fallen, his pocket vibrates.

Ah, cellular coverage has resumed. Pulling out his phone, he sees that he missed three calls while he was stuck underground. Predictably, one is from Bob.

The others are far more important.

Rowan was late getting home after spending fifteen minutes in the car talking to her sister. Mick was already upstairs when she got there.

Now she's back behind the wheel with him in the passenger seat, wearing his busboy uniform and a jacket she insisted he put on because it's chilly out. He grudgingly agreed.

"You begged me to buy you that coat," she reminds him as she drives toward Marrana's. "And it cost a fortune. Now you never want to wear it."

"That's not true."

Rather than argue, she changes the subject. "Did you eat?"

"Yeah, I had cereal. I couldn't find anything else."

"I'm sorry. I meant to get groceries over the weekend, but . . . you know. There was a lot going on."

"I know," he agrees, although of course he can't possibly know what's been going on: that his mother is neglecting to feed her family because she's been caught up in this . . . this ugly . . . *thing*.

"I'll stop at the store right now, and when you come home later, I'll make you anything you—"

"Mom, it's okay. I ate."

"Cereal isn't dinner."

"I'll get something at the restaurant later. It's fine. Really."

No. Clearly, it isn't fine. Mick has resumed staring out the window on his side of the car. Something is bothering him. She wants to ask what it is, but is afraid to.

What if he's figured out what she's been up to?

Oh, come on. Since when do kids his age waste two seconds brooding about anything that doesn't directly impact themselves?

Having raised two and a half teenagers, she's fairly certain that whatever is on Mick's mind has nothing to do with her. More likely it's something involving school, or basketball. Or a girl.

When she pulls up in front of Marrana's, he yanks down the visor and looks into the mirror. From the corner of her eye, she can see him finger combing his hair.

Definitely a girl.

He snaps the visor back up and pulls off the jacket, tossing it into the backseat before reaching for the door.

"Wait, Mick—it's cold outside."

"So? I'm not going to be outside."

"So . . . what, you're going to tunnel underground to get over to the door?" she asks dryly, and is rewarded with a brief smile, a flash of the easygoing boy he used to be.

"I'll be fine, Mom. You have to stop worrying about everything." Again, he reaches for the door.

"Wait." She touches his arm, reluctant to let him go just yet. "Anything special you want me to pick up at the store for you?"

"Nah. See you later."

With that, he's gone.

Watching him disappear into the restaurant, she basks in a moment of maternal normalcy as precious as the marital normalcy she'd appreciated on date night at Marrana's with Jake. If only she could go back to the time when her kids' tribulations were all that kept her up at night.

Whenever one of them decided the world was coming to an end, she felt the same way. Fretting along with her kids about breakups and SAT scores was nothing compared to realizing that someone might want to destroy her happily-ever-after.

She looks at the dashboard clock. She has plenty of time to go to the supermarket. Jake has a late meeting and won't be home for at least another hour, maybe two. She can make a nice dinner for a change. Not that she's hungry, despite the fact that she hasn't eaten since breakfast, and that consisted of a few bites of an apple.

Ah, stress: the most effective appetite killer there is. At this rate, her New Year's resolution will be to gain enough weight to fit back into her jeans.

She pulls away from the curb, winding back through the streets and around the traffic circle toward the Mundy's Strip Mall on Colonial Highway. It was built shortly after she and Jake moved back to town, on the site of the old Caldor discount department store where her mother used to buy all their back-to-school clothes. The boys and Rowan never minded much, but even as a little girl, Noreen longed for the designer brands they couldn't afford.

Noreen.

"I think you're blowing this whole thing out of proportion," she said when Rowan told her about the burnt cookies. "It had to be Rick who sent them. Of course he'd deny it."

"But why would he do it?"

"Who knows? Because the sky is blue? Because his wife died and he's lonely?"

"Ex-wife. And she died on the same day that—"

"I know, but the odds of that happening aren't really all that astronomical. Maybe he took it as some kind of sign that you and he were meant to be together."

"I doubt that. And I wish I knew how she died."

"Does it matter? The fact that she died was added stress for him. People get crazy enough when they go through a divorce. Believe me—I've seen it all."

"So you think it was Rick."

"Of course it was Rick. Who else could it have been?"

Well, it wasn't Vanessa, and it wasn't Noreen. And it wasn't Kevin, even though he knows what happened.

She shouldn't have been surprised when her sister admitted she'd shared the secret with her husband immediately after Rowan told her. After all, she herself has shared plenty of secrets with Jake.

Other people's secrets, anyway.

Her trustworthy, honorable brother-in-law is no more likely to taunt her or sneak around sending anonymous packages than her sister is. If Kevin is the only person Noreen told—and she swears that he was, and that no one could possibly have overheard the conversation—then Rick himself is guilty, or he lied about having kept what happened to himself.

"Can you just make sure Kevin never mentioned it to anyone else?" she asked Noreen before they hung up.

Noreen promised that she would, though she reminded Rowan that Kevin works long hours and she sometimes goes for days without seeing him.

Rowan refrained from warning Noreen that that's how she got herself into trouble back when she and Jake were living in Westchester. Her sister isn't a young stay-at-home mom pining away for her husband or fantasizing about the stay-at-home dad next door. Even twenty years ago, she would never have fallen into that trap.

Doing the right thing has always come so naturally to Noreen.

It must be nice, she thinks, sliding into the left-hand turning lane at the intersection in front of the large shopping complex.

"You need to tell Jake," Noreen advised. "Then your problem will be solved. This Rick guy will have nothing over you."

"You're kidding, right? If I tell Jake . . ."

"What? He'll leave?"

She hesitated. "I don't know."

"Jake isn't going to walk out on you because you kissed the neighbor fourteen years ago."

Noreen is probably right, she concluded. About that, and everything else.

Rick must have sent the package of cookies. Without

a spurned wife in the picture, he's the only person who would possibly have the motive to go to such lengths.

As she inches the minivan forward, her sister's words continue to ring in her head.

"You're lucky, Ro. Rejected men are capable of pulling a lot worse than this."

"But how is he rejected? I mean, maybe he was years ago, but . . . it just doesn't add up."

"He's nostalgic. It comes with age. He probably thinks of you as the one who got away."

"So he sent me a box of burnt cookies, because God knows that's the surefire way to a woman's heart."

"Maybe it seemed like a grand romantic gesture when he thought of it."

"When I told him about it, he seemed as shocked as I was."

"Of course he did. Because he'd probably come to his senses in the meantime and realized he'd look like an idiot admitting it. So he lied. He's a good liar. A lot of men are."

Not just men.

Some women are expert liars, too.

If someone asked Jake whether it was within the realm of possibility that his wife had spent part of Saturday having lunch with another man instead of at the outlet mall, what would he say?

He'd say that was impossible.

Because I went out of my way to make sure he wouldn't doubt me. I bought all those presents so that I could come home loaded down with bags.

But I did it because I love him. Because I'd rather die than hurt him.

At last, Rowan makes her left turn into the parking lot, snaking her way along behind a string of cars as if she's on autopilot, trying to convince herself that Noreen's theory makes perfect sense.

"Look, this guy started to stalk you and then he changed his mind and he lied about it," her sister told her. "Stuff like this happens all the time. It's tame in the grand scheme of things, believe me."

Rowan believes her. Noreen should know.

So should I.

Of course Rick sent the cookies. Of course he regrets it now. And of course he wouldn't pick up the phone this afternoon when Rowan called to confront him about it.

Well, good. That means the tables have turned.

All she said when she left her message in Rick's voice mail was "Call me. I need to talk to you."

Too bad she hadn't called her sister first. If she had, she probably wouldn't have bothered calling Rick at all.

Oh well. If he was embarrassed enough to avoid her call, he's sure as hell not going to return it.

As she pulls into a parking space near Price Chopper, she can almost see her way out of this mess. With any luck, it'll just fade away.

For the first time in a week, she's going to focus on what matters most: taking care of her family.

According to the forensics team, Sullivan Leary's latest Jane Doe wasn't your run-of-the-mill stabbing victim.

She was slashed to death. Her wounds were long and deep, had clean edges and neatly severed vascular structures, and lacked tissue bridges. They were consistent with a straight-edged razor, the kind you might find in a barbershop or your grandfather's medicine cabinet.

Not only that, but judging by the streaks of the victim's own blood found on her scalp—which was free of slash wounds—the killer appeared to have used the same razor to shave her head post-mortem.

The same was true of Heather Pazanno, who had lived just outside Erie, Pennsylvania. She went out one night last March to pick up a prescription for her sick mother and never came home. Her car was left in the parking lot. The store security cameras had captured a hooded figure on crutches trailing her out of the store, but the footage was grainy and the outdoor range didn't extend far enough beyond the front entrance to see what had happened next.

Having spent the last few hours painstakingly combing the online databases, Sully and Stockton have discovered two more slashing murders that bear similar details. One was in Rhode Island over the summer; another in Virginia back in January. Like Heather Pazanno and the West Side Jane Doe, both of the other victims were relatively young and attractive, and shared a striking physical characteristic: long red hair.

The local authorities in all three cases not only confirmed that the bodies were found wrapped in dry cleaner's plastic and that the hair had been painstakingly shaved off post-mortem, but that the murder weapon was most likely a straight razor and used to do the shaving. Those facts had been concealed from published reports in all instances, just as they have been here in New York.

It would have been difficult, if not impossible, for local police investigators to spot a pattern that would link homicides unfolding so many miles and months apart. Viewed individually, the cases would appear to be random, even when checked against a state's unsolved homicide database.

The federal databases are considerably more effective than they used to be, but they're far from ideal. Crimes continue to slip through the cracks.

Sully and Stockton alerted the FBI that they might have evidence of a highly organized serial killer crossing state lines. If this were a television show, a string of black government SUVs would immediately be dispatched to hunt down the killer. In reality, the bureau is as overburdened and understaffed as the NYPD, and it will take some time and red tape before they'll be able to assist in the case.

At least they're making progress on their own, although it's painstaking. None of the missing persons reports filed over the past couple of days fit their Jane Doe's description. The distinctive ladybug tattoo might help to identify her, but for now, they're holding that detail back from the public as well.

"You know what I could go for?" Stockton asks, leaning back and stretching.

"Coffee? Sleep? San Shan soup and shredded beef with spicy Asian green chili leeks and white rice?"

He groans. "Szechuan Emperor *again*?"

They've had takeout from her latest favorite Chinese place at least two days out of the past four.

"It's a serious craving, Barnes. I can't stop thinking about that beef."

"Maybe you're pregnant."

She snorts. "With my track record lately? Yeah, sure. It would be an Immaculate Conception."

Naturally that comment sets Barnes on a snarky roll until the phone rings on Sully's desk, cutting off his comment about the Blessed Virgin Gingersnap.

It's the desk sergeant, informing her that he's putting through a tip line caller. "She's the real deal. Got a missing roommate who fits the bill."

"Go ahead," she says, and grabs a pen and paper as the call clicks in. "Hello, this is Detective Leary."

There's a long pause. Then a halting female voice says, "I, um, just saw on the news . . . there was a thing about a . . . um, death, and I'm worried . . . I haven't been able to get ahold of my friend in a few days and when she blew me off the other night I thought she was just being annoying but now I'm scared that . . ."

"Okay, what's your name?" Sully asks, pen poised.

"Dana Phelps."

"And what's hers?"

"It's Julia. Julia Sexton."

Bob Belinke hasn't been stood up since . . . since . . .

Wait, has he *ever* been stood up?

Not that he can recall. But there's a first time for everything.

"Would you like to order your entrée, sir?"

The waiter has materialized yet again, the furrow between his brows deepening with every visit to this cozy table for two since Bob sat down over an hour ago. Clearly, he thinks Bob is waiting for a date—something he figured he and Rick could laugh about when Rick gets here.

But it looks like he'll be laughing alone—if at all.

"I'll hold off a little longer," Bob tells the waiter. "I'm sure my friend is coming."

"Shall I clear away the appetizer?"

"Why don't you leave it for now? My friend might have some."

Friend . . .

Remembering that Rick had used the same term yesterday to refer to his previous diner companion, Bob wonders again why he was so cagey.

As the waiter walks away, he checks his cell phone.

It's been nearly two hours since Rick texted to say he was leaving the office. He didn't pick up when Bob called to say he was going to be seated to keep the reservation, and he still hasn't called or texted back, which isn't like him.

At least, it *wasn't* like him.

How well do I know him now?

How well did I know him, ever?

Those are the questions that have been running through
Bob's mind for the past hour, as he sipped a beer and
nibbled the appetizer he'd felt compelled to order. The
restaurant is crowded tonight with several office Christmas parties occupying the private rooms and large tables,
along with crowds of shoppers who made their way across
the street from the Union Square Holiday Market.

He can't sit here much longer without either ordering
dinner or asking for the check.

He types another text to Rick—*Worried about you*, and
adds it to the stack of sent messages that include: *Where
are you?*; *I'm at the table*; *Can I order you a drink?*; and
Is everything okay?

No reply.

Ten minutes later, the waiter has pocketed a generous
tip, a pair of German honeymooners has happily settled at
the unexpectedly vacated table for two, and Bob is out on
the street. He pulls up the hood of his nylon jacket, wishing he had something warmer to ward off the chill and
knowing it would take more than a layer of down.

Rick's silence and failure to show up seem even more
ominous now that he's left the restaurant.

The sidewalk is teeming with people. It's still rush
hour, and this is one of the busiest neighborhoods in the
city. The NYPD presence is strong, with uniformed cops
directing traffic and pedestrians. Across the street, Union
Square Park is bedecked with garlands, flooded by warm
white twinkle lights, and lined by red-and-white-striped
canvas-covered market stalls.

If Rick had taken the subway to Union Square from his
midtown office as he'd claimed he was about to do earlier,
then he would have had to walk through or around the
market to get to the restaurant.

Maybe he got this far, was drawn over to . . . to pick up
a last-minute gift, and . . .

And lost track of time? For over an hour? And didn't notice his phone ringing or buzzing or vibrating?

It seems ludicrous to imagine that something happened to him along the way, though. Not here, anyway. This isn't a deserted outer borough street corner in the middle of the night. If there had been a violent crime or a serious accident in the vicinity, Bob would have heard sirens and there would be evidence even now: bystanders, commotion, flashing red lights.

Most likely, Rick never got this far. Maybe something came up at work.

He would have called or texted, though.

Okay. What else might have happened?

Maybe Rick lost his phone. He doesn't have a landline at his apartment. A lot of people don't these days—that's not unusual.

He still could have found a way to call—unless he kept Bob's number stored in his phone and not on paper or in his head . . .

That's possible.

Or maybe it was plain old cold feet?

That might have made sense yesterday, when they were about to see each other for the first time since Vanessa died. But not today. The ice was already broken. Rick seemed to want to talk.

Even if he'd changed his mind at the last minute for some reason, he'd have come up with a reasonable excuse. He was always good at telling white lies.

And I was always good at seeing right through them.

Rick may have teased him about playing detective, but Bob does have a keen sense of intuition. Right now, his instincts are telling him that something is wrong.

A gust of raw wind goes right through him, and he thinks longingly of his warm hotel bed thirty blocks north. He should probably head back there—but this time, he isn't going to walk. Having had no luck finding a cab on his way downtown, he can already sense that it's going to be a challenge to find one heading back up. He can take the subway, and keep an eye out for Rick as he makes his way toward it, just in case.

Shoving his chapped hands deep into the pockets of his light jacket, Bob crosses the street toward the maze of brightly lit stalls.

The rain has given way to a yellow haze drifting in the festive glow, fragrant with steamy cider and cocoa, rife with chatter and piped-in music and a chorus of sidewalk Santa bells.

Caught up in the slow-moving crowd of shoppers, Bob gradually makes his way toward the domed subway kiosk on the south side of the park.

"Todd!" a female voice shrieks a little too close to his ear. "There you are! Where have you been? I've been waiting an hour!"

"Sorry," calls a guy who's shouldering his way toward her. "Some guy jumped in front of my train and I've been stuck in the tunnel."

"No way, that's sick! Did you see it?"

Todd's reply is lost as the crowd propels him away, but a new realm of possibility has been introduced that Bob finds either comforting—or terrifying.

Maybe Rick, too, was delayed by the subway incident . . .

Or maybe he was the reason behind it, having chosen to take his own life just as Vanessa had taken hers last November.

From the *Mundy's Landing Tribune* Archives
Editorial
June 23, 1992

On Monday, researchers in Moscow announced
that they had used computer modeling to positively
identify the remains of Russian Czar Nicholas II and
his wife, Alexandra. Murdered by the Bolsheviks on
July 17, 1918, along with their five children, three
servants, and the family doctor, the Romanovs were
among nine skeletons unearthed last year in a shallow
grave in Yekaterinburg. Tests will continue on the remaining bodies, along with the search for the missing
two. That this development comes as a prelude to next
week's historical society fund-raiser is an interesting
coincidence.

Last year's inaugural gathering was such a re-
sounding success, drawing attendees and media
attention from across the globe, that the society determined that it will be an annual event whose purpose
is twofold. Primarily conceived to raise much-needed
funding for the non-profit, the event lured armchair
sleuths by extending an invitation to solve the so-
called Sleeping Beauty murders that took place here
in 1916. Never identified, the trio of young female victims is buried in Holy Angels Cemetery.

At last summer's event, sitting on a panel of sci-
entists and criminologists, chemistry professor Lina
Abu Bakr of Hadley College stated that it might very
well be possible now to identify those bodies using
modern scientific methods that were unavailable in
1916. The issue will be further examined at this year's
convention. Many locals are in favor of exhumation
in order to lay the mystery to rest at last. Yet perhaps
an equal number of us are opposed to disturbing the
remains, citing ethical or fiscal reasons.

Indeed, is it prudent, in this pivotal presidential election year, with an ever-tremulous economy and unemployment at levels not seen in nearly a decade, to devote significant resources to further investigate a crime whose victims have not only been deceased for three quarters of a century, but whose loved ones and yes, most likely the perpetrator himself, are likely also dead or infirm?

Chapter 11

Early Tuesday morning, Casey is back behind the wheel of the van, heading north and admiring the winter sunrise—the first actual glimpse of the sun in days—visible through the passenger's side window. Ordinarily on this journey, the speakers would be blasting "Sunday, Bloody Sunday." But today the radio is on, tuned to 1010 WINS, New York City's all-news station. Politics, sports scores, and even the traffic report hold little interest, but this morning, there are two reasons to listen.

The first is the weather forecast. When your livelihood depends—quite literally—on which way the wind is blowing, you pay close attention. The storm brewing out West is threatening to turn into a full-fledged blizzard. Naturally, the tri-state meteorologists are orgasmic at the idea that it might pick up steam and hit here by the weekend. Casey has been keeping tabs on the potential storm on television and online as well. But the day's most compelling news involves the latest updates on the West Side homicide victim. She has yet to be identified, but there are reports that she fits a missing persons report filed last night.

Looks like pretty soon, I won't be the only one who knows her name.

But that's okay, Casey decides, leaving the highway at

the familiar exit and heading west. Last night was an un-expectedly busy night. It may not have been a Sunday, but it was sufficiently bloody. Perhaps the experience wasn't quite as gratifying as Julia had been—or nearly as thrilling as Rowan will be—but it was satisfying in its own way.

Now Casey has a new secret, and the intoxicating af-terglow lingers like the faint streaks of red in the patch of eastern sky visible in the rearview mirror.

The ache lessened a bit after last night, though it has yet to subside completely.

How much longer can you hold out?

Not as long as you thought.

The storm might force a game change.

Up ahead, the bare branches, rooftops and steeples of Mundy's Landing are bathed in golden light.

The streets are stirring to life as Casey drives into the village proper. A couple of delivery trucks are parked along Market Street, unloading stacks of the *Mundy's Landing Tribune* at the deli and paper-wrapped loaves of fresh bread at the café. A few blocks away at the elemen-tary school, a green truck is just pulling into the parking lot, past the row of yellow buses that won't embark on their daily routes for at least another hour.

Casey drives on past the school, parks the van around the corner in the empty bank parking lot, and darts on foot through the woods that border the back of the school playground. From that spot, there's a clear view of the green truck parked alongside the back door of the school. The Wholesome & Hearty deliveryman is propping it open so he can roll in a hand truck bearing food service supplies.

Casey has witnessed this routine enough mornings to know that the delivery will demand four or five trips, and that each trip from the truck into the school and back again will take sixty to ninety seconds. That leaves a golden op-

portunity during the thirty-second safety window while
the deliveryman is busy stacking cartons in the cafeteria
kitchen.

Casey waits for the man to embark on the second delivery. The moment he disappears inside, Casey races
from the playground toward the door, counting down the
seconds.

Thirty . . . twenty-nine . . . twenty-eight . . .

The interior corridor is deserted and dark other than
the pool of light spilling from the lunchroom. Water is
running there, and the deliveryman's voice mingles with
that of a woman, probably a cafeteria worker. Beyond the
lunchroom, another hallway branches off into the main
part of the school.

Twenty . . . nineteen . . . eighteen . . .

Casey swiftly tries the handles of several doors that
line the service hallway. All are locked.

Dammit! . . . eleven . . . ten . . . Dammit!

Trapped in a dead end, Casey has two choices: either
head back outside, or scoot past the cafeteria doorway
and risk being seen.

Sometimes, you have to take the risk.

Seven . . . six . . . five . . .

Casey strides quickly down the hallway. Inside the
cafeteria, the water is still running but the voices have
ceased. Just as Casey reaches the doorway, the deliveryman steps through it and out into the hall, pushing the
hand truck.

They make eye contact.

Immediately slowing to a stroll, Casey forces a smile
and a casual "Morning."

"Morning." Bearded and burly, albeit much younger
than he looks from afar, the man nods and goes on his
way, apparently unaware that he's just encountered a tres-
passer.

Heart pounding, Casey follows the hallway to the end and turns, passing the gym, the auditorium, and the music room. All is shadowy and still. A window overlooking the back parking lot reveals Mr. Wholesome & Hearty rolling a fresh load of supplies toward the door as if nothing out of the ordinary happened.

Casey stays and watches until he returns again, this time to load the hand cart into the back of the truck and secure the doors. Then he climbs into the cab and drives away, obviously none the wiser.

Safe. For now, anyway.

Casey moves on to the stairwell and ascends to another deserted hallway lined with lockers and classroom doors. This is where Rowan's room is located, marked by the cardboard pencil cutout. Noting with interest that something is hanging from the doorknob, Casey walks closer and sees that it's a small gift bag imprinted with snowflakes. The matching gift tag is filled out in round, perfect penmanship.

To: Rowan

From: Your Secret Santa

A second golden opportunity.

Casey seizes it, opening the bag and finding a tube of almond-scented hand lotion—Rowan's favorite. She's been using it for years.

But I've got a much better gift for you.

Out of Casey's pocket and into the bag it goes.

A few minutes later, Casey is back in the van, weaving through the still quiet streets. Here a dog walker, there a jogger, and another, and another . . .

Driving past a female jogger on Prospect Street, Casey spots a long red braid dangling beneath the rim of her backward baseball cap. Belated recognition comes courtesy of the rearview mirror: the cute redheaded waitress from the restaurant where Mick works.

Brianna. Beautiful Brianna, with the long red hair and the fair, freckled skin. A perfect stand-in.

The hunger gains a stranglehold on Casey's soul.

If something were to happen to her now, Mick would be crushed with grief. And then to lose his mother on the heels of it . . .

Hmm. Casey circles back around the corner to drive by her again, this time slowing the van to a crawl.

Plugged into headphones, the girl is oblivious.

Casey clenches the steering wheel, running through possible scenarios.

A third golden opportunity in one morning shouldn't be taken for granted, and yet . . .

Mundy's Landing is supposed to be off limits until it's time. Time for Rowan.

It would be so easy, though, to pull up at the curb just ahead of the girl and then pull her into the van when she passes. So easy, and so perfect . . .

"Wow—I thought I smelled bacon but I figured I must be dreaming!"

Standing at the stove, Rowan turns to see Jake walking into the kitchen, black suit coat slung over one arm as he expertly knots his red necktie.

"Meatloaf for dinner last night and bacon for breakfast? Are you trying to kill me?"

She turns over a sizzling strip in the frying pan. "Eh, a little meat never killed anyone."

"Liar. But since you're dishing up hot breakfasts, I might throw in a couple of eggs to go with—wow," he says again, spotting the second skillet. "What's that?"

"An omelet." She gestures at the cutting board, still littered with the remnants of all the vegetables she'd chopped. "Scallions, red and green peppers, mushrooms, and cheddar."

"What's the occasion?"

"No occasion. I just thought you and Mick deserved a real breakfast for a change."

"Mick left."

"He left? What do you mean?"

"While you were in the shower. He said he had to be at school early today. I told him I'd drive him but he had a ride."

"From who . . . *m*?" she amends. Noreen would say *whom*.

"One of his friends, I guess."

"Which friend?" The good mood that settled over her last night, courtesy of her perfect sister's perfectly reasonable explanation for the cookie drama, is rapidly evaporating. "You didn't ask?"

"You know me when it comes to questions." Jake shrugs. "I never ask enough, do I?"

No, and he and the kids are always saying that she asks too many. Which, she suspects, is precisely why Mick waited until she was in the shower to head to school.

She lifts the bacon from the pan and presses it between layers of paper towels to blot the grease.

"Did Mick eat before he left?"

"I don't know."

"His medicine upsets his stomach if he doesn't eat."

"I'm sure he did, then."

"I doubt it. Did he say why he had to go early?"

"I think he had to take a test."

"For which class? Never mind. I know you didn't ask. I just hope it wasn't math, because if it was, it was probably a makeup test for something he missed or failed and I guarantee he didn't study last night."

She'd kept a plate of gravy-smothered meatloaf and mashed potatoes warm for Mick, but when he got home after work, he said he was too tired to eat and was going

straight to bed. When she looked in on him twenty minutes later, she found him tucked in and sound asleep.

Remembering that incident, and how preoccupied he'd
been yesterday when she dropped him off, she asks Jake,
"Have you noticed that something seems to be bothering
Mick?"

Expecting a no, she gets a yes.

"He was definitely quieter than usual over the weekend," Jake reports. "Maybe he's in love."

"That's what I thought. I bet he's meeting her before
school. Did he seem . . . you know, giddy?"

"He's not Katie. He's Mick. He seemed grumpy and
gloomy. Definitely not giddy."

"Maybe it isn't a girl, then."

"Or it is, and he knows she's not interested." Jake pours
a cup of coffee and adds a warm-up splash to the one she
was sipping.

"That doesn't explain why he left early, unless it really
was to take a test."

"It might be. Some people do tell the truth, you know."

Jolted by the words, even if he was just kidding, she
busies herself dishing up omelets, bacon, and toast.

Sitting at the granite counter, mindlessly eating the
hearty breakfast she intended for Mick, she makes conversation with her husband, worries about her son, and
wonders about Rick.

He never did return her phone call last night. If he had,
she was prepared to let it go directly into voice mail. It
was a relief to put aside a week's worth of toxic stress and
get a good night's sleep for the first time since the box of
burnt cookies arrived.

I don't want to go back to that, she thinks as Jake puts
their breakfast things into the sink and she steps over
Doofus to look around for her car keys.

Not on the counter, not in her bag, not in the door . . .

"Here they are." He puts them into her hand.

"Where did you find them?"

"Same place they've been every time you've lost them for the past twenty years. In the pocket of the coat you had on last night. You're welcome, and I know, you have no idea what you'd do without me, and you love me. I love you, too. Go, you're late. I'll walk Doofus. See you tonight."

He kisses her on the cheek, and she's out the door with a grateful grin, calling back, "Oh, and I'm making chicken Marsala for dinner."

"You're on a roll, babe. I'll be here."

Making the short drive through the village to the elementary school, Rowan drinks in the winter sun splashing through a canopy of bare branches against an ice blue sky and revisits her gratitude for the return of precious normalcy—marital, maternal, domestic.

Last night Jake opted for a nice cozy dinner in the kitchen with her over *Monday Night Football*. They made holiday plans, agreeing to stay home and invite Jake's aunt, uncle, and cousins who still live in the area, to come for Christmas dinner. The only vaguely unpleasant moment—for her, anyway—was when Jake suggested that they include Noreen and her family.

"I doubt they'll come, but I'll ask," she said, though she has no intention of doing that. Her sister's insight might have saved the day yesterday, but Rowan isn't eager to face her lone confidante in the near future.

Anyway, it's a moot point: Noreen would never spend Christmas in Mundy's Landing.

Rowan recalls the day she called her sister to tell her that she and Jake were moving back here.

"I have big news," she said.

Noreen laughed. "Are you serious? We're doing it *again*?"

"We're doing what again?"

"Being pregnant together!"

The sisters had been simultaneously pregnant with Braden and Sean and then again with Mick and Shannon. So when Rowan called with "big news," Noreen, who had just confirmed her fourth pregnancy the day before, was certain she was also having "an oops baby."

"You're pregnant? Congratulations!" Rowan said.

"You're not?"

"Are you kidding? No way. Three kids is enough for us. My news is that we're moving back to Mundy's Landing."

Silence, and then: "Why would you want to go back up there?"

"Because it's more affordable than Westchester, for one thing."

"A lot of places are more affordable. You don't have to—"

"It's not a terrorist target, either." The September 11 attacks were recent enough for most people to consider that a valid argument. But not Noreen.

"Come on, Rowan, you know the chances of—"

"Jake flies constantly on business. He won't have to do that if he gets one of the sales jobs he's interviewed for up there."

Noreen said nothing.

"For me, Mundy's Landing still feels like home," Rowan said simply. "Don't try to talk me out of it, okay?"

"I just feel that you, of all people, should move on and never look back."

"Why me 'of all people'?"

"Because you had a lot of problems when you were in Mundy's Landing."

"I was a kid. Every kid has problems."

"Not like that. I didn't. My kids won't."

"You can't know that."

"I can be pretty sure of it. And at least they're not living in a tiny, run-down village in the middle of nowhere." Talking over Rowan's immediate protest, she added, "I'm sorry. But you must know that I have your best interests in mind."

"Really? Because I—"

"Come on, you have to admit that there are better places to choose to live."

"I can't think of any."

"Whatever. Go ahead, move back there if you want to."

"We do want to, and we will, and gee, thanks for giving us permission."

They were snippy little girls again: one bossy, the other defiant.

It wasn't until a year later that Rowan confessed—in a misguided attempt to clear the air—the real reason she'd pushed for the move.

She regretted telling her sister the moment it was out there and she saw the condemnation in her sister's eyes. She should have known better, but . . .

People can change. I changed. She didn't.

At school, she stops in the main office to pick up her mail and spends a few minutes chatting with the secretary, who found a large pink poinsettia on her desk this morning, courtesy of her Secret Santa.

"Your Santa must be the custodian or a cafeteria worker if he managed to get into the building before you," Rowan says, flipping through her mail.

"No, there was a choral concert here last night, remember? The music and band teachers were here. One of them must have left it before they went home."

Those words echo in Rowan's head when she arrives at her own classroom to find another gift bag hanging on the doorknob.

This time, she doesn't hesitate to look inside.

Today's Secret Santa gift is jewelry: a strikingly unusual brooch, shaped like a snowflake and intricately woven in delicate strands of red silken thread.

What a difference a day makes, Bob Belinke thinks, once again at JFK airport.

Unlike yesterday morning at this time, the sun is shining beyond the windows of the plane, and air traffic is moving briskly.

As briskly as it can at one of the world's busiest airports, anyway. The boarding process for his flight to Tampa was delayed by only ten minutes. They pushed back nearly forty-five minutes ago and haven't taken off yet, but the plane is creeping along the runway lineup and should be airborne soon. A couple of hours from now, he'll have traded cold sunshine for warm.

In his window seat, he holds his cell phone. Ordinarily, he turns it off and stows it when he boards a JetBlue flight, happy to let the seatback television entertain him for the duration. But today, having texted Rick when he was waiting at the gate, he's keeping an eye out for a reply.

At least he knows it wasn't Rick who jumped in front of a subway train last night. Not long after the horrific possibility entered Bob's mind, he was relieved when Rick texted an apology for missing their dinner and attributed it to "subway problems."

Bob was still in Union Square Park when it came through, and texted back that it wasn't too late—he could meet him anyway.

That's okay, Rick wrote. *It's been a long day. Headed home. See you next trip.*

That should have been the end of it, but the situation just isn't sitting right with Bob. He slept restlessly and woke to find that his old friend was still on his mind.

Their last verbal conversation and Rick's avoidance of another has left him concerned. No, not concerned enough to put off his flight home—but when he gets there, he's going to invite Rick to come to Florida over the holidays. God knows a change of scenery would be good for him.

If Rick had just responded to that last text, Bob would feel a hell of a lot better about leaving New York.

Maybe I should call instead.

About to dial, he's interrupted by the captain's announcement. "Ladies and gentlemen, we've been cleared for takeoff."

Too late for phone calls.

Bob turns off the phone, puts it into his pocket, and leans back in his seat, staring out the window as New York City falls away below.

Operation Secret Santa isn't going very well.

Last night at the restaurant, Mick had anticipated that he'd be able to tell whether Brianna had received the gift he'd left at her house. He didn't expect her to come in wearing the single Trinkettes bead on a chain around her neck or anything, but he thought she might at least give off some kind of . . . vibe. Like maybe she'd be wearing a mysterious smile and daydreaming, something like that.

Instead, she was her regular old self, polite and attentive to the customers, polite but inattentive to Mick.

Zach wasn't his regular old self at all. He cold-shouldered Mick, who instantly regretted the way he'd treated him. He'd tried to apologize, blaming his moodiness on being tired, and Zach said it was okay, but he didn't act like it was.

Meanwhile, Mick really was tired, having lost sleep over Brianna. Just before he drifted off last night he came up with a new twist on Operation Secret Santa. It's complicated, but more efficient than following her around all day, and definitely preferable to cutting out of basketball practice to lurk around her house.

So this morning, he waited until his mother was in the shower to tell his father he had to be at school early. Unlike Mom, Dad doesn't ask questions or check to make sure he really does have a ride.

Nor does he remind Mick to take his morning medicine—which he remembered to do—and to eat breakfast with it. Which he did not.

Mick feels increasingly queasy as he walks down last stretch of Battlefield Road to school, but at least the sun is shining today. He arrives even before the morning driver's ed kids, when the school is nearly deserted. The boiler system hasn't yet kicked into overdrive in the main building, a three-story brick structure that everyone refers to as the sweatbox.

He scours the entire school for locales where he can plant clues for his Secret Santa treasure hunt—not just the main building, which houses the administrative offices, the auditorium, and gym, but also the classrooms and science and computer labs in the one-story, flat-roofed modern wings that were built in the sixties when the village was still booming.

Then, sitting at a table in the library alongside a bunch of kids he barely knows—the types who get to school early to study—he writes the notes in block letters.

The first one, which he pushes through the vents on Brianna's locker door, reads *Look behind the Toys for Tots flyer on the lobby bulletin board*.

Behind the Toys for Tots flyer, he hides a second note instructing her to go to Mrs. Miller's room and open *The Great Gatsby* to a certain page.

Mrs. Miller is the English teacher Brianna has for second period English. Mick never bothered to read *Gatsby* when it was assigned last year, but he quickly flips through Mrs. Miller's copy this morning and finds a romantic scene about a kiss. He imagines kissing Brianna the way the guy in the book kisses some girl named Daisy: "At his lips' touch she blossomed like a flower and the incarnation was complete."

And so it goes, until he's perfectly set the stage for Brianna's discovery of his day two gift, another bead charm for the Trinkettes bracelet she's going to get on Friday. He conceals it in the most secure spot he can find in the school on such short notice: behind the snack-sized bags of prunes in the cafeteria. He does so quickly, his empty upset stomach assaulted by the smell of something saucy simmering in the adjacent kitchen, and grabs a banana on the way out.

Steals a banana, actually. But there's no one manning the register at this hour and he's going to barf if he doesn't eat something, and it's not going to be prunes. Part of the new Wholesome & Hearty school lunch plan, they aren't exactly a big hit with the student body. Nor are they the least bit romantic. But at least there's zero chance that anyone is going to buy a bag with lunch today and stumble across the little gift box.

It seems like a great plan, and he could probably pull it off, but there's one major hitch.

Brianna is absent from school today.

The young woman who turned up dead—and bald—on Sunday morning was a twenty-eight-year-old aspiring songwriter named Julia Sexton.

Sully had been sure of that even before her distraught parents, fresh off a plane from Saint Louis, identified her an hour ago at the morgue. According to her former roommate, who reported her missing last night, she'd had long red hair and a ladybug tattoo just beneath her right collarbone.

Overnight, Sully and Stockton questioned the roommate, a couple of other friends, and an ex-boyfriend. According to them, Julia didn't have an enemy in the world,
with the possible exception of her landlord, who wasn't
thrilled about her unpaid December rent. But he lives in
California and has a pretty airtight alibi.

"I was at the Lakers game Saturday night," he told
them. "If you don't believe me, look at the game tape.
You can see me right behind Leonardo DiCaprio in the
courtside seats."

They looked. They saw. They were privately impressed.

"I'd sell my soul to sit courtside at a Knicks game,"
Barnes told Sully. "Think he has any connections at the
Garden?"

"Oh, I'm sure he's plenty connected," she said, and she
was right. It didn't take much detective work to link the
landlord to organized crime, but they'd quickly dismissed
any suspicion that Julia's death had anything to do with
that.

They're focusing their attention on identifying other
possible suspects, starting with her inner circle. Her ex-
boyfriend and her friends all seemed genuinely distraught
and none had any motive that Sully and Stockton could
uncover.

"Who would hurt my baby?" her mother sobbed this
morning.

Sully shook her head sorrowfully, not yet willing to
disclose that her daughter may have fallen victim to a
predator who might very well have been a total stranger.

"We're going to find out who did this," she promised
the Sextons after guiding them through the morgue nightmare. "We'll do everything we can to bring this person to
justice. I promise."

She knew it was little comfort to grieving parents about
to bury their only child, but it was all she had to offer.

Driving home after work on Tuesday afternoon, Rowan is focused on the prospect of tomorrow's field trip.

All the permission slips are in, thank goodness, and her students aren't the only ones looking forward to getting away from the daily classroom routine. Weary of teaching antsy kids about decimals and photosynthesis, she's hoping a break will help them get back down to business on Thursday in preparation for Friday's math and science unit tests.

On an even brighter note, visiting the historical society at this time of year always gets Rowan into the Christmas spirit. This year, she's been especially lacking in that department.

The director and curator, Ora Abrams, plays classical holiday music on a Victrola during her guided tours through rooms decked out to depict Christmas in bygone eras. And she serves cutout cookies and hot chocolate afterward.

Rowan remembers speculating as a child that it must be made from some secret recipe that's been handed down for generations, because it tasted so much better than ordinary cocoa. Naturally, Noreen burst her bubble, reporting that it came from a mix. It wasn't until years later that Rowan realized she was right. But when you're a child, anything—even powdered cocoa—tastes extra-special on a weekday morning when you're supposed to be in school.

As she pulls up in front of the mailbox, she remembers belatedly that she meant to stop in town and pick up a few boxes of Christmas cards . . .

Oh, and that she forgot to sneak tomorrow's Secret Santa gift into the library aide's mail slot in the office before she left school today. She won't have much time in the morning before wrangling the kids and chaperones onto the buses to the historical society.

She glances down at her own Secret Santa gift from this morning. She pinned the red snowflake to her gray winter coat, and two teachers stopped her to compliment her on it before she left the building.

One of them was Louise Flax, the music teacher, one of three people whom she suspected might have been the giver. "That's so unique! Where did you get it?"

"My Secret Santa."

"Well, your Santa has great taste," Louise said, either cleverly covering her own tracks or ruling herself out.

As she opens the mailbox, Rowan makes a mental note to leave extra-early tomorrow morning in order to deliver Marlena's gift before the field trip.

The thought is curtailed the moment she spots a package inside the box, sitting on top of the stack of letters.

Just like last week.

Again, she tells herself that it must be something she ordered and forgot about.

Except you haven't ordered anything lately. And you lied to Jake about Cyber Monday shopping, remember?

You lied to Jake about a lot of things.

Her hand trembles as she pulls out the package and sees the plain white label addressed to her. No return address. Manhattan postmark.

". . . still watching that blizzard as it makes its way over the central plains," the television meteorologist is saying in the background over the sound of running tap water as Casey stands at the kitchen sink.

According to the weather reports, the storm is gathering speed and strength. Interesting how that happens. You'd think it might be the opposite: that the storm would wear itself out, expending so much fury.

Then again . . .

It's the same with me.

If anything, the storm raging inside Casey is gaining momentum with every passing second. Even now, even after . . .

With a sigh, Casey washes the last traces of blood down the drain and reaches for the bleach.

From the *Mundy's Landing Tribune* Archives
Commerce
November 20, 2004

Shop Locally This Christmas

The Mundy's Landing Merchants' Association
has announced that most stores and restaurants in the
newly revitalized business district will offer extended
holiday shopping hours beginning on Friday, November 26, and continuing through Christmas.

Up and down the Common, special events are
planned throughout the season to draw shoppers to the
area from throughout Dutchess County and beyond.
Santa Claus will hand out candy canes and hot cider
and pose for photos with local children on the portico of the Dapplebrook Inn on Sunday, November
28. On Wednesday evening, December 1, Mayor
John Ransom will host the annual tree-lighting ceremony on the Common with music provided by the
Upbeats, Mundy's Landing High School's coed a cappella group. Over the weekend of December 11–12,
the Mundy's Landing Garden Club will sponsor tours
of several historic homes in the Heights that have
been beautifully decorated for the holidays. And for
the fourth consecutive year following its relocation to
the Conroy-Fitch mansion on Prospect Street, the historical society will offer a special exhibit throughout
December, with rooms decorated to represent holiday
celebrations in various eras during which the mansion
was a private residence.

Several new businesses have opened their doors
this fall, including Tru Blu, an upscale clothing boutique at 25 Fulton Avenue, Bell Tower Books at 16
Church Street, and Valley Roasters Bakery Café at
37 Market Street. Even long-standing institutions

have something fresh to offer: The Market on Market has added a line of organic artisanal chocolates, and Vernon's Apothecary is featuring framed, matted pen and ink prints of local landmarks.

"Area residents welcome the opportunity to shop closer to home, especially now that the Dutchess Mall is closed and Ames and Caldor are long gone," Merchants' Association president Stanley Vernon told the *Tribune*. "Why waste time and gasoline when everything you could ever need or want is right here at your fingertips?"

Chapter 12

Exhausted from a sleepless night and a stress-packed day at the office, Noreen is forced to take the long way home on Tuesday afternoon, detouring to pick up all three of her daughters at their schools and drop them all at various activities. If she didn't have to make the rounds to gather them all up again shortly, she'd crawl into bed right now and sleep till morning. Oh well. At least she can sit in peaceful solitude for half an hour, check her e-mail, maybe make a cup of tea . . .

But as she slows to turn onto the cul-de-sac, she spots Kevin's Lexus coming from the opposite direction. She has her right turn signal on; Kevin is flashing the left.

Faceoff. She has the right of way. Her first instinct is to complete her own turn and let him sit there and wait to make his left, which could take a while in rush hour traffic. Instead, she finds herself motioning him to go ahead. He waves his gratitude as he turns in front of her.

Apparently, her act of civility has resulted in a truce. As they step out of their respective cars in the garage, he actually stops to wait for her.

"How was your day?" He almost sounds like his old self.

He doesn't look like his old self, though. He's wearing his hair a little longer these days, brushing the collar of his recently purchased Italian leather coat. Plus he's lost the ten pounds that crept on over the past decade, and then some.

"My day was fine. How was yours?"

"Fine. Where are the girls?"

"It's Tuesday." Which means nothing to him. "It's Shannon's volunteer day at the animal shelter, and Sabrina has tennis, and Samantha has dance."

"Until when?"

"Five-thirty."

"All three?"

"Yes. You can pick up Shannon and Sabrina. I'll get Sam and take her to a drive-through because she has CCD at six-fifteen."

Silence from Kevin as the electronic door lowers itself.

That he doesn't protest carpool duty is a good sign. That he doesn't agree . . . not so much.

They step into the house. Goliath trots into the kitchen, wagging his tail at his long-lost master, who gives him a cursory pat. Noreen opens the patio door to let the dog out into the fenced yard, wishing she could kick Kevin out after him. She really wasn't in the mood for him right now.

"As long as no one's home for a change, I think we should sit down and talk."

"No one is ever home," she points out as he trails her to the hall closet. "Including you."

"I've been at the hospital non-stop."

"Mmm hmm."

"What? I have."

"I didn't say you haven't. I said mmm hmm."

They take turns hanging their coats and return to the kitchen. "What do you want to talk about?" she asks, resigned.

"Logistics."

"Are you planning military maneuvers? Invading a small country?"

"You're quite the comedienne."

"And you're quite the wordsmith."

He opens the fridge, removes a bottle of coconut water, and closes it without asking her if she wants anything.

She opens it, pointedly takes another bottle of coconut water, and closes it.

They sit facing each other at the table. She waits for him to speak, since he started this. All of it.

He clears his throat. "We need to figure out when we're going to tell the kids."

"I thought we already decided to wait until Sean gets home."

"Right, but when?"

"Do you want to make an appointment? Is that it?" she asks. "Calendar too crowded? Maybe you can squeeze us in between tennis and your massage."

"I haven't had a massage in weeks."

"Sorry, my mistake." Seeing Goliath at the patio door, she gets up to let him back into the house.

"His paws are muddy," Kevin observes, even as she reaches for the towel she keeps in a basket beside the door to wipe the dog's paws.

After a pause, he goes back to the matter at hand: deciding when they should break the bad news to their kids.

"I just think the sooner, the better. That's all I'm saying."

That isn't all he's saying, unfortunately. He goes on talking, and it's clear that he can't wait to get this separation out in the open so that he can move on.

As if he hasn't already.

Noreen's phone buzzes with an incoming text. She pulls it out of her pocket. It's from her sister.

Ignoring it for now, she asks Kevin, "What are you suggesting? Do you want to meet Sean's plane on the runway when it touches down and shout the news through a bullhorn, or . . . ?"

"Why are you so sarcastic all the time?"

Why are you such a jackass?

Her phone buzzes again. She checks. Rowan, desperately needing to talk.

Why does everyone suddenly need to talk now, when all she wants is to be left alone?

"When do *you* think we should tell them?" Kevin is asking.

"After Christmas. Let's let them have that, at least."

"Don't you think that's a little extreme? Pretending everything is okay and then dropping a bombshell on them the morning after?"

"I think it's better than ruining Christmas."

"It's not like they're five years old and we're going to tell them that there's no Santa Claus."

"You know what? It is like that," she says evenly, as her phone buzzes with yet another text. "It's exactly like that."

Sully and Stockton stare intently at the whiteboard where they've been scrawling details of the related crimes.

"All within a day's drive of here," she observes.

"So he travels as part of his job." Stockton circles the word they've already underlined several times. "Which rules out the barber theory."

"Unless he's a traveling barber. Or maybe he's being careful not to hunt too close to home."

"Home being . . ."

"Who the hell knows."

Sully studies the diagram showing New York in the center, with arrows fanning out in three different directions to depict locations west, south, and east of Manhattan. Pennsylvania, Virginia, Rhode Island.

"I've never been to any of these places," she tells Barnes. "Have you?"

"You've never been to Pennsylvania?"

"Philly. Not Erie."

"Yeah, that's different."

"You've been there?"

"Philly, Hershey, Pittsburgh . . . Pennsylvania's a big state. It's not, you know, Rhode Island."

"Ever been there?"

"Nah. Was supposed to go to Newport last July for the regatta, but—"

"Wait, you sail?"

"Hell no. But I was seeing this woman who does."

"You never told me that."

"I never tell you a lot of things. Anyway, there was that freak hurricane, and—"

"What was her name?"

"It didn't have a name, so maybe it wasn't exactly a hurricane, but it almost—"

"Not the storm! I meant the woman you were seeing. But I guess it doesn't matter."

"Believe me, it doesn't. Anyway, this storm knocked out the power and they closed the bridges and . . . wait, why am I telling you this again?"

"I have no idea."

"Okay. I'll stop."

They both fall silent, staring at the whiteboard again as Sully pictures Stockton on a sailboat with a leggy, outdoorsy New Englander.

"So is he still nearby," Stockton wonders aloud after a moment, "or has he already moved on?"

She jerks her focus back to the case, asking, "And why these places? What do they have in common, besides proximity to New York?"

"That might be easier to tell if we could just figure

out the trigger." Stockton rubs a few days' worth of razor stubble on his chin. "What's setting him off?"

"Hell if I know, but we'd better figure it out pretty fast."

If she's learned anything over two decades as a police detective, it's that sooner or later, whatever incident triggers a perp's homicidal rage is going to happen again. When it does, some other innocent person will pay with her life.

Sully stares at the diagrams on the whiteboard until the words are swimming before her eyes. Stifling a yawn, she reaches for the mug on her desk, tilts it, and finds it empty. Again. "I feel like I've been shot with a tranquilizer dart. I need more tea."

"You need something stronger than tea."

"You're right. I need dark chocolate. And tea. And the ladies' room. I have to piss like a racehorse."

"Nice. Oh, and do remember to extend that pinky finger when you're drinking your tea, Lady Leary," he adds in his fake British accent.

She often responds in a brogue that rivals her grandmother's, but today she can't muster the energy. She stands, picks up her mug, and tells him she'll be right back.

"You always are, aren't you."

"You say that as if it's a bad thing."

"You know I love you."

"And I love you. Solve this thing while I'm gone, will you?"

"No probs."

She swings by her desk to grab the loose leaf tea and strainer she keeps in her drawer, then heads to the kitchenette.

There, she notices that the Bunn coffee brewer on the countertop is giving off a burnt smell. The carafe is grimy and the filter basket is caked in crud. As usual, someone has left behind maybe a quarter of an inch of black liquid and put it back on the burner without bothering to make a fresh pot, leaving that task to whoever comes along and is desperate enough to drink the last of the bitter brew.

In a few hours, the scenario will play itself out yet again, and again . . .

Forever and ever, amen, she thinks as she fills her mug with hot water.

And Stockton wonders why she sticks with tea.

Leaving her mug in the microwave to heat, she heads into the bathroom.

Her mind is on the case and all the weighty implications—and responsibilities—that come with it.

If a predator isn't stopped in its tracks, he—she, it, any predator—will be compelled to kill again. It will happen over and over . . .

Forever and ever, amen.

The ladies' room door opens as she stands at the sink washing her hands.

"Hey, Sully."

"Hey, Brick." The female detective who just joined her in the ladies' room is never called by her real name: Flora. She's far more suited to her nickname, which she earned growing up in the South Bronx before she joined the NYPD. She's over six feet tall, tattooed, and is rumored to have killed a man—or two—without benefit of her weapon. Nobody messes with Brick. If she likes you, you're golden. If she doesn't . . .

Luckily, she likes Sully, and it's mutual.

"I hear you and Barnes are calling in the Feds," she says from behind the door of a stall.

"Bad news travels fast. Yeah. Barnes came across a case in Erie, Pennsylvania, that matches the MO and then we found a couple of others."

"Erie. I was there once, visiting my cousin who lives there. The weather's shitty. It snowed like hell."

"Yeah, well, winter's a bitch. Especially on the Great Lakes . . ."

"It was June."

"Mother Nature—also a bitch."

"No kidding. I guess it wasn't as bad as what happened there last spring. Remember the ice storm?"

"Where, in Erie?"

"Yeah. All along the lake up there. My cousin lost power for almost two weeks."

Ice storm. Sully remembers. It was epic. All over the news. "When was that?"

"March. I remember because she was supposed to visit me for Saint Patrick's Day but her flight was canceled."

Sully narrows her eyes at herself in the mirror above the sink, simultaneously remembering something and forgetting all about her mug of hot water in the microwave.

"Gotta go," she tells Brick, and hurries back to find Stockton.

"I thought you were getting tea and—"

"When was the regatta?"

"What?"

"The regatta? Newport? You said—"

"July. Yeah, I know, too early for hurricane season, but that storm was—"

"July what?"

"I don't know . . . mid-July. Why?"

"The storm. I just want to check something." She sits at her computer and enters *Rhode Island storm July* into the search engine.

A moment later, she's got it. "Barnes, give me the date on that Virginia case. Where was it, near Richmond?"

"Yeah, just outside. Why?"

"I need to check something."

A minute later, she's learned that there was a major snowstorm in the Richmond area a few days before a young woman named Emily Hines went missing. Her body—slashed, head shaven—didn't turn up until the spring thaw.

"So maybe our perp isn't a crazed barber," Barnes says, as she adds the storms to the whiteboard. "Maybe he's . . . what, a weatherman? A storm chaser? Is that what you're thinking?"

"I don't know. There was nothing major going on when Julia Sexton was killed."

"It was raining."

"Raining. But not an epic storm like the others. So if we're looking at weather as a trigger . . ." She trails off thoughtfully, shaking her head.

"The thing is," Barnes notes after a moment, "these other three women went missing a few days *after* big storms had passed. Not before or during. Maybe it's just a coincidence."

"Maybe. But probably not. Maybe he lives here. Maybe he's escalating. He came across Julia, and she fit the bill, and he didn't want to wait until he left town again."

"That would make sense. But there are probably others. I think we should take a look at recent weather events and see if there are missing persons or homicide cases that happened around the same time."

"Dammit." Rowan disconnects the call without leaving yet another message for Rick.

She probably shouldn't be surprised that he hasn't picked up his cell phone, yet somehow she expected him to.

Aware that he'll probably delete her voice mail messages without even listening, she decides to send him a one-word text message. Maybe he won't reply, but at least he won't be able to miss it.

Coward.

It feels good typing it, and even better after she sends it zooming through cyberspace.

Her phone vibrates a moment later with an incoming text, but it isn't from him.

Not now, her sister Noreen has written in response to the frantic *Can you talk?* text Rowan sent her a few minutes ago.

Just leaving court. Will call you in 10, her sister adds.

Cell phone clutched in her hand, Rowan paces back across the kitchen to the open package on the counter.

It's a snow globe. That's what he sent her today.

Not the store-bought kind like the one her kids bought her, with the built-in music box that plays "Winter Wonderland."

This one, which came wrapped in layers of yellowed fourteen-year-old newspaper dated November thirtieth, is crudely homemade from a glass jar that sits upside down. A pair of tiny figurines are glued upright to the inside of the lid, submerged in water and glittery fake snow.

She immediately recognized them as Polly Pocket dolls.

Katie had a whole collection when she was little, and Rowan spent hours crawling around playing with her. Each doll was about the size of her pinky finger and came with a name and personality.

The two dolls in the snow globe are glued together in a ghoulishly sodden and stiff embrace, faces locked in a plastic kiss, surrounded by swirling snow when you shake the jar.

The female has long red hair; the male is blond.

Rowan doesn't remember the name of the red-haired girl doll, but there were only a few boy Polly Pockets, and Katie owned this one. Rowan clearly recalls that her daughter got him for Christmas one year from Noreen and Kevin, along with a bunch of other Polly Pockets. By

that time they'd been living in Mundy's Landing for a few
years and neither Katie nor Noreen grasped the name's
significance. But it didn't escape Rowan then and it certainly doesn't escape her now.

The doll's name is Rick.

Mick was as pleasantly surprised not to find his mother
waiting at the bus stop today as he was yesterday when he
beat her to the house—even on foot—after dropping the
gift at Brianna's house.

Mom had no idea that he hadn't taken the late bus
home after practice yesterday, but he fully expected her to
be there to meet him on this sunny afternoon, maybe with
Doofus on a leash and definitely with a million questions.

Maybe she's already figured out that he'd lied about
having to go to school early this morning to take a test.
But that's the least of his worries right now. So is the fact
that he seems to have misplaced his good down jacket.

He can't believe Brianna was out sick today, of all
days. He kept thinking she must have shown up, because
he heard her name among those on the daily list of students called down to the office between periods. But at
the end of the day, there was still no sign of her.

Throughout basketball practice, he kept thinking
about the gift box he'd stashed behind the bags of prunes.
As soon as the coach blew the whistle, he took the world's
fastest shower and then raced from the locker room to the
cafeteria. The doors were locked, and the room beyond
the windows was dark. He had no choice but to leave the
gift there until tomorrow and hope the rest of the treasure
hunt clues remain intact overnight.

The minivan is in the driveway at home, and he braces
himself for the inevitable barrage as he steps into the
mudroom. But instead of questions, he hears his mother
let out a high-pitched cry.

"Mom?"

"Mick! You scared me," she calls from the kitchen. "I didn't realize it was so late already."

By the time he's taken off his sneakers and the light-weight jacket she's sure to point out isn't nearly warm enough for this weather—"and where is your good down coat that cost me a fortune?"—she's disappeared. Doofus is there, sniffing his empty water bowl and food dish.

Mick hears Mom's swift footsteps retreating up the stairs, and her voice calling, "There's leftover meatloaf in the fridge. I'll be down in a few minutes."

"What's the matter, boy? Did she forget to feed you?" Mick asks the dog, who responds with a forlorn gaze.

Mick pours food and water into Doofus's bowls, then puts a plate into the microwave for himself. As it heats, he notices that the kitchen is even messier than usual. There are dishes in the sink and a cutting board covered in veg-etable scraps alongside a chef's knife and unopened mail on the counter. Nothing interesting. Mostly catalogs and a stack of Christmas cards from people he either doesn't know or doesn't care about.

He thinks about last week, when Mom got that crazy package of burnt cookies. Caught up in Brianna drama, he never did remember to ask her again about it.

She shows up in the kitchen as he's eating his ketchup-smothered meatloaf and browsing the ski jackets in the catalog, wondering if he should ask for a new one for Christmas in case the old one is permanently lost. He ex-pects her to have changed into comfortable clothes, but she's still wearing a skirt, sweater, boots . . . and her wool coat?

"Are you going someplace?" he asks her.

"What? No." She looks down and quickly strips off the coat. "I got distracted when I came in, same as always in this crazy house."

Mick digests that. Some days are definitely hectic around here. But as far as he can tell, this isn't one of them.

"How was school?" she asks, draping the coat over a breakfast bar stool.

"Good."

"Good." She goes to the fridge, takes out a bottle of water, and stands silently drinking it, staring off into space.

He keeps his head bent toward the catalog but watches her, wondering if she's okay. She looks pale.

"Mom? Are you . . ."

"Hmm?" Snapping out of it, she looks at him, and he decides not to ask if she's okay. He's not so sure he wants to hear the answer. Instead, he changes his query to the first inane question that comes to mind.

"Are you . . . going to drive me to work?"

"Of course. How much homework do you have tonight?"

"Not a lot."

"As soon as you're finished eating, go start it. Okay?"

"Okay." He can't believe she didn't ask about the test he said he had to take this morning. Maybe Dad didn't mention it to her, and maybe she didn't notice he'd left early.

That's hard to imagine, though. When it comes to Mick and his brother and sister, Mom is so good at interrogation techniques that Dad teases her she should be a detective.

Mick finishes the meatloaf quickly, loads the plate into the dishwasher, and retrieves his backpack from the mud room. When he heads upstairs to do his homework, his mother still stands sipping water, absently looking out the window above the sink.

A half hour later, when he comes back down, she's in

her study with the door closed. He knocks and then opens it a crack.

"Mom? I have to go to work."

"Okay, I'm coming."

He hears her say, "I have to go. I'll call you back later," and realizes she's on the phone.

"Who was that?" he asks as she follows him to the kitchen.

"Aunt Noreen."

"What did she want?"

"Nothing. You know, we were just . . . catching up."

"We're not going out there for Christmas, are we?"

"No!" she says so quickly that Mick realizes she's no more eager to do that than he is. The funny thing about Mom is that she's always urging him and Katie and Braden to stay close to each other, but she barely talks to her own sister and brothers. Mick's uncles live far away and their kids are so much older that Mick's cousin Andrew is getting married next summer. Aunt Noreen is within a few hours' drive, but she and Mom are so different. Just like Mick and his siblings. Katie and Braden are pretty close to perfect, while he's . . .

Just *not.*

"Have you seen my keys?" Mom asks, rummaging around the kitchen.

"No."

She finally finds them in the pocket of the coat she'd draped over the stool earlier, and they leave for Marrana's.

Ordinarily, Mick looks forward to working, but not tonight. He knows Brianna won't be there and that Zach will. They'd passed each other a few times in the hall at school today, and Zach barely said hi.

Terrific. He probably screwed up a friendship he'd really come to value.

"What's going on?"

Mom's voice startles him, and he looks over to see that they're stopped at a light and she's watching him.

"What do you mean?" he asks.

"Something's bothering you. I'm going to guess it's a girl," says Mom the Psychic.

"Well, you're wrong." The lie pops out easily, but it doesn't sound very convincing.

"What is it, then? You don't have to tell me, but I know something's bothering you and I feel like I've kind of dropped the ball on this mom thing lately."

Caught off guard by that candid admission, he says, "What do you mean?"

"I've been so busy with . . . work. I don't think I've given you the attention you deserve."

"Mom, I'm good. With attention, I mean. And everything else."

"I was thinking maybe I can get you an appointment with a therapist, if you wanted someone to talk to about—"

"No! No way. No. I don't need a therapist. I'm fine."

The light changes and she starts driving again, looking at the road instead of him. "So your heart isn't broken?"

"No. I just . . . I had a stupid fight with a friend of mine."

"Who?"

"You don't know him." Another lie. She does know Zach, along with every other kid in Mundy's Landing.

"So what happened, Mick?"

"It's my fault. I did something stupid. Nothing horrible, you know, just . . . something I wouldn't have done if I'd stopped to think."

"Tell him that."

"I did, and I apologized but I don't think that matters."

"It happens to the best of us. You did the right thing when you apologized. All you can do is be accountable and hope he'll forgive you. If it wasn't horrible, he probably will. And if it was . . ." She shakes her head, not finishing the sentence.

But Mick does, in his head: *. . . then you probably don't deserve to be forgiven.*

"What was that about?" Kevin asks when Noreen walks back into the kitchen, cell phone in hand.

"Nothing."

"Nothing? Your sister starts texting you out of the blue and you drop everything to go call her at a time like this? That's not 'nothing.'"

No, it's isn't *nothing.* But it's not as urgent as Noreen made it out to be when she interrupted Kevin mid-sentence to say she had to call her sister.

"I'm sorry I bothered you while you were in court," Rowan had said.

"It's okay." She didn't regret the lie she'd sent her sister's way. Rowan would never know the difference, and Noreen wasn't about to admit that she and her husband had just sat down to have their first real conversation in weeks, about . . . logistics.

As it turned out, listening to her sister's concerns over a snow globe when her own world is unraveling wasn't much better than listening to her husband talk about the unraveling itself.

"She just needed to talk to me about something," she tells him now.

He's shaking his head. "I can't believe you told her."

"Told her what?"

"About us. We said we weren't going to tell anyone before we told the kids."

"Believe me, I haven't told anyone."

"You must have told your sister. Why else would she be texting you now?"

"She's my *sister.*"

He does have a point, though Noreen chooses to ignore it. She and Rowan go for weeks, sometimes months, without being in touch. "Believe it or not, she has a life that doesn't hinge on the state of our marriage," she tells Kevin. "So do I, for that matter."

"What's going on with her, then?"

"Why would I tell you?"

"Why wouldn't you?" he lobs back as expertly as if he were in tennis whites on the court at the club instead of sitting here on the couch in four-hundred-dollar midlife crisis jeans.

"My sister is none of your business anymore. If you're ending this marriage, then get used to the fact that she's my family, not yours."

He shrugs as if it's no great loss, and goes on talking about Christmas—or the lack thereof, really—with the kids.

Something has shifted for Noreen, who for the past few months has been wishing he'd change his mind about leaving, for the sake of the kids, finances, convenience, appearances . . .

Until now, she could think of countless reasons to stay married. But in this moment, they're outweighed by a single compelling reason to divorce.

I loathe him.

From the *Mundy's Landing Tribune* Archives
Police Blotter
June 12, 1979

Senior Prank

At 7:27 a.m. yesterday, police responded to a call from Mundy's Landing High School custodian Timothy Reynolds, who reported livestock loose on the premises. Upon their arrival, officers discovered several piglets running rampage through the halls and promptly evacuated the building. Animal Control Officer Lyle Timmons was summoned to the scene and apprehended three of the animals, marked with the numbers 1, 2 and 4. As arriving students and faculty congregated outside, officers carried out a lengthy and fruitless search for the missing piglet in what was presumed to be a quartet. Upon their failure to discover the animal, they determined that the incident was part of an elaborate hoax. Three local youths were being questioned pending charges of criminal mischief in the fourth degree in connection with the incident.

Chapter 13

Back home after dropping Mick at work, Rowan goes straight upstairs to retrieve the box containing the snow globe. When Mick startled her earlier, she'd dashed up the stairs and stashed it in the hall bathroom hamper beneath a pile of dirty clothes.

Again, she looks at the Polly Pocket dolls glued inside the jar.

Is it possible?

She carries the snow globe out into the hall, past her sons' bedrooms. Mick's door is closed, as always, to hide the mess and protect his teenage sanctuary. Braden's door is open and the room is tidy—but it would have been that way even when he was Mick's age.

How can brothers born of the same gene pool into the same household be so drastically different?

Her own mother must have wondered the same thing about her and Noreen.

Struck by a familiar longing for the woman who'd been yanked from her life far too soon, and for her father—not to mention for her firstborn son, and her daughter—Rowan feels as though most of her adult life has been spent missing the people she loves. Just when you think you've moved past one loss, bam! Another one takes its place.

But eventually, you figure out how to survive without

that person, and maybe you hold on a little tighter to the ones who are left.

When Braden first left for college, she couldn't walk by his empty room without sobbing. She kept the door closed and avoided it until he came home the following May with a heap of clothes and dorm room accessories that seemed to have quadrupled over the course of two semesters. When he left again the following fall, she missed him terribly all over again, but was nonetheless relieved to see the pile of stuff evaporate. She took advantage of his absence to paint the walls, update the bedding, and create space in his desk drawers for some of her school files.

Katie's departure last August brought another momentary wave of grief, but Rowan got over it quickly enough to move part of her accumulated wardrobe to her daughter's half-empty closet and stash some of her books on built-in shelves left barren in Katie's absence. She's been in and out of the room often enough these past few months to feel that she isn't violating her daughter's privacy as she crosses the threshold now.

Dusk is falling beyond the tall, lace-curtained windows that overlook the street. She flips the overhead light switch. It throws a bright yellow glare over the room. She quickly turns it off again, feeling oddly exposed and reaching instead for the bedside lamp.

There. That's better. Now the girly bedroom, decorated in pastel shades of green and lavender, is bathed in warm light, a sharp contrast with how she's feeling inside. The moment she saw that snow globe, a chill snaked through her and withered every glimmer of contentment she'd experienced on the drive home from school.

Talking to Noreen had helped a little, but her sister doesn't seem to grasp the gravity of this situation, and why would she? To her, it's ancient history.

Rowan drags Katie's desk chair over to the closet. Built on a swivel, the seat jerks back and forth beneath her weight as she climbs on it to retrieve a clear plastic bin from the top shelf.

Super-organized Katie keeps her belongings sorted and labeled. In some ways, she's cut from the same cloth as Aunt Noreen.

And Mick . . . poor Mick is so much like me.

The conversation in the car had left her worried. There were so many things she wanted to say to her son; so many things she probably should have said to him long before now.

She'd been so determined to put her troubled teen years behind her that she hadn't shared many details with the kids. Now she realizes that it might help Mick to know she gets it, gets him. That she knows exactly what it's like to do . . .

Something I wouldn't have done if I'd stopped to think.

Mick's words, but they could have been her own, thirty years ago and fourteen years ago.

She won't confess the most sordid sins of her past, but she'll share what she can and suggest that they find a therapist for him. Armed with a diagnosis, medication and therapy, he can turn things around now, while he's still young. Before he makes a reckless mistake that will have more serious repercussions than a friend's cold shoulder.

Ah, there it is—the bin marked in pink Sharpie: *Polly Pocket, Hello Kitty, & Barbie.* As she goes through the contents, she lays the entire collection of Polly Pocket dolls out on the lavender patchwork quilt. They're neatly organized in Ziploc bags individually marked with each doll's name and clothing and accessories. It looks like Katie kept them all.

All except two?

Rowan isn't sure whether her daughter ever owned the little redheaded doll glued inside the homemade snow globe, but she's a hundred percent certain about the male.

She goes through the box three times, just to be sure.

Yes.

The Rick doll is missing.

Beyond the screen walls of Bob Belinke's Florida room, the insect and amphibian chorus has taken up its nightly serenade. A gentle evening breeze stirs the palm fronds.

Ah, home.

He's been back for a few hours now—long enough to change into shorts and flip-flops, go through the pile of accumulated mail, and notice that there's nothing in the fridge fit for consumption.

He has yet to do anything about that, but is planning to head over to Publix as soon as he gets ahold of Rick, who never did reply to his text this morning or the voice mail he left when he landed in Tampa.

When he didn't pick up the phone then, Bob was slightly worried. When Rick doesn't pick up now, he decides to do something about it.

He goes into the house, sits down at the computer, and pulls up an e-mail from last winter. It was from Rick, and it lists all four of his kids' addresses. Bob had asked for their contact information after Vanessa died so that he could send individual condolences for the loss of their mother, since none of them was living with Rick at the time.

He sent four cards, writing messages telling every one of the kids that he would be there for them if they ever needed anything. He included his contact information. He heard back from the two oldest, Rick's stepsons. They thanked him for his concern. The younger kids, both in college, didn't respond.

The family might be fractured in the wake of Vanessa's suicide, but they need each other's support if they're going to heal.

Using the addresses of Rick's stepsons, Bob manages to locate phone numbers for both. Rick wouldn't be thrilled that Bob's reaching out to the kids directly, but it's for his own good.

That's what friends are for.

"Mick, have you talked to Brianna today?" Gina asks when he walks into the restaurant kitchen, wearing her telltale bursting-with-news expression.

His heart immediately starts pounding. Old Jiffy Pop may be privy to just about everything that goes on around here, but she can't possibly know he's Brianna's Secret Santa.

"No, why?" he asks as casually as possible.

"She didn't show up for work, and my mom can't get ahold of her."

"Oh well, she's sick," Mick tells her above the clatter of pots and pans, running water, and sizzling food. "She wasn't in school today."

"Then she should have called my mom. Now we're totally short-handed and there's a birthday party coming in with fifteen people in twenty minutes."

"Well, maybe she's feeling better. Your mom should call and—"

"She tried. Brianna's not picking up her cell phone and no one is answering at her house. Obviously she's not really home sick."

Mick's instinct is to snap at her, but remembering what happened with Zach—who barely greeted him when he walked into the restaurant a few minutes ago—he says only, "She's probably sleeping or plugged into head-phones. Happens all the time in my house."

Shaking her head and emitting sounds that may or may not be actual words, Gina grabs her order pad and heads back out into the dining room.

As Mick rolls silverware and steak knives into cloth napkins, he hopes Brianna isn't so sick she had to go to the doctor—or the hospital, even. She seemed fine last night, though.

Maybe she really is playing hooky. Maybe she snuck off to a Hadley dorm to be with her college boyfriend or something.

Disturbed by the thought of that, he fumbles the cut-lery and drops a steak knife onto the floor. He starts to bend over and pick it up, but someone gets there first.

If this were a romantic movie, Mick thinks, it would be Brianna handing him the knife, and their hands would brush and they'd look into each other's eyes.

But it isn't a movie, and it's Zach who hands him the knife that just dropped at his feet. "Hey, Lou—you missed."

"What?" Startled, Mick looks from the knife in his hand to Zach's face and sees that he's smiling.

"If you're gonna get rid of me, you're gonna need better aim, see?" Zach the wiseguy is back. "And you might wanna wait till there are no witnesses, or it's gonna get messy. Capiche?"

"Capiche. Thanks, Lou." Mick grins and takes the knife from him, glad that at least something is going his way today.

Sitting in her study, trying to make sense of what's gone on in her life, Rowan can't stop thinking about the carni-val that came to Mundy's Landing every summer when she was growing up. For one long weekend in June, an or-

dinary grassy field out on Colonial Highway would burst
to life with crowds and commotion and color.

In the early 1900s, an amusement park midway had
stood on that spot. In her childhood, you could still see
faint ruts in the grass where the penny arcade had been,
and rotting wood and pilings from the old boardwalk and
pier. Back in the woods, there were other ruins belonging
to the park, and the picnic grove structures and a stone
storage building remained intact, albeit covered by graf-
fiti.

In those days, there was talk of bringing a new theme
park to the site, but it never happened. Wistful kids of her
generation made do with the traveling carnival—and her
own wistful kids didn't even have that.

Too bad. Even when she was very young, Rowan rel-
ished the fleeting danger and decadence of it all: food
stands dishing up deep-fried, spun-sugared, gooey con-
fections; barkers convincing you to try your luck at games
that were impossible to win; wanton rides that rattled and
shook, flashing lights and blaring music as they hurtled
you into the sky or twirled you so fast that your brain
rattled.

Noreen always got sick on rides, even the carousel, but
not Rowan. She loved them. The higher, the faster, the
scarier, the better.

The barrel-shaped Gravitron was her favorite. She
rode it over and over, standing with her back against its
padded interior wall as the ride began to spin, picking up
speed, until the floor abruptly dropped out from beneath
her feet. Somewhere in the back of her mind, she always
expected to fall, but of course she never did, safely pinned
to the wall by centrifugal force.

It's been years since she's even seen a Gravitron.

But today, she feels like an unwilling rider, her back
against the wall as the world spins crazily.

And you know what's coming, don't you?

You know that any minute, the bottom is going to drop out.

The moment Rowan's first text message appeared this afternoon, Casey knew the snow globe must have arrived at last. Of course, she didn't mention it directly. But it was clear she was in distress.

Mission accomplished.

Does she realize that the miniature dolls inside the globe came from a box in her daughter's own bedroom? Casey found them there while browsing a month or two ago and knew that they'd be perfect.

Even if Rowan missed that connection, surely she knows that her secret is in jeopardy. Too bad she doesn't yet realize that her life is as well.

Maybe the gifts shouldn't have been quite so . . . benign. Maybe she should be made aware that this is life and death. It's not turning out to be nearly as much fun to imagine her squirming with discomfort as it would be to terrify her. The wait that promised to be so tantalizing has grown tedious.

Casey read online that the NYPD confirmed Julia Sexton's identity a little while ago. There was a teaser for the story at the top of the evening newscast. Sitting in front of the television in anticipation, especially on the heels of Rowan's text, Casey can't stop glancing over at the razor blade in the drying rack beside the sink. It might as well be flashing a neon beacon.

I'm bored. That's the problem. I need something else to do. Something constructive, to keep my mind and my hands occupied like when I made those little gifts for Rowan, and the time capsule scrapbooks, too.

I always was artistic. Too bad I never got to put my creativity to good use until lately.

Maybe Casey should become an artisan of some sort when this is all over. A sculptor or a painter, creating masterpieces that will hang on museum walls all over the world . . .

That might make up for the fact that I'll never get to take credit for this magnum opus.

The newscast is back from commercial with a chalk outline graphic. This is it. The shot of the news desk gives way to a reporter standing on the street outside a familiar Chelsea apartment building fronted by a grid of fire escapes.

Too bad I didn't get to climb them, Casey thinks, turning up the volume and leaning forward eagerly. *Rapunzel made it too easy for me. That's why I'm so tempted to get careless.*

Even the girl this morning made it easy.

"The victim in Saturday night's homicide case has been identified as Julia Sexton, a young singer-songwriter who, like many, came to New York City with dreams of stardom . . ."

It wasn't Saturday night, Casey thinks critically. It was Sunday morning. Sunday, bloody Sunday. Even the media can't get it right.

The reporter goes on talking about Julia, showing a montage of photographs: baby photo, little girl missing her two front teeth, in a cap and gown, on stage with a microphone. There's an interview with some guy carrying bags of groceries and standing on the stoop of her building, a neighbor who has frustratingly little to say about both victim and crime.

The lack of recognition is starting to get to Casey. Too bad the NYPD cops are too ignorant to realize that Julia Sexton has plenty of company. Maybe it's time to send them a note or make a phone call, something like that. Just so that they'll make no mistake about who has the

upper hand here. It can't hurt. Jack the Ripper and the
Zodiac did it, and they were never caught.

Casey watches with interest as the boring man-on-the-
street interview is replaced by earlier footage of a middle-
aged couple the reporter describes in voice-over as Julia's
parents. Heads bowed, arm in arm, they're being escorted
from the morgue by a couple of uniformed cops and
flanked by a pair of detectives: a tall African-American
male and a female with—can it be?—long red hair.

It's pulled back in a clip, but Casey can just imagine
what it would look like falling down her back; what it
would feel like . . .

Now there's a close-up of the woman—identified as
Detective Sullivan Leary—being questioned by the reporter.

"All I'm authorized to tell you at this point is that we're
working on a number of leads, and we're asking anyone
with information to call our tip hotline."

A phone number flashes on the screen.

Casey grins. Just what the doctor ordered.

As Rowan watches Jake's car pull into the driveway from
the window of her study, her stomach turns.

He thinks he's coming home to chicken Marsala, a
happy wife . . . normalcy.

"I think you should just tell him the truth, Ro," her
sister advised earlier, when she called back. "Then you
won't have anything to worry about anymore."

Her sister is delusional. Telling Jake she had a near-
miss with an affair fourteen years ago would open the
door to a whole slew of things to worry about.

When she said that to Noreen, the response was "Are
you sure you'd be worse off than you are now? Because
all you're doing is worrying. I can assure you that marriages have withstood much bigger issues than this."

She didn't say *This is nothing*, but she might as well have.

Rowan wished she hadn't called her, but she had to call someone. She has plenty of friends who are closer—much closer—than her sister is these days. But she can't bear the thought of admitting her secret to anyone else, regardless of whether they'd be less inclined to pass judgment than the almighty Noreen.

At least this isn't news to her. She's always known that Rowan is capable of terrible things.

The people in her life now—Jake included—only know the best side of her: the charade. She's carried it off for years now, aside from that momentary blip on a snowy afternoon fourteen years ago, when she reverted to her true character and got away with it.

No wonder someone wants to see her get what she deserves.

Someone?

Rick. It had to be Rick.

Unless Noreen was lying, or unless Kevin . . .

She's been thinking a lot about her brother-in-law today. About how he, like her sister, seems too good to be true.

"Ro?"

It's Jake, calling from the kitchen.

"In here."

She silences the ringer on her cell phone as her husband's footsteps cross the hardwood floors of their dream house. If Rick calls back now, she won't be able to pick up.

She hears the slight jingling of dog tags as Jake stops in the hall to pet Doofus. Then he's framed in the doorway, unknotting the tie she'd watched him tie this morning.

"I thought you were making dinner tonight. Chicken Marsala?"

"I didn't have time. I got home late."

"That's okay."

But it isn't. She let him down.

"I'm sorry. It's just been . . . a crazy day. And my field trip is tomorrow morning, so . . ." She trails off, implying that an impending field trip is sufficient reason not to follow through on a promised dinner.

"Which field trip?"

"To the historical society. You remember."

He nods. Of course he remembers. He grew up here. He'd know all about fourth grade and Ora Abrams and the hot cocoa even if he weren't married to Rowan and a parent whose three kids had gone through the local school.

That's the thing about Jake, Rowan thinks. The thing that Rick Walker could never have, or be, or share.

Mundy's Landing is Jake's home just as it is hers. More so, because he's a Mundy. Their shared roots are just one more bond that can never be broken. They belong here. Together. This—this village, this house, this man, this *life*— isn't just her past, or her present. It's her future. He's her future, and no one is going to take that away from her.

"It's just us for dinner, right? Mick is working?" Jake asks.

"Yes. Maybe I can throw something together."

"We can order takeout, or I can have leftover meatloaf."

Stop it! She wants to scream. *Stop being so nice to me, because you're only making things worse!*

I don't deserve you!

I deserve . . .

She takes a deep breath. It's not about what she deserves. It's about what Jake deserves.

The truth.

When Kurt Walker's phone rings, he's already in bed. It's not particularly late, but it's been a long day and all he wants to do is watch some television and get some sleep.

But when he sees the Florida area code accompanied by the name Robert Belinke in the caller ID panel, he quickly snatches up the phone. Bob is his stepfather's life-long best friend, and the one person in the world Kurt would expect to hear from if something happened to Rick.

"Bob? What's wrong?"

Like Rick, Bob is a pull-no-punches Midwesterner. He wastes no time on small talk, or trying to convince Kurt that everything is fine, because clearly, it isn't.

"Have you talked to your stepfather lately?"

"No, but I've been trying to get ahold of him for a few days. He left me a message on Sunday night."

"Really? What did he say?"

"Just that he needed to talk to me. But he left it on my home phone and I spent the weekend at my girlfriend's apartment, so I didn't get it until last night."

"I've been trying to reach him, too," Bob says, "and I'm a little worried. I was supposed to meet him for dinner last night—I was in New York for the past couple of days—but at the last minute, he couldn't make it."

"Why not?"

"Subway trouble, he said."

"There *was* subway trouble last night during rush hour," Kurt assures him, just in case Bob is doubting Rick's explanation. "Definitely." He chooses not to men-tion what he read in this morning's newspaper: that some-one jumped in front of a train. Suicide.

"I know," Bob says, "but I offered to meet him after that, and he didn't want to."

"So you heard from him later last night?"

"Yes, but not since then."

"That's good, though." That was just twenty-four hours

ago. Bob is jumping the gun on being alarmed. "How did he sound?"

"It was just a text. The thing is, he hasn't called me back today. I just want to make sure he's okay. I know you don't live right around the corner, but—"

"I'll try him again, but I'm sure he's fine. Sometimes he just sort of . . . drops out for a while. Especially since my mom . . . you know."

"I'm so sorry about your mom. I really am."

"Thanks. It's been a year, but it's still hard."

"I'm sure it is. On everyone. Including Rick."

Kurt's pulse quickens. "They were divorced."

"I'm aware, and I've been through it myself, so I know that kids take sides after something like that. But I hope you kids understand that what happened to your mother wasn't Rick's fault. It wasn't anyone's fault."

"Do you know how my mother died, Bob?" Kurt is up out of bed, striding across the small room. "Because it's not like it was from natural causes, or an accident. She didn't get hit by a bus or have a heart attack. She climbed into the bathtub and she *slit* her *freaking* wrists."

"I know that. I'm sorry."

"It didn't have to happen."

"Your father feels the same way. I talked to him about it over the weekend. He told me she'd started taking prescription antidepressants that came with a suicide risk, and he's blaming himself for that even though she'd been dealing with depression on and off for years. I just want to make sure you kids aren't blaming him as well."

Kurt stares at the framed photo on his cluttered dresser top. It shows his mother, young and pretty as a china doll, holding him on her lap. He was just a toddler. Both their faces are cast in shadow; it belongs to the photographer, his biological father, whose long silhouette falls over the photo.

Sure, she was depressed from time to time. Look what she went through. But . . .

"I can't speak for my brother or my half brother and half sister," he tells Bob after a long moment. "I promise you that I'm not blaming Rick for what happened to my mother, though. He's the only father I ever knew."

"I'm glad to hear that. I know he thought of you and your brother as his own sons, and your mom . . . well, it started out a really good thing, and it just didn't work out in the end. It happens. But—"

Exhausted, Kurt stops him there. "I know all that. It's okay."

God, it's been a long day. A long year. One year, one week, and one day since his mother died.

"Look, if I don't get ahold of him tonight, and if the others haven't heard from him, either, then I'll go over and check on him first thing in the morning," Kurt promises Bob. "Okay?"

"Okay. And when you reach him, tell him to call me right away. I'm going to talk him into coming down to Florida to visit me over Christmas. You can all come if you want. I've got plenty of room."

"We might just do that. Thanks. I'll call you tomorrow."

When Rowan told Jake to sit down—on the only uncluttered seat in her office, the antique fainting couch—she'd fully intended to start from the beginning and tell him the whole truth.

The problem: the beginning—the real beginning—was so long ago and far away that she kept getting sidetracked.

"Why are you telling me this?" Jake asks edgily, as she recounts the first time she ever cut class in high school.

"I just feel like . . . you know, I've done some not great things in my past, and—"

"We all have."

"You?" She shakes her head. "Please. The only bad thing you ever did was senior prank."

Jake and a couple of his friends were, in fact, elevated to folk hero status following the legendary "missing piglet" incident at the high school shortly before graduation.

"Anyway," she adds, "that was genius, and they didn't even press charges, so it doesn't count as getting into trouble."

"Not true."

"That it was genius?"

"No, that it's the only bad thing I ever did. It's the only one I've told you about."

"What else did you do? Chew gum in class?"

"Does this have something to do with Mick?"

"Mick? Why?"

"Because I've been thinking about him all day and I'm guessing you have too."

She flashes back to the conversation in the car when she drove her son to work.

"We both know he didn't really have to take a test first thing this morning, Ro."

"If we both know it, then why am I the only one who acknowledged it?"

"Because you're the mom, I guess." Seeing the look on her face, he adds, "Bad answer? Only one I've got. Sorry. I guess I've been preoccupied with work and I'm a little slow figuring things out."

"I talked to him this afternoon. He said he had an argument with one of his friends."

"And . . . ?"

"And that's why he's been upset."

He shrugs. "Maybe that's true, but it's not all that's going on with him. And even if it were—which it's not—it's no excuse for lying."

"You're right. There's no excuse for lying," she says quietly.

"He lied about coming home on time on Saturday night, too. I'll admit I was dozing on the couch, but I woke up a few times after midnight, and I know he wasn't here when he should have been."

"Katie missed curfew a few times, too."

"She never lied about it."

No. She wouldn't lie.

"Are you hungry?" Jake asks, looking at his watch. "I've had Italian food on the brain all day."

"I meant to make dinner. I just—"

"No, it's no big deal. Why don't we go over to Marrana's? We can drive Mick home when he's done with his shift. Maybe he'll talk to us."

"So you think he's in some kind of trouble?"

"Serious trouble? No. But he lied to us and his grades stink. I think we'd better sit him down and deal with it." He starts to get up off the fainting couch.

"Jake. Wait."

"What?"

"I didn't finish telling you what I was telling you."

"Oh. Right." He looks at his watch again. "Can we finish talking about it over dinner? It's getting late."

He has absolutely no clue that for perhaps the first time in their marriage, she's trying to tell him something so grave that it can't possibly be discussed in public over Cavatelli a la Mama.

She was planning to take her sister's advice and tell him what happened fourteen years ago—

"Fourteen years ago!" Noreen kept saying. "It's ancient history. Just get it out in the open, say you're sorry, show him the stupid snow globe, and move on."

She made it sound so simple.

The reality is anything but.

I can't do this right now, Rowan decides. If she does, it will blow up and envelop them both. They won't be able to deal with Mick, or . . . with anything.

Maybe it's an excuse.

Maybe it's a valid reason to wait to tell him until later, or tomorrow, or . . .

Maybe he doesn't need to know after all.

"Marrana's sounds good," she tells him, noticing that the desk drawer where she stashed the snow globe is open slightly. She pushes it closed as she stands.

Barnes went home to get some sleep an hour ago after extracting a promise from Sully that she'd do the same thing as soon as she finished her paperwork.

Now that it's done, however, instead of gathering her things and heading out into the night, she decides to spend a little more time searching the databases.

Having identified weather as a possible trigger or a draw that might have lured a transient killer, she and Barnes had identified several catastrophic storms over the past year. A few—a category 2 Caribbean hurricane and a deadly Oklahoma tornado—were likely beyond their perp's range. But she can't stop thinking about the massive Labor Day nor'easter.

All six New England states were affected, as was Long Island. There were no related homicides during that time frame, but they were searching a large area, both in population and in geography.

Wondering if they'd missed something earlier, Sully again combs the records for female slashing victims. This time, she finds one—a Boston prostitute—but she was brunette and of Asian descent, and doesn't fit the victimology. Anyway, her pimp was later arrested for the crime, had confessed, and is behind bars.

Turning her attention back to the missing persons files,

Sully embarks on a state by state search, focusing on the areas that were hardest hit by the storm.

In Vermont, she hits pay dirt.

A female college senior in Burlington has been missing since September 11, four days after the storm passed through.

She had long red hair.

She'd grown up in New York City and lost her beloved godmother in the World Trade Center attacks. According to the case file, her friends reported that the anniversary always brought her down, but she'd been more depressed than usual this year because their sorority house had been without power for several days. Suicide had not been ruled out, though no evidence of that had ever turned up; nor had her body.

At the time she disappeared, much of storm-ravaged Burlington was still flooded by Lake Champlain and littered with downed trees and power lines. The area was crawling with reporters, relief workers, repairmen, contractors, insurance inspectors . . .

Somewhere among them, Sully is now convinced, lurked a killer with a straight-edged razor and a deadly obsession with redheads.

From the *Mundy's Landing Tribune* Archives
Police Blotter
March 28, 1984

A Mundy's Landing teen is safely back home after a massive search that began Tuesday evening when her parents reported her missing. Believing she was safely in her bedroom, they had noticed nothing amiss throughout the evening, but called police when they discovered the bedroom empty shortly after eleven o'clock. Following an extensive overnight search, the teen returned to her parents' home mid-afternoon of her own accord. She stated that she had traveled out of state to a rock concert. Her identity is being withheld due to her age.

Chapter 14

Dressing for the field trip on Wednesday morning, Rowan can hear Jake singing in the shower.

He wouldn't be doing that if she'd had the chance to tell him what she wanted to tell him last night.

Now who's a coward? she scolds herself as she pulls a red sweater over her white blouse and zips her feet into a pair of warm boots.

It hadn't taken much for Jake to sidetrack her efforts to bare her soul last night.

All he had to do was offer to take her out to dinner, and she dropped the whole plan.

As they drove over to Marrana's, she toyed with the idea of continuing the conversation over dinner and even momentarily convinced herself that it wasn't as big a deal as she'd made it out to be. As Noreen had pointed out, Jake isn't likely to walk out of their marriage over something that had happened fourteen years ago . . .

Is he?

Wasn't Noreen the one who'd acted as though Rowan might as well sew on a scarlet letter back when she first confessed to having kissed Rick?

It *is* a big deal.

She realized she couldn't tell him about it in a restaurant over dinner. It would have to wait.

Marrana's was jam-packed last night, and short-handed. Mick was single-handedly bussing tables as the other busboy, Zach Willet, took orders.

"Did you get promoted?" Rowan asked him, surprised when he came over to wait on them.

"Nah, one of the waitresses didn't show up so they asked me to fill in. I've never done this before," he added nervously.

"I'm sure you'll do a great job," Jake said.

He was wrong.

Poor Zach fumbled their order and fumbled their plates—dropping Rowan's soup and Jake's dessert.

"The only thing he hasn't figured out how to drop is the check," Jake whispered after they'd sat waiting for it, yawning and trying to get Zach's attention.

When he finally brought it over, he apologized and said, "You don't have to tip me."

"Poor kid," Jake said to Rowan, pulling out his wallet as Zach hurried away.

"You're leaving him twenty percent, right?"

"Nope."

She frowned and started to protest.

"I'm leaving him fifty percent."

They smiled at each other, and she realized how much she loved him and how much she dreaded hurting him.

But she knew she had to do it, and she meant to, she really did . . .

As they drove Mick home from work, Rowan asked if he'd also been asked to pinch hit for the absent waitress.

"No, just Zach. I'm not good enough."

"Is that what they said?" Jake asked.

"That's what I say."

That evolved into a predictable and unpleasant conversation—between Jake and Mick, anyway—about taking pride in your work and being ambitious, which led to slammed car doors on the driveway and Mick stomping up the stairs to slam his bedroom door, too.

"We were supposed to talk about his schoolwork," Jake protested to Rowan, who could only shrug helplessly.

They were supposed to talk about a lot of things.

He walked Doofus, and she pretended to be asleep when he came to bed.

Long after Jake really had drifted off, she lay awake thinking about the snow globe.

She knows what she has to do today. She has to talk to Rick, and she has to talk to Jake. She's not sure in which order.

He comes whistling into the bedroom with a towel wrapped around his waist.

"Is that a new skirt?" he asks, gesturing at the gray wool plaid one she has on.

"I've had it forever."

"I like it."

Oh, Jake. Why do you have to be so sweet today, of all days? Why can't you pick a fight with me the way you do with Mick?

"Thanks," she murmurs, and heads for the hallway. "I've got to get going."

"Firing up the griddle? Bacon and omelets again? I'll take extra cheese this time."

"Jake! I told you, that was—" Turning back, she sees that he's grinning.

"I was kidding. Have fun on your field trip, babe. Don't forget that I won't be home until really late."

"I already forgot. Why?"

"The dinner."

"Which dinner?"

"The one at Hattie's."

Hattie's . . . ?

"You mean Hattie's in Saratoga Springs?"

"What other Hattie's is there?" he asks with a grin. Hattie's Chicken Shack is a Saratoga institution and one of their favorite places to eat whenever they get up that way for a long weekend—which they haven't done in at least a few years.

"Today is the regional sales meeting," he adds. "Remember?"

"Of course I remember. I just didn't know about Hattie's."

"I told you about it the other day."

Which other day?

The day I was sneaking around the city meeting Rick Walker for lunch?

I don't deserve Jake. And he deserves the truth. Tonight.

"Well—good luck with the meeting, and have fun at your dinner."

"Okay, I'll see you later. Love you," he adds, because they always do.

"Love you, too," she returns, and today she means it more than ever.

As the crow flies, Kurt's stepfather's Weehawken condo is less than a mile and a half from Kurt's Manhattan apartment. But it takes him nearly an hour to cover that distance in rush hour traffic, even though he's heading in the opposite direction of most commuters crossing the Hudson River.

He'd been surprised when his stepfather chose to stay in New Jersey after divorcing his mother.

"Why not the city?" he'd asked Rick the day he'd helped him move into a high-rise located on the wrong side of the river, as far as Kurt was concerned.

"Too expensive."

"Not everywhere." He'd managed to find an affordable

place a few years earlier, and so had his brother. Then again, they're both probably making more money than Rick is these days—or has in years.

He'd always seemed content to stay at home with the kids and Mom had been fine with that scenario. After Kurt's sister, Erin, started preschool, Rick went back to work. But his income was a drop in the bucket compared to Mom's.

She didn't mind. As far as she was concerned, Rick Walker had been her knight in shining armor at a time in her life when she was on her own with two little boys. She loved him.

And so did we.

Kurt will never forget the sunny afternoon when he and his brother came home from school to find Mom waiting for them on the stoop. The last time that had happened, she broke the news that their father had disappeared. This time, Kurt—then in first grade—braced himself for another bombshell.

"Rick wants to marry me," she said. "I won't say yes unless you guys want me to."

They were momentarily dumbstruck.

Kurt managed to speak first. "Will he live with us?"

Mom smiled. "He sure will."

"Can we call him Dad?"

"That's up to him. Should I say yes?"

Their answer to her was yes; Mom's answer to Rick was yes; Rick's answer to the dad question was yes.

He was the one who taught Kurt how to pitch a baseball and helped him with multiplication tables and made his lunch every day. He was the one who gave Kurt the Big Talk after the seventh-grade biology teacher sent home a note to all the parents that the reproduction unit was looming. He was the one who sat in the passenger's seat on the New Jersey Turnpike after Kurt got his driving permit; the one who tied his bow tie for his senior prom; the one who taught him how to shave, using an old-fashioned straight razor just like his own father had taught him.

"Those plastic safety razors are fine when you're in a hurry," Rick said, as they looked at each other in the bathroom mirror, faces lathered in preparation for the lesson, "but real men use real razors."

Kurt wanted to be a real man just like Rick, who wasn't his real father—not biologically, anyway—but was the only one who'd ever mattered.

His biological father did resurface a couple of times over the years, wanting to bond with him and his brother. But neither of them wanted anything to do with him, and neither did their mother.

She despised her first husband, but according to the suicide note she was clutching when she killed herself last November, she never stopped loving her second.

This morning's weather is as oppressive as yesterday's was luminous, with the threat of rain or snow hanging low in the sky beyond the turrets of the Mundy's Landing Historical Society.

Rowan stands beside the open doors of the yellow school bus parked at the curb in front of 62 Prospect Street, counting heads as her class files out onto the sidewalk.

The most important rule of a fourth-grade field trip— always count heads, always, *constantly*—seems particularly important this morning. She's seen more police cars than usual around the village and Bari Hicks mentioned that they're looking for a high school girl who never came home last night. She didn't remember the name, but had heard that the girl had a boyfriend at a college somewhere in New England.

"I just hope she wasn't kidnapped."

"Around here? I doubt that," the other chaperone said.

"I'm betting she'll turn up safe and sound in a dorm room," Rowan told them. The conversation unfolded well beyond earshot of her students, but Rowan wasn't about to confide that she herself had gone missing overnight back in her own high school days.

She'd climbed out a window and taken a joyride to a concert in Hartford with a couple of older friends. Prince— Purple Rain. That was the concert. She remembers the set list began with "Let's Go Crazy" and the first encore was "I Would Die 4 U," remembers that she sprayed her long permed hair purple, ratted it, and used a pair of violet tights as a headband, remembers everything except . . .

What the hell was I thinking?

She wasn't thinking. After the concert, no one was in any condition to drive home. They wound up at a party at some cabin, fell asleep at dawn, and arrived home the next evening to find search teams with dogs combing the woods surrounding Mundy's Landing.

She was grounded an entire summer for that stunt. That was the plan, anyway. Her mother died before she could see Rowan through the punishment, and although her father was too caught up in his grief to keep tabs on her, she didn't have the heart to resume her previous antics.

As certain as she is that today's missing girl will be found, and most likely grounded for life, she's not taking any chances with her students.

". . . twenty-three, twenty-four." Satisfied, she nods and holds up her arm, the signal for silence.

The excited chatter subsides, though not entirely. The kids are just too keyed up that it's finally their turn to embark on this local rite of passage, many of them having heard about it from older siblings and looked forward to it since kindergarten. Rowan gets that; she was once in their shoes.

Bari Hicks is on her cell phone, telling someone that she spent the "whole trip on the verge of vomiting . . . yes . . . yes, I'm serious! I know! But the teacher is giving me a dirty look so I have to run. I'll call you back in a few minutes."

Rowan sighs inwardly before she addresses the group. It's going to be a long morning.

"Okay, listen up, people. Before we go inside, I just want to remind you what we talked about. Use your manners, pay attention, hands to yourselves, and if I see *any* of you with a cell phone or an iPod or anything that has a screen, what happens?"

"You confiscate it," Amanda Hicks says.

"Confiscate!" Bari beams. "What a nice big word!"

Rather than pause to congratulate Amanda's literary skills, Rowan goes on talking, reminding the class of Miss Abrams's strict no-electronics policy in order to preserve an authentic atmosphere. She demonstrates that she's turning off her own phone, instructs everyone to follow suit, and knows that half of them, including a certain chaperone, will ignore the rule.

"Okay, let's go, guys. Just be on your best behavior. Got it?"

"Got it," most of them say in unison. The few who don't haven't got it and never will.

She marches the line up the wide steps of the stone building, with the three chaperones walking alongside them. Bari is, not surprisingly, only interested in interacting with her own daughter. The two of them are dressed identically in khakis and black North Face jackets, with ridiculously tiny matching purses slung from shoulder to opposite hip and clutched protectively close, in case someone tries to mug them between the bus and the steps.

Ora Abrams is framed in the doorway. She seemed elderly even back when Rowan was a girl, but always spry and lovely, with her snow white updo piled high above a pastel satin headband, making her look like a geriatric Cinderella.

She likes to say that history is her family business. Her father was a history professor at Hadley College and her great-aunt Etta was the longtime curator of the historical society before Ora took over back in the 1950s.

"Well, who have we here? Is that Rowan Carmichael?" she asks.

Not exactly. That hasn't been her name in twenty years. But despite seeing her often, Ora is one of those hometown folks who will always think of her as one of the Carmichael kids. Rowan can see the kids' ears perk up: *Rowan Carmichael? Who might that be?*

Realizing her mistake, Ora says, "I'm sorry! I meant Rowan Mundy! I mean *Mrs*. Mundy!"

Instant contradiction from—who else?—Amanda Hicks: "You mean, *Ms*. Mundy!"

"Yes, come in, come in, *Ms*. Mundy and . . . everyone." Ora holds the door wide open so that they can crowd into the majestic foyer, with its ornately carved woodwork, hexagon-shaped stained glass windows, and mosaic floor.

Rowan breathes a sigh of relief, ensconced, if only temporarily, in this familiar cocoon. Here, the old house scent that lingers in her attic at home blends with potpourri wafting from a cut-glass bowl near the guest book and the scented votives flickering on the marble mantelpiece. The imposing grandfather clock loudly ticks in time with its swaying pendulum, and Christmas music is playing courtesy of scratchy vinyl on a vintage Victrola.

In Rowan's house, the staircase is carved of the same dark wood, but it's angular with a landing. Here, the stairs curve in a graceful, unbroken arc to a second-floor balcony. Ora ducks beneath a velvet rope hung across its foot and ascends a few steps so that she can address the group from above.

At this time of year, visitors are restricted to the first floor, where it's all about mistletoe and holly. The notorious Mundy's Landing Collections—archives relevant to the village's bloody past—are housed in two large rooms above.

In one, among other seventeenth-century artifacts, is a cast-iron kettle that Jake's ancestors James and Elizabeth Mundy supposedly used to make stew from the disembodied limbs of their unfortunate fellow settlers. There are records from the trial and execution as well, written in pen and ink on crumbling parchment displayed beneath glass.

The other room contains a more extensive exhibit, given the relatively recent timing of the crimes. Included are bloodied clothing and hair ribbons that were found on the Sleeping Beauties' corpses, and notes that were purportedly left by their killer. There are yellowed newspapers—the story made national headlines—and police reports, along with dozens, perhaps hundreds, of original photographs.

Rowan remembers poring over the collection as a child, when the historical society was crammed into the library basement. She was particularly captivated by the macabre images that showed the corpses tucked into beds that weren't their own, arms folded neatly on the coverlets, faces serene, looking for all the world like sleeping children.

When she was growing up here, that exhibit was far more disturbing than the other one. Not so for Jake, though, or for their kids.

The overachieving descendants of James and Elizabeth Mundy stretched well above and beyond the realms of good citizenship in their efforts to redeem the tainted family name, and it's paid off.

For the most part, anyway.

Years ago, forensic testing was conducted at Hadley College on skeletal remains that showed indications of having been crudely butchered—including the fractured skull of a young female. The lab results revealed that the fracture had occurred before—and most likely had been the cause of—the girl's death.

It's one thing to be descended from Early American settlers who valiantly resorted to the unthinkable in order to stave off death by starvation, and were cruelly executed in front of their children. It's another to be descended from cannibals who murdered their prey in cold blood.

"The truth has been lost in the mists of time," Ora Abrams always concludes dramatically when she relates that chilling tale during the special exhibit tours during the summer convention.

Today, however, she tells the students only about the first-floor exhibits.

"The front parlor is decorated to portray a typical Christmas Eve in 1860; the back parlor depicts what Santa would have left for the children of an upper-middle-class family in 1880; the scullery is in the midst of preparing breakfast on a Christmas morning in 1900, and the dining room is set for a formal New Year's Eve dinner in 1910. Any questions?"

There are plenty, as always.

"Where can we put our coats?"

"I suggest you leave them on," Ora says. "You'll find that it's quite chilly in here."

"Why don't you turn up the heat?"

"Because it's very expensive to warm this huge old mansion."

"When do we get to eat cookies and drink cocoa?"

Ora chuckles delightedly. "So you've heard about the cookies and cocoa. Very soon, I promise."

One last question—an earnest one that comes from Billy: "How old are you?"

"Younger than I look and older than I feel," is the good-natured reply. "Shall we get started?"

She descends the staircase and begins leading the group toward the front parlor nestled in the base of one of the turrets.

"You have a nice bunch of students this year," she tells Rowan. "Very well behaved."

"They are. There are always a few live wires."

"The live wires are my favorites . . . and as I recall, you were one yourself, my dear." Eyes twinkling, she reaches out to touch the snowflake brooch pinned to Rowan's coat. "Oh my goodness. Where did you get this?"

"It was a gift from my Secret Santa. Isn't it unique?"

"It is. We have a few pieces in the collection, but nothing like this. I'd love to know where your Santa got it when she reveals herself."

"I'll let you know. You have pieces like this in the museum? So you think it's an antique?"

"I'm sure it must be. Mourning jewelry was wildly popular in the late Victorian era."

"I didn't know that's what it was called. I guess I'll have to make sure that I don't wear it at night."

"Oh no, not morning. *Mourning*. The Victorians wore jewelry made from the hair of their dead loved ones."

Taken aback, Rowan looks down at the intricate snowflake she'd assumed was crafted from red thread. "You think this is made from *hair*? Human hair?"

Ora nods. "I inherited a similar brooch from Great-Aunt Etta but it's not nearly as striking. Yours is a rare piece. That's why I'd love to know where your Secret Santa got it."

"So would I," Rowan murmurs, as the Gravitron picks up speed.

As Kurt covers the last few steps between the parking garage and his stepfather's Weehawken apartment building, he belatedly wonders whether he should have asked someone to come with him.

But who? This is a family matter, and he's the only one in the family available to tend to it right now. His half sister is at college in California, his half brother in Texas, and his brother, though he lives nearby in Brooklyn, is working.

"Daddy did leave me a message on Sunday," Erin said when she returned Kurt's call late last night—late for him, anyway. "But he didn't answer when I got back to him Monday night, and I left him a message but I haven't heard back."

His brother said almost the same thing: Rick had left a message on Sunday saying he wanted to talk, but when he got around to returning the call Monday night, Rick hadn't answered.

As for Liam, who knows? He's ensconced in an Austin fraternity house and didn't pick up when Kurt tried to reach him last night. Nor did he answer his texts. Typical college kid.

Not that Kurt has much experience in that area. He'd lasted two semesters at Rutgers. Mom was dismayed when he flunked out, but Rick had his back.

"You mark my words. He'll make something of himself even without a college degree, Vanessa."

She was dubious, but Rick was right.

Kurt fishes Rick's spare set of keys from his pocket as he walks into the lobby. The doorman, typing on his cell phone behind a desk, doesn't give him a second glance. Maybe he's new and assumes Kurt lives here. Maybe he just doesn't give a crap.

So much for security, he thinks, riding the elevator to the third floor.

"I know what you're thinking," Rick said the first time he showed Kurt around the place, almost two years ago now. "Believe me, I was hoping for something with a better view."

"I don't know how you can beat this," Kurt said dryly, gazing at the brick wall across the way and Dumpster below. "Wasn't there anything on a higher floor? There must be awesome skyline views up there."

"Maybe, but the price is right for this place. I can afford it."

Maybe not. Last time he saw Rick, he had his doubts that his stepfather was even holding down his latest job. He'd been pretty broken up after Mom died.

Yeah, well, who hasn't been?

Heart pounding, Kurt walks toward apartment 3C, jangling the keys.

Maybe he should have waited until his brother got out of work to come here. Maybe he shouldn't do this alone. Maybe . . .

No. It was Rick who taught him how to be a man—a real man. "You don't run away from the tough stuff. You face your responsibilities head-on and you do what needs to be done."

He takes a deep breath.

He turns the lock, opens the door, takes a few steps over the threshold—and screams himself hoarse.

From the *Mundy's Landing Tribune* Archives
Sports Page
May 25, 2009

Local Team Wins Soccer Tournament

The Mundy's Landing River Rats defeated the Catskill Wildcats 7–1 in yesterday's championship match at the Youth Soccer Tournament in Albany. Led in scoring by Julia Williams and Carmichael "Mick" Mundy, the team, a co-ed mix of ten-to-twelve-year-olds, went into the final game with a pair of round robin wins.

Coach Ronald Calhoun told the *Tribune*, "These kids played hard and I'm proud of each and every one of them."

Chapter 15

After waiting around near Brianna's locker again this morning, Mick was forced to give up when the first bell rang.

She must be really sick, he decides as he sits through English class, chin in hand, staring absently at the teacher.

He's not feeling so great himself today, having remembered to take his medicine but forgotten, once again, to eat something with it.

He'd better grab a banana from the cafeteria when he goes to retrieve the gift box from behind the bags of prunes in the lunchroom. Operation Secret Santa will have to wait until Brianna's back in school.

When the bell rings, he heads swiftly down the hall to make the detour to the cafeteria before his next class. Above the noise of chatter and slamming locker doors, Mrs. Dunlop, the principal's secretary, is talking on the PA system.

"Will the following students please report to the main office immediately . . ."

As she begins naming names, all of them female, Mick recognizes that they're close friends of Brianna's.

Both his heart and his feet pick up their pace. The cafeteria is quiet and empty other than Denise, one of the workers, who's putting milk cartons into the refrigerated case near the register.

"Hi, Mick," she says, looking up. "What's going on?"

"I just wanted to see if I could grab a healthy snack."

"You know we're not open till fourth period."

"I know, but . . . I missed breakfast this morning. Please?" Mick offers her his most charming smile, when it's the last thing he feels like doing.

Denise, who graduated from Mundy's Landing High School back in the eighties with Mick's dad, shakes her hairnetted head but smiles back. "Go ahead and grab something," she says, "and I'll bill it to your account when I open the register."

"Thanks."

"No problem. Tell your parents I said hello."

His stomach is churning but he bypasses the bananas, making a beeline for the prune display.

The gift box isn't there.

Frowning, he roots around trying to find it, but it's definitely gone. Realizing Denise is watching him, he grabs a bag of prunes just as the bell rings signaling the start of next period. He shows it to her, saying, "I'll take this. Bill me for a banana, too, okay? I grabbed one yesterday when no one was here. Thanks, Denise."

"No problem. Now get moving." As he heads for the hall, he hears her laugh and repeat, "*Get moving.* Hah! Good one."

Mick is too concerned about Brianna and the missing gift to be mortified.

Passing the bulletin board in the empty hallway, he pauses to lift the Toys for Tots flyer, intending to remove the written clue he'd left there for Brianna.

It, too, is missing.

Since he's already late for class, he detours past a few

other spots where he planted notes, only to find that all
have been removed.

Even more disturbing: through the glass window of the
main office, he can see a pair of uniformed police officers
along with several of Brianna's friends—all of whom are
crying.

After spending the night combing case files, Sully got
home at four in the morning to find that her upstairs neighbor was apparently spending the night at her boyfriend's
because her teenage son—an avid drummer—was having
a party. And the insomniac old man downstairs was blasting his television so loudly that she could hear every word
of *Life Begins for Andy Hardy* on Turner Classic Movies.

Reminded of her father, who had been a big fan of old
movies and Mickey Rooney, she downed a shot of Irish
whiskey, crawled into bed, and managed to sleep soundly
until nine. She'd have kept right on sleeping if she hadn't
been awakened by a call from Barnes, reporting that a
teenage girl had gone missing up in the Hudson Valley
and she might have crossed paths with their redhead
stalker.

Maybe. But probably not. Brianna Armbruster is
younger than the other victims, still living at home with
her parents. She vanished on a sunny morning, not on the
heels of a catastrophic storm.

When small-town teenage girls go missing, the vast
majority of them disappeared voluntarily. Often, they've
had a fight with their parents or boyfriend, or they're
simply in the mood for a change of scenery or searching
for some big-city excitement.

Still, she lived on the Hudson River just up the Taconic
Parkway from New York, and she's an attractive girl
whose most striking feature is her long red hair.

At that news, Sully bounded out of bed and jumped into the shower. Now she's juggling rest stop tea and a bagel in the passenger's seat as Stockton follows the foggy gray ribbon of highway stretching along the Hudson River with the Catskill Mountains looming to the west. They're well aware that the trail is fairly cold by now. The girl had likely been missing for hours before anyone realized she was gone. No one had seen her since she'd gone to bed on Monday night.

"Those poor parents." Sully shakes her head. "Can you imagine the guilt?"

"I can. That's why I've never had kids. It doesn't mix with this job."

Both Armbrusters are successful professionals, with demanding state government careers in Albany. They'd assumed when they left for work yesterday morning that their daughter was out jogging, as was her early morning habit.

"At least they're both cleared as suspects," Barnes points out. "That saves everyone a whole lotta extra anguish."

Yes, the couple's solid alibis spared them the unique hell Sully and Stockton have encountered many times in the past. Parents often fall under the umbrella of suspicion in a child's disappearance, and it's a challenge to stride the fine line between compassion and skepticism when investigating a case like that.

"It's just incredible that in this age of overcommunication, the system failed so spectacularly," Sully says with a sigh, giving up on the bagel and shoving the remains into Barnes's coffee cup parked in the console.

"Hey!"

"It's empty. This is garbage."

"I thought you were starved."

"I was. But even I have to draw the line somewhere.

Like I said, that's garbage. You can't get a good bagel north of the George Washington Bridge."

She brushes the crumbs from her hands and pulls out her notes, going over the facts of the case.

When Brianna didn't show up at school yesterday morning, the attendance office assumed she was out sick and followed procedure, which was to leave a message at the house to confirm the absence. No one was home.

After school, her younger brother was wearing gaming headphones and parked in front of the Xbox console in his room, too engrossed to notice that his sister hadn't come home as usual. When the parents arrived later that night, they found nothing amiss and assumed their daughter had come and gone to her waitressing job. It turned out she'd never arrived there, either, but when the restaurant called looking for her, the twelve-year-old video game junkie never heard the phone ring.

"The thing that gets me is that the parents never checked their voice mail when they got home," Barnes comments, shaking his head.

"I don't bother to do that very often, either," Sully tells him. "If people want to reach me, they call my cell. Lately, only the telemarketers bother calling my landline."

"But you don't have kids."

"True. But I can imagine these people are probably like every other working parent we've ever met. Over-extended, overwhelmed, overtired from a long day, long commute . . ."

"You're right. And they really didn't have any reason to think anything was wrong until they realized their daughter hadn't come home from work."

She nods. It was well past ten o'clock when the Arm-brusters began to worry, belatedly discovering the messages from the school and the restaurant. They panicked and called the police.

The village is small enough that the police chief lives a few blocks away and was once their daughter's soccer coach. He wasted no time in ruling out a runaway scenario. That conclusion seems based not just on assumption and emotion but on intuition, and Sully has been in this business long enough to respect that.

"If our perp is escalating," she muses, "then he's not holding off until he has a weather-related reason to travel farther from home. He either found himself up here for a different reason, or he singled out the girl because she crossed his path somewhere else and he hunted her down."

"Maybe online. Hey, what's the exit number? These mountains are messing with the GPS signal."

She quickly opens a search engine on her phone and Googles the name of the village, Mundy's Landing.

"That's why it sounded familiar," she says, more to herself than Barnes.

"What? Why?"

"It's that town where they have that big murder festival every summer."

"*Murder* festival? What?"

"Unofficially known as Mundypalooza," she reads off her phone. "Crime buffs gather from around the world in an attempt to solve the Sleeping Beauty murders of 1916."

"Oh, right." Barnes nods. "That's the case where people were waking up in the morning to find dead girls in their beds. It doesn't get much creepier than that."

"No, it doesn't. Do you think what happened to this Armbruster girl has anything to do with it? Maybe it's a copycat killer. Next summer is the hundredth anniversary of the murders and the three-hundred-fiftieth anniversary of the town, and they're already gearing up for a media circus."

"I wouldn't put that past some sicko. But at least this

girl hasn't turned up dead in someone else's bed. She's just disappeared."

"I know." Sully stares past him at mountains cloaked in somber gray. "Let's just pray she doesn't turn up bald and shrink-wrapped."

"Mr. Walker? I'm so sorry for your loss."

Kurt looks up to see a middle-aged man standing over him. Everything about him is puffy: curly blond hair, navy down jacket, even his face and breath, both of which bear the florid evidence of boozy nights.

He lowers himself into the seat opposite Kurt. They're in a small office just off the building lobby, where the first cops on the scene escorted Kurt to get him away from his stepfather's dead body.

That was almost an hour ago. He has no idea who summoned the police. Most likely one of the third-floor neighbors called in response to his screams. Or maybe the doorman heard the commotion from two floors below.

Still huffing a little and mopping his brow with a hand-kerchief, the man in the chair introduces himself as Detective Lindgren with the local police force. Kurt wonders whether he's sweaty and out of breath from the exertion of taking an elevator and walking a few yards, or if the bloodbath upstairs got to him.

"Can I get you anything?" the man asks. "Glass of water?"

"No, thank you."

One of the cops had asked him the same thing, and so did the doorman. It happened when his mother died, as well. Why, he wonders, do people assume that proximity to death is accompanied by great thirst?

"I need to tell my brothers and my sister what happened," he tells Detective Lindgren.

"Are they close by?"

"One is. I'll go tell him in person. I'm going to have to call the younger two. They're away in college. They're going to have to make travel arrangements, and . . ." He looks at his watch. "They'll want to come right away. Today."

"I understand. I just have a few questions for you, if you feel like you can answer them right now? I know this is a terrible time but the sooner we get this out of the way, the better."

He inhales and exhales shakily, nodding. "I'll answer them if I can."

"Thank you. When was the last time you saw your father?"

"I don't know . . . it's been a while."

"Why did you come over here this morning?"

"To check on him. None of us had heard from him since . . . I don't know, Monday, I guess."

"None of us . . ."

"Me, my brother, my half sister and half brother. And my dad's friend, Bob—he's in Florida. We were all worried."

"So he was your stepfather, correct?"

"Yes, but he adopted me and my brother when he married our mother."

"When was that?"

"Twenty years ago last summer. I was six, and my brother was four."

"And your father's friend Bob—who is he?"

"Bob Belinke. He lives in Florida."

The detective wants more information, including Bob's contact information.

As Kurt answers the questions, he realizes his mouth is dry. Now he wants the glass of water, but if he asks for it, the cop might think it's an attempt to distract his line of questioning.

Why is he questioning me anyway?

Rick committed suicide. He slit his wrists and he left a note, just like Mom. There can't possibly be any question about that . . . can there?

"What about your father?"

"What do you mean?"

"Your biological father."

"What about him?" Kurt presses his hands against his cheeks, suddenly exhausted. "I haven't seen him in at least ten or fifteen years."

"His name?"

Why does that even matter here? What the hell is going on?

He answers the question: "It was Kurt. Kurt Clark."

"Same as yours."

"My name is Kurt Walker." Now, anyway. But even as a child, long before Rick came along, he resented being named after his deadbeat dad. His mother and brother called him by any number of nicknames that evolved from God only knows where—Cookie, Kiddo, Buddy, KitKat . . .

"And you're estranged from your biological father?"

"We all are."

"All?"

"Me and my brother . . . and my mom was, too, before she died."

"And she took her own life, just as your stepfather did?"

"Yes." He finally manages to swallow. Hard. Remembering. "Exactly the same way. Exactly. She slit her wrists with a razor. Rick's razor."

The moment Ora Abrams told Rowan the snowflake was a piece of Victorian mourning jewelry and made of human hair—red hair—she knew it had to be from Rick. She has no idea how he got it to her classroom doorknob, but there isn't a doubt in her mind that he managed.

"I've always had a thing for redheads," he'd said on Saturday.

Not only that, but he'd remembered her passion for the Victorian era.

This is creepy. He's gone too far. She's got to talk to Noreen about it. Maybe there's some legal action she can take against him.

That would mean Jake will have to be told, but she was already prepared to tell him tonight anyway. She owes him the truth, even if it is fourteen years late in coming.

As Ora steers the group from the front parlor to the back, Rowan whispers to one of the chaperones that she has to step outside for a moment. The kids will be so engrossed in the array of antiques beneath the tree—tin soldiers and porcelain dolls, a rocking horse and an elaborate little theater complete with puppets—that they'll never notice she's gone.

Out on the porch, she sees that snow has begun swirling in the air. A police car is parked down the street with its red lights flashing. The officer behind the wheel has his window open and is talking to a pair of pedestrians.

They must still be looking for the missing girl. Rowan had temporarily forgotten all about that. Now, well aware that it's most likely one of her former students, she feels a renewed sense of concern. What if the girl didn't just take off to visit her college boyfriend? What if . . .

No. Rowan shakes her head, pulling her cell phone from her pocket. One crisis at a time.

Waiting the few seconds for her phone to power up so that she can call Noreen, she gingerly unpins the brooch from her coat.

This isn't a crisis. But it's just as disturbing to think

that it's made from someone's hair as it is to imagine Rick Walker violating her professional space the way he's violated—

Her phone buzzes to life and she sees that a text came in a little while ago.

Speak of the devil. It's from Rick.

It's about damned time.

As she reads it, her anger gives way to a new wave of concern.

We have to talk. I'm driving up there this afternoon. I'll text you when I get there.

Mick shouldn't have bothered going to class after seeing Brianna's friends crying in the office.

He should have marched right in there and demanded that someone tell him what's going on. Instead, his feet went on autopilot and carried him to the next classroom on his daily schedule. All he has to show for it now is a failing grade on a quiz that was handed back, a late slip that needs to be signed by his first-period teacher in order to avoid detention, and a pounding headache courtesy of staring unflinchingly at the teacher for the past forty-four minutes.

Brianna must be sicker than he thought. Maybe she has some kind of horribly contagious disease, or—God forbid—cancer.

Whatever it is, he's certain she can get through it, and he'll be with her every step of the way.

The moment the bell rings, he rushes out into the hall and heads toward the office, intending to burst in and demand some answers. Halfway there, his friend Van flags him down.

"Mick . . . did you hear?"

"Hear what?"

"Brianna Armbruster disappeared."

"What?"

"No one's seen her in a couple of days. She's gone."

Gone . . . gone . . . gone . . .

Stepping off the elevator again on the third floor of the Weehawken high-rise, Detective Steve Lindgren pauses to take a deep hit off his asthma inhaler.

The hallway is bustling with activity. At the far end, an officer is talking to a couple of neighbors who knew the victim. A crime scene investigator is removing equipment from a duffel bag as an officer stationed at the open door of apartment 3C talks into his cell phone.

Steve tucks the inhaler back into his pocket alongside his Marlboro Lights. Ordinarily, he'd have stepped outside to smoke both before and after meeting with Kurt Walker, but he's cutting back to a pack a day. Doctor's orders.

Well, actually, doctor's orders were to quit altogether. "You have asthma and you've had one heart attack already. You have a death wish?"

Steve doesn't have a death wish, no.

Apparently, Richard Walker did.

Suicide is the immediate assumption when someone slits his wrists in a bathtub and is found with note—in what is almost definitely his own handwriting—that reads: *I can't do this anymore. You'll be better off without me. I'm so sorry.*

Still, all unattended deaths are investigated as potential homicides when accidents and natural causes have been ruled out, and in this case, they have.

There's always a suicide spike at this time of year, and it's not a stretch to think that this guy might have been depressed. Divorced and living alone, he'd been laid off back in October, which was news to his son. Plus, his ex-wife killed herself almost exactly a year ago using the same means, according to her son. Maybe even the same razor. Kurt Walker seemed to think so.

Losing one parent to suicide is bad enough, but two? And only a year apart? Steve feels for the guy, he really does.

He offered to accompany the poor guy to notify his brother in Brooklyn, and also offered to send local law enforcement in Texas and California to notify the younger siblings.

"No, thank you." Kurt shook his head, eyes solemn behind his glasses. "I have to tell them myself. It's my responsibility. My father taught me to do whatever has to be done, no matter how hard it is."

"He sounds like a wise man. I'm sure he'd be proud of you."

As they shook hands in the lobby, Steve promised to be in touch later today. "You let me know if you or your family need anything at all, okay?"

Kurt nodded and walked out into the cold, head bent, hands shoved deep into his pockets.

Thinking of what lies ahead for him and his siblings now, Steve sighs to himself as he reenters apartment 3C. The place is bustling with investigative activity, most of it centered around the body in the bathtub.

"The ME will be here in about twenty minutes," one of the officers, Jimmy Hogan, informs Steve. "I'm just confirming we've got an ID on the victim and it's Richard Walker, the guy who lives here?"

"Yeah, that's him, according to his son. He's the one who found him."

"That's rough."

Steve shakes his head. "You don't know how rough. The mother did the same thing, same way, last year at this time."

Jimmy's response is a colorful curse—followed by an

even more colorful one as he steps back to let a police photographer pass by and knocks a water glass off a table in the process. It shatters on the parquet floor.

"Cleanup on aisle six," Steve announces through cupped hands.

"Yeah, yeah, funny. See if there's a broom in that closet behind you there."

Steve opens the door. The closet is jammed. He begins pulling things out, finds a broom, and hands it to Jimmy.

"Got a dustpan?"

"What do I look like, Molly Maid?" Steve continues rummaging in the closet.

He doesn't find a dustpan; he finds something that's a hell of a lot more interesting.

"What the hell . . . ?"

He swiftly pushes his way into the bathroom to take another look at the body in the tub.

"Hey, hey, careful, Lindgren," the photographer protests. "I'm setting up a shot here."

"Sorry, hang on. I just gotta check something." Steve checks, and nods. "Hey, fellas? I think this one's a homicide after all."

From the *Mundy's Landing Tribune* Archives
Community Notes
June 14, 1916

Young and old persons alike anticipate the arrival
of summer for refreshing delights no other season
can offer. Envision the perfect day: open-air lun-
cheon in a shady picnic grove, donning a bathing
costume and splashing away a sultry afternoon at
the water's edge, indulging one's sweet tooth with
a bowl of rich, delicious ice cream or an effervces-
cent root beer, and winding down the evening with
the fox-trot in an open-air dance hall, a vaudeville
performance, or a ragtime serenade beneath the
stars.

One can fulfill all of these desires and more at the
new Valley Cove Electric Pleasure Park in Mundy's
Landing. Now open for the season and just in time
for next month's Sestercentennial Extravaganza, the
riverfront park is accessible via streetcar to the end
of the River West Line and is located adjacent to the
1665 settlement monument.

Amusements include a carousel, a Ferris wheel,
and a figure-eight thrill-coaster. Along the boardwalk
are an arcade, a shooting gallery, and a food conces-
sion pier, including a root beer stand and confec-
tioner's stall. Strolling the well-lit grounds, parkgoers
will find modern bathhouses, picnic shelters, a roller-
skating rink, bandstand, theater, and dance pavilion.
Plans for expansion include a baseball diamond, a
grandstand, and a swimming pool.

While there have been concerns among the upstanding citizenship of our fair village—particularly
those of a gentle female persuasion—that the park
might draw vagrants and unsavory characters from

far afield, management offers utmost assurance that this is a family-friendly endeavor. Undesirables shall be refused admittance. All others are invited to visit at ten cents for the day.

Chapter 16

Ordinarily, Noreen doesn't leave the office at lunchtime, opting to stay at her desk and eat Greek yogurt or a protein bar, if anything at all. Today, however, she heads home at noon to grab a brief she'd left behind in her haste to clear away the breakfast things and get out the door with the kids.

Luz helps when she's here, but she's off on Wednesdays. Kevin wasn't working, but had reserved an indoor court at the club and was already gone when she got up at six-thirty.

She was hoping he wouldn't be home now, but sees his Lexus parked in the garage when she raises the electronic door. Terrific. It's already been a lousy day after a sleepless night on the guest room mattress, and she's dreading this afternoon's meeting with one of her more difficult clients.

Having come to terms not just with the separation, but with the likelihood of a divorce, she wishes he'd just get out of her house and her life. But of course he can't. Unfortunately, neither can she, not even just overnight. She doesn't have the luxury of an escape chute to the hospital, a rented condo, or wherever the hell it is that he sleeps when he's not here.

Walking into the kitchen, she finds a mess. An array of

chopped fruit sits on a cutting board, rinds and peels litter the sink, and the juicer is filled with a pumpkin-colored sludge that's spattered on the counter and backsplash.

Goliath's muddy paw prints are tracked over the floor, and the dog himself apparently toppled his bowl of dry food and is undoubtedly cowering someplace in shame.

She fights the urge to grab a sponge and start cleaning, instead striding through the house to the foot of the stairs.

"Kevin!" she calls.

No answer.

She stomps up the flight and sees that the master bedroom door is closed.

What if he's in there with someone?

That gives her pause.

Then, realizing her heart wouldn't be broken and it would be ammunition for the divorce settlement, she embraces the scenario and strides toward the room.

Opening the door, she braces herself to see her husband in the arms of another woman.

Instead, she finds him sound asleep—wearing his shoes—on top of the white silk comforter.

The scream that's been building inside her for months bubbles dangerously close to the surface.

"Are you kidding me? Are you freaking *kidding* me? You're sleeping? In the middle of the day? After making a disgusting mess and leaving it there for someone else to clean up?"

He blinks, sitting up. "What are you doing home?"

"I live here! Remember? I live here!" She wishes he'd yell back, wishes he'd do something other than sit there and stare at her. "My God. Don't you have anything to say?"

"What else do you want me to say?"

"I don't know. 'I'm sorry' would be a good start."

"For what?"

"For destroying the kitchen!" *And our lives.*

He has the nerve to dismiss that with a wave of his ringless left hand. "You're a lunatic when it comes to stuff like that. You make us all crazy with your nitpicky neat-nicky—"

"Us *all*? Who *all*?"

"Me. The girls. Sean, when he's here. Even Luz."

"That is not true! Don't you dare tell me how my children feel about me unless you want to hear how they feel about you!"

"Go ahead. Tell me. How do they feel?"

Oh no. No way. She's not going to drag the kids into this ugliness.

She shakes her head and leaves the room. As she descends the stairs, her throat aches fiercely with the effort of swallowing the scream.

Her eye falls on the wedding portrait in the Baccarat frame, angled a little too close to the table's edge.

She reaches out to straighten it and gazes for a moment at herself as a young bride, eyes filled with confidence. Not tears, not hope, not misgiving, just confidence. She was so certain on that day about what their future would hold.

So wrong.

She can no longer hold back the scream. It erupts from her throat and she picks the crystal frame and hurtles it with all her might against the wall.

It explodes into glittering shards that seem to hang in the air for one long moment before raining onto the floor.

As the scream dies away, punctuated by Goliath's alarmed barking, her cell phone rings in her pocket.

After chain-smoking three or four cigarettes in the falling snow while making twice that many phone calls, Steve Lindgren rides the elevator back up to the third floor.

"What'd you find, Jimmy?" he asks Hogan, who has an

array of papers spread out on the kitchen counter. They contain various examples of Rick Walker's handwriting: on a grocery list, medical insurance forms, and plenty of unemployment paperwork. Visible through a transparent evidence bag, the suicide note found next to the bathtub is laid out alongside the papers.

"I'm no handwriting expert, and I know you're going to run this by one," Jimmy says, "but this thing looks like a match to me. What do you think?"

Steve leans in closer to study it. Jimmy's right.

"I think that's Rick Walker's handwriting. That's what I think. But that doesn't make this a suicide," he adds, heading back into the hall. There, he spots the telltale blond ponytail of Mary Ellen Kramer from the medical examiner's office. She's standing in the bathroom doorway talking to one of the patrol officers.

They've worked together on a number of cases over the past couple of years. He's come to appreciate her professional opinion almost as much as the other guys on the force appreciate her good looks.

Not that Steve doesn't appreciate a beautiful woman, but he's been happily married longer than Mary Ellen's even been alive.

"What's the word?" he asks her.

"We're past rigor mortis. This happened over thirty-six hours ago, but probably no more than forty-eight."

"So . . . sometime late day Monday, Monday night?"

"That's my guess. And the wounds are suspicious, just as you thought. Keep in mind that this is just my initial impression."

Well aware that nothing is conclusive at this stage, Steve nods. "Tell me what you see."

"There are no hesitation wounds. The cuts on his wrists appear to be of equal depth and were made with equal pressure appear to have severed the tendons."

"Meaning it would be impossible to use the hand on whichever side was done first to do the other side with that much precision. Meaning he definitely didn't do it himself."

" 'Impossible' and 'definitely' are strong words, Steve, but you're probably on the right track. Pretty impressive that you were suspicious about the wounds just at a glance."

"He's holding the knife in his left hand, and he's left-handed."

"And you know this because . . . ?"

"Because there's a set of left-handed golf clubs in the hall closet."

"Maybe someone else is storing them here," Mary Ellen points out.

"His name is on the tag on the bag. Anyway, he'd instinctively make the first cut with the dominant hand—the left—and then switch to the other hand, the right. That's where the knife should be."

"Whoever killed him must not have known him very well, then."

"Or knew him—and was so caught up in the emotion that went along with killing him—that he slipped up. Even the most meticulous killers make mistakes. And there are a few other things that don't add up to suicide."

"Like what?"

"Like we didn't find a cell phone here and we searched every inch of the place."

"Maybe he doesn't have one. Maybe—"

"There's no landline, and there's a cell phone charger plugged into that outlet on the kitchen counter."

Again, Mary Ellen plays devil's advocate. "Maybe he lost his phone."

"Or maybe there was something on it that someone didn't want anyone to see."

"**W**ait, so you're just leaving?" Kevin asks, as Noreen tosses toiletries into an overnight bag in the master bathroom.

"I'm going to see my sister, like I said. For one night."

"What about the girls?"

"What about them?" She strides back into the bedroom and opens a bureau drawer to find something warm to sleep in. Rowan's house was cold and drafty the one time she visited—much too cold for the silk nightgown she was wearing.

"What am I supposed to tell them?"

"Tell them the truth: that Aunt Rowan needed me to come help her with something and I'll be back tomorrow."

"What, exactly, are you helping her with?"

She shrugs and shakes her head, already having informed him—twice—that she can't tell him that and it's none of his business.

"Are you sleeping with someone?" Kevin demands.

If the mighty scream were still lurking in her gut, that question, under these circumstances, might have set it free.

She merely laughs and shakes her head. "No. I'm not sleeping with anyone."

Not tonight. Not in a while, actually.

Her last dalliance was with a horse trainer at the barn where Sabrina rides, and that was last August. Even if she'd had the energy or the heart to fool around since Kevin told her he wanted to separate, she's much too smart for that.

Bag packed, she heads for the hall. He follows her down the stairs.

"What the hell is that?" he asks, catching sight of the shattered picture frame.

"Leave it. I wouldn't want to drive you crazy with my neat-nicky nitpicking."

She slams the door behind her, climbs into the car, rests her forehead against the steering wheel, and exhales. Perhaps for the first time in months.

Then, as she pulls out of the driveway, she starts making phone calls. She has to cancel her meeting, clear her calendar, let the carpool moms know that Kevin will be driving tonight instead . . .

She starts with her partner, telling Jennifer that something came up—family emergency—and she has to leave town.

"Oh no. Are the kids okay?"

"They're fine. It's not the kids, it's—a long story. I'll explain later."

She hangs up and lets out a deep breath, oddly calm now that the scream is gone.

Her sister didn't ask her to drive up there. She seized the opportunity like a parachute in the midst of a harrowing freefall.

"Are you serious? You'll really come? I can't believe I don't have to deal with this alone. I know how busy you are and can't believe you'd do that for me."

I wouldn't, Noreen thinks, as she pulls out onto the main road, ready to begin the long trip back to Mundy's Landing. *I'm doing it for me.*

Standing by his open locker, Mick reaches for his jacket, then thinks better of it. He still can't find his good down coat, but this building is too overheated to consider putting on even the lightweight windbreaker he wore this morning. He fights back another wave of nausea, thinking that he can't get sick now. He has to find Brianna, has to—

"Going somewhere, Mr. Mundy?" a voice asks as he puts one arm into his sleeve.

He turns to see Mr. Goodall, the principal.

He isn't alone.

"We'd like to have a word with you, please." The uniformed police officer with him is familiar. He's the same cop who offered Mick a ride home from Dunkin' Donuts last Saturday night. The Eagle Scout who once knew Braden.

He isn't smiling today.

"Is it about Brianna?" Mick asks, heart pounding.

The two men exchange a glance.

"We'll talk in my office," Mr. Goodall says.

"But—"

"Come on." The cop rests a strong hand on Mick's shoulder. "Let's go."

For Casey, the decision to take care of Rowan Mundy today was born of frustration and practicality. The storm in the west is bearing down on the country's midsection. If it hits with its projected ferocity, that would mean being away from here for days, maybe longer.

And that wouldn't be good.

Casey was in Rhode Island for weeks last summer after that storm. Free moments were scarce, but every one of them was spent searching for a suitable stand-in. It was dangerous to strike in such an insular location.

Yet you took the chance.

And now you've been taking chances again. If you take another one now—the wrong chance—you'll never get back to Rowan.

Funny—Casey almost doesn't care much what happens after that. The plan was to make things right, and then put all this in the past and move on.

But maybe a fresh start someplace else, as an artist or a craftsman, is too ambitious or too . . . mundane.

If this is going to be your claim to fame, why give up now? Why not continue?

This might have begun as an effort to punish Rowan Mundy, and that hasn't changed. Rowan Mundy will die. But she doesn't have to be the last one.

Especially not now that Detective Sullivan Leary has reared her lovely red head.

Cobblestone streets lined with charming old houses, mom-and-pop shops, vintage lampposts, and towering trees: Mundy's Landing is precisely the kind of village where Sully imagines herself living whenever she's fed up with homicide and city stress—which isn't, surprisingly, every single day of her life.

"Are you kidding? You'd go stir crazy in a place like this, Gingersnap," Barnes informs her as they park in a diagonal spot along the town square, decked out for the holidays and dotted with fountains and statues, benches, and an old-fashioned bandstand that currently houses a lit Christmas tree.

"I would not go stir crazy. I'd sit in that nice park with a book."

"You can do that back home."

"Yes, but here, no one would bother me. Look how peaceful it is. No crowds, no panhandlers, no naked raving lunatics—"

"There was just one naked raving lunatic and that was a few years ago."

"That's one too many. Plus," she continues, "there are no sirens, there's no construction . . ."

"Because the weather's crappy and it's a weekday." He zips his coat as they get out of the car. "I bet this place is jammed at high noon on a Saturday in July."

"I bet Central Park is jammed right now," she returns, noticing an Apartments for Rent sign in the window of a mansard-roofed mansion that houses law and dental offices.

Reading her mind, Barnes says, "You don't want to live there. It's got to be haunted."

"Ghosts? Pfffft." She shrugs. "That's nothing compared to what we've seen. And I'm not even talking about the naked lunatic."

He can't argue with that logic—which ordinarily doesn't stop him, but this time, he refrains. Instead, he points out that it's starting to snow.

"See that? It's just like I told you the other day. This isn't city snow."

"Sadistic snow."

"Right. This isn't sadistic snow. It's a Christmassy snow. Kind, gentle small-town snow. You have to admit that there's something to be said for this Main Street USA stuff."

"You have to admit that if you lived here, you'd never find a decent bagel, or a black and white cookie."

"Sure I would. Look at that." She points to a painted shingle hanging alongside the door of a bakery. "It's called the Gingersnap Sweet Shop. I think it's an omen."

He raises an eyebrow. "Okay, well, try finding San Shan soup and shredded beef with spicy Asian green chili leeks and white rice around here."

"There's more to life than food, Barnes."

"You're right. There's sex."

"Leave it to you." She rolls her eyes, grinning.

"Well, come on. Who are you going to date when you move up here? Them?" He points at a trio of elderly men chatting in front of the café, and another one getting out of an enormous white car. All are wearing the suburban great-grandpa uniform: newsboy caps and galoshes.

"They're a step up from my dating pool back home. Anyway, don't worry. I'm not going to do it, because then there would be no one around to keep you in line."

"I didn't even know moving here was an option until now."

"Neither did I."

Barnes shakes his dark head. "You'll never leave New York."

He's right, of course. Yet as they walk down the steps to police headquarters, she can't help but compare it to the chaotic, strictly functional precinct back home. This one is housed on the basement level of a stately brick building that was once, according to a historic placard, an opera house. Now it's a movie theater showing an art house film that just opened in New York.

Five minutes later, they're seated in a cozy office with the darkly handsome Lieutenant Nick Colonomos and clutching fragrant, steaming beverages: coffee for Barnes, tea for Sully. Not whole leaf, but she had her pick of Earl Grey or chamomile. The chairs beneath them are vintage and upholstered, facing a sidewalk-level window high in the wall. There are no bars on the glass, and beyond it, the locals are visible strolling—not scurrying—about their daily business.

Colonomos quickly briefs them on the case, then asks, "Did you find any evidence that Julia Sexton had a stalker in the days leading up to her murder?"

Sully and Stockton look at each other and shake their heads.

"Well, Brianna Armbruster was receiving gifts from someone calling himself her Secret Santa," Colonomos informs them. "A neighbor says she saw someone lurking around her house on Monday afternoon."

"What were the gifts?" Sully asks.

"Those bracelet beads the girls are collecting . . . you know what I mean? Painted, enamel, with little stick figures. Trinkettes, I think they're called."

She shakes her head and Barnes informs Colonomos, "You're asking the wrong person. That's not really her thing."

"What's not really my thing? I love bracelets, and beads. And . . . trinkets."

"Since when?"

"Since always. I mean, I'm not going to wear that stuff to work, but . . ." She scowls at Barnes before asking Colonomos—who really is drop-dead gorgeous—to tell them more about the beads.

He spins his chair around to face the polished wood console perpendicular to his desk. After pulling up an image on his laptop, he turns the screen to face them.

"This is the Trinkettes Web site, just to show you what they are."

"You have to buy them online?"

"No, some higher-end boutiques carry them, too, but they're still catching on so there aren't many. A store right here in town sells them and I have an officer over there right now." He clicks from the array of painted enamel beads to a search screen and types something in, talking the whole time. "When we searched Brianna's locker at the high school, we found that he'd set out a whole treasure hunt for her. We confiscated a bead he'd hidden in the cafeteria. This is the one."

He zooms in on an image of a stick figure depicted in a classic runner pose, with the word *Runner* etched beneath. "Her parents found another one in her bedroom. It was this."

Sully's eyes widen as he zeroes in on the design: a stick figure crowned by long crimson curls and etched with the word *Redhead*.

From the *Mundy's Landing Tribune* Archives
Lifestyles
October 1999

Historical Society Acquires
Conroy-Fitch Mansion

When she stepped in to helm the Mundy's Landing
Historical Society upon the retirement of her great-
aunt Etta in 1956, Ora Abrams inherited a subter-
ranean closetlike office, a heap of unpaid bills, and
a trove of artifacts relegated to numbered bins in a
cramped space between the boiler and the janitor's
sink.

She also inherited her aunt's fondest dream—one
that wasn't meant to come to fruition in Etta Abrams's
lifetime. But it's about to be realized in her niece
Ora's. Housed for nearly a century in the basement
of the Elsworth Ransom Library, the society is at last
about to move into a home of its own with the pur-
chase of a grand stone mansion that dates back to the
late nineteenth century.

Built in 1891 at 62 Prospect Street on the site of the
former Penrod Hotel, which burned to the ground several years earlier, the home was a lavish wedding gift
from banker Barnaby Fitch to his bride, Edith Conroy.
Childless and widowed young, she bequeathed the
home to her only heir, great-nephew Rudolph Conroy,
a concert pianist. Mr. Conroy resided there until his
death in 1985, leaving it to his longtime companion,
Kenneth Stone, from whose estate the historical society purchased it. "Over the past eight years, the profits
from our annual summer fund-raiser have exceeded
my wildest dreams," she said, "and not only were we
able to buy this lovely property, but we'll be able to
put some much-needed work into it."

Ms. Abrams detailed planned restoration and renovation, including plumbing and electrical updates and tearing down a crumbling carriage house to make room for a parking lot. While the home itself will remain as period-authentic as possible, she envisions building an annex equipped with state of the art technology, where the society can hold event-related meetings, seminars, and panel discussions. For now, however, she's focused on moving the exhibits to the new quarters in time for next summer's convention.

"Aunt Etta would be thrilled about this," Ms. Abrams noted, adding, with perhaps a glint of a tear in her gray eyes, "And so, of course, am I."

Chapter 17

Rowan was hoping the sing-along in what was once the Conroy-Fitch mansion's music room would banish "I Would Die 4 U" from her head. It's been playing in the back of her mind all morning, ever since she thought about the time she ran away to the Prince concert in Hartford.

But as Ora jauntily plays carols on the upright piano, Rowan finds that "I Would Die 4 U" mingles discordantly with old favorites like "I Saw Mommy Kissing Santa Claus," which has suddenly taken on an ominous significance.

She can't stop thinking about Jake, and the conversation she's going to have with him the moment she sees him. It feels wrong that whatever is about to unfold with Rick will have happened before Jake even has an inkling about it.

"You better watch out, you better not cry," she sings, well aware that Santa Claus isn't the only one who's coming to town.

In the midst of the cacophony, the strange mourning brooch on her coat catches her eye every time she moves her head, standing out like a scarlet letter. Is that what the sender had intended? Had she branded herself an adulteress when she unwittingly pinned it on? Has he—whoever *he* is, if not Rick—been gloating from afar? Or, God help her, from nearby?

Her instinct was to hurtle the brooch into the bushes when she took it off outside after she discovered what it was. But it's evidence, just like the cookies and the snow globe. She has to show it to Noreen. Plus, sharp-eyed Ora Abrams would immediately notice that it was missing. With great reluctance, she pinned it back on before reentering the mansion.

At last, the sing-along is over and it's time to move on to the kitchen for cookies and cocoa. Again, Rowan goes through the motions, chatting with the chaperones and their hostess as the students descend on the treats.

"You know, Rowan, you really should consider volunteering here next summer during the convention," Ora tells her. "It's the hundredth anniversary of the murders, and the town's three-hundred-fiftieth birthday, and we'll be opening the time capsule that was buried in 1916. We're expecting record crowds. We need all the help we can get."

"Mmm, maybe I will," she says absently.

"I hope so. I'll be training the extra guides, and with your built-in knowledge of our history—and your last name—you'd be a big hit. We really need more locals to be involved so that we can keep it from becoming . . ."

"Aren't all the volunteers local?" Bari asks when she trails off.

"Pardon my phrasing—I should have said *natives*," Ora says, fixing her with a gaze that informs her that the *natives* distinguish themselves from the collective population.

Undaunted, Bari jerks Rowan back into the conversation. "So Ms. Mundy, as a teacher in our district, you don't find it the least bit inappropriate to take part in an event that celebrates the deaths of innocent young girls?"

"What? No, it isn't—"

"It's not a celebration, my dear," Ora cuts in sweetly, but her gray eyes have hardened into flint as she addresses Bari. "It's a commemoration. That's very different."

"Not really. We moved here last summer and I was shocked at what I saw. All those people invading our town, talking and laughing like it was one big . . . party."

Invading our town? Our town?

"Whenever people come together, even to mark a solemn occasion . . . there are going to be moments of enjoyment," Miss Abrams tells her. "Have you never been to a Memorial Day parade or barbecue?"

As Bari claims that she has not, Rowan reminds herself not to say or do anything she'll regret later. This might feel personal, but it's nonetheless a professional situation.

She picks up a tree-shaped cutout cookie from the platter to keep her mouth busy. Iced and painstakingly decorated, it's probably delicious, but it tastes like the flour and salt dough she'd used to make ornaments as a kid, and the cocoa chaser might as well be water.

All she can think about is what lies ahead.

Noreen is on her way to Mundy's Landing.

So is Rick.

If he isn't behind any of this . . . who is?

When Sully's cell phone rings with a call from the precinct, she quickly excuses herself from Lieutenant Colonomos's office.

The waiting room beyond has hardwood floors, plaster walls, and dark wood moldings. The furniture is entirely devoid of plastic, metal, and particle board. Nice. Really nice. Not just nicer than the precinct, but nicer than Sully's apartment—and a hell of a lot bigger.

She answers her phone. "Detective Leary."

"Where are you?" It's Jin Kim, the on-duty desk sergeant.

"In Mundy's Landing."

"Okay, listen. A call came in to the tip line a few minutes ago about the case you're working."

"The Sexton case?"

"Right. Some guy said he had some information and he wanted to talk to you."

"What else did he say?"

"Nothing. Not a damned thing, other than that he wanted to talk to you and only you."

"Why?"

"No clue. But he wanted your personal number."

Her heart is pounding. "Did you give it to him?"

"No! I told him to call back in five minutes and I'd patch him through. He agreed. Can you sit tight until he calls back?"

Of course she can.

"Did you get his name, location, anything like that?" she asks Jin.

"He was on a cell phone and he tried to block the number, but of course we traced it right away."

"Of course." Cakewalk compared to some tech-related tasks.

"It was a Jersey area code. We got his name."

"What is it?"

"It's Richard Walker."

The final segment of the historical society tour, after the cookies and cocoa, takes the class into the small modern annex behind the kitchen. It feels strikingly ordinary after the sumptuous mansion.

Everything about the meeting room is monochromatic and rectangular: the furniture, windows, tile floor, drop ceiling, and beige-painted cinder block walls.

"All right, boys and girls," Miss Abrams says, "now we're going to see how well you were paying attention. We're going to divide into two teams and play a trivia game."

Predictably, Amanda Hicks immediately waves her hand in the air. "I want to be a captain!"

"No captains," Rowan says firmly. "We don't do schoolyard picks."

Predictably, Bari Hicks protests. "Why not? It's the only fair way to do it."

"Because it's *not* fair. It's a popularity contest, and someone always has to be picked last."

"So? That's life," she says, apparently confident that her own daughter would be among the first chosen.

Somehow, Rowan refrains from telling her that the opposite would be the case, but it's getting more difficult to control her temper when she's already under enough duress. She excuses herself from the room after the kids count off numbers, odds versus evens, and line up on opposite walls for the showdown.

Outside, snow is coming down harder. She turns on her phone again.

There are no new texts and no messages. But that's not why she's here.

She takes a few deep breaths in an ineffectual effort to steady her nerves, then shakily dials Jake's number.

"Why you?" Barnes asks, predictably, when Sully tells him and Colonomos about the tip line caller's request. "We were both mentioned by the media in connection with the case."

"Yes, but I'm the one with the sparkling personality."

"You're also the one with the red hair."

"Yeah, no kidding."

She and Barnes exchange a long look. He's obviously

thinking the same thing: that the caller, Rick Walker, might very well be the killer.

Her phone rings right on cue.

She picks it up immediately. "This is Detective Leary."

"Hello there, Detective." Rick Walker's voice is mid-range, pleasant, unaccented. There's music playing in the background.

"With whom do I have the pleasure of speaking?"

Ignoring her question, he asks one of his own: "Where are you?"

"I'll tell you if you tell me."

"Very clever, Detective," he croons in a tone that sends shivers down her spine. Not good shivers. Creeped-out-by-a-psychopath shivers.

"Do we have a deal, then?" she asks him, recognizing the background music.

It's U2. "Sunday, Bloody Sunday."

Bloody . . .

She wonders if he's trying to send her a message.

"You'd have to promise to be honest with me if we do this, Detective Leary."

Sully looks at Barnes, who nods.

"Absolutely. And you'd have to promise to be honest with me."

"Of course, although . . . promises. Promises are never quite as convincing as proof. Do you agree?"

"Absolutely," she says again.

"Well, you really are brilliant. We can text photographs to prove our locations. Make sure that yours is a selfie. I'd dearly love a photo of you."

"And I'd love one of you."

He laughs. "Nice try. A photo of my surroundings will have to suffice."

"It wouldn't prove anything unless you're in it."

Barnes jots something on the pad and shows it to

Colonomos as the caller laughs again, saying, "Now that would be stupid of me, wouldn't it? To send you a picture of myself? I enjoy my anonymity. Really, I do."

Yeah, so did I, she thinks grimly, realizing she's going to be looking over her shoulder until they catch this guy.

Colonomos nods at whatever Barnes wrote on the pad. Barnes slides it toward and mouths, *Keep him talking*.

The call is being recorded, of course, back at the precinct, and they'll be attempting to trace it. The longer she keeps the guy on the line, the better.

"If you sent a photograph, how would I even know you took it right now?" she asks. "It could be any old picture stored in your phone."

"You're right. It could. I have to admit, you're very, very clever, Detective."

The way he says it suggests that he's certain she's not as clever as he is.

We'll just see about that.

She glances at the note on the pad in front of her, and nods at Barnes and Colonomos.

"Okay," she says into the phone, "here's what I want. I want you to pull up a map on your phone that can show GPS coordinates of your location. And then I want you to take a screenshot and send it to me."

"A screenshot?"

"Yes. One that shows a bull's-eye of your location, and it has to be time stamped, obviously."

She fully expects him to refuse, well aware that the NYPD would instantly put out an APB and, given the population-dense tri-state area, probably have an officer at just about any location in the city or its suburbs within seconds. There are so many security cameras in the area that even if it took a few minutes to get a live person on the scene, they'd have a virtual eye on his location right away and track him if he tried to get away.

"Fair enough," he says, to her surprise. "You tell me, and then I tell you."

"No, you tell me, and then I tell you."

"I may be accommodating, but I'm not stupid, and neither are you. You first. And I want a photo. Deal?"

She hesitates for only a moment, glad she's well over a hundred miles away from the city and the New Jersey suburbs where his phone is registered. It's not as if he's going to materialize here in a matter of seconds, even if he is by chance responsible for Brianna Armbruster's disappearance.

"Deal," she says.

"Good thinking. Where are you?"

"I'm in a little town in upstate New York called Mundy's Landing."

The statement is met with silence, followed by a long, hard laugh—and then a click.

"Bastard," she whispers.

A moment later, her phone buzzes with an incoming text.

It's a screenshot of a map—with a GPS bull's-eye located a few blocks away, right here in Mundy's Landing.

It takes Jake a few rings to answer Rowan's call, and when he does, he sounds harried. "Hey. What's up?"

"Where are you?"

"Don't tell me you forgot again."

"No, I mean, I know you're in Saratoga Springs, but I meant . . . are you in the meeting?"

"We broke for lunch. We're about to go back in. What's up?" he repeats.

"I just needed to talk to you about something. It's important. Otherwise, I wouldn't have bothered you there."

"What is it?"

Hearing the impatience in his voice and the hubbub of

background voices, she knows she made a mistake. Why did she think it was a good idea to have this conversation over the phone? Especially when he's in the middle of an important sales meeting?

"Never mind. I'm sorry. I shouldn't have—"

"Are you okay? The kids?"

"The kids are fine," she says quickly.

"You're not fine, though."

"How do you know that?"

"I didn't, but you just confirmed it. What's going on?"

"Nothing. I'll talk to you when you get home tonight."

"It's not nothing, Ro. I can tell by your voice. And I won't be home until really late. Tell me."

His tone is so gentle, despite the fact that he's in the midst of an important meeting. She opens her mouth to tell him to forget it, but a choked little sob is all that comes out.

"Hang on."

She hears him tell whomever he's with that he has to step outside, and the background noise fades away.

"Okay," Jake says quietly, "you're scaring me. Are you sick? What's going on?"

Her attempt to stammer a reassurance and a good-bye is met with a stern "Tell me. Now."

"You're in the middle of a meeting."

"Right, and if you don't tell me now, I'm going to think the worst and I won't be able to focus on my presentations."

"It isn't . . . the worst," she tells him—and reminds herself—as she clutches the phone hard against her ear. "It's just something that happened a long time ago and it popped up again. Something bad. I should have told you back then, but you need to know now, because . . ."

"What is it?"

This is it. Confession time—if she has the nerve.

The moment Casey heard that Detective Sullivan Leary is here in town, he had to hang up the phone. He could scarcely speak, overwhelmed by joy and temptation.

First things first—he did send the screenshot she'd demanded. A deal is a deal, and how could he resist?

Then, of course, he left the area immediately, heading away from the business district, out to the strip malls on the highway. He pulled into a crowded Home Depot parking lot, where his van was one of many.

They won't be looking for it, of course, or for him. They have no idea what he's driving, or who he is.

He just needs a moment to blend into the scenery and collect his thoughts. It might be time to revise the plan yet again, but he doesn't want to make a rash decision. Things have been moving too quickly as it is.

He leans his head back against the seat rest, catches sight of himself in the rearview mirror, and grins.

Hey there, stranger.

The beard is gone. He'd forgotten all about that. He'd lathered up and shaved it off this morning before he left his apartment, using the freshly sharpened antique blade.

It was time. He'd started growing it over a year ago— not deliberately, of course. He'd never been a fan of facial hair. But after someone you love slits her wrists with a razor blade, you don't handle one lightly.

No, not at all. Not on yourself.

He'd stopped wearing his contact lenses, too. When you've been through a loss like that, you find yourself crying at any random moment, and tears make contacts cloudy.

But today, Casey was finally ready to put all that behind him. He shaved off the beard, and he swapped the glasses for contacts.

Now he looks like his old self, the man he was one year, one week, and three days ago.

Hearing sirens, he looks up and sees a police car racing along the highway toward town.

Are they looking for him?

Or are they looking for Brianna?

He drove her up into the mountains and left her far off the trail. When the snow comes, it'll cover her. Chances are, they're not going to find her for a long, long time.

And they're never going to find me.

And Rowan Mundy and Sullivan Leary . . . what about them?

Imagine having them both at once: two beautiful redheads, one representing good, the other evil. Which would win in the end?

Neither.

I'm in control. I decide who wins and loses, lives and dies.

I decide how, and when . . . and where.

So. Maybe it should be right here in Mundy's Landing after all. Maybe two of them together will be enough, so exquisite that when all is said and done, he'll be satisfied at last.

If that's the case, why not stay?

Why not live right here among the locals? They'll never suspect that the most brilliant killer of their time is right there in their midst.

For all he knows, the Sleeping Beauty Killer did the same thing.

"Do you remember Rick Walker?" Rowan asks Jake, her voice shaking as she says the name.

It's met with a moment of silence. Then a taut, "What about him?"

"He . . . I . . ."

Jake curses softly. "I knew it."

"What? What did you know?"

"I knew you and he were . . . I *knew* it."

"No! We weren't—we didn't—"

"Then what?"

She hesitates, hearing someone calling Jake's name in the background.

"It wasn't like that. It wasn't—"

"It wasn't what? You didn't what?"

Now she can't find her voice at all.

"Did you sleep with that guy, Rowan?"

She swallows hard. "No. I didn't sleep with him. I stopped it before it went that far. He made a move on me, and I . . ."

"Slapped him across the face?" he asks. "Did you slap him across the face?"

"No."

"And you didn't tell me so that I could slap him across the face, or—" He breaks off to call to someone on the other end, "I know, sorry, I'll be right there."

"Jake, listen—"

He cuts her off. "How long did it go on?"

A little more than eight minutes.

Eight minutes, and I burned the cookies.

"It wasn't like that, Jake. It didn't go on. He made a pass, and I didn't stop it right away, and . . . it didn't go any further than that. I barely saw him again after that day."

"But you did see him."

"Not that way. The kids were friends. He lived next door. And after we moved away, I never saw him again . . ." Dammit. She swallows miserably before concluding the sentence: ". . . until last week."

"You saw him last week? Where? Did you run into him?"

"No. I got a package in the mail, and I thought it was from him."

"Why?"

"Because it arrived on the exact day that he . . . you know. The anniversary."

"So you remember the exact date, after how many years?"

"Fourteen. How could I forget it? I was so upset after it happened. It was horrible."

"Yeah. I'll bet."

"Jake—"

"So you didn't see him for fourteen years, and then out of the blue, he sent you a gift on your anniversary."

"I don't have an anniversary with him, Jake. It was *the* anniversary. And it wasn't a gift. It was something stupid that he knew would remind me of him."

Mercifully, he doesn't ask what it is. She can't stomach the thought of painting a vivid verbal image involving the smoke alarm and burnt cookies.

"So you saw him . . . when?"

"Saturday."

"Saturday," Jake echoes, and she can sense the wheels turning. "So you lied about going shopping? You were with him instead?"

Oh, how she wishes she could lie again.

Those days are over. Own it, dammit. Own what you did. Ask for forgiveness.

"I really did go shopping. But I saw him, too. Only to find out why he'd sent the package and to tell him to leave me alone."

"And did you?"

"He didn't send it."

"Yeah. Sure."

"I know. I don't believe him, either. I mean, I didn't. Now I don't know what to believe. I've gotten two other weird packages since then, and if they're not from him, I don't know who they're from."

She waits for the logical follow-up question: *Who else did you tell?*

But he doesn't ask it. She can picture him sitting there outside some hotel conference room, trying to process it all. If he weren't there—if they were together, alone, at home—would he be so quiet? Or would he be ranting at her? Walking out on her?

"I'm so sorry I didn't tell you what happened, Jake. I was afraid to. I was afraid you'd think the wrong thing. I was afraid of losing you. But you have to believe me— what I've just told you is the entire truth. I have nothing else to hide. Please believe me."

Silence. And then: "How can I ever believe you again, when you kept something like this from me for all those years? How could you?"

"You were never around back when it first happened, and I—"

"Because I was working to keep a roof over our heads, just like I'm doing right now," he says over someone calling his name in the background, "so if you're trying to blame this on me—"

"I'm not. I'm blaming it on myself. It was one hundred percent my fault. But what you asked me was how I could have kept it from you, the answer is that it wasn't very hard."

She pauses.

Silence, interrupted after a few moments by "I'll be right there, sorry," but he isn't talking to her.

"Jake, remember how it was back then? You were gone for days on end, and nights, too. When you were around, our time together and with the kids was either so hectic or so precious that I could never find the right moment. I knew we wouldn't have had time to heal something that huge. Was that the right decision? No. I'd never make that decision now. But I was a different person back then. We both were."

"I've never lied to you. Never. "

She absorbs that. "If you had ever come right out and asked me if something like this had happened—back then, or in the years since—I wouldn't have lied about it."

"How would I know to even ask something like that?"

"You wouldn't. I'm just saying—"

"I get it. I have to go."

She wants to protest, needs to keep talking until they've found resolution, until they've healed.

Well aware that it's not going to happen right now, or today, or maybe even soon, she says only, "I'm so sorry. Please forgive me. The last thing I'd ever want to do is hurt you."

"But you did."

"I know, and I'm sorry, and I love you." She waits for him to say it back.

He doesn't. Not this time. She hears only a click as he disconnects the call.

From the *Mundy's Landing Tribune* Archives
News
July 15, 1916

Sestercentennial Festivities to Resume
Memorabilia Chest Will Be Buried

The spate of inexplicable murders over recent weeks put a grisly halt to the merry celebration of our two-and-a-half-century-old village, which will recommence tomorrow.

"The tragic and mysterious deaths of three anonymous schoolgirls notwithstanding," Mayor Cornelius Holmes said from his office in Village Hall, "we ought not ignore our first settlers, who courageously arrived in Mundy's Landing 250 years ago and deserve, upon this momentous occasion, to be fêted in a grand manner befitting their tenacity."

Gently reminded that the first settlers arrived a year prior, the mayor returned that the village has perennially recognized its official birth date as 1666.

Indeed, it was then that the vast majority of our forebears arrived on an overdue supply ship from England, only to discover that nearly all members of the existing colony had succumbed to starvation over the course of their first treacherous winter in the New World.

The aghast newcomers determined that two of the surviving quintet—James and Elizabeth Mundy—had butchered and cannibalized their fellow settlers. After their parents had been executed for their dastardly crimes, the couple's three children were mercifully allowed to stay on in the home their father had built. Charity Mundy passed away in her teens, but Jeremiah Mundy and his sister Priscilla lived well into their dotage after marrying and raising children of their own.

Many of their descendants live and work among us to this day—most notably, Horace J. Mundy, one of several prominent American financiers who met with J. P. Morgan and the late Senator Nelson W. Aldrich on Jekyll Island, Georgia, to draft legislation for the new Federal Reserve System that was subsequently signed into law by President Wilson. Although he passes the winter months in Georgia, Mr. Mundy summers at his Prospect Street mansion and shall preside as honorary chairman of tomorrow's festivities as planned.

At two o'clock in the afternoon, a parade featuring the award winning Dutchess Fife, Drum, and Bugle Corps will step off from the Mason Street schoolhouse and march to the Village Common. There, Miss Etta Abrams will deliver a noble oration covering the town's history. Mrs. Mildred Haynes, president of the Ladies' Aid Society, will then step forward to close the treasure chest containing pertinent vestiges of our time. Surely, just as we would regard the relics of 1816 as quaint antiques, so shall our progeny view the assemblage of items deemed representative of our life and times in the year 1916.

The handsome metal chest, donated by Westerly Dry Goods Co. of Market Street, will be sealed at precisely midnight and lowered into its temporary tomb, not to see the light of day again until our ancestors unearth it on the sixteenth of July in the distant year 2016.

Chapter 18

Steve Lindgren has been trying unsuccessfully to get in touch with the doorman who was on duty in the Weehawken high-rise from early Monday evening through Tuesday morning. Now, in a small office adjacent to the room where he'd spoken with Rick Walker's son Kurt, he's hoping to have better luck with the building's security camera footage.

Artie Vance, the brash, middle-aged building manager, operates the remote control as they work their way through the past forty-eight hours. They're watching it on fast forward, pausing it every time someone enters the building, looking for anything out of the ordinary.

"Whoa, whoa, stop," he says, yet again, and Artie freezes on a hooded figure entering the lobby.

"Nah, that's Bobby Shaw," he tells Steve. "He lives here."

"Okay, keep going. Sorry."

"Hey, this is a lot more exciting than what I'd be doing if I were at home right now with my wife. This is how she watches those stupid reality shows she tapes on the DVR. She keeps stopping them, backing them up, playing them, stopping them—" He interrupts himself to freeze the footage, exclaiming, "There! Look at that! That's him!"

"That's who?"

"That's Richard Walker, just coming in the door, see?"

Steve leans in to get a better look at the video monitor, noting that the time stamp is Monday evening at 8:17 p.m.

That's Richard Walker, all right. And he isn't alone.

Immediately after Sully received the text message from Richard Walker's phone, Mundy's Landing police officers were dispatched to the location at the edge of town.

"What did they expect?" Barnes mutters to Sully after Colonomos received the call that they'd found nothing out of the ordinary. Now he's down the hall, summoned by one of the detectives, leaving Sully and Stockton to mull things over.

"It's not like this guy was going to be standing by the side of the road flagging them down," Barnes says. "You know?"

"But he's here someplace."

"Only if the GPS screenshot was legitimate."

"You think he faked it?"

"It wouldn't be all that hard to pull something like that together."

"But in a split second? He couldn't have known I was going to ask him for a GPS location screenshot ahead of time. And he couldn't have known I was going to be in Mundy's Landing. I didn't even know it myself until twenty minutes before we left New York, unless . . ."

"Unless what?"

"Do you think he followed us up here?"

"No." Barnes is decisive. "There's no way. Half the time we were on the road, there was no one behind us at all."

"Okay, but if this guy was responsible for Brianna Armbruster's disappearance, he might have expected us to tie it to Julia Sexton's and assumed we'd come here to investigate."

"Or maybe he's been here all along."

"He lives in New Jersey," she reminds Barnes just as her phone rings again. She hesitates only a moment before answering it.

Jin Kim again: "Are you ready for this?"

"I doubt it. What's up?"

"We found Rick Walker."

She sighs in relief. "Thank God. You traced the call? He was down there after all? Barnes and I were just trying to figure out how—"

"No, wait, back up. That's not what I meant. I just got off the phone with the New Jersey police. Rick Walker's dead."

"They *killed* him?"

"No. He died. In his apartment. Yesterday, maybe the day before. And it's looking like a homicide."

"But . . . if he's dead, then who the hell just called me?"

"I don't know, but he's nearby. Watch yourself, Sully."

Please, please, please let him call me back . . .

She clings tightly to her phone inside her coat pocket, willing it to ring. With blatant disregard for Miss Abrams's restriction, Rowan left her cell phone powered on after the conversation with Jake.

It vibrates with an incoming call just as she's leading the class back through a curtain of falling snow to the bus.

But it isn't Jake.

Frowning, she steps away from the class to answer it, ignoring questions from the kids and blatant disapproval from Bari, who makes a comment about teachers who make a "big stink" about rules but don't follow them.

"Rowan?"

"Yes . . . ?"

"This is Joe Goodall."

Joe is the principal of Mundy's Landing High School. Close to retirement age now, he was a student teacher at the middle school back when Rowan was in eighth grade, and had moved on to teaching science at the high school by the time she graduated. She never had him for class, but he was a hall monitor who handed her quite a few cut slips back in the day. They've laughed about it since but it's always a little strained on her part, even though she's long since redeemed herself, and Braden and Katie were stellar students.

"What's going on, Joe?" she asks nervously.

"I need you to come over here as soon as possible."

Once Noreen has crossed the Whitestone Bridge from Long Island to the Bronx, traffic is surprisingly light.

She makes it to Mundy's Landing in record time, speeding the whole way, despite the snow that starts falling north of the New York City suburbs.

It isn't that she's eager to get to her hometown so much as she's eager to leave her life behind for a little while.

Funny—that's the opposite of how she used to feel driving back to Long Island after visiting Mundy's Landing when her father was still alive and ailing. She could never get home quickly enough to Kevin and the kids.

Now Kevin is leaving, and Sean is gone most of the time, and soon Shannon will be away too. The younger girls aren't all that far behind.

What then?

She's never lived alone in her life; nor has she ever wanted to. It was never part of any plan.

Her mother's words, the ones Noreen had repeated to her son on his commencement day, echo in her head as she passes the chamber of commerce billboard welcoming her to Mundy's Landing.

It's easier to say good-bye if you focus on what lies ahead instead of what lies behind you.

For once, Noreen isn't so sure she agrees.

Being summoned to the high school by the principal can mean only one thing.

Rowan's heart sinks as she stands in the falling snow, clutching the phone to her ear. She's lost track of Mick and his grades in the past ten days. He must be failing something. Maybe everything.

"I'm on a field trip with my class," she tells Joe Goodall, "but we're right here in town and—"

"When can you get here?"

"We're on our way back to the school now."

"Rowan, listen, you need to come as soon as possible. This is serious."

"I know it is," she says glumly. "I've been trying to make sure he studies, and I know there was a chem lab last week that he—"

"It's not about academics."

"What? What is it?"

"Mick has gotten himself into some serious trouble. I tried Jake's cell, but it went straight into voice mail."

He must have turned off his phone after he spoke to her. He never does that, even when he's in a meeting.

"Did Mick cut class or something? Did he get into a fight?" It must be serious if Joe tried to reach Jake before her. He knows Jake doesn't work right here in town.

"It's—the police are involved."

She closes her eyes. *Dear God, no. Please, no. Please don't let it be drugs, or theft, or . . .*

What else could it be? What could he have done?

Come on, Rowan. Who knows better than you what kind of trouble a hotheaded, impetuous high school kid can get into?

"Okay," she tells Joe resolutely. "Okay, I'll get my class back over to the school and find someone to cover for me. I should be there in fifteen, twenty minutes."

It isn't until after she's hung up that she remembers, with a flicker of apprehension, the missing girl.

As Noreen drives through the outskirts of Mundy's Landing, she tries to recall the last time she was here. Two years ago? Three, maybe?

She didn't make it here for her niece or nephew's graduations, even though her sister was in Oyster Bay for Sean's.

That's different, Noreen remembers telling herself at the time. Rowan wasn't nearly as busy as she was, and visiting Long Island didn't mean confronting childhood memories at every turn.

Noreen passes the deserted roadside stand where her mom used to buy homegrown tomatoes and corn every August; the site of the drive-in movie theater that closed when she was in high school and was torn down shortly after; the barn where she took her first—and only—horseback riding lesson before her parents realized they couldn't afford it.

When I have a daughter, Noreen decided then, reeling with disappointment, *she'll take riding lessons.*

They did; all three of them. According to plan.

She drives past the turn that would lead her to Rowan's house, choosing instead to drive into town. *Not* according to plan.

The business district has perked up quite a bit in the past couple of years. Vacant parking spots along the Common are few and far between and the municipal lots are crowded. The ugly oversized vinyl candy canes that adorned the light poles every December have been replaced with simple green wreaths. Formerly deserted

storefronts have transitioned into shops and restaurants.
Just off the Common, the three-story Dapplebrook Inn on
Prospect Street, once the Gilded Age mansion of Jake's
ancestor Horace J. Mundy, has been restored to its Victorian grandeur. The houses on neighboring streets are
well-kept, with only one or two in need of a paint job.

There's a noticeable police presence in town: plenty of
cops patrolling the streets on foot and in cars.

Pulling up to a stop sign, Noreen flicks her turn signal
to drive down State Street, past the house where she grew
up. If you're doing the memory lane thing, you might as
well go big or stay home.

She hasn't been back to The Heights since she and her
sister packed their childhood into boxes and garbage bags.

She tried to keep a level head that long weekend
almost two decades ago, but sentimentality kept seeping
in, much like the damaging spring thaws that had infil-
trated fissures in the foundation of their childhood home,
only to later freeze and crack the stone.

She remembers warning Rowan that the house wasn't
going to be an easy sell between the structural damage,
the cosmetic issues, and the location. Rowan disagreed.
Surprise, surprise.

"A lot of people want fixer-uppers," she said, and she
was right about that. The couple who bought their parents'
Dutch Colonial were planning a complete renovation.

Parked at the curb, Noreen can't tell what went on
inside, but the outside looks exactly the same, other than
having gone from white with black shutters to gray with
dark blue shutters. She approves of the new paint scheme,
but the maroon bow on the door wreath clashes, and the
lawn is patchy even for December.

She sits staring at the house, lost in her memories of that
final day there with her sister. Noreen had long dreamed
of creating order from that household chaos, but when the

time arrived, she was unexpectedly emotional—and of
course, frustrated by her sister, who was, well, chaos in-
carnate.

Standing on a wobbly chair in the kitchen, Rowan
reminisced about every damned thing she pulled from the
cupboard. She wanted to keep it all—or wanted Noreen to.

"No room," Noreen said to just about everything.

"You're kidding, right? Your kitchen is five times the
size of mine. I'm the one who has no room."

Rowan protested about everything she put into the dis-
card carton, even a noticeably chipped red pitcher. "Don't
you remember how Mom always made us homemade
lemonade in that on hot summer days?"

"I remember her making it from a powdered mix in
one of those." Noreen pointed at a couple of dime store
plastic pitchers they'd already tossed into the carton.

"That was later, after she went back to work. But when
I was really little, she'd let me help her squeeze lemons
and stir the sugar into that pitcher. I'll take it if you don't
want it."

"I thought you had no room."

"I'll make room. Add it to my box."

Rowan's box of kitchen keepsakes was already overflowing with everything from a stack of plastic cereal
bowls that had been obtained by collecting cereal box
tops forty years ago to an entire set of tin cookie cutters.

Noreen carefully wrapped the pitcher in several layers
of newspaper as her sister went back to rummaging in the
cupboard, saying, "Whoever would have imagined that
this day would come?"

"It was inevitable, Ro. Parents pass away. We can't
keep the house."

"I know, but it breaks my heart to get rid of it. You'd
think at least one of us four would have stayed here in
town."

"It's a dreary place. I'd never raise my family here."

"Dreary? It's not dreary." Rowan waved a hand around the kitchen, with the blue and white gingham curtains Mom had sewn and the old cabinets and paneling she'd talked Dad into painting white years ago, because they couldn't afford to replace or even refurbish them.

"I don't mean the house. I mean the town itself. The weather is crappy and everything is so shabby and there are no businesses left downtown and the schools are going downhill and there are no jobs . . ."

"Oh, you and your rose-colored glasses," Rowan quipped.

"Well, it's the truth."

"Times are tough everywhere. A lot of towns are in the same boat. Things will turn around here eventually. Places can change, you know, just like people."

"Not always for the better."

"Sometimes, though."

"Come on, the only reason Mundy's Landing is even on the map is because a lot of people died horrible, bloody, violent deaths here."

"It's on the map because it's a historic place."

"It's a tragic place."

"A lot of historic places are."

"But these were heinous, bloody crimes. Unsolved crimes. That casts a pall."

"So now you're on the bandwagon with all those people who think Mundy's Landing is cursed? Mom and Dad always said that was ridiculous. How can you—"

"I don't think it's cursed. I just think it's depressing. You can't argue with that."

Rowan could, and tried. Unsuccessfully.

"So what are you saying?" she finally asked Noreen. "After today, you're never coming back here again?"

"There's nothing to come back to."

"Mundy's Landing will always be home to me. It's your home, too."

"Not anymore." Not with their parents gone and the house on the market and a burgeoning life on Long Island.

A perfect life.

For a while, anyway.

Rowan was right. Places change, just like people.

Not always for the better, but sometimes . . .

With a sigh, Noreen reaches for her cell phone and dials her sister's number.

Rowan snatches it up on the first ring. "Noreen?"

"I just got to town."

"Okay, go over to my house and let yourself in. There's a key hidden under the pot on the back steps. I'm on my way over to the high school."

"Why?"

"I just have to . . . take care of something. I'll be home as soon as I can."

"Okay. Where's Rick?

"He just texted that he's on his way to my house."

"You told him where you live?"

"No. But obviously, he's figured it out, because he didn't ask me for an address. If he gets there before I do, just . . . deal with him."

"Deal with him? What does that mean?"

"I'm sorry, I've got to go."

Rowan might as well have said, *You're the big sister. Just do whatever you have to do to fix things and get me out of trouble.*

Noreen hangs up with a sigh.

Yes, some people change—and some never do.

Trying not to panic, Mick sits in Mr. Goodall's office under the watchful gaze of the principal and a man he's been addressing as Coach Calhoun since his youth soccer league days. Today, however, he's not wearing a red team shirt and a whistle around his neck; he's in uniform as the chief of police here in Mundy's Landing.

That Brianna is missing is a nightmare. That anyone thinks Mick could possibly have something to do with it is crazy.

Coach—Chief—Calhoun asked about the gifts he left her, though he didn't come right out and say Mick is suspected of being anything other than a stupid, stupid, stupid Secret Santa. But why else would he be here, with the other cop, Officer Greenlea, standing guard just outside the door?

The office is unbearably hot and stuffy despite the window being cracked open a few inches. Snow is falling outside.

In the distance, a salt truck rumbles, but the room is so silent he can hear the two men breathing and swallowing. By comparison, his own breathing and swallowing sound deafening.

He wishes they'd say something, or even interrogate him like they do in movies, but they seem to be waiting for Mom to get here.

He keeps wondering if he should just come right out and proclaim his innocence. Or maybe ask for a lawyer.

But that might make him seem guilty of . . .

What? What the hell is happening?

Where's Brianna?

The dread that something terrible has happened to her mingles miserably with terror over his own predicament, so acute that any second now he might pass out or throw up, or—far worse—start to cry.

At last, the phone on the desk rings. Mr. Goodall answers it, says, "Okay, good. Have her wait right there," hangs up, and looks at Mick. "Your mom is here."

He can only nod mutely as a surge of emotion mixes with the lump of nausea threatening to burst from his throat. If anyone can fix this, it's his mother. She'll set them straight, whatever it is that they're thinking.

"Let's have a word with her alone," Chief Calhoun tells Mr. Goodall. "Son, you can step out and wait there with Officer Greenlea."

Mr. Goodall opens the door, gesturing for Mick to make his exit. As he steps over the threshold, he sees Mrs. Dunlop, the young cop, and his mother clustered in the small reception area.

"Mick! What's going on?" Mom is windblown, red-faced, wide-eyed.

He finds his voice. "I don't know, but I— "

"Officer, this young man is going to sit here with you," the chief cuts in.

This young man—as if Mick is some juvenile delinquent off the street instead of the kid Coach Calhoun affectionately called Striker because of his skills on the soccer field. Bile pitches and rolls in his empty stomach.

"Mick, are you okay?"

There's no easy way to answer his mother's question. He shrugs and bows his head to avoid the confused concern in her eyes, afraid she'll see the tears that have sprung to his. All he wants is to escape this overheated little room, but it's his mother who gets to do that, ushered away into the principal's office.

Hearing the door close, Mick lifts his head at last. Mrs. Dunlop is back at her desk, shuffling papers around as if she's suddenly very busy, or just pretending to be. Officer Greenlea gestures at a chair.

"You can have a seat."

"Can I . . . I don't . . ." Vomit is pushing into his throat. "I'm going to . . ."

He lurches toward the wastepaper basket beside the desk, lowers his head into it, and retches as Mrs. Dunlop cries out in dismay.

Miserable, he looks to see Officer Greenlea wordlessly holding out a handful of tissues. He accepts them and mops his mouth, and then his eyes. If he could speak, he'd probably feel compelled to explain that they're watering because he's sick. But you shouldn't lie to a cop and anyway, another tide of bile is pushing ominously at his throat.

"Here . . ." Mrs. Dunlop pulls a key out of her desk drawer and hands it to Mick. "There's a faculty restroom right outside the door. You can use it."

"Come on, kid." The officer puts a hand on Mick's shoulder and propels him away from the offending wastebasket, toward the hallway.

He's relieved to see that the corridor is deserted. Everyone is in class right now, so there's no one to see him let himself into the faculty restroom as a police officer stations himself right outside.

Locked inside, he tosses the key on the sink, kneels in front of the toilet, and vomits again. Then, racked by dry heaves, he thinks about what's waiting for him beyond the door, and he thinks about Brianna.

This is crazy. If he could just find her, everything would be okay. More than okay: he'd be her hero—hers, and everyone else's.

He stands on shaky legs, reaches out to flush the toilet, and hesitates with his fingers on the handle, noticing something.

There's a window above the sink.

It's propped open with a stick and it's large. Much larger than the high, small windows in the boys' restrooms in the building's newer wings. Large enough for someone to climb through?

Conscious of the police officer stationed outside the door, Mick makes another loud retching sound as he walks over to examine the window. In his own house, they use propped sticks to keep some of the old windows from crashing down, and others are almost impossible to open at all.

Mick tugs to see if it will open wider.

It does.

Without stopping to consider the wisdom of his new-found plan, he scrambles onto the sill, climbs out, and hits the ground running.

Either Rick's stepson forgot about his promise to check in on him, or he did check in on him, but forgot to update Bob afterward.

Those are the two conclusions Bob drew as he spent the morning on the endless errands that are necessary after a long absence. He went from the bank to the pharmacy to the post office to the dry cleaner, with long lines at every stop, then met a couple of friends for a late breakfast that stretched past lunchtime.

Now he's home again, checking the voice mail in the futile hope of finding a message that will put his mind at ease.

Frustrated, he tries—yet again—to call Rick. No answer.

Bob scrolls through his recent calls, finds the number he dialed last night, and hits redial. So what if Rick's stepson thinks he's a pain in the ass?

The phone is answered with an automated outgoing message.

At the beep, Bob says simply, "Casey, it's Bob again. Did you check in on Rick? Call me back as soon as you can."

The Gravitron spins on.

An hour ago, Rowan would have bet her life that there was nothing—absolutely nothing—that could make what had happened with Jake, and with Rick Walker, seem insignificant.

She'd have lost.

Visiting the high school principal's office for the first time in thirty years, she's reverted right back to the bad old days: full-blown denial.

"No," she says, shaking her head vehemently. "No way. Absolutely not. There's just no way."

"Rowan, we have a witness," Ron Calhoun, the chief of police, gently tells her. They've known each other all their lives; he graduated with her brother Danny and was both Braden and Mick's soccer coach. He doesn't want to believe this any more than she does, and yet—he seems to. So does Joe, who is saying very little and nervously toying with a pen.

Beyond the closed door, Mick is waiting in the reception area with Officer Greenlea, who was once a fourth-grader known as Ryan G. There were two other Ryans in Rowan's class that year: Ryan K. and Ryan L. Ryan G. was the round-faced one who lisped and smelled like Fritos.

Now, in a bizarre twist, he's armed with a badge and standing guard over her son.

Of course, Rowan didn't realize that when she walked in. Her heart lurched when she saw the cop, but she assumed Mick had done something mischievous, not . . .

Not what they think.

This is crazy. There's no way.

"One of the neighbors was out walking her dog," Ron is saying, "and she saw Mick lurking around the Armbrusters' house late Monday afternoon, looking suspicious."

"He has other friends who live on Prospect Street. It doesn't mean that he—"

"He was on their driveway, and when the neighbor spoke to him, he was acting strange and evasive."

"He's a sixteen-year-old boy! They all act strange and evasive around adults."

"Look, no one is saying that he's responsible for Brianna's disappearance," Ron says. "But a clerk at Vernon's confirmed that he bought the beads that were anonymously left for Brianna."

Spinning . . . faster . . .

Back against the wall . . .

"But you said yourself that they were from a Secret Santa!" she protests.

"As far as anyone knows, Brianna wasn't involved in any kind of Secret Santa exchange."

She remembers the day she explained to Mick what a Secret Santa is; remembers the bizarre gift supposedly left by her own Secret Santa . . .

What if . . .

Can Brianna's disappearance possibly be connected to Rick?

It seems crazy, but right now, what doesn't?

Spinning . . . faster . . .

She'll have to tell Ron about Rick Walker. Just in case. Privately. Now that Jake knows.

Oh God. Jake knows. He knows about her and Rick—but not about Mick's trouble at school.

She'd tried calling him as she drove over here from the elementary school parking lot. It went directly into voice mail every time. She didn't leave a message, not wanting to tell him there was a problem with Mick until she knew how serious it was.

Dammit. It may be more serious than she ever imagined.

Spinning . . . spinning . . .

She needs to be with her son. She needs to hug him

and let him know that someone is on his side, and . . . yes, and hear what he has to say for himself. And after that, she can pull Ron aside and tell him about Rick.

Rick, who's on his way to her house right now.

Noreen can deal with it.

She can deal with anything.

So can you.

"All right," she says abruptly, "I think it's time we get Mick in here and hear his side of the story."

"He admitted he was leaving gifts for Brianna."

Okay. Deep breaths.

"That doesn't mean he had anything to do with her disappearance."

"No, it doesn't." Ron nods. "But—"

There's a sharp knock on the door, and then it jerks open. A voice—Mr. Goodall's secretary—calls, "He's gone! Hurry! He took off! Ry— Officer Greenlea went after him. Hurry!"

After letting himself into the Mundys' empty house with the key hidden beneath the flowerpot, Casey picks up the orange prescription bottle sitting on the kitchen windowsill.

He noticed early on in his surveillance that the first thing Rowan does every single afternoon when she walks in the door is take her ADHD medication.

Casey has been sneaking capsules out of the bottle over the last few months. Not enough for her to miss, but enough to suit his purposes.

Now, he dumps the contents of the plastic bottle into his pocket and replaces them with the identical capsules he'd stolen from her. He'd emptied their contents and re-filled them with the same medication—the so-called date rape drug—he'd slipped into Rick's drink the night he died, to make things easier on both of them.

He'd been caught off guard when his stepfather left him a message on Sunday wanting to talk. He was certain Rick must have somehow figured out what was going on, and he knew he'd have to do something about it.

He didn't want to kill Rick. But he had no choice.

Rick sounded glad to hear from him on Monday night and claimed he only wanted to reestablish the connection that had been lost in the year since Vanessa had died. He said he'd been on his way to meet a friend for dinner but his plans had changed last minute, and suggested that they connect for a drink.

Thinking quickly, Casey lied that he was in Jersey City on a local job and offered to meet Rick at his apartment.

He arrived at the building just as Rick did, and his stepfather greeted him with a warm hug. He didn't seem suspicious . . . but maybe he was covering up.

Casey proceeded with the plan, but there was no joy in it.

When Rick had passed out, he dragged him to the tub, ran a bath, and slit both his wrists with Rick's straight razor from the medicine cabinet. It wasn't the one Vanessa had used, though Casey had kept that.

Casey had kept a lot of things.

One memento he'd preserved in Vanessa's scrapbook had come in especially handy.

Rick had left her a note when he walked out on her the first time. She'd crumpled it and thrown it away, but Casey had plucked it from the trash.

I can't do this anymore. You'll be better off without me. I'm so sorry.

It was the perfect suicide note. Rick had written it himself.

Casey hated to part with that keepsake.

But now he has an even better one: Rick's cell phone.

Fleeing the school, Mick has no idea where he's going, exactly. He only knows that he has to find Brianna.

He starts out running at top speed. A safe distance away, he slows to a trot and then a walk, feeling weak and still a little nauseated. He's panting, and his heart seems to be beating in time to the mantra in his head.

Find her . . . save her . . .

He pulls his phone from his pocket to see what he can learn from social media.

Great. His phone battery is almost dead—again.

At least it lasts long enough for him to find several links to an official missing persons bulletin that features a photo of Brianna and a physical description. She hasn't been seen since she went to bed on Monday evening. A few of her friends mentioned having heard from her late that night. The presumption is that she got up and went jogging as usual.

Find her . . . save her . . .

Where does she go when she runs? What if she fell and hit her head and is wandering around with amnesia? Worse yet, what if she's lying unconscious somewhere?

He shoves his dead cell phone back into his pocket. As he strides along Highland Street toward town, Mick realizes two things: he has no idea where to start looking, and it's snowing even harder than it was when he first glimpsed it from Mr. Goodall's office window.

She's going to freeze to death if he doesn't find her.

Find her . . . save her . . .

Rowan tells herself she shouldn't be alarmed when Mick's phone, like Jake's, rings directly into voice mail. She knows too well that her son frequently forgets to charge it. The battery could have run down.

Even the fact that he skipped out of school wouldn't be alarming under ordinary circumstances. Not if he felt trapped, and sick to his stomach, and if he thought he was in trouble.

Ordinary trouble—the kind of trouble ordinary teenagers get into. Because her son, of course, is an ordinary teenager.

Then again, what does she know?

She had no idea he was buying gifts for a girl or visiting her house when he was supposed to be at basketball practice. Apparently, Mick has a whole secret life.

The apple doesn't fall far from the tree . . .

Regardless of what she doesn't know about him, though, Rowan is positive of one thing: he isn't responsible for Brianna Armbruster's disappearance. Not in the way the police chief and principal are insinuating.

That Mick is suddenly nowhere to be found—with Rick Walker here in town— strikes her as ominous.

It's time to tell the police chief the rest of the story.

Clutching her cell phone tightly, praying it will ring and she'll hear her son's voice, she looks at Ron Calhoun.

"I need to speak to you," she says urgently. "In private."

When Steve Lindgren saw the security camera footage of Rick Walker coming home on Monday evening, it took him a moment to recognize the man beside him. He was bearded, and wearing glasses . . .

But it was Rick's stepson, Kurt Walker.

Kurt Walker, who—according to the neighbors who heard his screams—was distraught when he discovered Rick's body.

When Lindgren last saw Walker, he claimed to be on his way to notify his siblings of their father's so-called suicide. He never did.

That was evident after a few phone calls. All three—Derek, Liam, and Erin—were stunned and devastated by the news. Steve broke it as gently as he could.

Now, trying to piece together the rest of the story, he sits across from Derek Walker, Kurt's brother, in the Brooklyn loft he shares with a roommate.

Steve was taken aback, meeting Derek.

Kurt Walker had struck him as intense and socially awkward, but he'd attributed that to being in the midst of a personal crisis. Derek, while he didn't walk in on his stepfather dead in a bathtub this morning, is dealing with the same loss. But he's much more likable, and comes across as an average Joe.

Of course, he most likely has nothing to hide, and he doesn't seem to realize that his brother does. Steve hasn't told him yet that Kurt not only already knows about their stepfather's death, but might very well have caused it.

"This is going to be really hard for Casey," Derek says.

"Casey?" Steve makes a mental note. "Is that what you call him?"

"Yeah. He was named after our father. He's Kurt Clark, Junior. But he hated that. He hates *him*. We both do, and so did our mom."

That part of the story rings true, and understandably so: Steve's earlier search revealed that the elder Kurt Clark is a convicted felon now serving twenty years for first-degree assault.

"So Casey was your brother's nickname."

"Yeah. It's his initials. K.C.—Casey. Rick came up with it. He even made the teachers in school use it when we were little, because my brother would get so upset whenever anyone called him Kurt."

"So they got along pretty well, your brother and Rick?"

"Always. I mean, he was the dad we never had. My brother worshipped Rick like a superhero and they were inseparable, even after the divorce, until . . ."

"Until . . . ?"

Derek's blue eyes cloud over. "Until, you know . . .

Mom died. She killed herself, too. My brother almost lost it."

"Lost it?"

"You know . . . he had a rough time. He kind of went off the deep end."

"In what way?"

"He couldn't sleep, he lost weight and he didn't want to see anyone, not even Rick."

Understandable. Some people react to a sudden loss by holding on tightly to their remaining loved ones; others by letting go for fear of losing someone else.

"He's the one who found her," Derek adds.

Steve pretends he wasn't aware of that when, in fact, he looked into Vanessa De Forrest's death before he headed over to Brooklyn.

She had, indeed, slit her own wrists in a bathtub, on November thirtieth of last year.

She was discovered by her eldest son, who'd gone over to check on her after she failed to show up at work. Her doctor had recently prescribed an antidepressant that carried a risk of suicidal tendencies, and she'd left a rambling, handwritten note that both blamed her ex-husband and professed her love for him.

That isn't unusual after a divorce. The timing isn't unusual either: she killed herself on the Sunday after Thanksgiving.

According to Derek, Rick had custody of the younger half siblings on that first Thanksgiving after the divorce. Derek went to Mexico with friends, so Vanessa cooked a turkey for herself and Casey. When Derek called her that night, she was alone again, had been drinking, and was upset and resentful.

"At you?" Steve asks.

"Kind of. At everyone, really. But mostly at Rick."

"Why did they split up?"

"They were so different. Looking back, I'm more surprised they ever got married in the first place than I am that they got divorced."

"Did your brother feel the same way?"

"Probably. I don't think anyone who knew them wouldn't feel that way."

"Yet your mother didn't want the divorce."

"No."

"Because she was still in love with him?"

"That, and I think she felt like a failure. She was a real perfectionist, and . . . you know. Both her husbands left her."

Steve shifts gears.

"When was the last time you saw your brother?"

"It's been a while. Probably not since . . . I'd say it's been almost a year."

"That's a long time when you live in the same city."

"I know, but he's . . . not that social. Plus, he travels a lot for work."

"What does he do?"

"He's an electrical lineman—he does power restoration in areas that have been hit by storms."

From the *Mundy's Landing Tribune* Archives
Front Page
July 8, 1916

Second Young Woman Murdered
Bloodied Corpse at G. H. Purcell Residence
Village in Uproar at News

At approximately ten-thirty this morning, Mrs. Florence S. Purcell of 46 Bridge Street was greeted by a horrific sight upon entering the second-floor guest room to prepare it for weekend visitors. A young woman lay beneath the coverlet with her head resting upon a pillow, eyes closed as if in slumber. Had Mrs. Purcell not been aware of a similar discovery earlier in the week at the home of Dr. and Mrs. Silas O. Browne of 65 Prospect Street, she might have approached and attempted to awaken the sleeping intruder as did the unfortunate Mrs. Browne.

Correctly surmising that the bed's occupant was deceased, Mrs. Purcell began shrieking, which greatly frightened her children, Miss Augusta A. Purcell and Master Frederick G. Purcell. Hastening to the scene were Mr. Homer M. Sampson, who resides across the way at 49 Bridge Street, and Niall Devlin, a stable hand at Harrison's Livery on Fulton Avenue, whose barns are located adjacent to the rear of the Purcell property.

After ushering the distraught Mrs. Purcell and her children to the safety of a neighboring home, Mr. Sampson dispatched the Devlin lad to fetch both the police and Mr. Purcell, who at the time was in his office at the First National Bank on Fulton Avenue.

This follows the aforementioned incident that took place last Friday morning, when the lifeless body of an unidentified young girl was found in the former bedroom of Miss Maude Browne, the eldest daughter of Dr. and Mrs. Browne, who is spending the year abroad. In that case, as in this one, there were no witnesses to the dastardly deed, no assassin was readily apprehended, nor were any suspects questioned.

At press time, a full investigation was under way. Asked whether the two crimes were linked, Officer Ernest B. Vestal informed the *Tribune*, "It would be imprudent to offer speculation."

Chapter 19

After noticing several police cars in town, Mick decided to search along the bike path that follows the river north of the Schaapskill Nature Preserve. He's pretty sure that at this time of year, no one else would think to look over here for Brianna—or for him.

When Mom and Dad were growing up in Mundy's Landing it was a rail track, but neither of them remember it ever being used. It's since been paved over and it's where he jogs every morning, accessing it via a shortcut behind his house. During the summer, it's busy with bike traffic, but at this time of year, it's nearly deserted.

He's never crossed paths with Brianna here, but that doesn't mean anything. Maybe she goes earlier or later than he does. He can't keep tabs on her every move, though he regrets that now.

He moves slowly, searching the grayish-brown scrub along both sides of the paved trail, determined not to leave until he finds her.

Waiting for the water to fill the tub in Rowan's master bathroom, Casey regrets that it isn't an old claw-foot model that you might expect to find in a house like this.

Ironically, you wouldn't expect to find a claw-foot tub in a Hoboken condo, but there was one in the master bathroom of the place they'd moved into after leaving West-chester County thirteen years ago.

"Are you going to start taking bubble baths?" Casey remembers asking his mother when he saw it.

Rick answered for her. "Are you kidding? Your mom would never sit around soaking in a tub. She doesn't like to waste time."

"I don't have time to waste," Mom said in the brittle tone she was using more and more often when she spoke to Rick.

Casey was still just a kid then—thirteen—but he was old enough to recognize the ever-escalating tension be-tween them. It had worsened right before they moved away from Westchester, with a fight about Rowan Mundy.

Rick felt bad that she had moved away; Mom accused him of being in love with her. Casey overheard every-thing.

By that time, he'd been indulging his voyeuristic ten-dencies for years—with his mother and stepfather, his siblings, the neighbors . . .

He was addicted to eavesdropping on people's private conversations, watching their most intimate moments. There was tremendous power in omniscience.

The habit had originally been born out of paranoia, back when his biological father was still around and fre-quently threatening Mom that he was going to leave town with Casey and his brother. Terrified that it would actu-ally happen, Casey monitored his father's every move, looking for signs that he was getting ready to take off.

Mercifully, when it finally happened—when Kurt Clark, Senior, finally left—he went alone.

Casey kept spying, though. At first, just on his mother. He was afraid she was going to leave, too. That fear eased when Rick came along, but watching the two of them to-gether was so titillating that he couldn't stop. Finally, Rick caught him peeking through a crack in the door one night when he and Mom were in bed together. Casey didn't let on that he'd been watching them and pretended he wasn't feeling well. They bought it. But they began locking their bedroom door after that.

There were ways around that for a precocious kid like Casey. When they still lived in the city, he'd crawl out the fire escape outside the bedroom he shared with his brother and peek through the window into the room next door. His parents never bothered to close the blinds; the apartment faced an alley and an unbroken concrete wall.

When they moved to the house in Westchester, the master bedroom was on the ground floor, making it even easier for him to spy from outside. But as time went on, he rarely caught his mother and Rick naked in each other's arms. Most nights, they were just sleeping.

That was okay. By then he'd discovered Rowan.

He wasn't much interested in her when they first met. She was just a mom, hugely pregnant.

But one day, soon after she had the baby, she bared her breast to nurse him right there in front of Casey. He was mesmerized, watching the baby suckling, his tiny fingers toying with his mother's long red hair. Mesmerized, and insanely, irrationally jealous.

From that moment on, he watched Rowan Mundy every chance he got and pleasured himself to fantasies that involved her.

From the tree house, he could see over the fence into the yard next door. Sometimes, at night when the lights were on, he could see directly into her house from his own. Having spent so much time inside the house during the day, he knew the layout of the rooms, well aware which windows belonged to the master bedroom and which to the bathroom. The curtains were always closed at night, so he never glimpsed anything more erotic than Rowan nursing her baby, but his imagination conjured plenty of tantalizing scenarios that were undoubtedly unfolding across the way. He longed to glimpse her showering or disrobing or making love with her husband . . .

It didn't happen.

Something else did.

Always a stickler for details, for numbers, Casey remembered the date clearly. November thirtieth.

That was the day his stepfather finally did what Casey had long fantasized about doing to Rowan. Naturally, he was spying on them from the next room. In the throes of adolescence, hormones raging, he didn't blame Rick for finding her irresistible. Nor did he resent the woman in the arms of his mother's husband.

Not at first.

But that day was the turning point. Afterward, everything changed. She changed.

Until November thirtieth, Rowan was always so open, so affectionate—not just with Rick, but with Casey. To be fair, she was that way with everyone: Casey's younger brother Derek, his half brother Liam, and his sister Erin, too. But overnight, she went from loving and warm to ice cold.

Not long after, a For Sale sign went up, and she was gone.

Eavesdropping on his mother and Rick's argument after the Mundys had moved away, Casey felt torn. He loved his mother more than anything in the world, and he didn't want her to be unhappy. But he loved Rick, too, almost as much. Rick was his hero. He'd saved Casey from being the kid with the loser dad, or the kid with no dad at all. He'd made everything okay.

"Don't worry, you can do no wrong in his eyes," he once heard Mom telling Rick, laughingly, when they were behind closed doors talking about how Rick had grounded Casey for a week. As his new stepfather, Rick was afraid Casey was going to hate him for the punishment, but was adamant about teaching him a lesson.

Casey can no longer remember what he'd done. Not that time, anyway. He only remembers that no one ever caught him doing anything that was truly wicked, like stealing a pocket knife from Kmart and using it to skin small, furry animals. Live ones. Well, not live for long. His hand, back then, wasn't nearly as steady as it is now.

But I was much too smart to get caught. Smarter than Mom and Rick, smarter than Derek and Liam and Erin, smarter than the teachers . . .

Just like I'm smarter than the police. Even Sullivan Leary.

The thought of the redheaded detective jars him back to the present.

The tub is filled with steaming water.

Casey turns off the tap just in time to hear a car pulling into the driveway. She's just in time.

He smiles, pleased, and takes out Rick's cell phone to make a quick, final call.

Biting into a flaky apple pastry dusted with cinnamon and sugar, Sully forgets, momentarily, about the disturbing screenshot, and about the homicide, and even about bagels. Good bagels, bad bagels . . . who needs bagels? She could live here, and subsist on this pastry.

"That's not lunch," Stockton points out as he unwraps a ham and cheese sandwich on a croissant. "That's dessert."

"It's not lunchtime," she replies with a shrug. Anyway, there's nothing wrong with dessert for lunch. Especially when it's mid-afternoon and you had absolutely no appetite when you placed your order.

But the secretary stationed outside Colonomos's office

had encouraged her and Stockton to order something when she'd passed around a menu earlier. "It's going to be a long day."

Every day is a long day where they come from, but in the few hours they've been here, they've become well aware that the Mundy's Landing police force isn't accustomed to this intense state of overdrive. They're efficient, but small. From what Sully gathers, they deal mostly with petty crimes, parking tickets, and crowd control during the summer festival.

Now they're dealing with not one, but two missing teens. They identified a high school kid who was reportedly stalking Brianna Armbruster, only to have him slip away before they could question him.

"Mick Mundy?" Sully echoed, when she heard the name. "As in . . . Mundy's Landing?"

"Right. His dad's family is descended from the first settlers here."

That they were executed as accused murderers wasn't lost on Sully, but Colonomos assured him that Mick Mundy is a good kid from a good family.

Theoretically, all he did was give a girl a couple of gifts. Sully would be inclined to believe it was totally innocent if one of the beads hadn't been etched with the word *Redhead*.

Even that might be innocent; a coincidence.

Brianna Armbruster aside, it's hard to imagine that a sixteen-year-old small-town kid—regardless of what his ancestors might have done three hundred and fifty years ago—is responsible for the heinous serial murders. Too bad he took off before he could be questioned and cleared.

Her cell phone rings as she takes another bite. She hurriedly chews and swallows when she sees that the call is from the precinct.

"Detective L—"

"Sully." Jin again. "He called back. Can I patch him through?"

She doesn't have to ask who. "Go ahead."

"Okay. And he says it's urgent. Life or death."

Yeah, whose? Sully wonders, and then he's on the line.

Stepping through the back door into her sister's kitchen, Noreen is aghast.

Dishes in the sink, clutter on the counters, dirt tracked on the floors, spilled food and water around the dog's bowls . . .

Her first instinct is to start tidying up. Still wearing her coat, with her purse and overnight bag hanging from her shoulders, she begins with the coffeemaker. After pouring this morning's stale brew down the drain, she dumps the cold, wet grounds into the nearly overflowing—of course—garbage can, and opens the dishwasher. It, too, is full, and someone—*Gee, I wonder who?*—forgot to run it. The dishes inside weren't rinsed so they're caked in crud. Among them is the chipped red pitcher from their childhood home.

Noreen closes the dishwasher and steps away.

She's not here to clean up this mess. She's here to clean up the bigger one.

Maybe, if she can set this loser Rick Walker straight and help her sister get past this marital setback, she'll feel better about all the things she can't fix in her own life.

Still, she walks through the first floor with a critical eye. Throw rugs are slightly askew, closet doors ajar, coats draped over chairs, shoes are scattered on the floor . . .

The dog, when she comes across him napping on the sofa, shouldn't be shedding on the furniture, and he should be barking at her presence.

And there are far too many framed family photos, she

decides when she reaches the front hall. Especially on the wall leading up the stairs, where they're hung in mismatched frames of all shapes and sizes.

Hearing a rustling sound behind her, she spins around.

No one is there.

She never did like old houses. She doesn't believe that they're haunted, but they do creak and groan. Settling noises, her parents used to call them. Which never made sense to Noreen, because old houses should have had plenty of time to settle.

Again, she hears the sound.

Again, she whirls around.

This time someone is there.

This is the moment Casey has anticipated for months, years. Yet now it's finally arrived, it isn't quite right. It isn't right at all.

Coming face to face with Rowan Mundy at last, Casey confirms that all the familiar components are accounted for: the compact build, fine bone structure, speckled green eyes, long, lovely cinnamon-colored hair . . .

It's all there, but . . . different. Off.

Why? Casey wonders, his brain muddled in confusion. Is it because of time passing? Proximity? Perspective?

It's been a few weeks now since he last glimpsed her even from afar, but still . . .

Close up, she seems taller and leaner than she should. There's not a hint of freckle on her face. Her hair—her beautiful hair—is pulled back in a severe ponytail. She never wears it that way.

But it's her eyes—the expression in her eyes—that is most startling. She isn't just wary or even frightened or furious. Her gaze is calm and cold. Stone cold. So is her voice when she addresses him; the pitch lower and barely recognizable.

"You're not Rick Walker."

"No." He pushes aside his confusion, forcing a laugh. "I know you were expecting him, but he's . . . incapacitated."

"Who are you?"

"Oh, Rowan . . . you don't recognize me? Really?"

"I'm not—"

"I'd be insulted," he goes on, cutting her off abruptly, "if I believed you."

"You don't?"

"Of course not."

There's a subtle shift in her gaze as she stares at him. She tilts her head, studying him, and then shakes it. It's obvious that she's stalling, buying time by pretending not to know who he is, but that's okay. He's the one in control here.

"My memory isn't what it used to be," she says. "People change."

"You have a point. I *was* just a boy the last time we saw each other. Now I'm a man. A real man."

He stretches a hand toward her. As if she senses that his intent is not to shake hands, but to caress her, she recoils quickly—too quickly. That, too, is wrong. Her reflexes should be slowing already. Maybe she forgot to take her medication when she came in.

If so, then she's going to put up a fight. It could get messy.

But that might be more fun, anyway.

"What are you doing?" she asks him as he reaches into his pocket. "You need to keep your hands where I can see them."

He laughs, pulls out the razor, and snaps it open.

Cold, wet, tired, hungry . . .

That's it. I've had enough.

Mick has found no sign of Brianna along the paved trail by the river.

He's not giving up the search entirely, though. No way. She needs him.

He's just taking a short break. He needs to change his clothes, eat something, and rest for a little while in a warm, dry place.

Luckily, home is right down the path. He heads in that direction.

The first strike catches Noreen in the arm as she tries to get away from the intruder. The razor blade slices neatly through the sleeve of her blouse and into her flesh. Stunned, she looks down to see blood seeping over the white silk fabric. The stinging pain doesn't hit her for a few seconds after that.

Those seconds are spent realizing that the attack was meant for her sister. If she corrects his mistaken assumption that she's Rowan, he might stop and flee.

But he might not. He might continue to hurt her, and then go after Rowan, too.

Rowan's not as strong as Noreen. She won't be able to fight him off. She'll get hurt.

I told her I'll deal with this, and I will.

There's searing pain now in her right arm where he cut her, and he's holding her left so tightly that she can't wrench herself free. She lifts her leg and kicks him, hard, going for the groin.

Not hard enough, not high enough.

The razor flashes again.

Suddenly, Noreen is afraid.

What if he hurts her badly?

What if . . .

It's easier to say good-bye if you focus on what lies ahead instead of what lies behind you.

Her mother hadn't realized what lay ahead when she said those words years ago, before she got sick, before she died.

For all her planning, maybe Noreen, too, is destined to—

She feels the blade slash into her side.

No. Her kids. The girls, Sean . . .

They need her. Nothing can happen to her. She won't let it.

She lifts her leg to kick him again and the blade catches it. More pain, more blood . . .

"You son of a bitch!" As she goes down, she kicks him with the other leg.

But then he's on her again, and this time, the blade slashes into her throat.

In the parking lot of the high school, Rowan unlocks the door of the minivan with shaking hands, then shoves the keys back into her pocket.

This is crazy.

She just revealed her deepest, darkest secret to Ron Calhoun, and what did he say?

"I'm sure that doesn't have anything to do with this."

That's what he said, and she could see the disapproval in his eyes. "But we'll look into it," he added. "I promise."

Too little, too late.

I shouldn't have told him. Why did I tell him?

Maybe he's right.

Maybe it's a stretch to think that . . . what? What does she even think? That Rick Walker kidnapped Brianna Armbruster?

What, exactly, would that accomplish in the grand scheme of things?

Nothing. Absolutely nothing. It makes no sense. She's just dizzy with stress and exhaustion, and that damned song is still looping through her head: *I Would . . . Die 4 . . . U . . .*

As she climbs behind the wheel, she catches sight of the red snowflake still pinned to her lapel and lets out a frustrated cry. She strips off the coat and tosses it into the backseat.

She needs to get home. Thoughts spinning, she quickly texts Noreen that she's on her way. Rick must be there by now, but she just has to find Mick. Noreen can help her.

Her keys . . . where are her keys?

Why can't she ever find her damned keys?

She slams her fists against the steering wheel and leans her head back, eyes closed.

Get a grip. You can't fall apart now. Come on.

Okay, her keys . . . keys . . .

Pocket of her coat?

She can't reach it from here. She gets out of the car, opens the back door, kneels on the backseat to retrieve it . . . and finds Mick's down jacket.

Caught off guard, she grabs it and presses it to her face. She breathes in the faint scent of some kind of body spray he must have used the last time he wore it, probably trying to impress a girl: Brianna?

Even so . . .

I know my son. I might not know what he's doing every moment of every day, but I know who he is.

Determined to find him—to help him—she gets back behind the wheel, starts the engine, and grimly drives toward home.

In the split second before Casey slashed Rowan's throat, a single word escaped it.

Why?

Now, standing over her, watching her bleed all over her scuffed hardwood floor, he answers it.

"Because you destroyed us! That's why!"

She doesn't reply, of course. She's too busy bleeding, moaning. Soon she'll be unconscious. But on the off chance she can still hear him, he explains.

"Before you came along, we were a family. My mom and Rick were so happy, and we were normal, and . . . and then you ruined everything. You and your stupid . . ." He kicks her in the head, the *hair*, with his work boot.

She groans a little.

She's still alive. Good. She should hear this.

"Nothing was ever the same after that. You moved, we moved, but it was like you infected us with some kind of virus. And my mom . . . she knew you were trying to take him away from us. She *knew*."

Years later—on that lonely Thanksgiving weekend when it was just the two of them—Mom tried to convince Casey that Rowan hadn't caused the divorce. She acted as though she barely remembered Rowan.

But he knew better.

You couldn't forget a woman like that.

He never had. And he was certain, when Rick left his mother a few years ago, that Rick never had, either.

On Monday night when Casey asked him about her, he admitted he'd seen Rowan again recently, but claimed it was innocent, and insisted that Mom's death wasn't her fault.

"How can you say that? She killed herself on the same day that you . . . that you and Rowan . . ."

"It had nothing to do with that. She was overwhelmed at work. The days were getting shorter and darker, winter was coming. Your mom always hated that time of year. And she'd just gone through a miserable holiday and a miserable weekend."

"So she *killed* herself?"

"Come on. She struggled with depression all her life.

And that date wasn't just meaningful to me and Rowan. It was meaningful to me and your mother. We met on November thirtieth."

That gave him pause. He'd never realized that.

"So it was your anniversary?"

"Not of our wedding, of the day we—"

"I know, I heard you. But then why would you choose that day to . . . to . . ."

Rick sighed heavily. "Every year on November thirtieth, we . . . celebrated. At midnight." He was slurring his words a bit by then. The medication was beginning to take hold. "We stayed up late, and we had champagne, and we . . . toasted. You get it."

Yeah. He got it. He'd seen it.

"That year, your mother got home late from work, and she was in a pissy mood, and she fell asleep early. I tried to wake her up, you know, at midnight, but she got angry and I got angry and . . . you know. We went to bed angry and we woke up angry and then I . . ." He shrugged droopily. "I did something stupid. Casey, come on. It was fourteen years ago and—"

"Don't call me Casey!"

"All right, so what do you want me to call you . . . Kurt? Are you going by Kurt again now?"

He shrugged. Might as well. One name had been given to him by the father who'd abandoned him, the other by the stepfather who'd promised he would stay and then ultimately did the exact same thing. And why?

Because of *her*.

"It was your fault!"

He kicks Rowan again. She makes a whimpering sound, like a wounded animal.

He kneels over her, grabbing hold of her hair to lift her head. Her throat is bleeding, but the cut isn't deep enough. One more slash will put an end to her suffering, and to his.

As long as she walks this earth, he won't be free.

She ruined Casey's life, and she ruined his parents' marriage, and she lured Rick away, and . . . and . . .

And she had lured his biological father away, too. She must have. Who else, what else, could it have been? It was all part of her plan to destroy him, and he—

Someplace in the house, a door opens, closes. Footsteps.

She's here. She really came, just as he'd instructed her to.

Detective Sullivan Leary.

"Noreen?" a voice calls . . .

A familiar voice . . . but it isn't the one he heard on the phone a short time ago.

It belongs to Rowan Mundy.

Then who . . . He stares at the woman on the floor.

"Noreen?" she calls. "Noreen?"

Walking up the driveway, Mick sees his mother's minivan parked alongside an unfamiliar car: a Mercedes SUV.

Uh-oh.

He stops short, regarding it uneasily.

Whatever it means, it can't be good.

As he stands there wondering whether he should leave again, he hears a shriek from inside the house.

It's his mother.

He starts to run toward the scream, but a pair of strong hands close on his shoulders.

"Stay right here," a deep voice says, low in his ear. "Don't move, and don't make a sound."

Frozen in the archway, Rowan gapes in horror at the scene before her.

Her sister is lying on the floor near the foot of the stairs, covered in blood. She's alive, moaning. But a man is kneeling over her with a blade in his hand, pressed against her bloody neck.

He looks up at her.

Who the hell is he?

Rick is supposed to be here, but he's too young to be Rick; he doesn't look like Rick at all, but there's something about him . . .

She gasps.

Casey. Rick's stepson. He was always a quiet kid, shy, kept to himself . . .

Rick's shadow. That's what she used to call him.

And now he's here, and Rick is not, and her sister . . .

Her sister . . .

She finds her voice, shrieks, "What are you doing? What are you doing?"

He scrambles to his feet, momentarily confused, caught off guard. "You . . . You're . . . Your hair! What did you do to your hair?"

She hurtles herself at him without stopping to think. They topple to the floor, rolling, grasping . . .

The blade slices through the air, searching for its mark, but she won't let it hit her, she won't . . .

In one violent motion, he lifts her off him and throws her down, flat on her back. He straddles her, and she sees the madness burning in his eyes as he glares down at her, sees him raise the hand that clutches the blade, sees it arc through the air toward her chest, her heart . . .

Grasping that this moment is her last, she tilts her head back; she can't bear to watch. Her eyes settle on the gallery of framed portraits above the stairs. They're upside down, but she can see them: Braden, Katie, Mick, Jake . . .

Her heart.

Her heart, her soul, her life.

I would die for you . . .

She takes her last breath, but she won't close her eyes.

Fixated on the photo, she wants their smiling faces to be the last thing she sees on this earth.

There's a blast of sound, and then she can't breathe, and there's blood in her mouth.

This is what it's like to die, she realizes. It will be over soon, and then . . .

It isn't.

Time goes on, and she can taste blood, smell it, but it isn't her own. It's Casey's.

He's on top of her, crushing her, because . . . because . . .

A muffled, far-off voice shouts something that sounds like "Sully!"

"I got him, Barnes!" a female voice shouts, closer and clearer. "We need the medics right away. Hurry! There are two females here, and one's in really bad shape!"

She hears a commotion, and then the dead weight is being lifted off Rowan, and she sees a redheaded woman standing over her.

"Are you okay?" she asks, holstering a gun and leaning in. "Did he hurt you?"

"My sister . . . please help my sister . . ."

"It's okay. Let me take a look at you. Take deep breaths. Just breathe."

Breathe. She breathes. She can breathe; she's alive.

Paramedics lunge through the door toward Noreen. One twists a tourniquet onto her arm; another takes her pulse; another crouches beside her, talking to her, telling her to hang on, hang on, hang on . . .

There are cops now, too, swarming in, closing around the man on the floor. He's bleeding from a gunshot wound to his chest.

Rowan doesn't give a damn whether he's alive or dead; she only cares about her family. Dammit, dammit, he tried to hurt her family, tried to . . .

"Noreen!" she calls. "Noreen!"

The woman turns back toward Rowan. "Shh, she's going to be all right."

"Are you . . . who are you?"

"I'm Detective Leary. Here, can you sit up?" She stretches out a hand, and Rowan grasps it. The woman's grip is warm and reassuring.

"You've got to help me, Detective. Please. I need to find my son . . . He disappeared, and they think . . ." She pauses, closing her eyes just for a moment, trying to collect her thoughts.

Mick. She has to find Mick.

"Your son disappeared?" The detective is solemn, but there's a little twinkle in her eye. "Can you describe him?"

"He's six-two, lanky, with green eyes and red hair . . ."

"Red hair? I'm kind of partial to that. Hmm, let me see what I can find out." The detective steps closer to the door and calls, "Hey, Barnes? Can you come in here now? And bring your pal?"

A moment later, a large black man steps through the front door, his arm around Mick.

Rowan closes her eyes, this time in silent, thankful prayer. Then her boy is there, hugging her.

"He got here just as we did," Detective Leary tells Rowan. "He heard you scream and he was running toward the house but my partner Detective Barnes here stopped him so that he wouldn't get hurt."

"What happened?" Mick asks, over and over as the paramedics rush Noreen out the door on a stretcher. "What happened?"

Rowan just shakes her head, spinning, spinning . . .

She has a feeling that it will be a long time before she can answer that question.

Right now—as long as she has her boy back safely, and her sister is in good hands, there's only one other thing that matters.

On her feet at last, she steps away from the bedlam, through the doorway into her study.

She dials Jake's number. This time when it goes into voice mail, she'll leave him a message. She'll just say . . . she'll say . . .

What the hell are you going to say?

But it doesn't go into voice mail.

"Jake? You answered. I've been . . . trying to call you."

"Yeah. I've been in a meeting, but now I'm out. I saw that you called a few times. Listen, I can't talk about this right—"

"It's not that. It's something else. It's . . ."

"What?"

She looks around, spinning on the Gravitron. Spinning, spinning, and it's all a blur: Mick, the detectives, Casey, the blood . . .

"Rowan?"

"Can you come home? I . . ." Her voice cracks. Dammit.

"I'm in Saratoga."

"I know, but . . . something happened, and . . ." She swallows a sob. "I need you, Jake."

"What happened? Is it Mick? Is he okay? Are you okay?" Concern nudges the anger from his voice.

The spinning slows.

Her gaze settles on a framed photo of herself and Jake on her desk. Arm in arm, smiling, wearing jeans and holding shovels: the day they planted the oak tree to replace the one felled by the storm.

She hesitates.

No more lies.

"We're . . . not exactly okay. Not right now. We just . . . we need you home. Please."

"What happened? What's wrong?"

"Please, Jake . . ." Her voice breaks. "Please just come home."

"Okay, I'm on my way." Before he hangs up, Jake adds two last words: "Love you."

At last, the world stops spinning. The ground is solid beneath her feet once more.

"I love you, too."

From the *Mundy's Landing Tribune*
Front Page
December 24, 2015

Local Teen Remains Missing

As the holidays close in, the search goes on for Brianna Marie Armbruster, 17, of Prospect Street in Mundy's Landing, in the wake of her suspected abduction by Kurt Walker over two weeks ago.

Speaking through Police Chief Ronald Calhoun, Brianna's parents, Charles and Michelle Armbruster, expressed fervent hope that their daughter will be found alive and offered gratitude to local law enforcement for continuing in their tireless efforts to locate her.

Walker, who remains in serious condition at Mid-Hudson Regional Hospital recovering from a gunshot wound, has refused to cooperate with the investigation. He has been charged with the murder of his stepfather, Richard Walker of Weehawken, New Jersey. Other charges are pending following the NYPD announcement yesterday that preliminary DNA evidence found in his van has been linked to Ms. Armbruster along with several missing women.

Speaking on behalf of the Walker family, which has gone into seclusion at his home in Venice, Florida, Robert Belinke issued the following statement: "Richard Walker's sons Derek and Liam and daughter, Erin, express their sorrow and concern for the families whose lives have been impacted by recent events involving their brother, Kurt Walker. They request privacy at this time to grieve the loss of their father."

Epilogue

Christmas Eve

Beyond the kitchen windows, fat white snowflakes drift from a gray morning sky. The air is fragrant with the freshly cut Frasier fir tree in the living room, and Rowan hums along with the carols playing in the background as she kneels in front of an open drawer, rummaging through the contents.

They must be here someplace . . .

Except, they're not.

She crawls to the next drawer and begins searching it, looking for the set of tin cookie cutters she kept when she and Noreen cleaned out their parents' house. She uses them every December, but this year, things have been so crazy that she hasn't gotten around to the holiday baking yet.

School was in session right through yesterday, and every spare moment she wasn't working was spent in survival mode. Having endured the darkest month of her life, she's finally, *finally* certain that both her marriage and her sister are going to make it.

Noreen is in the hospital right here in Mundy's Landing. Yesterday, her condition was upgraded at last and she was moved out of the ICU. It's going to be a long road to recovery, though, in more ways than one.

A few days ago, Kevin told Rowan privately that he and Noreen had been planning to separate after the holidays. She was stunned.

"So she didn't tell you?"

"No."

"The kids don't even know yet. We were waiting until Sean came back from Europe."

Sean is home now, but all four of Noreen's kids are so shaken by their mother's injuries that the news of an impending separation will have to wait.

Rowan was initially hoping that her sister and brother-in-law might be able to work it out, but it isn't looking likely. Kevin had spent the first few days at his wife's bedside, but now that she's pulled through the worst, he hasn't been as vigilant. He's working at the OR tomorrow, Christmas Day, but Rowan's nephew and nieces are coming to spend the holidays in Mundy's Landing. They'll be here later today.

The full house, with Braden and Katie both home as well, will be good for Mick. He's been seeing a therapist since that awful day, shaken by what happened to Brianna Armbruster.

Every time Rowan thinks of what almost happened to her own family—and what *did* happen—she wonders how life can ever be normal again.

But they're all still alive, still here . . .

Jake is still here—and he's promised he's not going anywhere.

Their first days together after his return from Saratoga were consumed by the crisis at hand. Noreen's life was hanging in the balance. Rowan and Jake didn't talk about what had happened between them until she was stabilized. They're still processing it all with the help of a marriage counselor. But Jake has forgiven her, and they're going to get through this.

She closes the drawer, drags a chair across the kitchen, and climbs onto it to reach the cupboard above the stove. Those cookie cutters must be here someplace . . .

"What are you doing up there?"

Jolted by the voice behind her, she shifts her position. The chair wobbles, tilts, and she falls . . .

Right into Jake's strong arms.

She laughs. "Good catch."

"What were you looking for?"

"Cookie cutters. I thought I'd bake some cookies," she says, and regrets it when pain shadows his eyes like a cloud crossing the sun. She'd told him a few details about the burnt cookies, and Rick.

"I'm sorry, Jake. What a stupid idea."

"Climbing on chairs without a net?" He smiles faintly.

"Baking cookies. It was a spur-of-the-moment thing, and I should have known better. Why don't I ever stop to think things through?"

But Jake is shaking his head. "You do think things through—the things that count. It wasn't a stupid idea. It's Christmas. You always bake cookies for Christmas."

"I know, but—"

"Look, I don't think we should spend the rest of our lives tiptoeing around things that might remind us of what happened. It's over. We're healing. We're moving on. Right?"

"Right." She smiles, and he smiles, and the light is back in his eyes.

"Oh, and by the way," he says, "You're under the mistletoe, so . . ."

"What? I'm not under the mistletoe."

He lifts his hand and dangles a plastic sprig of green over their heads. "You are now."

"Hey, where'd you get that?"

"It was in the pocket of my sweatshirt when I put it on. I have no idea how it got there."

She knows how. He'd let her wear the sweatshirt to warm up the morning they were in the attic getting the boxes of Christmas decorations. She'd been so worried he'd discover her secret.

But Jake is right. It's over. They're moving on.

And they're under the mistletoe.

Don't miss the next thrilling book in the
Mundy's Landing trilogy from
New York Times bestselling author
WENDY CORSI STAUB!

BLUE MOON

Coming Summer 2016

Prologue

Sunday, October 25, 2015
Mundy's Landing, New York

As the real estate agent slows the car in front of 46 Bridge Street, Annabelle Bingham, seated in the leather passenger's seat, might as well be seeing the place for the first time.

She'd literally grown up right around the corner, but she'd never imagined she might actually live under that mansard roof, in the shadow of the century-old unsolved crime that had unfolded beneath it.

"Here we are," the Realtor, Lynda Carlotta announces. "It really is magnificent, isn't it?"

Against a gloomy Sunday morning sky, the Second Empire Victorian presides over neighboring stucco bungalows and pastel Queen Anne cottages with the aplomb of a grand dame crashing a coffee klatch.

"Magnificent isn't exactly the word that springs to my mind." That comes from Trib, Annabelle's husband, whose lanky form is folded into the seat behind them.

For the past few days, they've taken turns talking each other into—and out of—coming to see this place. They're running out of options. Local real estate prices have skyrocketed, unlike the Binghams' income. The only homes in their price range are small, undesirable fixer-uppers across town by the highway. They saw seven such properties yesterday and another this morning, a forlorn little seventies ranch that smelled of must and mothballs. *Eau d'old man*, according to Trib.

Lynda smiles at him in the rearview mirror. "I'm not quite the professional wordsmith you are. I'm sure you can come up with a more creative adjective."

Annabelle can think of one. She's been trying to keep it out of her head, but everything—even the tolling steeple bells from nearby Holy Angels Church—seems to serve as a grim reminder.

"Gargantuan," pronounces the back seat wordsmith. "That's one way to describe it."

Murder House, Annabelle thinks. That's another.

"There's certainly plenty of room for a large family here," Lynda points out cheerily.

Optimism might be her strong suit, but tact is not. There are plenty of families that don't care to grow larger; many, for one heartbreaking reason or another, that couldn't expand even if they wanted to; and still others, like the Binghams, whose numbers are sadly dwindling.

Annabelle and Trib are only children, as is their own son. As of this past summer, all four of their parents are gone. Trib's father, the last to pass away, left them the small inheritance that led directly to this long-awaited house-hunt.

They've outgrown the gardener's cottage they've been renting since their newlywed days, and have been longing for more space. But this?

This is crazy. This is way too much house for three people.

Lynda, whose strong suit is also not intuition—waxes on. "There are fourteen rooms, including the third-floor ballroom and servants' quarters, and over thirty-five hundred square feet of living space—although I have to check the listing sheet, so don't quote me on it."

That, Annabelle has noticed, is one of her favorite catch phrases. *Don't quote me on it.*

"Is she saying it because you're a reporter?" she'd asked Trib after their first outing with Lynda. "Does she think you're working on an article that's going to blow the lid off . . . I don't know, sump pump function?"

He laughed. "That's headline fodder if I ever heard it."

Lynda starts to pull the Lexus into the rutted driveway. After a few bumps, she thinks better of it and backs out onto the street. "Let's start out front so that we can get the full curb appeal, shall we?"

They shall.

Parked at the curb, they gaze at 46 Bridge Street.

Gargantuan—yes, there's no disputing that.

The house looms, with a full third story tucked behind the mansard's scalloped slate shingles. Its grillwork crest mirrors the pronged black iron fence encircling the property. A square cupola rises from the flat roof, its arched cornices perched atop paired windows like the meticulously sculpted, perpetually raised eyebrows of a proper aristocratic lady.

Fittingly, the house—rather, the events that transpired within its plaster walls—raised many an eyebrow a hundred years ago.

"Would you mind handing me that file from the seat back there, Charles?" Lynda asks Trib, who had been born Charles Bingham IV.

As one of several Charlies at Mundy's Landing Elementary School, he was rechristened "Trib," courtesy of his family's longtime ownership of the *Mundy's Landing Tribune*. The childhood nickname stuck with him and proved prophetic: he took over as editor and publisher after his dad retired a decade ago.

But Lynda wouldn't know that. She's relatively new here, having moved to Mundy's Landing sometime in the last decade.

Annabelle and Trib had been born here at the tail end of their hometown's midcentury boom years and had watched it succumb to economic decline.

Lynda wouldn't remember the era when the grand mansions in The Heights had fallen into shabby disrepair and shuttered storefronts lined the Common. She'd missed the dawning renaissance as they reopened, one by one, to form the bustling business district that exists today.

"Let's see . . . I was wrong," she says, consulting the file Trib passes to the front seat. "The house is only 3300 square feet."

Can we quote you on it? Annabelle wants to ask.

"I can't imagine what it cost to heat this place last winter," Trib comments, "with all those below-zero days we had."

"You'll see here that there's a fairly new furnace." Lynda hands them each a sheet of paper. "Much more energy efficient than you'll find in most old houses in the neighborhood."

Annabelle looks over the list of specs, noting that the "new" furnace was installed about fifteen years ago, around the turn of this century. The wiring and plumbing most likely date to the turn of the last one.

There are two parlors, seven bedrooms, three bathrooms, two porches, an eat-in kitchen, and the aforementioned ballroom, plus the only privately owned indoor pool in town. Some potential buyers might view that as a burden rather than the luxury it is for Annabelle, a lifelong daily lap swimmer.

Still, the house lacks plenty of key items on her wish list. There's a ramshackle detached garage instead of the two-car garage she and Trib covet. There is no master suite with a bathroom. The lot is relatively small, like many in this historic neighborhood. It's probably too shady for a vegetable garden like the one Annabelle happily tends where they live now.

"You're never going to find exactly what you want," Lynda has been reminding her and Trib from day one. "You have to compromise."

They're trying, searching for a home that will fit a happy medium—literally. Not too big, not too small, not too old, not too new, not too expensive, not a rock-bottom fixer-upper . . .

Goldilocks syndrome—another of Lynda's catchphrases.

This house may be too old and too big, but it isn't too expensive despite being located in The Heights, a tree-lined enclave adjacent to the village common.

"Since you both grew up here, I don't have to tell you about how wonderful this neighborhood is," Lynda says, as the three of them step out of the car and approach the tall iron gate. "Have either of you ever been inside the house?"

"I trick-or-treated at the door when I was a kid," Annabelle says. "That's the closest I ever got."

Trib shakes his head. "I never even bothered to trick-or-treat here. Old Lady Purcell—that's what everyone called her, because she was ancient even back then—never gave out good candy. Her nephew was the one who went out and got it for her, and he was a real cheapskate."

Maybe, but Lester Purcell isn't being much of a cheapskate now.

He'd inherited this house upon the death of his great-aunt Augusta, who died over a year ago, reportedly in the same room where she'd been born back in 1910. He could have sold it to the Historical Society for well above market value, but he refused to entertain a longstanding preemptive offer from the curator, Ora Abrams.

"I'm not going to cash in on a tragedy like everyone else around here," he grumbled, adamantly opposed to having his ancestral home exploited for its role in the notorious unsolved Sleeping Beauty case.

Murder House—that's what everyone in Mundy's Landing has called this place and two other homes in The Heights, for as long as Annabelle can remember.

Back in the summer of 1916, 46 Bridge Street was the second home to gain notoriety as a crime scene. The first had been a gambrel-roofed fieldstone Dutch Manor house just around the corner at 65 Prospect Street; the third, a granite Beaux Arts mansion at 19 Schuyler Place.

The series of grisly crimes unfurled in the relentless glare of both a brutal heat wave and the Sestercentennial Celebration, marking 250 years since Mundy's Landing had been founded.

As far as anyone knows, no actual murder took place inside the three houses. But what had happened was profoundly disturbing, especially for the people living there at the time.

From late June through mid-July of 1916, several days and several blocks apart, three local families awakened to find the corpse of a young female stranger tucked into a spare bed under their roof.

The girls' throats had been neatly slit ear to ear. The investigation determined that they hadn't died where they lay, nor in the immediate vicinity. No, they had been transported to the houses by someone who was never caught, someone whose motive remains utterly inexplicable to this day.

Ghastly death portraits were printed in newspapers across the country in the futile hope that someone might recognize a sister, daughter, niece. In the end, their unidentified remains were buried in the graveyard behind Holy Angels Catholic Church in The Heights.

The residents of the Murder Houses lived out their lives without further incident, most right here in Mundy's Landing, and some, like Augusta Purcell, in the very homes where the terrible events had transpired.

Is Annabelle really willing to move into a Murder House?

A year ago, she'd have said no way.

This morning, when she and Trib and their son Oliver were crashing into porcelain fixtures and each other in their tiny bathroom, she'd have said yes, absolutely.

Now, staring up at the lofty bracketed eaves, ornately carved balustrades, and curve-topped couplets of tall, narrow windows, all framed against a blood red foliage canopy and an oppressive sky . . .

I don't know. I just don't know.

A brisk wind stirs overhead boughs. They creak and groan, as does the gate when Lynda pushes it open. The sound is straight out of a horror movie. A chill slips down Annabelle's spine, and she shoves her hands deep into the pockets of her corduroy barn coat.

The brick walkway between the gate and the house is strewn with damp fallen leaves. For all she knows, someone raked just yesterday. It is that time of year, and an overnight storm brought down a fresh barrage of past-peak foliage.

Yet the grounds exude the same forlorn, abandoned atmosphere as the house itself. It's the only one on the block that lacks pumpkins on the porch steps and political signs posted in the yard.

Election day looms, with a heated mayoral race that reflects the pervasive Insider versus Outsider mentality. Most residents of The Heights visibly support the incumbent John Elsworth Ransom, whose roots extend to the first settlers of Mundy's Landing. Support for his opponent, a real estate developer named Dean Cochran, is stronger on the other side of town, particularly in Mundy Estates, the upscale townhouse complex he built and now calls home.

A *Ransom for Mayor* poster isn't all that's conspicuously missing from the leaf-blanketed yard. There's no For Sale sign, either.

Noting its absence, Trib asks Lynda—not entirely tongue-in-cheek—if she's sure it's on the market.

"Oh, it is. But Lester prefers to avoid actively soliciting the 'ghouls'—not the Halloween kind, if you know what I mean."

They do. Plenty of locals use that word to describe the tourists who descend upon the town every summer in an effort to solve the cold case.

Trib turns to Annabelle. "That's something we'd have to deal with if we bought this place."

"You're right. We'd be inundated with curiosity seekers. I don't think I want to—"

"Just in the summer, though," Lynda cuts in quickly, "and even then, it's not a big deal."

Trib raises an eyebrow. "I wouldn't say that Mundypalooza isn't a 'big deal.' Especially this coming year."

Mundypalooza is the colloquial name for Ora's annual Historical Society Fundraiser, which has taken place ever since 1991. That's when, in conjunction with the seventy-fifth anniversary of the cold case, Ora extended a public invitation: *Can You Solve the Sleeping Beauty Murders?*

She hoped the event would draw enough attendees to put a dent in the nonprofit's efforts to move from their unceremonious digs in the library basement. It exceeded her wildest dreams: before the decade was over, the Society purchased the elegant Conroy-Fitch mansion on Prospect Street.

These days, the nonprofit organization turns a hefty profit, even offering an as-yet unclaimed reward to anyone who can unmask the killer. The dollar amount has substantially increased with every passing year, along with the size of the crowd and media attention.

With next summer marking the twenty-fifth annual Historical Society fundraiser and the hundredth anniversary of the murders, there's bound to be more hype than ever. People and press will be poking around the Murder Houses, invading their residents' privacy.

"Let's just walk through the house before you rule anything out," Lynda tells them. "A comparable house at any other address in this neighborhood would sell for at least six figures more. I'd hate to have someone snatch this out from under you."

The odds of that happening are slim to none. Lester, who insists on pre-approving every showing, requests that prospective buyers already live locally. Not many people fit the bill, or are willing to sign the required restrictive covenant to the sales contract stating that they'll use the house solely as their private residence.

Annabelle and Trib passed muster and they're here, so they might as well look.

As she steps through the massive double doors into the dim, chilly entrance hall, Annabelle realizes she's not going to be able to get past what happened here during the summer of 1916.

Then Lynda presses an antique mother-of-pearl button on the wall. "There, that's better, isn't it?" she asks as they find themselves bathed in the glow of an elegant fixture suspended from a plaster medallion high overhead.

Surprisingly, it *is* better.

"Just look at that mosaic tile floor!" Lynda exclaims. "And the moldings on those archways! And the woodwork on the grand staircase! We haven't seen anything like this in any of the houses we've looked at, have we?"

Annabelle and Trib agree that they haven't.

As she runs her fingertips over the smooth cherry wood of the carved newel post, she envisions twelve-year-old Oliver sliding down the banister that curves above.

She can see him walking through those big doors after school, dropping his backpack on the built-in seat above the cast-iron radiator with a "Mom? I'm home."

One by one, doors creak open. Spaces beyond brighten courtesy of wall switches that aren't dime-a-dozen rectangular plastic levers. No, these are period contraptions with buttons or brass toggles or pull-pendants dangling from thirteen-foot ceilings. Lynda presses, turns, pulls them all, chasing shadows from the rooms even as Annabelle's imagination strips away layers of faded velvet and brocade shrouding the tall windows. Her mind's eye replaces Augusta's dark, dusty furnishings with comfortable upholstery and modern electronics.

Instead of mustiness and cat pee, she smells furniture polish, clean linens, savory supper on the stove. Instead of the ticking grandfather clock, dripping faucets and Lynda's tapping footsteps, she hears the voices she loves best, echoing through the rooms in ordinary conversation: *Mom, I'm home! What's for dinner? I'm home! How was your day? I'm home . . .*

Yes, Annabelle realizes. This is it.

This, at last, is home.

FROM *NEW YORK TIMES* BESTSELLING AUTHOR

WENDY CORSI STAUB

"Wendy Corsi Staub is an author who is not to be missed."
—Joe Hartlaub for Bookreporter

"Staub is a master storyteller!"
—*NY Times* bestselling author Brenda Novak

In search of a fresh start after her husband's death, Bella Jordan and her son Max arrive in Lily Dale, New York—a town teeming with psychics and mediums. When the owner of the town's local hotel is found dead, Bella agrees to step in for her. But, when it's uncovered that Leona was murdered, Bella must track the killer down in order to save her new home.

Available on **October 27th 2015**
Visit **crookedlanebooks.com**

SPINE-TINGLING SUSPENSE FROM
NEW YORK TIMES BESTSELLING AUTHOR

WENDY CORSI STAUB

NIGHTWATCHER
978-0-06-207028-9

Allison Taylor adores her adopted city, New York. But on a bright and clear September morning in 2001, the familiar landscape around her is savagely altered—and in the midst of widespread chaos and fear, a woman living upstairs from her is found, brutally slaughtered and mutilated. Now a different kind of terror has entered Allison's life . . . and it's coming to claim her as its next victim.

SLEEPWALKER
978-0-06-207030-2

The nightmare of 9/11 is a distant but still painful memory for Allison Taylor MacKenna—now married and living in a quiet Westchester suburb. She has moved on with her life ten years after barely escaping death at the hands of New York's Nightwatcher serial killer. But now here, north of the city, more women are being savagely murdered, their bodies bearing the Nightwatcher's unmistakable signature.

SHADOWKILLER
978-0-06-207032-6

Nestled in the warm, domestic cocoon of loving husband and family, Allison finally feels safe—unaware that a stranger's brutal murder on a Caribbean island is the first step in an intricate plan to destroy everything in her life.

WCS1 0615